P9-DEI-981

Advance Praise for
Radiant Fugitives

"*Radiant Fugitives* is a rare marvel, an intimate epic of faith and family, love and politics, knit together by a magical omniscience of profound compassion."
—PETER HO DAVIES, author of
A Lie Someone Told You About Yourself

"Elegantly crafted and luminously written, Nawaaz Ahmed's first novel is a fearless exploration of the clash between identity, sexuality, and religion."
—MANIL SURI, author of *The City of Devi*

"With a fine sense of the complex relationships among women kin, Nawaaz Ahmed has crafted an exquisite tale that explores the contradictions, love, compassion, and forgiveness in a family divided by tradition, sexuality, rivalry, religion, patriarchy, and geography."
—SUSAN ABULHAWA, author of *Against the Loveless World*

"A tender and heartbreaking love letter to San Francisco, to family, faith, tradition, and all the ways we get lost in them, *Radiant Fugitives* is richly drawn, poetic, and mesmerizing. Nawaaz Ahmed is a marvelous and intricate storyteller."
—NATASHIA DEÓN, author of *The Perishing* and *Grace*

"*Radiant Fugitives* indeed glows. This is such a beautiful novel, full of light and luminous sentences. Reading it felt like basking in a generous and lucid intelligence. Ahmed writes his characters and their worlds with honesty and compassion. This is a writer to watch, a voice we need."
—MATTHEW SALESSES, author of *Disappear Doppelgänger Disappear*

RADIANT FUGITIVES

Radiant Fugitives

A NOVEL

NAWAAZ AHMED

COUNTERPOINT

Berkeley, California

Radiant Fugitives

Copyright © 2021 by Nawaaz Ahmed
First hardcover edition: 2021

Library of Congress Cataloging-in-Publication Data
Names: Ahmed, Nawaaz, author.
Title: Radiant fugitives : a novel / Nawaaz Ahmed.
Description: First hardcover edition. | Berkeley, California : Counterpoint, 2021.
Identifiers: LCCN 2020048936 | ISBN 9781640094048 (hardcover) | ISBN
    9781640094055 (ebook)
Subjects: LCSH: East Indians—United States—Fiction. | Muslim families—Fiction. |
    Estranged families—Fiction. | Newborn infants—Fiction.
Classification: LCC PS3601.H577 R33 2021 | DDC 813/.6—dc23
LC record available at https://lccn.loc.gov/2020048936

Jacket design by Jaya Miceli
Book design by Jordan Koluch

COUNTERPOINT
2560 Ninth Street, Suite 318
Berkeley, CA 94710
www.counterpointpress.com

Printed in the United States of America

10 9 8 7 6 5 4 3 2 1

For my family

Prelude

I

My life outside my mother's womb has just begun.

But what a beginning: I'm bathed in a harsh light, buffeted by jarring noises from all directions, and besieged by cold hands and instruments that prod and squeeze.

Doctors and nurses circle me. They apply suction to clear my airways of fluid and pump air into me to trigger my breathing. But my lungs have so far refused to cooperate.

Consider this: I've spent nine months cradled in my mother's body. During that time I was mostly asleep, suspended in a warm amniotic sea, my head and body and limbs secure. I was soothed by the regularity of my mother's heartbeats. My world was small and safe and familiar, interrupted only occasionally by lights and sounds from the outside. And even those arrived muted by my mother's flesh and bone, the light tinted by her blood. I knew my mother's voice, and little else.

Yet, I'm now expected to welcome a world I know little about, wrenched from my mother's embrace.

A mother who is already dead. Her heart no longer pumps what little blood remains in her body, lying splayed on the operating table. Beside her, a doctor is furiously trying to revive her, his hands massaging her heart via the six-inch incision in her abdomen through which I was lifted out just a minute ago.

The doctor compresses her heart's chambers to coax them into action again, all the while issuing commands that others rush to carry out. They're working hard, these men and women, as if they believe—and fear—they still hold my mother's life in their hands.

As for my attendants, they're anxiously awaiting a sign from me. Particularly, a lusty cry that will indicate my lungs have inflated and that I've accepted my admittance into this world.

2

Is this to be the extent of my experience of my mother—these few moments in the operating room when I still feel linked to her, the umbilical cord only just severed, the oxygen that flowed through her body still flowing through me? Taking a breath and crossing the threshold of this world will sever my remaining connection to her and consign her to the shadowy regions of my subconscious.

I would like to think I have more choice: I could hold my breath and be granted a longer respite. A few moments more, to grieve what I've lost, to appraise what I'm about to enter. For what world handicaps a child at the same time it receives him?

My mother's name is Seema. Which means *face*, something of her I will never see, or *frontier*, something I must leave behind.

How twisted it is: to be able to properly mourn her, I must not cry, for with the very breath I take to cry, I will leave her behind.

All that I will carry of her is what she has left imprinted deep within me.

And the name she's given me: *Ishraaq*.

Sunrise. Radiance.

3

What cosmic irony that I, who am birthed at my mother's darkest hour, am to be named for the day's rosiest light.

Wasn't the warning evident in the hour of my conception, during an obscured dawn?

The night before, my yet-to-be mother Seema returns to a home that's barely visible in the fog. It's early February in San Francisco. The fog has already rolled in, and it now shrouds Twin Peaks, so there is no house to see, only its faint outline.

The living room is dark; the kitchen and dining room beyond are an orange glow. A bottle of red wine stands open on the dining table next to two empty glasses. My yet-to-be father Bill is not downstairs—the air is too still, the light too steady.

Seema busies herself in the kitchen, transferring the food she's brought—takeout from Pakwan, Bill's favorites: lamb saag, achaar chicken, and naan—into serving bowls. She doesn't turn at the familiar tread of Bill's steps down the stairs, not even when she senses him directly behind her in the dining room.

"I could smell the food the minute you entered," he says, standing by the table, pouring out wine. She'd parked in the driveway so as not to announce her arrival: the garage door creates a racket when it winches up.

He hands her a wineglass, kissing her lightly on the cheek. He hasn't changed much in the two months since she's last seen him. He's even wearing his favorite tan sweater, which he may have worn the day she left. One difference—he's back to wearing glasses, like the very first time she saw him, looking more like a professor than the lawyer he is. She sips the wine, glancing around the kitchen and dining room for other signs of change. Everything is preserved the way she remembers. She's sure she'll find little changed in the rest of the house too.

As if by unspoken consent, they slip into familiar routines. Seema sets the table, while Bill reheats the food in the microwave. They help themselves to the naan and curries and raise their glasses in a silent toast. They bend their conversation to safe topics—the literal fog enveloping their home, the metaphoric fog blanketing the country.

"I didn't miss the fog here one bit," Seema says. She's been subletting in fog-free Mission.

The other fog has been harder to avoid. The drama over the Affordable Care Act—the Democratic Party's plan to extend health insurance to the uninsured, a signature priority of President Obama's first year in office—has dominated news cycles for the last six months. She lets Bill hold forth about it: Bill works at an insurance company as in-house counsel and is privy to the latest insider information regarding the wheeling and dealing happening in Washington.

"He'll get it done, see if he won't," Bill says.

Seema has less faith. The opposition seems to have already won. Obama has ceded too much—both to insurance companies and to his political rivals—without a fight; what's left may perhaps not be worth having at all. But she doesn't want tonight to devolve into another argument about this. That's not what she's here for.

"Bill—" she says, interrupting him, holding the wine to her nose, inhaling, letting the fumes flood her brain in a dizzying rush. She sets the glass down and extends her hand toward him.

He stops talking, pats his lips with his napkin with extra care, his hand evading hers. "You're right," he says. "I don't think this is going to work."

These are exactly the words she was about to utter. She's not sure if he's still talking about the healthcare bill, though he's no longer looking at her. Her voice cracks as she seeks to confirm: "What isn't going to work?"

"I don't think you'll ever be ready for a child."

She swallows all the words she practiced on the drive up the hill. She hadn't expected him to give up so readily. He's making it easy for her, as he's always done. She should be relieved, but she's surprised at how much the words hurt, coming from him.

"I agree," she says, as if they're discussing weekend plans.

They turn their attention back to the food. Bill returns to his pet subject. The healthcare bill will be the best thing since FDR's New Deal, he says. She lets his voice lull her. Bill's confidence is calming, comforting, as always. She reaches across the table to take his hand, and this time he doesn't draw back. They finish the food, one hand clasped in each other's, like lovers.

When dinner is done, they clean up and put away the dishes. They finish the bottle of wine and open another.

"Stay," he says, when they've finished that one too. "You can't drive back like this."

She's glad he asked her to stay. She'd been thinking she'd have to call for a cab if he didn't, though technically this is still her home. They change into their nightclothes and fall into a bed they haven't shared in two months, holding each other as they fall asleep.

But the wine, after the initial soporific effect, wears off, and Seema wakes up earlier than she normally would, restless with the beginnings of a hangover. She gets out of bed without waking Bill, opens the door to the fire escape, and lets herself out onto the narrow landing.

She stands high above the city. From here she could see the entire sweep of the bay if not for the fog. Instead, there is no city, no sky. There is only this— the shivering fabric of her nightdress, the wet fingers of the fog, the landing's cold steel rungs pressing up against the soles of her feet. The earth and the sky pass in and through her.

Whenever the fog thins she can make out the house down the hill. A light is on, and through the window, two figures—indistinct, like ghosts—sit at a table, cups in their hands. But it is herself she sees as unreal, insubstantial—a wandering sprite, enviously peeping in on the warm reality of other people's homes.

She turns when she hears the door to the fire escape open. She tenses as Bill joins her at the railing. They stand side by side, only their little fingers touching, staring at whatever part of the city the winds choose to reveal. Now the faint necklace of the Bay Bridge, now the lights of cars dipping and rising on Market Street.

"It's a very lovely view," Bill says.

It's the view that sold them on this house, despite its location in the fog belt. "I'll miss it," she says.

"I'll have to look for another place too."

"Do you have to?" A sense of loss sweeps over her now, as she imagines their home stripped bare. She has moved a lot in her forty years. From Chennai to Oxford, to New York, to San Francisco, to Boston, then back to San Francisco. And within these cities so many dwellings she so briefly called home, only to pack everything up in neat little boxes and move again. She's become an expert at that.

"It's too big for a single person," Bill begins, but stops when he notices her crying. Now the city is doubly blurred. He holds her as she sobs on his shoulder. He massages her fingers.

"You're cold," he says. "Let's go back in."

Is it love, or is it the chill embers of love flaring one last time before dying out? Is it just bodies seeking warmth and shelter, turning to what's nearest? They're back in the bedroom, in bed, the comforter pulled over them. They're clinging to each other, their faces proximate, their lips touching. Their whispered words are swallowed by their mouths.

4

By chance—or is it fate?—my mother ovulated the night before. An ovarian follicle ruptured, releasing an egg, which nestled at the end of her fallopian tube. Ordinarily, her hormone-releasing intrauterine device would have prevented the sperm my father ejaculates into her from reaching the egg. But Seema had the IUD removed the very first week into their two-month separation, so she could imagine herself once again as the woman she was before she met him.

Of the more than a hundred million sperm that start their way, a tiny fraction reach the egg. It requires the collective efforts of hundreds of sperm to dissolve a path through the cloud of cells that surround the egg, so that one sperm can fuse with it. How they whip their tails and swing their heads in frenzy, activated by the chemicals the egg secretes!

Finally, one sperm succeeds, transferring its unique genetic cargo from my father, which combines with my mother's DNA and determines me.

What a miracle of conception, even if unintended and unwanted.

5

Now, not quite nine months later, my mother lies lifeless in an emergency ward in San Francisco, while my father treads the marbled floors outside, a dark silhouette pacing the stark hall. Bill never expected to be here, having had little contact with Seema over the term of the pregnancy, and none yet with me.

He can't help but wonder: Did he in some way have a hand in delivering us to this fate, by severing all relations with Seema on their divorce and signing away his parental rights to me?

6

Two other people in the hospital also claim kinship to me.

My mother's mother, Nafeesa, waits with Bill. She's pressed against a far wall, tiny in that cavernous room, subdued as a shadow in diffused light. Her thoughts are focused and obstinate, continuing a precise litany of hopes and dreams for Seema and me, as if to keep from considering any future that doesn't include us all together. For how can she even bear to speculate that she who came to assist in a birth has instead precipitated death?

Somewhere in the hospital, my mother's sister, Tahera, is searching for us. She doesn't yet know the extent of the crisis, but because she's a doctor herself, her mind is already mired in the looming possibilities. How is she to face Nafeesa and Seema after the events of the day? And if something were to happen to Seema, how is she to keep her promise and assume responsibility for me, consumed by guilt and remorse at her part in the evening's tragedy?

7

Grandmother, did you know that the immature egg of me was present in Seema's developing ovaries when you were pregnant with her, by the time she'd grown to the size of your palm? My future was being initiated within you even as Seema's was beginning to unfold. And just as you could never have imagined then the shape Seema's life would take—a shape that includes the two decades you barely got to see her—you can't begin to imagine now the shape being impressed on mine.

Grandmother, do I have you to thank—or blame?—for summoning your other daughter, Tahera, to meet us in San Francisco? For it seems now that it is Tahera who will hold and feed me, her lullabies that will rock my sleeping, her words that will guide my first steps. It is her I will come to call *mother* when I am able to utter the word.

I see her clearly, this substitute, running toward me through a maze of hospital corridors, her hijab fluttering, her jilbab tripping her up, her face flattened and blanched by unforgiving fluorescent light.

One

2010

I

Tahera came into my life barely a week ago, joining the two other women already awaiting my arrival in San Francisco: Seema, my mother, and Nafeesa, my grandmother, who came all the way from Chennai, India, to be by her daughter's side, defying her husband Naeemullah's wishes. Tahera flew in from Irvine, Texas, leaving behind her husband, Ismail, and her son and daughter, Arshad and Amina, to fend for themselves. The three women are gathering together for the first time in more than fifteen years.

Here is Tahera, last Thursday evening, waiting at the baggage carousel at San Francisco International Airport. She stands a little distance away from the grating steel plates, while passengers mill around the circling luggage. Her black hijab is pulled low over her forehead, pinned at the neck, framing her face. She has tucked away escaping strands of hair. Her jilbab is a muted indigo, its soft folds falling to her feet, the fraying hem trailing on the floor. Only the tips of her dull black shoes can be seen.

She's told her mother she'll take a cab to Seema's apartment; they're not to bother coming to the airport to pick her up. So the sight of Seema and Nafeesa walking toward the carousel startles her. Instinctively she shrinks back, pressing herself against a nearby pillar. Then, hoping they haven't seen her yet, she attempts to lose herself in a clump of passengers by the conveyor belt, feigning preoccupation in identifying her luggage so she can buy herself a few extra minutes in which to ready a smile and a greeting. The tap on her shoulder comes quicker than she expected. Nafeesa stands behind her, smiling. A smile—saintly tired—plays on Seema's lips too, her arm draped proprietorially across Nafeesa's shoulders.

"I knew it," Tahera says, throwing herself at her mother, forestalling thought with action. "Ammi, I knew you'd come even though I told you not to. You shouldn't have."

Her mother feels pencil thin in her embrace. She's reminded of the stick figures in her daughter Amina's drawings. Her arms can encircle Nafeesa, and still there is more arm to go round. She holds her mother in her embrace longer than she needs to.

She's aware of Seema's impatience. Seema shifts from one foot to another, waiting her turn, but Tahera ignores her. "Let me see how you look," she says instead to her mother, holding Nafeesa away from her.

Nafeesa frees the edge of her saree from under her sweater and raises it to her face, dabbing at the corners of her eyes, now sparkling with unshed tears.

"Still my sweet, beautiful Ammi," Tahera says.

Yes, beautiful still, but how shrunken her mother has become since the diagnosis, how skeletal—all skin and eyes and teeth, scalp showing white between thinning hair. The piteous smile her mother rewards her with spears her, and she turns away hurriedly, toward Seema finally, nuzzling her face blindly against Seema's, arms tight around Seema's shoulders.

Tahera squeezes hard. I feel the pressure, a compression of the amniotic fluid firmer than any I've experienced before.

Seema stiffens in Tahera's arms. "Careful," she says, pulling away and smoothing her top over her stomach.

Tahera lets go. A jolt shakes her as she's returned abruptly to the glacial lighting of the baggage claim.

"Sorry, I wasn't thinking," she says, trying to smile, working to keep the anger out of her voice.

2

Where does the anger come from?

Consider this: Tahera has not seen Nafeesa and Seema together for nearly sixteen years. Seema, after all, was cast out of their family by their father. The intimacy that Tahera observes between mother and sister—walking arm in arm down the aisle of the baggage claim, laughing at some private joke, leaning on each other for support—is unexpected, almost a betrayal.

And consider, too, Seema smoothing her maternity frock over her belly and pushing Tahera away during their embrace. The first sight of the ravages that time and disease have wrought on her mother had tricked Tahera into turning to Seema more warmly than she'd intended. She'd become her agitated twenty-year-old self, come to the Chennai airport to receive Seema, returning for the very first time after leaving for England for her master's. The very same embrace, but—

Careful! What a cutting, rebuffing word.

As soon as they reach Seema's apartment, Tahera insists her first priority is prayer, her maghrib namaz. It's a refuge she can count on. The ritual of wadu begins to calm her down, the sensation of water on her wrists and elbows, her fingers skimming her hair and down the neck and under the ears. She feels a little more at ease each time she repeats the movements, each gesture small and precise and contained, and completely in her control. After wadu, she spreads her janamaz in one corner of Seema's living room. Facing the sage walls, the maroon of the janamaz under her feet, she is cloistered in her own private sanctuary. She focuses on her rakaat, the raising of the arms, the clasping of the palms, the bending down to the knees, the prostration, the whispered verses, till everything falls away. Only when she's kneeling in sajda, after her final rakaah, her forehead and nose to the floor, does she let the sounds of the apartment seep back into her consciousness. Seema and Nafeesa are laying the table for dinner. She sits back on her knees, and breathes out her apprehensions to the right and left, before she gets up to join them, some degree of equanimity restored. She folds the janamaz carefully, precisely, smoothing down the wrinkles, and places it squarely in the corner, claiming the territory as her own.

3

In the kitchen, Seema helps Nafeesa reheat the dishes for dinner. There's the pulao, and the chicken, neither of which Seema made. Seema rarely cooks Indian food, or any other cuisine for that matter. The spices and provisions in her well-stocked cabinets are a concession to her mother's visit, purchased at the Indian store the week of Nafeesa's arrival. Everything she can remember from her mother's kitchen: rice and dal; chili, coriander, cumin, turmeric; cardamom, clove, cinnamon; tamarind. Yet, over the week, she's had to add to them daily under Nafeesa's instructions. Her mother has been cooking every dish she can remember Seema liking.

"Ammi, you should not be spending so much time in the kitchen," Seema has protested, but only half-heartedly. The mulish set of her mother's jaw does not invite discussion. Then, too, Nafeesa's eyes frequently tear up, and Seema knows what her mother leaves unsaid: *This is to make up for fifteen years of not mothering you. This is the only chance I will have.*

Also, Seema cannot deny herself a taste of everything she missed those motherless years, including the mothering.

But tonight's chicken is from the supermarket. Nafeesa insisted on cooking Tahera's favorite dish for dinner. Seema meant to find chicken from a halal store earlier that day, but it slipped her mind, and Nafeesa used the chicken in the fridge, waving aside Seema's concerns. "Tahera won't mind this one time, because *I* made it."

Seema is uneasy. Tahera has, in fact, refused to eat non-halal meat before, during her visit to San Francisco earlier that year, in spring.

That was the first time Seema saw Tahera after a decade and a half, her only time meeting Tahera's husband and two children. The day Seema spent showing her sister's children around San Francisco was the happiest she'd been in some time. It awakened hopes she didn't know she still harbored.

But there's no misinterpreting what Tahera signaled by deliberately ignoring her at the airport: *I'm here for Ammi, not for you.*

In the kitchen, Seema is aware of the throaty whispers of Tahera's prayers issuing forth from the living room. The whir of the microwave drowns her out, but when the microwave stops, Tahera's voice in the kitchen sounds like the mutinous hum of a swarm of bees.

A clear warning: *Keep away.*

4

The pungent smell of fenugreek and roasted fennel from her favorite curry makes Tahera's mouth water. Her mother has already served the food, and her plate is heaped with chicken curry and rice and raita. But what is the source of the chicken? In her new mood of conciliation post-namaz, Tahera decides she won't make a fuss. She'll leave the chicken alone, and hope Nafeesa won't notice.

She takes her seat as Seema starts eating. Before taking a bite herself, Tahera murmurs self-consciously, head bowed, "Bismillah wa'ala barakatillah."

Seema freezes, her hand halfway between plate and mouth. It's clearly been ages since Seema uttered *bismillah* before eating.

"It just means in the name of Allah *and* with the blessings of Allah," Tahera explains her addition to their childhood invocation. "We should be grateful to Allah whenever we receive anything. Especially a meal cooked by Ammi's own hands after such a long time."

"How did you know I didn't cook?" Seema says.

Before Tahera can reply, Nafeesa steps in. "Yes, *I* cooked the chicken, specially for you. Eat."

Tahera notes the quick look that passes between Nafeesa and Seema. Nafeesa shakes her head almost imperceptibly as if to warn Seema off.

"Smells delicious, Ammi," Tahera says, conscious that something's afoot. "I never can match that aroma, though I follow your recipe. You must cook it again while I'm here so I can figure out what I'm missing." She tastes the gravy gingerly, and it is delicious.

But by now it's too late to ask about the chicken. Nafeesa is watching her with anxious eyes. To distract her, Tahera starts talking about her children, how dutiful they are, and how well they're doing at school. Nafeesa is diverted to inquiring about them. Amina likes writing and spends hours forming her letters with patience and concentration. Arshad likes science, but he's as bad at mathematics as she once was, except he's disciplined and works extra hard on it with his father.

Seema shows interest as well, and Tahera remembers how the children couldn't stop speaking about their aunt after their visit to San Francisco. "Enough about me and my children—what have you been doing for a week? Seema, were you at work?"

"I took most of the week off," Seema says. "I'm on maternity leave now. But I'm still doing some volunteering—for an election campaign. I took Ammi with me to some meetings." She smiles at Nafeesa. "Hopefully Ammi wasn't too bored."

Nafeesa shakes her head. It was interesting, she says, especially since the candidate—What's her name? Kamala something?—is Indian. She'd enjoyed seeing so many different people at the meeting, so many young people, Indians too. And she'd listened with pleasure to Seema addressing them from the podium.

"Half-Tamil, half-Black," Seema corrects. "Her mother's from Chennai and her father's from Jamaica." She explains to Tahera that she knows San Francisco's district attorney through her friend Divya and has been advising her campaign for state attorney general on public relations issues. The race is very close. In fact, Obama is in San Francisco that very evening to drum up funds and support for the midterm elections. "How is it in Texas?"

Tahera shrugs. "I don't have time to follow politics. I've enough to do at the clinic and at home. Wait till you have patients and children and a husband to take care of. It's three full-time jobs."

She knows she's gone too far when Nafeesa shoots her a glance. They're not to allude to Seema's husband, Bill, or her divorce. Tahera subsides but is pleased when Seema bites her lip and pretends to search through the chicken for a choice piece.

Tahera's triumph is short-lived. "Here's the neck, Tahera, your favorite part. Do you want it?" Seema says, the spoon poised over Tahera's plate.

"No, let me finish what I have first." Her mother has noticed now that she hasn't touched the chicken. She should have hidden a portion in the rice.

An awkward silence follows. With the silence, Nafeesa's actions get slower and slower. Her bony fingers idly push the rice and chicken around. The few small mouthfuls she takes remain long in her gaunt cheeks. Her hand falls lifelessly back to the plate.

"Are you okay, Ammi?" Seema asks.

"Just a little tired. I didn't sleep well last night."

"Go rest, Ammi. Seema and I'll clean up." Tahera can't bear to watch her mother wilt any more.

Nafeesa rises. "Yes, I think I'll go to bed. You both should eat some more. There's also kheer in the fridge."

Seema follows Nafeesa out of the kitchen. "I'll be back, just making sure Ammi has everything she needs."

The momentary solitude soothes Tahera. There's the cleaning up to do, and then she should plead exhaustion and retire for the night. Sleep, such a haven, like namaz. Before Seema returns, Tahera slides the chicken on her plate back into the serving dish. She hears low voices coming from the bedroom, and she strains to make out what's being said.

Seema returns with an audible sigh. "She shouldn't have exerted herself so much today. She gets tired very easily." She hesitates, stirring the chicken dish with the spoon. "I told her you wouldn't eat the chicken if it wasn't halal. But she wanted to cook your favorite dish. She thought you wouldn't mind this once."

"Are you saying I upset her?" A mixture of remorse and anger surges through Tahera. If her mother had indeed made the chicken for her, why hadn't she at least tried to persuade Tahera to eat some?

"You didn't even touch it."

"Am I to blame? You knew, and yet you tried to serve me more."

"Tahera, Ammi just wanted to do something nice for you."

"Did she say she wanted me to eat this? Do you want me to eat this?" Tahera heaps a spoonful of the chicken back onto her plate. "Will it make both of you happy? Tell me, I'll do it." Even to her own ears, she sounds strident.

Seema backs down. "Let's not fight, Tahera. It's my fault. I shouldn't have let her use the chicken."

It's too easy a victory for satisfaction. Tahera stalks to the sink, scrapes the remains of her plate into the garbage can beneath it, and starts soaping the dirty dishes. "I'll wash up, just bring the dishes over." She doesn't wait for an answer; she attacks the sink with vigor.

5

"Do you want some tea?" Seema says.

Chamomile for Seema, black for Tahera. Caffeine no longer affects Tahera—the many long nights in Irvine have taken care of that. Tahera's night starts after her children go to bed—the dishes, the laundry, the tidying up, the next day's meals, everything she can do so she'll have more time with her family during the day. The previous week has been particularly exhausting. She cooked enough meals to last her family two weeks, labeling packets by day, week, and person; gave the house a thorough dusting and cleaning; typed up and stuck lists, reminders, and phone numbers to the fridge door. All this, apart from squeezing as many patients as she could into her calendar at her clinic.

Opposite her, Seema sits engorged, squat fingers clasped around the cup, her face still unlined, as if her forty years have left little mark on her. She appears lost to the world, sipping her tea and stroking her pregnant belly with a smile of contentment and accomplishment, which Tahera knows from their childhood days. So smug and untroubled, while their dying mother sleeps in the next room.

"How's Ammi?" Tahera asks, despite her resolution not to discuss their mother.

Seema rouses herself. The chamomile has begun to relax her, and the sensation of tautness and solidity as she moves her hands over her stomach has its usual comforting and stabilizing effect. The kitchen, even with Tahera seated across the table from her, glows with a languorous warmth.

"She's not been sleeping well. I found her awake the other night, sitting here in the dark. I'd gotten up to go to the bathroom, and she wasn't in bed. I heard these weird sounds—like a mouse squeaking. I thought she was crying, but no. Just hiccups and jet lag."

"Has she said anything at all?"

"She's been telling me about her school days." Seema and Nafeesa talked for almost three hours that night. "Did you know she used to recite poetry, like you? Urdu poetry. She wanted to be a poet. Used to write and sing ghazals. How come she never sang for us when we were growing up?"

Against the light Tahera looks surprisingly like Nafeesa, the same shape of the head poised birdlike over the same small frame. Seema notices other similarities: the thin, tight lips, the thin nose, the thinning eyebrows. Seema is also reminded of Amina, who she knows will grow up with a strong resemblance to her mother and grandmother. "You two look so alike. I hadn't noticed before. I haven't seen you together in so many years. It makes me happy and sad at the same time."

"Why?" Tahera asks.

"What makes me sad?" Seema repeats. "Isn't it obvious?"

She suspects in Tahera's question a suggestion that she has renounced all rights to her family. Over the phone the last two months, the sisters have discussed mainly the logistics of Nafeesa's visit: when, where, how. Tahera has consulted with their father and other doctors in Chennai, and is a doctor herself, but she has remained tight-lipped about her mother's condition, answering Seema's queries with curt, cryptic replies. Seema has since stopped asking. What she knows she's gleaned from Nafeesa and by consulting her physician friends. "You know Ammi doesn't have much time, right?"

"Of course I know," Tahera says.

"We haven't talked about it."

"There's nothing to talk about. Did Ammi say how long she's going to stay?"

"No. And I haven't asked her. She can stay with me as long as she wants." She's aware of Tahera's eyes boring into her, but she can't resist the taunt, like with the chicken neck earlier.

The room feels charged again. My mother returns to what she knows will calm her—placing her palms on the shell of her body around me and taking deep breaths. She slides her palms slowly along the dome of her belly, naming parts of me she thinks she recognizes—elbows, knees, skull. There's security in the promise of me. But Tahera's anger is growing palpable. "What?" Seema says, without looking up.

"I've read her case reports," Tahera says. "She shouldn't have come."

Seema puts a finger on her lips to remind Tahera of their mother sleeping in the next room, but the gesture infuriates Tahera further. She stands up, face clenched and lips quivering. "It was very selfish of you to ask her here. What happens if she suddenly becomes worse? Will you be able to take care of her?"

Seema struggles to rise. "Why are you upset with me? I didn't ask Ammi here. I tried to convince her not to come. She wanted to." She pushes herself off her chair with a jerk. "I didn't ask you to come either."

It happens in a flash—she stumbles, the chair totters. She's falling backward, and for a moment it seems that the world is swiveling out of control. She throws her hands out, seeking purchase on the tabletop, but it's smooth. In her panic, she's sure there's to be no reprieve for her. *Ishraaq*, she calls out to me in her mind, as though she can warn me to safety.

Who or what saves us that first night? It's Tahera flinging herself across the table and grabbing Seema by the arms. The momentum brings their heads together with a crash that resounds in the kitchen. Seema sits down with a gasp. The world slowly rocks back into place.

"I'm sorry," Tahera says. She hurries over to Seema's side. A bruise is already beginning to show on Seema's forehead, but she turns away as Tahera reaches for the spot. "Let me see," Tahera persists.

She bends down, blowing on the bruise, much as she would on her daughter Amina's.

For the second time that day, Seema pushes her away. "Let's see about setting up the futon. Ammi is sharing the bed with me. I'll get you pillows and a blanket."

In the living room, Tahera insists on making up the futon herself. She wants—no, *needs*—the futon to be uncomfortable, the blanket inadequate: something of a penance. Something to erase from her memory the image of Seema's paralyzed face as the chair teetered. Something to expunge from her mind the thought that accompanied it, however fleetingly. In the instant before she threw out her hands to grab her sister, she'd wanted the chair to tip over, she'd imagined Seema arcing back, her head striking the floor.

Even the isha namaz cannot quite eliminate the guilt and shame that burns her now.

6

Oh, Grandmother, you're not asleep yet. The voices from the kitchen are no lullaby. Your daughters are fighting, and you blame yourself. There must have been something you could have done, before the rifts widened to such chasms.

It's your elder daughter you're agonizing over, it's my not-yet-born self. Who's there to care for us? You abandoned Seema when she needed you most, and you won't be there when she needs you again. You have little time to make amends—a few months, perhaps a year—and there's little you can do for Seema now other than persuade Tahera to take back her sister. But Tahera is stubborn, like her father. How unbending she has become over the years, sequestering herself behind her hijab and her five-times-a-day namaz. You're afraid you no longer know how to reach her. You're afraid you have failed them both.

You pretend to be sleeping when Seema returns to the bedroom, turning away when she climbs into bed, so that she can, as she's been doing the last few days, snuggle into you, her belly pressing into your back, one arm resting on your waist. This connection is precious to you—three generations: mother, daughter, and grandson—and somehow its very existence gives you some hope, the sense of life persisting and persevering. There is tomorrow, even if there are not many more tomorrows for you.

7

Tahera's alarm wakes her at five fifteen Friday morning, so she can speak with her children on the phone before they leave for school.

She calls from the kitchen with the door closed to avoid waking up her mother and sister. Ismail is getting the children ready. Amina is crying, he says, missing her mother and refusing to cooperate. Tahera croons into the phone, "Ammi's little sweetheart. You have to be a good girl, you have to do what Abba tells you."

Hearing her mother's voice, Amina's sobs become all the more anguished. She calms down only after Tahera promises to return soon. But how soon? Tahera wishes she could squeeze herself into the cell phone and magically appear on the other side to ease her daughter's distress. To avoid having to lie, she distracts Amina by talking about everything they'll do together when she gets back, like sewing new dresses for Asma doll, painting and coloring, baking cookies. She manages to coax Amina into letting Ismail dress her in her navy blue tunic and new sky-blue hijab.

After the half hour with Amina, there's little time left to talk to Arshad, who is as usual self-sufficient: he's done his homework, he's studied for his test, his lunch is stowed in his backpack. She tells her son to take care of his younger sister, not to tease her.

"Why would I tease her?"

"Just saying you should be extra kind to her while I'm away. Look how she's crying."

"You don't need to tell me to be kind. I always am."

He sounds older than his eleven years, his voice slightly amused, which Tahera invariably finds a little disconcerting. As though he's aware of her partiality to Amina but is inclined to overlook it. Tahera works hard at concealing it, but whenever she even thinks of Amina, a deep yearning stirs within her that Arshad doesn't elicit. Toward him she has always maintained an affectionate rectitude but has never showered him with the outpouring of love that Amina receives. Arshad is his father's child—Amina is hers. That's how she's always viewed them.

"Go, go to school," she says. "And don't forget to practice your tajwid. You have only one day left before the competition."

Afterward, Tahera prepares for fajr namaz. The namaz at dawn is the one time of day she and Ismail always spend together. Praying alone now, she misses their comforting communion. Their two janamazes side by side. The rustle of their clothes, the combined rhythms of their inhalations and exhalations, the mingling of the verses muttered under their breath. And the synchrony of their movements, as though bound together in time and space by some invisible impulse that brings them dropping to their knees in unison, then sinking to their haunches, then rising to stand. She catches herself glancing at the spot to her left, where Ismail's janamaz would be, flustered to encounter empty space instead.

She's glad she can return to sleep, not having her usual morning chores. She'd like the extra minutes of seclusion before her mother and sister wake up.

8

Tara!—star!—is how you wake your younger daughter, Grandmother, a cup of coffee in your hand. Tara from *Tahera*—pure, chaste. The way Tahera's three-year-old tongue struggled with her name. By calling her Tara, you're invoking the girl of your memories, firm-limbed and pigtailed. And as if in answer, it's that Tahera who props herself on her elbows and gazes back at you. Her face is soft, unlined, yet to assume its adult creases and severity.

Which mother is she seeing? You've showered, and made yourself up with care, sandalwood soap for your body, talcum powder for your face, kohl for your eyes. You've chosen a sweater to conceal your caved-in chest, and you've arranged your saree to minimize the bulk of the tucked-in folds against your shrunken waist. You've braided what's left of your hair, together with an extension, and drawn it into a bun. All this to hide the sense of decay you're afraid escapes from you. At least today you're free of the pain you sometimes wake up with, too challenged to drag yourself out of bed.

Tahera pulls her nightgown over her knees and takes the coffee from you. You watch as she takes a sip and sighs appreciatively. It's the brand you bid Seema to buy, knowing Tahera's fondness for it. A memory: Tahera waking at four in the morning to study for her twelfth-standard public exams, and you bringing her coffee. Getting a seat in a medical college was highly competitive, especially the college she wanted, the one her father attended.

"Coffee with chicory," Tahera says, smiling up at you. "I was afraid Seema would only have the American kind."

She pats the place beside her on the futon. You perch on the edge, as though afraid to take up more space.

Tahera scoots over. "Sit comfortably, Ammi. Why are you sitting like a bird, ready to fly away?"

"I can look at you better from here."

But she insists, and you settle in closer, as she drinks her coffee. Halfway through, she holds her cup out to you, a ritual of sharing from the past. You take a sip, and she lays her head in the hollow of your lap.

"I could lie like this all morning," she says.

The last time you remember her lying in your lap was before your grandchildren were born, a decade or more. You stroke her hair with your free hand. Once luxuriant and lustrous, her hair was the envy of all her female relatives, but it's much thinner now, and much streaked with gray already, and she's not yet forty. You try to tease the tangles out, but she won't let you—she holds on to your stroking hand tightly and closes her eyes.

You're grateful: you'd been worried that she'd hold on to her anger from last night.

When she opens her eyes, you look at each other, both suddenly bashful, tongue-tied. "Do you want me to heat up the coffee?" you blurt out, and simultaneously she says, "What shall we do for breakfast?"

There's so much you want to tell her, so much you mean to ask. But can you speak, knowing that Seema is in the next room? And will Tahera listen? You worry that the day will fritter itself away in inconsequences. Cups of coffee and tea will be brewed and drunk. Breakfast and lunch and dinner will be cooked and served and eaten. Another day will have passed ordinarily, as if you still have a lifetime's supply of them.

"Seema's still in bed," you say. "She's complaining of backache."

"That's not unusual in the ninth month," Tahera says. "Her baby seems big."

She has less concern for her sister than she'd have for a patient. You recall the argument you overheard last night. "Go to her, Tahera, ask her how she is," you plead.

Tahera draws herself up with a jerk, knocking over the cup in your hand. The coffee spills onto the futon.

"Look what you made me do." She brushes aside your apology, yanking from under you the sheet covering the futon. Some coffee has soaked through already. She runs to the kitchen to fetch a roll of paper towels and begins to scrub at the patch. The spreading stain on the futon stares back at you.

9

My mother's backache is real, a result of carrying my substantial weight, but it's also an excuse to stay longer in bed, for the rest of the apartment already feels like territory Tahera controls. Seema regrets having given in to her mother's appeal: "I want to see both my daughters at the same time." An implicit "one last time" had trailed Nafeesa's request, and she couldn't refuse. But Tahera's fraught presence has now made Seema an exile in her own home. She decides to claim an unavoidable appointment and stay out for most of the day.

When Seema's dressed and ready to step out, she finds the living room tidied up, Tahera's bedding cleared away, the futon restored, the coffee stain caused by the altercation barely visible. Tahera's bags are stashed away behind the futon, out of sight. There are only a few signs of Tahera's presence: A Quran resting on a rehal in the bookshelf, a janamaz in one corner. Tahera's hijab and jilbab benignly draped over the back of a chair.

In the kitchen, her mother and sister sit in companionable silence, like childhood friends. There's a smell of cooked eggs and the whiff of brewing tea.

"Come, have breakfast," Nafeesa says, and Tahera rises and pours out juice—freshly squeezed orange juice!—for her. "I asked Tahera to get me oranges from the corner store."

"You two have been busy. What else have you planned for today?"

They are excited to cook lunch together. The fridge is well stocked, and they plan on making a sambar with eggplant, a curry with capsicum and potatoes, a stir-fry with beans. They can find a halal meat store later, Tahera says, if Seema doesn't mind being vegetarian today.

"No, that's great," Seema says. Their plan absolves her of any guilt about abandoning them. "I need to go out for a while. I'll try to be back by lunch, but don't wait for me if you become hungry."

She first takes a cab to the Kamala Harris campaign office, where there'll be a buzz about Obama's presence at the fundraising event the previous evening. She also hopes to run into Divya, who probably attended the fundraiser and whom she hasn't seen in a few days. Divya can always be counted on to boost her spirits.

It's around ten in the morning, the phone banks haven't yet started, and there's a chattering crowd at the doughnuts-and-coffee table, mostly volunteers, surrounding Divya and peppering her with questions about the fundraiser. Three years ago, Divya started South Asians for Obama, and she's distinguished herself since as one of his top bundlers in San Francisco, adroit at hitting up Silicon Valley's South Asian entrepreneurs and newly minted engineer millionaires for big donations. She catches sight of Seema. Excusing herself, she leads Seema to her office.

"Didn't go well?" Seema asks, when Divya shuts the door behind her and leans against it, sighing. Divya is striking in her maroon scoop-necked dress and a frilly pigeon-gray sweater—Divya dresses as stylishly for work as she would for an evening out—and Seema would have felt frumpy by comparison if she hadn't worn her favorite maternity top, sunflowers in a turquoise sky.

"The fundraiser was fine enough," Divya says. "But things are not looking good." Divya works on campaign finances but is well informed about most of the issues the campaign faces. An internal poll has just shown them slipping even further behind than the public polls indicate. With less than three weeks to the election, the team's mood is quite somber.

It shouldn't have been this difficult—any other year they'd be coasting to victory. But now it isn't even clear if Obama's visit helps or hurts. Divya describes the scene outside the fundraiser venue: not only Tea Partiers, waving placards of *Wall Street Traitor*, *Obamanator*, *Kills jobs, kills hope*, and *No death panels*, but also leftists, with their *Repeal Don't ask, Don't tell* and *Stop the discharges*. The fundraiser attendees, too, challenged Obama, quite aggressively, accusing him of broken promises—to be tough on Wall Street, to close Guantanamo. And even about his pledge to work with Republicans, to unite the nation. "As if he hasn't been trying," Divya fumes.

Seema lets Divya rant—it's a distraction from her other worries. Seema personally thinks Obama is trying too hard at conciliation. She also suspects that some of Obama's inaction is opportunistic, with an eye toward reelection. But Divya still has faith, still believes his election is proof that the country has turned a corner. An African American as president, then two years later an Indian American woman as California state attorney general—Divya will have worked on both their campaigns—the world is surely changing.

"How's Kamala doing?" Seema asks when Divya finally runs out of steam.

"She'll hang in there, she's a fighter." Kamala is campaigning in Los Angeles, appealing to her Black roots, making a round of the megachurches.

A knock on the door, and Divya reverts to her usual self, confident and in control. She taps on her computer, looks up information, gives directions, while Seema looks on, admiringly.

"I wish I could do more to help," Seema says when they're alone again, "but as you can see—" She pats the pronounced globe of her stomach.

"Oh my God, Seema, you must be due any day now," Divya says. "I'm sorry, I haven't even asked how you're doing. And your family is here. What a bad friend I am, let me make it up to you."

She cocks her head at Seema, her dimples popping a question. Then, ignoring Seema's finger wag, she heads to the door to lock it and lets the blinds down. But Seema doesn't protest when Divya, returning, enfolds her in an embrace from behind.

They sway like this for a minute, Divya's hands supporting the weight of me. Seema says, "Is this what friends do?"

Divya murmurs, her lips by Seema's ears, "Just say the word Seema, and I'll swoop in and save you from anything that's troubling you."

"You won't be able to save me from my mother and sister." Seema tries to disentangle herself, but Divya wishes to hold on a little while longer, and Seema lets her.

"And the twenty-year-old? Is she still pestering you?"

"She's not twenty!" Seema laughs, pulling herself free. "Though sometimes she does make me feel twice her age."

"That's what you get for dumping me for someone younger. Will you manage to see her while your family's here?"

"Yes—she's waiting for me."

10

Seema first met Leigh at a product release party that she'd organized for a software company, a client of her consulting firm. I was all of four months old then, barely showing, a small bump in my mother's body.

Leigh is a journalist, working for a nonprofit news organization serving the ethnic communities in the Bay Area. She sees Seema across the space of a ballroom and makes a beeline for her. Seema is dazzling that day: in her sapphire-and-silver dress, Seema outsparkles the glitter and glitz of the release party. At the first opportunity, Leigh asks to meet later, ostensibly to interview Seema about her client. At the end of that interview, Leigh asks her out on a date. Only later does Seema realize that she accepted because Leigh reminds her of Reshmi, her first teenage crush.

Leigh is half-Chinese, half-Irish. Leigh is lanky, lightly freckled, black-haired. Leigh is fifteen years younger than Seema and a head taller.

What Seema likes about Leigh: Her youthful nonchalance, her tousled hair, her spindly-muscled frame, the way her pale shoulder blades jut from her back like the hidden stubs of wings. The bowler hat that gives her face an impish insouciance. Eyes that are no color Seema has ever seen before—neither black, brown, blue, nor green but at various times all of them. A smile that welcomes everything, and her frank excitement every time they meet. The gentleness with which she cradles Seema's growing stomach, the tender firmness with which she clasps Seema to her as they lie cuddling in bed.

It's been agreed that while Nafeesa and Tahera are visiting, Leigh will take time off work if necessary to wait for Seema in her studio apartment in Oakland. Today Leigh is ready at the door to draw her in. First a kiss and an embrace before words are spoken, a rocking of bodies from side to side, forehead touching forehead, eyes melting eyes. Then Seema kicks her shoes off, and allows herself to be led to the bed, the only furniture in the room that can accommodate two people.

Ensconced between Leigh's tented knees, Seema leans back.

"My poor babe," Leigh says, "has it been very stressful?"

Seema nods and leans back even further, her entire weight now borne by Leigh. When Leigh presses her for details, she says, "Let's not talk about my family." Some degree of loyalty holds her back, toward Nafeesa mostly, but Tahera as well.

They lie in bed, body against body. At some point, as it usually happens, they are down to their undergarments, and then to skin.

There are no windows in the room. Leigh's bedside lamp bathes the room with dappled blues and greens. They are deep in a forest, by a stream, and the outside world recedes to the edges of consciousness. Now there is a place only for lips and breasts, for scent and sweat, for voices that speak not in words but in a more primitive language—in croons and cries, in urgent whispers.

II

Afterward, Leigh suggests they get a bite to eat, and Seema says she can't, she needs to return home.

Leigh grumbles that she'd been waiting for Seema for more than an hour. "Why were you late then?"

"I had to stop by the campaign office."

"Did you see Divya there?"

"Yes, we spoke about the fundraiser."

Leigh sits up, pushing the comforter off. "I'm your lowest priority," she says, arms locked around her knees.

"Don't be silly. I'd stay if I hadn't promised my mother I'd be home for lunch." But Seema knows that she's still unprepared to answer the question Leigh will want to discuss: Is Leigh to be present at the delivery? Seema has managed to stall the discussion by pleading that they wait and see how things turn out when her family's here.

"You're avoiding me. You didn't call me once last week—I called you each time."

"I cannot neglect my mother."

"What I don't understand is why you worry so much about what your family will think. They've already disowned you."

"Not my mother. And I have very little time left with her. I don't want it to get complicated."

Leigh turns Seema's face toward her. "Do you want me at the delivery or not?"

"Yes, of course"—Seema pauses—"if it won't rock the boat." The issue is not only Leigh's role during the delivery but her role afterward as well. Seema is relieved that Nafeesa and Tahera provide an excuse to hold Leigh from weaving herself inextricably into her life before she has figured out what Leigh really means to her.

Leigh swings out of bed and fishes her clothes off the floor. She wriggles into her briefs, facing away, her body pale and shimmering, vulnerable— narrow sinewed shoulders, jutting hip bones, high buttocks, hollowed-out butt cheeks. As always, Seema finds the curve of Leigh's spine expressive. The groove along the backbone ripples now with barely contained emotion— heartache, despair. She wants to touch it, to console Leigh, who is standing just beyond reach.

"We'll figure it out. I promise." She knows she's promising more than she ought to.

Without replying Leigh pulls on the rest of her clothes.

12

There are many aspects of Seema that remain mysterious to Leigh. They've never discussed Seema's marriage to Bill, for example. Seema rarely speaks about her pre-Bill past either.

But Leigh knows more about Seema than she's let on. She's had a crush on Seema since her college days, when she was required to view an interview between Seema and Deepa Mehta, the maker of the movie *Fire,* for a paper in her gender and women's studies minor at Berkeley. Her paper's focus is the dialogue Seema engages in with the filmmaker—about Mehta's decision to subordinate lesbian desire to themes of women's equality and emancipation in India—but it's Seema's sparkling eyes and lips Leigh ends up paying more attention to. For days afterward she wastes the time set aside to research the paper by searching instead (obsessively) for trails of Seema on the internet, spurred by the proximity of the vision, just across the bay.

Seema's name pops up, associated with various queer South Asian groups all over the country: Trikone in the Bay Area, SALGA in New York, Masala in Boston. There are photos of Seema with June Jordan, with Urvashi Vaid, with Pratibha Parmar, luminaries Leigh has only read about in class. Seema appears to have volunteered with queer organizations across the country and has even written articles for *The Advocate* and other queer publications.

Over the next few years, at random moments, Leigh scours the web for Seema, as she does for her celebrity crushes—Yang Li-Hua (thrilling in both her male and female roles in Taiwanese opera), Michelle Yeoh (Leigh has seen all her kung fu movies, and has watched *Crouching Tiger, Hidden Dragon* at least half a dozen times), and Salma Hayek (since that amazing tango with Ashley Judd in *Frida*). When—many years later—she spots Seema at the party, she recognizes her instantly. Seema seems to have aged little. That evening, Leigh hunts for her again on the internet. To her surprise she finds little new, only tidbits about Seema's recent professional activities, as if the queer Seema has ceased to exist. Leigh puts out feelers to her South Asian lesbian friends and her journalist friends, on the pretext of working on a piece. Various rumors filter back to her: Seema is a hasbian, Seema has married a man, Seema is divorced, Seema is pregnant. If she's puzzled how someone so involved in the queer scene for a decade could have turned her back on her past so completely, she doesn't let it discourage her. She goes to interview Seema giddy-eyed. She's prepared for rejection when she asks Seema out; Seema's bemused acceptance drives her ecstatic.

Every one of their initial dates—a stroll among roses in Golden Gate Park, an open-mic evening at a local Mission café, a Chihuly glass exhibit at the de Young Museum—is a roller coaster. For, surely, each would be the last one; what could possibly continue to interest Seema in her? Yet each is followed by another.

After their fourth date, a dinner at Leigh's favorite Chinese haunt in the Inner Sunset, where she orders in Mandarin a meal that delights and impresses Seema, they take a cab to Dolores Park and end up on a bench at the very top. And there, with the lights of the city spread at their feet, they kiss for the first time. And later that night, while Seema lies in her arms blissfully spent, she summons every ounce of courage she possesses to whisper, "If you ever get tired of me, you should let me know. I promise I won't make a fuss, you can send me away whenever."

Had she uttered those words merely to allay Seema's likely misgivings about her youth? For now that Seema is finally tiring of her—what else could explain her recent remoteness?—persistent anguish has eroded her resolve to back off from pressuring Seema, as she'd promised, as all her friends have advised. But every moment away from Seema is crushing; every moment with her is punishing.

13

Leigh is present when Nafeesa calls about the diagnosis.

It's a Sunday, about a month ago, and they have spent the afternoon in Seema's apartment poring over a list of names for me. A name is the first decision Seema is called to make on my behalf, and she finds the responsibility stressful.

Seema has never forgiven her parents for her name, which means *face, expression*, or *likeness* in Urdu. Not *beautiful face* or *sweet expression* or *likeness to a flower*, but those plain and ugly words, vague and ambiguous, as though her parents had been unsure what she'd turn out to be. The meaning in Hindi is worse—*limit, boundary, frontier*—restrictive and constraining. And though her father had finally placated her—she can be the expression of anything she wants to be, and as for the limit, she's unsurpassable—in some corner of her mind she believes her name is linked to the trajectory of her life. So she has roped in Leigh to share in the burden of picking a name for me, even though she worries that Leigh may infer from this invitation a depth to their relationship that she's not yet ready to grant.

Leigh goes over each name, ponders its meaning, labors over its pronunciation—they're all Muslim names. She gets Seema to speak them aloud. She makes a game of it: Speak it softly, she says, speak it loudly. Now as though you're waking him up. You just caught him with his hand in the cookie jar—scold him. He's crying—comfort him.

They take turns calling out to me. Some names are easier to reject—too harsh, too many syllables, too much of a strain on the vocal cords. Some names Leigh rejects—she assures Seema that no American tongue can wrap itself around those specific combinations of consonants and vowels. She also nixes names with corruptions that would deliver my future American school life into the hands of bullies: "No, not Faqr."

They come finally to the name they'll pick. "Ishraaq, where are you?" Seema calls out from the futon where they're sitting, and Leigh echoes it, producing a passable match for the *q* at the end. They pause, looking at each other—there are no obvious objections.

"What does *Ishraaq* mean?" Leigh asks.

"Radiance. Light of the rising sun."

"A new beginning." Leigh puts her lips to Seema's belly and whispers the name, now a caress, now a low growl, running her kisses along the skin stretched taut as a roof over me.

My could-be mother Tahera would never have chosen that name for me. Consider the names of her children: Arshad—rightly guided; Amina—faithful.

Do I choose that moment to kick? My mother is sure she feels something.

The phone rings. Seema answers, cautioning Leigh that the call is from her mother, but Leigh pays no heed as she continues her kisses down the slope of the belly and toward the thighs. It's only when Seema stiffens that Leigh looks up.

"What?" she mouths, but Seema doesn't answer, jerking her T-shirt down and scrambling off the futon.

Leigh becomes fearful. The Seema who drifts around the room is not the Seema of a few minutes ago but rather the Seema who seals herself off. This Seema doesn't see her even when looking in her direction, this Seema brushes past her as if she were not in the room at all. Whatever Seema hears over the phone is clearly distressing, but when Leigh tries to comfort her, she is shrugged off, recanting the intimacy of the previous hours.

Seema doesn't notice Leigh leave the apartment. Seema's world has contracted to her mother's trembling voice, the delayed echo of her own, the words they both struggle to form, and the silences that are more threatening than the words themselves. She'd been aware of the tests her mother had undergone; she cannot believe that something this devastating could be established merely by ruling out more likely and more testable conditions. There must be a mistake somewhere, there must be questions she can ask that would expose the lie. But she's ill equipped to find the right ones, and anyway her mother is not the right person to ask.

Only then does she notice Leigh's absence. All at once the present and the future reveal themselves to her—she is to be left utterly and devastatingly alone, with only me as anchor.

14

Tahera and Nafeesa have spent the morning in chai and cozy gossip about relatives in Chennai and are now cooking lunch together. Tahera has ordered her mother to rest, so Nafeesa sits by the kitchen table, chopping some vegetables and directing her daughter, who keeps up a commentary of everything she's doing on the stove. "I am adding the onions now, the mustard seeds have just spluttered."

It reminds Tahera of the Saturday mornings in Chennai after Seema left for college, when she was allowed into the kitchen to help her mother. She falls back easily into her old role of assistant, deferring to her mother on the quantity of spices to add, how long to stir, when to cover the pot. Occasionally she mentions the changes she's made to the recipes over the years: "It's simpler to do the seasoning right in the beginning."

Nafeesa sometimes accepts the changes, other times explains why her method is superior. Sometimes she insists Tahera do it her way, because that's how Seema likes it.

Tahera doesn't argue. She promised herself she would not let Seema spoil the time she has left with her mother.

She has forgotten, too, how enjoyable cooking is when not crammed between her practice at the clinic and domestic chores. Here she doesn't need to optimize every step—preparing and refrigerating boiled dal, steamed vegetables, fried onions, spice mixtures, all in bulk quantities—and there's nothing else she needs to keep an eye on in parallel.

But it's impossible to ignore how slow and halting her mother has become with the progress of her symptoms. Nafeesa grasps the knife tightly as though it could slip from her hand at any moment, sometimes needing to steady one hand with the other. And she takes frequent breaks, though only behind Tahera's back, the silent knife giving her away. But Tahera's offers to take over the chopping are met with resistance, much like how her daughter, Amina, would resist if some conferred responsibility were retracted.

Amina has recently taken to pleading with Tahera to be given chores in the kitchen. Tahera was inclined to be strict at first, insisting the child finish her homework before getting distracted. But now she enjoys having Amina there, with her books and crayons, enjoys instructing Amina in the small tasks she gives her—shelling peas, picking mint leaves, counting out raisins and cashew pods. She loves the care with which her daughter applies herself to these, her small fingers busy, her face furrowed with concentration. Much in the same way her mother now chops the tomatoes, slices and cubes the eggplant.

A rush of affection overcomes Tahera. She bends down and kisses her mother on her forehead before sweeping up the chopped vegetables and adding them to the pot. They are good together, good mothers and good daughters.

15

Inevitably, whenever Tahera thinks about Amina, an image of Arshad presents itself in contrast. This bothers Tahera, because there's nothing about her son to merit the anxiety he provokes in her.

In every way he's an exemplar: solicitous toward his parents, caring toward his sister, studious in his schoolwork, proficient in sports, disciplined.

And he's responsible beyond his years—he can be trusted to look after the house or babysit Amina whenever Tahera is called away on an emergency with a patient.

And now that he's old enough, he's thrown himself with equal fervor into his Quran studies and his namaz. He wakes up before dawn for fajr with his own alarm, refusing her offers to rouse him, and performs his wadu and is ready to unfurl his janamaz beside his father's without morning fuss, something that Ismail himself is sometimes guilty of. At these moments she can't help feeling proud, but then she also regrets that her one daily intimacy with Ismail is diminished by the boy's presence.

Perhaps it's Arshad's self-sufficiency that makes her feel superfluous, as if she has little to contribute to his well-being. "Masha'Allah," Tahera says, every time she recounts Arshad's many virtues to friends, but she wishes that her feelings for him were as uncomplicated as her love for Amina.

16

"How different daughters are from sons, don't you think?" Tahera says.

Grandmother, you don't answer immediately; your fingers continue to slowly feed the beans to the knife. There is a meditative aspect to the chopping, and it prevents the cramps that can shoot through your hands when you keep them idle too long. You reply only when Tahera repeats the question. "I wouldn't know. I only have you two."

"Do you ever regret not having a son?"

"Your Abba may have wanted a son at one point. I'm satisfied with my daughters." You fumble on the *satisfied* and hope Tahera doesn't notice.

"Poor Ammi—no sons or daughters to take care of her now." Tahera says it laughing, but you catch the sharp edge of something else under her words.

"I don't need anyone to take care of me."

But that's a lie. Already there have been days when your husband made chai, his bitter overboiled chai, because you couldn't manage even that, and your sister bustled about your home, preparing meals, sorting out the laundry, tidying up. And soon—perhaps even in a matter of months—you'll be too debilitated to move. But you know you can't burden yourself on your daughters the same way in America, nor can you expect them to leave their lives and return to Chennai to look after you.

An augury: your fingers spasm, and you must put down the knife. Despite the pain, you automatically begin separating the cut pieces from the uncut, forming two piles.

Tahera sits down and pulls the knife and cutting board toward her. She says, "How is Abba taking—all this?"

You know from her gesture that Tahera is asking about her father's reaction to your visit to San Francisco. You reach to take back the knife from her hands, but she refuses you and begins slicing the beans. "What am I supposed to be doing now?" you protest.

For the next few minutes the only sounds are the clacking of the knife against the cutting board, the pot bubbling on the stove, the hiss of the gas flame. It's just the two of you. "Your Abba didn't want me to come here. You know how he is when he doesn't want you to do something. He stopped speaking to me for a few days."

"How did you change his mind?" Tahera asks.

"We went back for a second consultation. The results were the same. I said I wanted to see my daughters while I still could. They should come here, he said. Even Seema? I asked. He didn't say anything, but he let me call Seema from our phone. It still makes him angry if I speak to Seema from home."

"Seema wanted you to come to San Francisco?" The knife flashes in her hands, the beans reduced to thin green rings.

You want to complain that she's cutting too finely, but her expression warns you against it—she's waiting for your reply. "I said I wanted to be with her for the delivery. She said she'd visit Chennai later with the baby. She can be quite stubborn—just like you, you're both like your Abba, don't deny it." Tahera winces at that, and you rush on, before she derails what you need to finish saying. "That's when I told her. She called home the next day, and your

Abba answered. They didn't speak, he just handed me the phone. Seema said she'd buy my ticket. He refused. He'd pay for my ticket or I couldn't go."

"You told her before you told me." Tahera has gone rigid, knife paused midair.

"I had to tell her, Tahera. Otherwise she wouldn't have agreed. I was planning to tell you both when I came here. I didn't want to break it over the phone."

"I've been a good daughter, haven't I?" Her words are clipped, matching the rhythm of the knife as she resumes, hewing through the beans. "I would have come to Chennai. I didn't because you said you were coming here. You didn't give me a chance. Are you even planning to come to Irvine?"

Now you understand the earlier bitterness in Tahera's voice. You do want to visit Irvine, perhaps after a few weeks of helping Seema with the baby—but who knows what your condition will be by then. "Seema's alone," you say. "How could I let her go through the delivery by herself?"

"You could have come to Irvine first."

You're on the brink of tears. Why hadn't Tahera suggested that earlier? You knot and unknot the edge of your saree, biting into your lower lip to stop it from trembling. Tahera is a blurred outline.

But her voice is sharp, knife-edged. "Is it our fault she's alone? Did we ask her to call herself a lesbian, then get married, then have a baby after deciding to get divorced? She's always done what she wanted. Yet it's Seema you come to spend your last days with, while I, who've always done what you wanted, am treated like an afterthought, like I don't matter."

Words fail you. They've always failed you. When you need them the most, Grandmother, they shrivel up somewhere deep within you and die.

Seema's voice cuts through the moment; neither of you noticed her return. Peeking warily into the kitchen, she says, "Who doesn't matter?"

"Nobody." Tahera plunks down the knife and sweeps the beans onto a plate. "We're just gossiping about Chennai." Her eyes are downcast and hooded, but you can't miss their angry glitter.

You soak up your half-formed tears with your saree before showing your face to your daughters.

17

How airless the apartment feels that afternoon, how strictly its space seems carved up among the three women.

After a meal that is almost as uncomfortable as the previous night's, Nafeesa tosses restlessly in the bedroom, Seema shifts restively in her seat by the window in the living room, while Tahera, trapped in the kitchen, speaks to Khadija, her partner, in whose charge she's left their family practice in Irvine.

It's Nafeesa who suggests a walk, giving up on the elusive nap, not able to unhear Tahera's accusations from the morning.

Seema and Tahera leap at the idea. But will the walk be too tiring for their mother? It's obvious she will not be turned down. Tahera has to finish her asr namaz first, though.

The mid-October sun drips honey, doling out its warmth liberally, San Francisco's vaunted fog still crouching behind the hills to the west. The two sisters flank their mother, each holding on to one of Nafeesa's hands.

"Like when we were kids, no?" Seema says.

Tahera concurs warily, because she has contrived to take hold of Nafeesa's right hand. As girls they'd squabble over who got to walk on their mother's right, settling the matter by taking turns the way out and back. But Seema has forgotten this preoccupation from their childhood, and Tahera relaxes, gripping her mother's hand, a hard-won, justifiable trophy.

What a picture they make! Tahera covered hair to foot, black gown billowing in the breeze; Seema rotund in a tight ochre top and flowing brown pants; and sandwiched between them, Nafeesa's slight figure in a green saree and white sneakers, pink sweater and blue shawl, a combination completely deficient in color coordination. The sisters burst into laughter on catching sight of their reflection in a storefront window.

"What?" Nafeesa says, baffled by their sudden mirth, but they don't stop laughing. And though Nafeesa knows she's in some way involved in their merriment, perhaps even the target, she is secretly delighted.

Some tension is eased, some old intimacy begins to take hold as they stroll through the Mission's sun-drenched streets, past multicolored murals and buildings painted orange and purple and cyan, past grocery stores and florists exhibiting brilliantly hued wares on sun-splattered pavements. An almost natural chitchat springs up among them, Seema sharing lively anecdotes about the landmarks they pass, and Nafeesa and Tahera listening and pointing and inquiring with an almost natural enthusiasm.

They're walking slowly—Seema slower than her pregnancy dictates, keeping an eye on her mother for signs of exhaustion. Before long they find themselves crossing Market Street and are confronted with the rolling hills of Lower Haight.

"Shall we turn back?" Seema asks.

Nafeesa denies fatigue, wanting to prolong the truce the outing seems to have fostered. They continue, stopping at each intersection to pick the direction with the easiest incline. Even so, her breathing soon grows ragged, and she has to remind herself not to grip her daughters' hands so tightly every time she feels the need to take an extra deep breath. When she finally agrees to take a break, her daughters exchange glances of relief.

They rest on a bench in a bus stop for a brief moment before a store selling baby apparel across the street catches Nafeesa's eye. Inside, she flits from shelf to shelf, exclaiming over blankets and sweaters, socks and shoes, despite Seema's protests that the baby has all the clothes he needs. Nafeesa's taken in by a particularly soft blanket, sky blue and embroidered with a smiling moon and many winking stars. She has brought clothes for me from India but nothing she thinks will last me beyond the first few months. Alas, she has left her purse behind in Seema's apartment. She strokes the blanket, reluctant to give it up.

"I have baby blankets already," Seema says.

"I'll get it," Tahera says. "I didn't get anything for the baby yet." She takes the blanket from Nafeesa, glad to make up for her behavior that morning. She's shocked at its price—she'd never have bought anything as expensive for Amina or Arshad. "What else would you like, Ammi?"

Over Seema's objections, she leads Nafeesa through the store, and they rummage through baskets and racks, adding to their purchases—a nightcap and a pair of gloves and socks for me, the same blue as the blanket, bibs, and sleepwear.

Next door is a bookstore. Nafeesa, energized now and finding a ready ally in her younger daughter, begins browsing the children's section.

Seema follows reluctantly, leery now that her mother and sister have joined forces. She'll have to put her foot down, or she'll be railroaded by them the rest of their stay. "My son is not going to read books any time soon," she tells Tahera.

"Stop saying that," Tahera whispers sharply. "It will remind Ammi and make her sad. Let her do what she wants. See how happy she is."

Indeed, Nafeesa darts around with an armful of books—alphabets and numbers, farm animals and fairy tales—unable to stop herself, intent on showering me with an entire childhood's worth of books.

The store has an international section too. There are no books from India, but Nafeesa finds a shelf with a smattering of books from England. "Look, they have the entire Faraway Tree series." These are the books her daughters read repeatedly—about three siblings who find magical lands at the top of a tall tree reaching into the clouds—before they moved on to more mature fare. There are still shelves in their home in Chennai lined with books they'd devoured during their school years, even if the lending libraries they'd frequented had one by one disappeared.

Tahera exclaims over the series, pulls out her favorite, and sits down to read. Nafeesa searches for Seema to tell her of her discovery and finds her in the poetry section.

"They've changed the names," Tahera complains when Nafeesa returns with Seema. "Bessie is now Beth, and Fanny is Frannie."

The disappointment is fleeting. Soon both daughters are flipping through the books, reading snippets to each other, recalling other favorite passages that they must read immediately, and even—here Nafeesa chokes up, for it has been years since she's witnessed anything like this—even peeking over each other's shoulders to read a page. How often she saw her daughters reading this way as children. Her heart pounds with the pleasure of the sight.

Seema buries her nose in the pages and inhales, green apple and dried wood. There's something so essentially bookish about that smell that she can convince herself it's the same smell her own well-thumbed copies once possessed. Were they still there gathering dust on some shelf? Or did her father get rid of them as she'd been told he got rid of everything else that belonged to her?

She collects a copy of each book in the series. "Tahera, will Arshad and Amina like these?"

Tahera ponders the question. Amina is the right age for the series. But magic and pixies and goblins? She has not permitted Arshad the Harry Potter books, which have been hard to ignore, with posters everywhere of the movie series, dark images of grimy kids and wizards and witches brandishing knobbly wands. Ismail is not concerned they'd corrupt Arshad, but he leaves decisions about books and movies to her.

"No, they don't read such books," she tells Seema. There are probably better—more Islamic—books she could buy for Amina. She resolves to look for these when she's back in Irvine, reshelving the book she holds in her hand.

"I'll buy them for myself then," Seema says.

They find the city transformed when they leave the bookstore. The sun has sunk behind the hills to the west, the blue of the sky replaced by pale pinks and violets. A faint mist, the beginnings of fog, has nosed its way into the neighborhood. Lights dot the streets, and farther east blink hazy lights across the bay. The flushed city of the afternoon is no more.

"This is beautiful," Nafeesa says, but she shivers.

"I didn't realize it was so late," Tahera says, flustered. "I must get back for the maghrib namaz, then call Amina and Arshad before they go to bed."

And Seema, who'd wished earlier that the day would pass quickly, is sorry that it's ended. The past has been an oasis.

They hail a cab, and squeeze in, quiet now. Nafeesa has suddenly shrunk, as though with the light—the sky has turned a deep unrepentant purple—her strength has drained away. She sits huddled between her daughters, clutching to herself the blanket and the books and a fluffy yellow duck she persuaded Tahera to buy for me. Each sister looks out a window, lost in her own thoughts. Each sister lurches between vexation and hope that the cab will take all evening to arrive.

18

Tahera is folding the janamaz after the maghrib prayers when Seema holds out a book, smiling. "For you. I got it at the bookstore."

"What is it?" Tahera continues folding without glancing at the book.

"Poetry," Seema says. "I remembered how much you liked Keats. Your favorite poet, no?"

"I don't read poetry anymore," Tahera replies, which is true, if one didn't count the Quran. She has neither the inclination nor the time to waste on frivolous, self-serving indulgences.

"It has that poem you loved—*There was a naughty boy*. Only you changed it to *girl* whenever you recited it." Seema flips through the book trying to find the poem.

Tahera's first impulse is to deny Seema, pretend she doesn't recall. How dare Seema invoke their shared history after renouncing all rights to it. She already regrets her sentimentality from earlier, the false comfort of those books from their past, the delusion of continuing sisterhood. But the opening of the Keats poem comes back to her too vividly to ignore.

"There was a naughty girl, a naughty girl was she, she would not stop at home, she could not quiet be," she recites involuntarily, taking the book from Seema.

"You used to recite it everywhere. You did that funny skip at the end, hopping from one foot to the other. How did it go?"

"She stood in her shoes and she wondered. She wondered. She stood in her shoes and she wondered."

"You could teach Amina the poem. She'd look sweet doing it."

Tahera thumbs through the book. The complete poems and selected letters of John Keats. Her father had many collections of Keats's poems, but none that claimed to be complete. She recognizes many of the titles, some of her favorite poems. How foolish she'd been, so taken with poetry, convinced there was nothing more important in the world. And surely Seema is raking it up now to make some disparaging point, to attack and ridicule her. She'd seen the look on Seema's face when she declined the Faraway

Tree books on her children's behalf, as if she pitied the children their close-minded mother.

She thrusts the book back at Seema. "All that is in the past. You should keep it for yourself. Or for *your* children."

Seema's thwarted expression is very satisfying.

Besides, she'd never been the naughty girl in the poem. The poem fit Seema better. It was Seema who initiated the scrapes they got into, who created a scene if she didn't get what she wanted, who finally ran away from home.

"I have to call home," Tahera says, turning away. "Amina will be waiting."

19

Hearing her mother's voice, Amina becomes teary-eyed again. But the busy evening, errands with their father topped by dinner at Hot Breads, where her brother let her have the bigger share of chicken nuggets, has mostly succeeded in distracting her from the approaching motherless weekend.

"I miss you," Amina says to Tahera. "Do you miss me?"

"I miss you too, Ammu," Tahera says, blowing a kiss into the phone.

"I love you," Tahera says to Amina. "Do you love me?"

"I love you two, Ammi," Amina says.

This is a game they play often. Amina giggles, playing along with her mother.

I love you ten, like a chocolate bar.

I love you hundred, like a pickle jar.

I love you thousand, like a room full of dolls.

I love you million, like a sky full of stars.

20

Lately, my could-be father Ismail has visited the mosque most nights after the children go to bed to participate in discussions of the Quran, led by Imam

Zia. Tonight he cannot. Their mother isn't home, and Amina insists he stay by her bedside. She has sniffled her way to sleep, but her hold on his hand hasn't loosened enough to extricate himself.

Tonight, Ismail especially wishes to visit the mosque. There's the fund-raiser tomorrow, and perhaps a conversation with Imam Zia, and an extra namaz there, would dispel his anxiety.

Imam Zia is a recent addition to the mosque and Islamic center. He's from Pakistan but brought up and educated in England, with a PhD in Islamic theology. He has won several international competitions, both in Quran re-cital and in Quranic exegesis. Since his arrival two years ago, he has instituted many activities: besides the Friday sermons, there are nightly discussion groups and regular lectures and study sessions. He even maintains a blog on living a life of Islam, answering anonymous questions from the congregation.

Another innovation: weekly soccer matches. Imam Zia is an avid soccer fan. Every Tuesday, after the isha namaz, carpools from the mosque drive to a rented indoor soccer field, where he leads a training session, followed by a match. Imam Zia is thirty-eight, but he runs faster and dribbles more wickedly than those half his age. The soccer matches have attracted many Muslim men from Irvine and the surrounding towns. Ismail, too, has become a regular at them.

Imam Zia is keen to develop the grounds around the Islamic center for sports—a soccer field and volleyball and basketball courts—and to extend the center to include a gym with locker rooms and showers, to make the center a place where the youth can congregate, find community and Allah, while having clean fun at the same time. Imam Zia believes such a space is essential to ensure the youth don't stray from their faith, and that they—including the girls—grow up strong and confident. A plan has been drawn, and Ismail is on the fundraising committee, spearheading its efforts, to culminate in the event planned for tomorrow, in less than twenty-four hours.

Ismail now considers himself Imam Zia's right-hand man. He has worked hard the last few months, calling on Muslim businesses and wealthy members of the community to ask for donations and pushing the organizing committee to implement as many fundraising ideas as possible—securing sponsors for the event in exchange for publicity, a magazine to sell advertising space, a silent auction, etc.

The target is finally within reach. Ismail is no longer anxious about the fundraising itself. The logistics of the event are also under control. What perturbs him now is the potential for trouble. They've heard no reports of specific protests planned for tomorrow, but recent incidents in Manhattan, Murfreesboro, and Yorba Linda have been very disquieting.

Ismail believes that hatred of Obama is being exploited to revive the fear of Muslims and Islam that had appeared to fade slowly in the decade following 9/11. How else to explain the widespread belief that Obama is a Muslim or that Islam is taking over America? Though he'd been excited by Obama winning the presidency, even tantalized by the possibility that Obama's win was a sign of Allah's intentions for America, Ismail has since come to the conclusion that Obama's background is not just a distraction but a setback for Muslims everywhere. Obama, though born to a Muslim and stepson to another, is no Muslim, and despite Obama's many speeches regarding tolerance and respect, Ismail does not expect him to pursue any policy that would put American interests second, especially regarding the Middle East. America will always want more oil and will always support Israel. But what Obama's presidency has done is to rally half the country against him, and the American right wing—hardcore Christians and Jews—has seized this opportunity to further its crusade against Islam.

Sitting in the children's bedroom—Arshad and Amina share a room, Amina still unwilling to sleep alone—Ismail can feel the dread weighing him down. If only he could do something—go for a drive, go to the mosque, talk to Imam Zia, pray. But he's stuck here. Of course Tahera must go to her mother's side, like any caring daughter, but did it have to include this weekend, knowing that anything could happen at the fundraiser tomorrow?

Across the room, Arshad isn't yet asleep. He's lying rigid in his bed, knees up, staring at the ceiling as though it holds mysteries. Which in a way it does, for glowing faintly green—faint because the light from the bedside lamp is overwhelming—are glow-in-the-dark stickers of constellations and galaxies that Arshad had Ismail fix to the ceiling above his bed years ago. Glimmering amid the ghostly universe are Arshad's favorite verses from the Quran, a more recent addition, projected onto the ceiling. There's the ayat Al-Kursi from the surah Al-Baqarah, and the last three surahs from the Quran—Al-Ikhlas, Al-Falaq, and An-Nas. His son's lips move, as though he's reciting.

"Recite a little louder," Ismail tells Arshad, although it could wake Amina up.

Arshad starts out softly, with the surah he's memorized for the Quran recitation competition in the fundraiser, his voice thin and high. As he grows more confident, he grows louder. Arshad has been learning Quran recitation in his Sunday school and plans to memorize the entire Quran. The class is run by Imam Zia, who's complimented Arshad on his progress. Arshad's tajwid has improved remarkably since he started practicing pronunciation accompanying the computer program his mother found for him, which displayed renderings of the correct shape of the mouth and placement of the tongue alongside the corresponding syllables. Arshad's control of pitch and tune, though, is still diffident and unsteady. It will take years, of course, to master that, but even so, Ismail can already hear Imam Zia's characteristic vocalizations in Arshad's fledgling style.

Arshad stumbles a few times in recalling some ayats. But there's an earnestness to his efforts, a natural piety to his recitation, that fills Ismail with pride. Subhan'Allah, this son of his is truly a blessing, an example of how to practice faith in this day and age. How much time Arshad is willing to expend on his desire to master the Quran, time that his friends squander on video games and the internet. That too of his own volition, with no compulsion from his parents.

Isn't this the reason why the community center is important? Would Ismail have wasted his youth if he'd had access to such a community? All those years straying away from the true path of Islam, not knowing what he was missing, not even realizing how he was harming himself. Yes, there are challenges—and is not what's happening in America now just such a challenge?—but challenges are meant to be faced, not run away from, and surely Allah, subhanahu wa ta'ala, would steer His believers to safety, as He had steered the Prophet, peace be upon him, through those dark initial days at Medina. There's no reason to be beset by doubts—his son's faith puts his to shame. He listens to Arshad, marveling at the quiet poetry, wishing the moment never to end.

But it does. Arshad finishes and falls silent. Ismail notices that Amina's grasp has slackened. Her brother's voice has succeeded where his had failed, although her forehead is puckered, as if she's still concentrating on what she's heard. He smoothes the creased skin and, rising, tucks her blanket around her.

He places a kiss on his son's forehead. "Go to sleep. We have a long day tomorrow."

When he turns off the bedside lamp, the stars and galaxies burn instantly brighter, as if the universe has come to life. And emblazoned across its skies are Allah's verses.

21

Seema has asked her friend Fiaz to take them sightseeing around San Francisco. She's counting on him to entertain her mother and sister and act as a buffer and deterrent. Surely the three women will have to behave themselves in the presence of an outsider.

Fiaz arrives at ten on Saturday morning, punctual as always. He's sharply dressed, colorful: gray jacket, maroon shirt, teal jeans, brown shoes.

"What?" he says, catching Seema's look as she lets him in. "I did tone it down."

And he has, for he looks irreproachably harmonious. The gray in his jacket is streaked with just the right hint of the dark teal of the jeans, and his maroon shirt is echoed by the rich mulch brown of his shoes.

He gives her a peck on her cheek, before looking around and mouthing, "Where are they?" As though he's inquiring about aliens from outer space.

Seema is forced to laugh. "Ammi, Tahera—Fiaz is here." She's eager to hurry everyone out of the confines of the apartment.

But Tahera is still getting ready, and Nafeesa will not allow Fiaz to leave the apartment without offering him something. "But Fiaz is being so good taking us around. It's terrible if we don't offer him even chai. It'll only take a moment."

"Don't put yourself out, Aunty," Fiaz says. "I like being a tour guide. That's the only time I remember how beautiful San Francisco really is."

Fiaz works with Seema. But he's more than just a colleague—he's also her oldest and best friend in the city. Nafeesa has already met him; he accompanied Seema to receive Nafeesa at the airport and drove them home.

What Seema has not told Nafeesa is that Fiaz is gay. He lives in the Castro with Pierre, his French boyfriend of many years. Seema met Fiaz when she'd moved to San Francisco the first time, at a potluck hosted by Trikone, the first South Asian gay and lesbian organization in the United States, or in the world, for that matter. It was Fiaz who'd alerted her to an opening in his firm when she was considering returning to San Francisco, after breaking up with Ann, the girlfriend she'd moved to Boston for. Fiaz is one of the few friends from Trikone who remained after she married Bill.

Nafeesa makes chai, while Tahera clears away her things in the living room. Fiaz and Seema sit across from each other at the dining table, like kids awaiting punishment.

"How're you holding up?" Fiaz whispers.

"We'll talk," Seema signals. Conversation is difficult, given the two extra pairs of ears.

"How do you like San Francisco so far, Aunty?" Fiaz asks, taking the proffered cup.

"I'm happy to be here," Nafeesa says.

She does look happy, for this simple act of making and offering chai. Nafeesa fusses over Fiaz, over the amount of sugar and milk in the chai, thrusting cookies at him. Fiaz submits gracefully to her ministrations. He compliments her: "This is the best chai I've had in San Francisco, Aunty!" He keeps up a lively spiel about the places they're going to visit and is a fount of amusing anecdotes about the history of the city and the gold rush that propelled its growth. Seema relaxes. The day will go smoothly enough, she thinks. Her mother is clearly smitten: Fiaz can be very charming.

His charms don't work on Tahera, though. Entering the kitchen in her jilbab and hijab, she replies to his greeting with a brusque salaam, ignoring the hand he holds out to her. She accepts Nafeesa's offer of chai but drinks it in large gulps, as if swallowing a tonic. Fiaz attempts to engage her in a conversation, asking about her last trip to San Francisco, offering to alter the itinerary if she's visited any of the spots he's planned for them, but she declines: "Ammi hasn't seen them. It's kind of you." She smiles perfunctorily at his jests—"What do Texans think of our Muslim president?"—and replies to other inquiries with monosyllables.

Soon Fiaz gives up. "Shall we leave?" he asks, putting his cup down. "The car is parked around the corner."

Tahera and Nafeesa go down first. Fiaz helps Seema lock up and follows her.

"What have I got you into?" Seema tells Fiaz.

"Relax, just relax," Fiaz says. "Everything will be okay."

22

Grandmother, you watch Fiaz help Seema into the passenger seat as he holds the door open and waits till she buckles her seat belt before shutting it, and you think: What a sweet man! He's handsome and obviously fit. His black hair is glossy and slicked back, his eyes sparkle. He sports a precisely fashioned beard. But he's younger than Seema, you think, probably by five years.

You wonder how he got to the United States, to San Francisco. There is a confidence to him, a way of carrying himself that suggests he is native to the city and the country. Yet he speaks flawless Urdu, without an accent.

"Seema's Urdu is poor," he says. "She should be ashamed of herself." He says this in Urdu.

Seema swats him but cannot deny the allegation. Neither can you, Grandmother, and you're ashamed too: your daughters never learned to read or write Urdu when they were children. The Urdu they grew up with is colloquial and mongrel, with English and Hindi handily substituting for words they didn't know and couldn't be bothered to learn, despite all your attempts to instruct them.

They were never interested. They went to an English-medium convent school. They grew up on books from England—beginning with Enid Blyton's adventures, before progressing into the world of Charles Dickens and Jane Austen and the Brontë sisters, then Thomas Hardy and George Eliot, Byron and Shelley and Keats. All their father's influence.

You have a BA in Urdu literature and would have continued with an MPhil, or even a PhD, if you hadn't married my grandfather. His love of everything English easily drowned your own love for a language that was "only good for love poetry," as your husband put it after marrying you, though he didn't deny it was your recitation of Urdu ghazals the evening he came bride-seeking that had so captivated him.

"That's the only woman I want to marry," he'd said, turning down many flattering offers from prospective fathers-in-law with account balances large enough to bankroll a hospital for him. And you, Grandmother, flattered by his lovesick adamance, allowed your whole world to be turned upside down. Giving up Urdu was only one of the sacrifices you made—and perhaps the most unnecessary, for couldn't you have continued in your love for the language, even if you'd been forced to give up dreams of making a career studying and teaching it?

Sitting in the back seat with Tahera, you try to remember what you can of phrases and courtesies that had once slipped easily off your tongue but now feel so strange that you're afraid you'll trip over them, should you be called on to exhibit your past mastery. But your daughters seem to have forgotten all about your degree, just like you had until this moment.

The first destination is the Golden Gate Bridge. Fiaz points out various landmarks as he maneuvers the car through the light weekend traffic, but you're not really paying attention. You're lost in past drives with your daughters and their father—always this same way, father and elder daughter in the front, mother and younger daughter in the back, the father holding forth on some topic or the other. Fiaz's voice rolls over you, and the city sinks into the earth with you barely noticing, to be replaced by trees and shrubs and rocks and water.

You're at the Golden Gate Bridge, under its looming skeletal towers and massive cables. To the left and the right are the Pacific Ocean and the San

Francisco Bay, two hundred feet below. You're more excited by this glimpse of the Pacific than you're impressed by the bridge. You can't believe that the sliver of water you see between the two tongues of land is really the largest ocean on earth. That sliver extends all the way west, wrapping itself around the globe and merging into that other ocean by your homeland's feet. You're transported in an instant to Kanyakumari, to that tip of India's peninsula where three bodies of water meet.

You're standing on the stippled beach with your daughters and husband. Your daughters each hold on to one of their father's hands as the trio edges toward the waves, churidars and pants rolled up to their knees. You're guarding their footwear.

"There," he says, pointing toward the east, lifting one of the girl's hands along with his, "that's the Bay of Bengal." Now lifting the other daughter's hand: "That's the Arabian Sea." Finally, lifting both their hands, and gesturing to the south: "And there's the Indian Ocean."

"Where, Abba?" asks Tahera.

"How can you tell?" says Seema.

"Can't you see?" he says. "Look, the Arabian Sea is muddy. The Bay of Bengal is green. The Indian Ocean is blue."

Seema claims she sees the difference, but Tahera can't. Father and eldest daughter take turns waxing on how blue, how green, how muddy each is, until your youngest daughter is reduced to tears. She comes running back to you, asking whether you can tell the seas and ocean apart.

"No, I cannot." You console her. "It's just the sun." The sun is in the west and the waters closest to the sun glint differently.

"It's just the sun," Tahera shouts to her father and sister, who have waded a little deeper into the water by now. "You're both lying."

She runs after them, skirting the edge of the waters, jumping back every time a wave advances. "Abba, Seema, I want to come too."

They eventually return for her, and the trio stands for a long while in the churning seas, as the sun is slowly swallowed up by the hungry line of the horizon. Father and daughters are an outline silhouetted against it, distinguishable only by their height.

The ground beneath you shifts, as though the earth is being drained away, and in a flash you're standing on the Golden Gate Bridge again.

Tahera holds your hand to steady you against its sway and steers you around a couple by the railing, kissing. "Careful, Ammi."

A chill wind has begun blowing. You clutch Tahera's hands for warmth but also as a precaution—as if the wind could carry you away, over the bridge and across the bay.

Seema and Fiaz stand in the shelter of a tower, leaning into each other as they share a laugh. They smile, beckoning you and Tahera to join them.

"How good they look together!" you're moved to exclaim.

23

"Your sister is nothing like you," Fiaz says. "But anyone can tell you're sisters."

"Really?" Seema grimaces. "How?"

"Your voices. Your eyes. You both have similar expressions." He studies Tahera approaching them. "Does your sister ever smile?"

"I suppose she must." Surely there were moments when Tahera should have smiled, not a mechanical curving of the lips, but a genuine transfiguration of her face—on birthdays, while receiving prizes after winning competitions, on vacations, at treats. "She was always serious."

Had Tahera really been so solemn, or had Seema paid so little attention to her sister that she can't recall even one joyful image of her? The thought is distressing.

Her sister and mother tread ponderously. Nafeesa's shawl and Tahera's jilbab are plastered to their bodies, the edges fluttering wildly. There's the same concentration in their faces, the same determination as they struggle against the wind. How small and fragile they look, like birds stranded in a storm. She left them behind in order to speak with Fiaz alone. She'd only have memories of silent, serious faces if she kept fleeing from them this way.

"Isn't this lovely?" she calls out, smiling a welcome at them, and gesturing toward the red towers and the cables, the blue skies and the water. "The last time I was here was with your children, Tahera."

She'd ended up here with Amina and Arshad as the sun set, unexpectedly happy with their day together.

She'd been beyond surprised when she'd received a call from Tahera in March. Their last conversation was more than a decade earlier, when she called Tahera to wish her well on her marriage to Ismail, after Tahera moved to Dallas to join her husband. The letter Tahera wrote her after made it clear she wanted no more contact.

It turned out Tahera was in San Francisco attending a conference hosted by the American Academy of Family Practitioners, invited to give a talk on healthcare for Muslim women. Her husband had accompanied her, for a day of meetings at his company's Silicon Valley headquarters in Santa Clara. They'd brought the children along.

Then: "I heard you're getting divorced."

So the call was clearly obligatory, imposed on Tahera by Nafeesa, their go-between, relating news of one sister to the other. Yet, hearing Tahera's voice after such a long time, Seema immediately yielded to the lure of the past, craving that sympathy from her younger sister, so soothing and familiar from her childhood. She found herself narrating details of the breakup—brave and telling—calculated to arouse that past sister's solicitude. She even considered disclosing something she'd learned barely a week earlier, and was still grappling with—that she was pregnant as well.

But Tahera displayed neither sympathy over the phone nor exulting vindication, only the sense of duty. Seema was to be denied any satisfaction—neither the knowledge that her sister was gloating at her misery, nor the catharsis of reconciliation.

After listening mostly in silence, Tahera asked, "Do you need any help?"

"No, I'm fine," Seema replied, hearing the effort it took Tahera to frame the question. To prove to Tahera, and to herself that she was really fine, she'd agreed to meet the visiting family for dinner.

I had been all of an inch then, my presence made real only by the accompanying symptoms—morning sickness, heartburn, the ripening tug of my to-be mother's breasts. She had no concept of me except as cells quickening in her body, cells she could still choose to expel if she wanted. I was a to-be child she hadn't decided yet to keep.

What did she see in her sister's children that trip that made up her mind?

24

At the Thai restaurant by their hotel, Tahera and her family are already seated when Seema arrives. Tahera stands up as though for a hug, but changes her mind and scoots over to make space for Seema. Ismail raises his hand to his forehead in a silent salaam.

Tahera introduces Seema to her children. "This is your Seema Aunty. Remember I said Ammi has a sister? Say salaam."

"Assalamu Alaikum, Seema Aunty," the children intone. They are seated opposite Seema, with their father between them. Amina is shy, and hides her face in her father's kurta. Ismail smooths her hijab over her head and asks her not to behave so bashfully—what will her aunt think of her?

The more interesting question: What do *they* think of Seema?

Tahera hasn't seen Seema for fifteen years. She first notes what Seema's wearing: a long skirt and a demure full-sleeved top, brown and beige. She's both relieved and irritated by Seema's choice—she'd expected Seema in jeans or pants and in brighter colors. She wonders what Seema makes of her own attire, of Amina's hijab.

In the quick appraising glance Ismail gives Seema, he sees that she is stylishly dressed, poised, sure of herself, matching Tahera's various accounts. The prospect of a divorce seems to have had little effect on her—she is cheerful, unflinching, unabashed.

Arshad can't stop staring. He notes the differences: his mother is in a hijab, his aunt isn't; there are dark circles around his mother's eyes, while his aunt's face has makeup and lipstick. His mother is like a moth, his aunt like a sparrow, sharply etched. "This is your sister, Ammi?" he asks.

Seema replies, "Yes, I'm your Ammi's sister."

"Are you Ammi's *little* sister?" Amina asks, chewing the tip of her hijab to allay the vague sense of trepidation Seema produces in her. Seema's smile appears welcoming, but Amina holds back, uncertain. She associates warmth and motherly attention only with the flowing curves of a jilbab and hijab.

"No, I'm your Ammi's *big* sister." Seema laughs, tapping Tahera on the shoulder. "I'm two years older."

Tahera smiles back, a quick piqued smile. It irks to acknowledge that Seema does appear younger. How fresh her sister looks, while she is already tired, wishing the visit to San Francisco were over. She reminds herself that she's added the stress of this meeting to the stress about her talk the next day at the conference. She says, "Wait till you become a mother yourself."

Seema winces, and Tahera assumes Seema is reminded about her divorce. Her sister is clearly not as happy as she looks, nor as invulnerable as she pretends to be.

They study the menus, a welcome diversion. Arshad and Amina already know what they want—fried rice! Thai fried rice is one of Arshad's favorite dishes. Seema decides on a chicken dish with basil and green peppers. Arshad and Amina glance over to their father.

Ismail is familiar with that glance: Are they allowed to order chicken here? He shakes his head. Arshad is already forming words: "But Seema Aunty—!" Ismail tries to preempt Arshad but is too late. He sits back, letting Tahera deal with this misadventure. After all, this dinner is on her insistence. He'd given in with reluctance.

Seema looks up from her menu. "What?"

"You can't eat chicken here," Arshad says. "It's not zabiha."

"Your Seema Aunty can order what she wants," Tahera says. "We won't be sharing."

"Oh, I can order tofu," says Seema. "I don't have to eat meat."

Arshad is disappointed he can't display his newly acquired knowledge, the relevant ayats from surahs Al-Ma'ida and Al-An'am regarding the rules of slaughter. Large questions foment in his mind. Why did his mother say Seema Aunty could eat nonpermitted meat? Won't Allah punish Seema

Aunty for this sin? And doesn't his mother care what happens to her sister, as he cares for Amina?

25

When the children greet her with "Assalamu Alaikum, Seema Aunty," Seema is taken aback by how easily the response, "Alaikum Assalam," rolls off her tongue. She remembers using only the first half of the greeting as a child toward her elders, never the response. And here she is, responding to the children so naturally. She senses a collapse in time: for the moment, she's both adult and child, both here in San Francisco and back in Chennai.

This sensation is heightened by seeing Tahera and her daughter side by side. Amina's face is Tahera's from years ago, while Tahera looks shockingly aged and drawn now.

Both mother and daughter are wearing hijabs, and Seema thinks: The girl is so young, give her a chance to decide for herself. Neither father nor brother is wearing a prayer cap, after all. Ismail is in a white kurta and a leather jacket, Arshad in a bright yellow T-shirt and black jeans. Ismail's beard is trimmed.

Uncomfortable silences persist till the food arrives. The curries are spicy but delicious, and the fried rice is served in a hollowed-out pineapple, which draws cries of delight from the children. Arshad and Amina grow animated as they crunch happily on cashews and pineapple chunks that stud the rice. They compete with each other for their Seema Aunty's attention, excitedly recounting the day's adventures—the barking sea lions, the bungee trampoline, the carousel ride at Fisherman's Wharf—interrupting each other, amplifying, disagreeing.

Arshad is wistful about the Ripley's museum they were unable to visit. Amina wishes they'd gone to the aquarium. Their father had promised to take them the next day, but he now has a meeting in Santa Clara, and they have to accompany him, since their mother will be busy at the conference. How lucky Seema Aunty is to live in San Francisco! Does she live near the Wharf?

They've anointed her best friend already. She is asked to settle disputes, to explain mysteries, to exercise her authority as a local. Their high spirits infect her. She slips into the role of a much-loved aunt easily—much preferable to excommunicated sister—reveling in the ready intimacy that she's rarely felt before with the children of her friends.

"How would it be," she exclaims, surprising herself, "if I take tomorrow off and show the children around San Francisco?"

The table thumps to a halt. The children look at their parents, their parents look at each other.

After a moment's hesitation, Tahera says, "Your father must decide."

Ismail is clearly reluctant. The children immediately train their entreaties at him: they were promised the sights! They clutch at his arms. When he finally agrees, the children erupt in celebration. Seema realizes that, like Amina, she too has been holding her breath.

But the next morning, waiting in the lobby of the Fairmont Hotel to pick up the children, Seema feels only anxiety. What caprice has she yielded to? Here's Tahera stepping out of the elevator, clad head to toe in rigorous black—black hijab, black jilbab, black shoes. Clutching her mother's hand, Amina is in a pink dress embroidered with white flowers, a pink sweater, pink-and-white shoes, and a matching pink hijab framing her face and flowing over her shoulders. Arshad trails after them, in blue jeans, a tan fleece pullover, and white Adidas shoes, but on his head today: a white prayer cap.

Ismail has already left for his meeting, Tahera says, and she's late for her session. She hands Seema a booster seat for Amina, gives her a few instructions—Don't spoil the kids!—warns her children not to pester their aunt, and hurries away.

"Shall we go?" Seema asks, but the children continue to stand there, the intimacy of the previous day forgotten. To break the ice again, Seema lists the treats she's planned for them: the aquarium, the exploratorium, the Golden Gate Bridge, ice cream.

Seema has picked right: the exploratorium excites Arshad, and he's ready to make that the first stop. But Amina is not won over yet. She hugs her booster seat to herself, eyes scanning the lobby for her mother, resisting Arshad's efforts to steer her toward the doors. Arshad lures her with the promise of visiting the aquarium first and makes a big fuss over the car—how like a toy it is!

It's Fiaz's Mini Cooper actually, borrowed for the day, since Seema has sold her car, like she's sold or given away almost everything that reminds her of her life with Bill. She's thankful Arshad can install the booster seat, since she knows next to nothing about it.

All formality evaporates as soon as they climb into the car and head out to the aquarium, down one of the steepest slopes in San Francisco. Amina closes her eyes and squeals. Arshad begs they do it again. Seema obliges, going around the block to repeat the same vertiginous descent. The car is filled with shrieks and laughter as they roller-coaster their way down to the Wharf.

The children slip their hands into hers as they cross the road. This recalls to Seema walking to school with Tahera. They'd continued to hold hands even after they became too old to draw a sense of safety from the act, for there'd been a distinct pleasure to walking into school hand in hand. They were striking as a pair—the same heart-shaped faces, framed by hair tightly pulled back into twin plaits with white ribbons, the same cut to their starched blue pinafores, the same puff to the sleeves of their white blouses. They were everywhere recognized and admired—*the Hussein sisters!*—and even the head-mistress would stop to greet them.

But the differences now, three decades later, leading her sister's children through the Wharf! Seema is acutely aware of Amina's hijab, and Arshad's prayer cap, and the accosting glances of the other tourists. Are they confused by her attire of jeans and sweater and what she's doing accompanying these children? Pretending she's cold, Seema shivers self-consciously, and pulls out a shawl from her bag, which she drapes over a shoulder and loops around her head. She's aware Arshad has noticed, though he says nothing.

At the aquarium, a yellowtail balances on the tip of its nose, and Amina's laughter is infectious. Everybody experiences gooseflesh at a wolf eel's glare. A sleek seven-gilled shark slices through the water. There are rows of suckers on an octopus's arms, like coins thrown at a fountain—but a swish, and they're all gone!

For lunch, they have fries and grilled cheese sandwiches, Cherry Coke. Later ice cream, a banana split for Arshad, a chocolate cone with sprinkles for Amina that she doesn't finish and ends up with Seema.

In the afternoon, the exploratorium. Here Arshad flies suspended in a mirror like Superman, and Amina joins him, his Supergirl. Later, a movie about the origins of the universe—whirling masses of gas, galaxies like far-flung roses—and Arshad watches transfixed, while Amina wanders off. They find her at an exhibit on sound, with unusual musical instruments made of wires, disks, balloons, and rubber bands. With her quick little fingers she improvises a tune on one of them.

"She can sing too," Arshad says. "She sings very well."

He urges his sister to show Seema, and Amina complies, without a trace of embarrassment or shyness, in a light clear voice. An Urdu song, an old melody from Seema's childhood!

"She sings like an angel," compliments a listening woman. "What's she singing?"

It's a song Tahera and Seema used to love, about a rocking horse that springs to life and runs away. Amina's eyes shine with a soft concentrated happiness. When she finishes, Seema can't help but lift her up and smother her with kisses.

The day ends on the Golden Gate Bridge. The bridge is a tongue of fire, lit by the sun's dying rays. The children shiver in the stiff breeze blowing off the Pacific, but Arshad is adamant about walking the length of the bridge, and Amina is his willing follower. Seema gives in. Arshad wants to run ahead, but Seema insists the children hold her hand—the bridge is thronging with visitors, the curling waters of the bay are a steep drop below.

See them promenading down the bridge. Anyone would think them a family: a mother and her two children, walking hand in hand. Arshad's cap glows in the golden sunset. Amina's hijab flutters in the breeze, as does Seema's shawl. Seema has wound it tighter around her shoulders and head now, no longer pretending to be chilled. She's glad for the children's hands, warmth shared between them. The warmth reaches the inch of me, burrowed deep in her body.

Soon she'll have to return the children, like books borrowed from a library. They sense the end nearing too. Amina clings tighter. Arshad becomes urgent with questions about growing up in Chennai with their mother. Seema answers, hesitantly at first, then loosening up. She talks about two girls who slept in the same bed, who went to the same school, who read the same books, who played the same games, who sang the same songs—including the one about the rocking horse that escapes.

"Why haven't we seen you before, Seema Aunty?" Amina asks. "Will you come to Irvine to visit us?"

Before Seema can think of a lie, Arshad replies, "No, silly. If she'd wanted to, she'd have come before." He glances sidelong at Seema, but Seema senses no hostility in his remark and is baffled.

"Don't you like us, Seema Aunty?" Amina says. "I like you."

"Why did you say that?" Seema asks, directing her question at Arshad.

They come to a halt under one of the towers of the bridge. Arshad hops onto the lower railing and peers over at the water.

"Don't," Seema says sharply, and he jumps off the railing back onto the bridge.

"Why did you cover your head this morning?" he asks, looking directly at her.

"I was cold," she replies. "San Francisco's cold." She shivers involuntarily.

"Ammi says you don't practice deen."

"She told you that?"

"I asked her why you eat nonhalal meat. Why don't you practice deen, Seema Aunty? Why don't you submit to Allah?"

"Well, why do you?" The question slips out of her even as she recognizes the absurdity in interrogating a ten-year-old.

The three of them are protected from the wind by the tower, and they don't have to struggle now to be heard. The world seems to be holding its breath.

"Because," he says. He looks around, then points to the tower spearing the sky. "Because this is awesome. We couldn't have built it without His help."

"Muslims didn't build it."

"We're all people of the Book. We all pray to the same God."

"Do we all have to pray the same way?" she asks. "Do we all have to live the same lives?" She is alarmed by the bitterness in her voice, its vehemence. Why pick a fight with a child? This would earn her Tahera's ire if she learned of it.

He doesn't answer her but doesn't appear fazed by her questioning either. Instead he says, "I'll tell you why you covered your head."

"Why?"

"Because you saw people looking at us. You were afraid of what they'd think."

"Why should I be afraid? Why should I care what people think of me?"

He looks at her with a sly grin. "No, you were afraid of what people would think of Amina and me. You don't like us covering our heads." He pulls his cap off his head and twirls it around on his fingers. "People are scared of us. They think we'll become terrorists."

Seema looks at them, Arshad fiddling with his cap, Amina adjusting her hijab. They are waiting for something from her: some acknowledgment perhaps, some reassurance?

She can't trust herself to speak. She's angry: at Tahera and Ismail, for their pigheaded choice of a lifestyle that made outcasts of their children. But also: at Amina and Arshad, as if she blames them for accepting unquestioningly the life their parents imposed on them. But aren't they more to be pitied than blamed? Growing up, she hadn't much choice either, not until she left home.

"People are just stupid," she says. "It's easier to control them if they're scared. And it's easier to make them scared of those who are different."

"You shouldn't call anyone stupid," Amina says.

"What do you call a Muslim who prays five times a day and offers zakat to the poor?" Arshad asks.

Seema shakes her head. "What?"

"*A problem.* What do you call a Muslim who prays five times a day, offers zakat to the poor, and grows a beard and wears a cap?"

"I don't know."

"A *big* problem. What do you call a Muslim who uses swear words and drinks wine and eats pork and chases after women?"

She's startled by how fluent he is, how self-possessed. She detects no rancor in him, only wry amusement. And he doesn't seem to care that there are people milling around them.

"A problem *solved*!" Arshad chortles. "What, Seema Aunty! Surely believing in Allah is not the worst thing one can do."

He throws his cap into the air. As it reaches the zenith and starts to fall, a gust of wind picks it up and carries it over the edge of the railings.

"Bhaiya, your cap!" Amina cries.

She runs to the railings but Arshad stops her. The cap billows as it is lifted, catches the sunlight as it leaves the shadow of the tower, and glows like a lightbulb.

"It doesn't matter," he scoffs. "It's just a cap."

"What will you tell Ammi?" Amina whispers.

"Nothing. It doesn't matter," Arshad says, this time less surely. He gives Seema a quick smile. "Look how lovely it is. Everything is by Allah's grace."

They watch as the wind buffets the cap and carries it out toward the bay. It hovers for an instant and then plummets like a stricken dove, until another gust sweeps it farther away.

26

Seven months later, at pretty much the same spot on the Golden Gate Bridge, Seema stands with her sister, their backs to the tower.

"Arshad lost his cap here," Seema says. "The wind blew it away."

But Tahera is not paying attention to her, straining instead to listen to Fiaz. With the wind whistling through the bridge, they can hear only snatches of what he tells their mother by the railing, holding his jacket open to protect her from the wind.

"Your *friend* seems very knowledgeable about many things," Tahera says.

Seema is amused by Tahera's slight questioning emphasis. "Yes, he can talk your ear off on any topic." She calls out to him, "Fiaz, come closer. We too want a share of your infinite supply of useless information."

He puts his tongue out at her but submits dutifully, shepherding Nafeesa toward them. He's talking about jumpers. The bridge, he says, is the most popular site in the world for committing suicide. More than a thousand have climbed over its railings to plunge down to its icy waters.

"Why would anyone choose this way to die?" Tahera steps onto the lower railing to peer over, as Arshad had done. "That must be at least two hundred feet down. Has anyone survived?"

"A few. But they usually end up with a broken body."

Nafeesa shudders, as though the prospect of living with a broken body is more horrifying than the prospect of death.

"Why are we talking about this?" Seema complains. Fiaz should know better than to speak about death when their mother is so close to it, but he continues, describing a documentary dealing with the suicides from the bridge. The filmmaker had caught jumpers in the act, collecting video footage of two dozen leaps over the course of one year.

She grabs Fiaz's arm to interrupt him. Fiaz yelps, and Nafeesa and Tahera turn to look at her, her mother concerned, her sister surprised. "It's nothing. I thought I felt a contraction," she says.

They head back to the car. She puts pressure on Fiaz's arm to slow him down, ignoring Nafeesa's anxious glances as they fall behind. Beneath them, a ship emerges from under the bridge, as though appearing out of nowhere.

"I'm sorry I got carried away," Fiaz says.

She rubs his arm where she'd tweaked him hard. "All this talk about death and dying—I'm scared, Fiaz."

"Why?"

"I don't know how much longer my mother will be here. Tahera's lucky, she has her family. I'm alone, and I'll have to bring up my child alone."

"You have me, you have Leigh."

"You I'm sharing with Pierre. And Leigh—" She can't bring herself to complete the thought. Completion implies a decision made. "What if I can't do this by myself?"

She's had this conversation with him before, knows what he'll say—"You can," he says, "you're the strongest person I know"—and she's always found his words reassuring, but today she feels strangely empty. A life is turning within her, and what has she to offer it?

She's not strong the way Tahera is strong, the way she suspects Arshad is. All her childhood she'd been confounded by Tahera's enthrallment with things she remained blind to: a perfectly purple jamun, a line of poetry, a rainbow. Arshad had stood on this bridge, his eyes focused on the cap being swept away by the breeze until it was no more than a glittering speck. They have something she doesn't have, never had, may never have. Even Amina—she recalls the look on Amina's face as she sang.

They are like this bridge—anchored, and held upright and strong by their unshakable faith in the rightness of their devotions and their ecstasies and in their capacity to bear the weight of them. Her strength, on the other hand, lies chiefly in her ability to raise anchor and sail away, and reestablish herself elsewhere, in more favorable waters. They're the bridge, she's the ship beneath, tramping from port to port.

Fiaz puts an arm around her, gives her shoulders a squeeze. "You know you can always count on me to play the doting uncle. As long as I don't have to change dirty diapers."

"What use are you then?" She swats him, masking her disappointment in playfulness.

Fiaz jokes, but this is his way of hinting at the limits of what he's willing to do for her child. Pierre doesn't want children, and Fiaz doesn't regard himself as free to make a choice for himself. Would he agree to more if he weren't with Pierre? That's not a question she can ask him. Fiaz will continue to show her and her child many kindnesses, and she has to be satisfied with that.

She's startled by the ship's warning horn as it sails into the bay. The kite-surfers and sailboarders zipping back and forth by the bridge race to get out of its path.

She leans against Fiaz and lets him bear some of her weight as they walk up the incline from the bridge to the parking lot.

27

Nafeesa's comment—how good Seema and Fiaz look together!—unsettles Tahera. It hadn't occurred to her to suspect more than friendship between them. There's something about Fiaz that is too reassuring—too nice, too normal—to imagine him as Seema's lover. But perhaps her mother knows something that she does not.

Tahera now watches Seema's every interaction with Fiaz with suspicion. Throughout the morning, at the Golden Gate Bridge, and later on the crooked Lombard Street and at Coit Tower, every time their bodies draw close, she takes note. She edges closer to eavesdrop; she insinuates herself into their conversations under cover of interest; she projects innocent curiosity even as she asks questions: How did they meet? How do they like working together? Do they see each other often outside work?

Their replies are wary, evasive, giving her little to go on. There's no denying that some (deep) connection exists between them. This much is evident in the easy familiarity that marks their intercourse, the conspiring smiles Seema gives Fiaz, the readiness with which he cooperates. There's a tenderness too in his concern for Seema; he helps her into the car and bends to whisper something into her ear, and Tahera burns. She needn't have abandoned her family. Seema has already found herself a willing servant, if not a new suitor.

It's close to 1:00 p.m., and Fiaz and Seema discuss lunch at one of the Pakistani places around Union Square. It'll be halal, Seema tells Tahera.

"But it's time for my zuhr namaz."

Fiaz offers to drive her to a mosque.

"If we're going to Union Square, I can pray there. I've prayed before in parking lots and lobbies. I just need a place to spread my janamaz." She's brought it with her, for just such an eventuality. The passersby in Union Square won't faze her; in fact, today she'll relish the challenge. She feels combative. She's ready with an answer if anyone in the car chooses to question the advisability of praying in public: people pray on the roads in Mecca all the time, both men and women!

Nobody speaks until they pull to a stop in front of a building. "I bring my mother here," Fiaz says. "The mosque's on the second floor."

The neighborhood looks sketchy. There's litter on the pavements, and shabby loiterers lean against the garbage can. If it weren't for the inscription across the building's nondescript entrance, Tahera wouldn't believe it housed a mosque. A small prayer space, likely, in this large commercial building, nothing like their mosque in Irvine, stand-alone and impressive, with its green dome and tall decorative arches.

She clambers out from her side, chagrined. "I told you not to bother. What will you all do now?"

"We'll wait here for you, if you won't be long," Fiaz says. "Or I can drop your mother and Seema off at Union Square and return to pick you up."

"Don't wait for me. If they're hungry, they should go ahead and eat." She immediately turns around and heads for the entrance, not waiting to see what they do.

But the mosque is not what she'd expected. The prayer hall is spacious, occupying the entire second floor of the building. It is carpeted in red and aglow with light streaming in through large floor-to-ceiling windows. The light reflects off the carpet and suffuses the space with a ruby hue. Nothing she's seen this morning matches this, not the Golden Gate Bridge, not the view of the city from the top of Coit Tower. Nothing she knows of San Francisco has prepared her for this.

"Subhan'Allah," she exclaims involuntarily, before realizing that the congregation has already started the prayers. The zuhr is recited quietly, there's only the buzz of the verses whispered, the takbir barely audible: Allahu Akbar. She'd interrupted the namaz.

She stands by the entrance to the prayer hall, watching. She is awed, dazzled by the light. The space seems to pulse, the walls receding and then closing in, for every time the worshippers bend forward or genuflect, the room flares instantly brighter, from the reflections off their backs. Like crystals in a chandelier. The ayat from surah An-Noor comes to her mind: Allah is the light of the heavens and the earth. His light is like that of a crystal lamp in a niche, burning brilliant like a star, even the oil glowing. Light on light!

Only then does she notice that there are women praying in the hall as well. Unlike in Irvine, where the women have their own room, here they're all gathered to one side, while the men occupy the area in front of the mihrab. There's no barrier separating them.

It's the same surah An-Noor that enjoins modesty, chastity, fidelity.

"Yes, they'll do that in San Francisco," she can hear Ismail say, deriding this lack of separation as an unnecessary innovation, a false notion of equality trumping every other consideration. How familiarity breeds contempt—contempt for the purity of the body, contempt for the merit of Allah's decrees. She wouldn't be surprised if Seema and Fiaz are having an affair after all. The affair could even be the reason for Seema's divorce, adultery just another transgression added to her already long list.

But instead of the punishment that the surah decrees, Seema is to be rewarded. A new baby and a new husband—Muslim, good-looking, smart, successful—and Seema is all set for a prodigal daughter's welcome. No doubt their mother will now broker a reconciliation between estranged daughter and father. No doubt Seema's many lapses will be forgiven, and Seema will soon be reseated on her pedestal.

Tahera won't join this perverse San Francisco congregation but will pray after it finishes. Seema, Fiaz, and her mother must wait. She pictures them in the car driving away without her: it only needs her father now to join in their complicity.

There's this consolation: Seema may have been her father's favorite but is not one of Allah's favored. For the surah also says: Only by Allah's bounty and mercy could anyone attain purity. And Allah decides who will and who won't. He guides His light to whom He wills.

Why then does it feel to her, watching the worshippers move through the light—aglow as if they were made of that very light, like angels—that she stands in the shadows while they are blessed, transformed, redeemed?

28

Grandmother, the morning has energized you. You see your daughters together, behaving cordially if not affectionately, and you're greatly heartened. They're finally talking to each other, not using you as their intermediary. Your scheme of forcing them to spend time together seems to be working.

San Francisco is so unlike Chennai, with its picture-postcard blue skies and emerald-green waters, a perfect miniature city secure in its glass globe, except for the occasional panhandler or loiterer. Yet, all morning you've been reliving the past, with many former selves of Seema and Tahera and your husband walking beside you, resurrected by the most ordinary of occurrences. Here—in Union Square—you see two sisters skipping up and down the stairs holding hands; on a cable car you see a teenage girl leaning out, waving at passersby; at a store, a father holds his child up so she can better see the mannequin's painted face. The past seems not the past—untouchable, unchangeable—but something that floats just beyond your fingertips, something that you feel you can reach and perhaps reshape.

These visions fill you with hope. Already, Seema's life feels more real, her future more promising. While waiting for Tahera, Seema has encountered more friends at a campaign booth in Union Square. Three women and a man—all Americans you think, by their accents, two Black, one White, one Indian—rush to surround Seema as soon as they catch sight of her. Clearly Seema is not living the isolated and cheerless life you sometimes imagined her to.

If her father could see her now, so engaged and animated, and surrounded by well-wishers! Perhaps it will be Seema running for election one day. You picture Seema's face on the poster instead of the candidate's, even though it was your husband who'd nursed these ambitions for your daughters. All you wanted for them were happy, fulfilled lives.

The Indian American friend introduces herself as Divya. She's very pretty and dressed more fashionably than the rest. "I'm so glad to have a chance to meet you," she gushes. She praises Seema to you and thanks you for flying all the way over to help Seema with the delivery. "If it weren't for the election, I would be there to help anytime she wanted."

"I'm so glad Seema has such a good friend," you say.

She draws Seema aside to discuss some matter. They whisper to each other, and you note that Seema seems a little uneasy, glancing over as if to reassure you. You wonder what they're discussing.

Fiaz returns with Tahera. She looks a little downcast but makes no objection to the restaurant chosen for lunch. Divya can't join you—she apologizes profusely, taking leave of Seema with an embrace—but the other two women can.

The six of you walk to the place—you can't call it a restaurant, since it's so shabby. It's smoke-filled and sharp with the smell of stale curries, with cheap tables and chairs strewn in disarray on not particularly clean flooring. Seema's friends don't seem to mind, though, continuing their chatter on politics. Tahera keeps mum. You let her choose dishes for you. The dishes arrive floating in oil, but, apart from Tahera, everyone finds them delicious. You eat a little to not call attention to yourself, but you decide that you'll have to cook a proper meal for Seema's friends—to treat them to a real feast, to thank them for supporting your daughter.

After lunch, Fiaz takes you all back to Seema's apartment, none inclined for further sightseeing.

"Thank you so much, son," you tell Fiaz when he's leaving, in Urdu, in as perfect and chaste a diction as you can contrive. You're brimming with gratitude, for the morning of course, but also for his reassuring presence in Seema's life. "You must come to dinner. I must feed you something I've cooked with my own hands."

"You shouldn't put yourself to so much trouble, Aunty. All the pleasure was mine." He replies in Urdu too.

You grasp his palms in your bony fingers, unwilling to let him go without securing his consent. It will be harder later, for you sense Seema shift uncomfortably, ready to intervene. "You must come. Otherwise I'll be very disappointed."

"Of course. Just say the word, and I'll come wearing a pajama, with drawstrings to loosen."

When he's gone, you start planning the dinner you'll cook. You'll ask

Seema to invite her other friends too. You'd like to feed them all, at least once. You know Seema will resist, but you're determined to override her. You have little time to make amends for all the sorrow and pain that your silence and inaction have perpetuated.

29

It's late afternoon. The ghosts of the morning still torment the two sisters.

Seema is seated by the bay window in the living room with the book of poetry she'd bought Tahera, while her mother naps in the next room. She reads what she remembers as her sister's favorite poems, recalling the intensity and earnestness with which Tahera used to recite them. But the poems evade her—she remains unmoved by their lyrics or music. She has recited poetry herself in competitions at school, but they'd been mere performances, to be crafted and perfected. She stares outside the window, idly stroking her stomach, while she works on shoring up her will to talk to Tahera. Are there traces of the childhood sister still lurking in the stranger moving about the apartment?

Tahera is restless, too stirred up to remain idle. The asr namaz doesn't take long, even with all the voluntary rakaat in addition to the obligatory ones. She calls Ismail, but he is busy at the mosque, overseeing the arrangements for the fundraiser that evening, and the children are having too much fun in the air castle set up in the parking lot to remain on the phone for long, even Amina. At least there's no sign yet of any trouble. Tahera throws herself into tidying the apartment. She puts away her stuff and straightens the living room; she cleans the kitchen, and washes and shelves the dishes in the sink; she even mops the kitchen floor. When she's done, she looks around for something else to do.

"Tahera, you're making me tired just listening to you," Seema says. "Come sit down. I want to speak with you."

Tahera is thrown off balance by Seema's request. "I don't want to talk about Ammi right now."

"No, not about Ammi." Seema notes Tahera's pinched face, which shows more anxiety than the hostility her voice suggests. "Please?" Almost unconsciously she employs the tone her younger self would use with Tahera to get her way.

It still seems to work. Tahera hesitates, then says, "I'll make us some chai first."

While Tahera brews chai, Seema counts fetal kicks. Her hands slide slowly over her stomach inch by inch, fingers spread wide. Both sisters are intent on their tasks as the minutes drag on, as though the future somehow depends on how conscientiously each carries them out.

Tahera returns and places one cup by her sister's feet, then pulls another chair to the bay window and sits down, studying her. "How many so far?" she asks.

"Good boy," Seema murmurs to me, reacting to a particularly vigorous kick. "Ten in fifteen minutes," she tells Tahera. "He seems very active."

They sip their chai deliberately, with exaggerated care, as if that were the sole reason for their sitting together.

The sun streams in through the window, the rays cutting into the living room, glancing off the hardwood floors, bathing them in a golden afterglow. The light softens them, making them appear less substantial, almost translucent.

To Tahera, Seema looks slight. The light has shaved off mass from the edges of her frame, stripping her of her pregnancy, rendering her small and oddly vulnerable. And in Seema's eyes, the light masks the lines and wrinkles on Tahera's face, smoothing out its textures—her sister could be any age now, twenty or eighteen, fifteen or thirteen. A window to the past has unexpectedly opened.

"Tara," Seema says, and the word feels so awkward on her tongue that she falters. She has not used this nickname in more than two decades.

Tahera's heart stills. Seema has only ever called her Tara when asking a favor or cajoling her into a shared exploit. She has never heard Seema utter it this way before, stuttering, unsure of herself.

A sudden hope flares within her, and it sets the very light in the room quivering. Tahera is reminded of the mosque that morning, of the worshippers shimmering in the light. The morning and the afternoon mingle and fuse in an incandescent moment: confession—supplication—absolution.

"What is it?" Tahera clutches at her cup to steady herself, gazing at her sister over its rim.

"Tahera"—Seema enunciates the word carefully so as not to slur it and have it sound like the diminutive again—"I know we haven't exactly been close for some time now. But I'll be very grateful if you'll consider this carefully before you say no."

"Say no to what?"

"I never thought anything would happen to Ammi, at least not this soon. She's only sixty-two. But look at her—it happened so quickly, in less than three months."

"We agreed, no talking about Ammi." Tahera sets the cup down.

My mother plunges ahead. "I'd like you to bring up Ishraaq if something were to happen to me. I'd like to name you as his legal guardian in my will."

And how does my could-be mother react? The enormity of the ask takes Tahera's breath away. Whatever Tahera had expected, it hadn't been this. Surely not even Seema has the audacity to make such a request, with so little acknowledgment of the hurt and pain she'd inflicted.

A stream of questions eddies in Tahera's mind: Why her? Why now? What is being asked of her?

"How long have you been thinking about this?" she asks.

"A couple of months."

"Since Ammi's diagnosis?"

Seema nods.

"What about the father?"

Seema bites her lip. "I don't want him involved."

"I don't know," Tahera says.

"I don't know what to say," she says.

"I'll have to talk to Ismail," she says, finally.

What she notes: a hint of a teardrop clinging to her sister's eyelash. It trembles there gathering mass before it embarks on its perilous way through the lit and glowing air.

30

At the fundraiser that evening, Arshad is Superkid in his royal-blue kurta pajama and his crocheted white prayer cap. He's miraculously at hand whenever someone is needed—to carry messages between organizers, to track down particular members of the community, to guard the video camera during the videographer's breaks. Now he directs attendees to the spaces for various events, now he hands out pens and ink and paper for the calligraphy competition, now he works the slides on the laptop during Imam Zia's speech about the future of the center. He's a whirlwind in blue, streaking through the swelling throng, the men in suits and salwars and jeans and caftans, the women churidared and jilbabed and abayaed and hijabed, the young boys and girls dressed to their parents' tastes in bright and shiny traditional outfits of every gaudy hue.

He has time for little else the first half of the evening—no time to hang out with his friends, to be dejected about not winning a prize for his recitation, to keep an eye on his sister. Thankfully, Amina is under Najiba Aunty's care, playing with her friend Taghrid.

After the isha namaz there's only one event left: the Quran *Jeopardy!* Originally his father was supposed to conduct it. Arshad had helped him put the quiz together, and he's excited. But Ismail has since assumed post outside to supervise the activities in the lot, and the role of quizmaster has fallen to Imam Zia. Three contestants have been selected: the father of Arshad's friend Jemaal, a senior from his school, and his mother's business partner, Khadija Aunty.

Imam Zia, elegant in his navy blue robe (blue like his!) begins with a disclaimer in his rueful British accent: "Pardon me if I botch this, I'm not too familiar with this American format of answering with a question. And as I didn't prepare this quiz, I may not even know all the answers myself. But, ah, Brother Arshad, over there, definitely does. A round of applause for him, please, he helped create this quiz."

The audience claps, turning to look at him, and he's thrilled at being singled out for praise, and for being addressed as "Brother." It almost makes up for his failure at the recitation competition and for missing all the fun earlier.

But what could be more fun than the contest that unfolds? His father could never have been as entertaining as Imam Zia, who is funny and can quote from the Quran and narrate incidents from the Hadith to support the answers. He teases the participants good-naturedly, especially the two males, when they get an easy question wrong.

Once he tsk-tsks when nobody gets the question right, and he points to Arshad and says, "Why, even a twelve-year-old knows this!"

Arshad is called to shout out the answer: "What is *iqra?*" He adds, "And I'm eleven."

"Yes, *iqra!* To read, to recite—the very first word of the glorious Quran as revealed to the Prophet, peace be upon him, by Allah subhanahu wa ta'ala's messenger, the angel Jibreel. That is the first command that Allah bade the Prophet, and all Muslims. But more than just to read—to understand the Quran, to follow the Quran."

Every time after that, when the contestants are stumped, Imam Zia eggs the audience to chant, "Even an eleven-year-old knows this." And Arshad gets to call out the answer.

He roots for Khadija Aunty, admiring the competitive spirit with which she responds to the clues, eyes flashing like the sequins in her hijab as she pounces on the buzzer. But unfortunately, she makes as many mistakes as she gets questions right, and the senior from his school ends up winning.

Afterward, his father compels him to return home with Amina, though he wants to stay to help with the cleanup. Amina is tired and falls asleep almost immediately once Najiba Aunty takes them home. Arshad is too keyed up for that. He practices his recitation in the living room, working on the ayats he'd stumbled over during the competition. He'd recited surah Al-Qiyamah, his all-time favorite.

The Sunday Quran class when he'd first heard Imam Zia recite the surah, he'd felt his limbs tingle the moment the opening word, *la*, resounded, in what seemed to him not Imam Zia's usual voice but verging on a cry: *No!*

Thereafter, each ayat seemed to reach toward him, a solar flare that surged with each prolonged vowel, seeking him out as if to sear him, receding only when sounding the final rhyming syllable. It started up again with the next ayat. He'd felt himself grow feverish. Even the ayats with only short vowels were awful and awesome, the flare engorging itself with each percussive rhyme, as if pumping itself up in preparation. Finally, at the word *raq* that concluded one ayat, Imam Zia sustained the vowel so long that the flames succeeded in reaching Arshad. He'd felt burned, branded, effaced, and ecstatic.

Later, during the tafsir, listening to Imam Zia's explanation of the surah, he'd marveled at how, even without knowing its meaning, he'd been so affected.

Do you think Allah cannot resurrect you from the dead? No, He can reassemble the very tips of your fingers. On that day, when every eye will be astounded, when the moon turns dark and plunges into the sun, every disbeliever will ask, "Where can I hide?" But there is no place of escape. Only with Allah will you find refuge the day of Qiyamah. Allah alone is the cure that day—*raq!*—Allah alone is the healer.

He'd vowed to master the surah. Its terrible beauty, and its power to call to Allah anyone who listens to its recitation, proof of Allah's glory and compassion. But he's only now comprehending the immensity of the task ahead. The competition has laid bare his shortcomings. He's far from catching up with some of the other participants, some only slightly older than him, let alone matching Imam Zia.

It's beyond midnight when his father's car pulls into the garage. "You still up, buddy?" Ismail asks, coming in and hanging up his keys.

"I didn't win anything for my recitation, Abba," Arshad says, stopping the practice track he'd been listening to on his MP3 player.

"It's okay, I'm sure you did very well. It's not about winning."

Just the consolation Arshad expected. Yes, it's not all about winning, but surely there's some value to becoming perfect. Isn't it every Muslim's responsibility to learn to recite the Quran correctly, and beautifully, and doesn't such a recitation hold the power of swaying unbelievers' minds, guaranteeing him a place in Jannat? Abba knows too few of the rules of tajwid to even be aware when he commits a basic mistake. Last night, Abba hadn't stopped him a single time, though he'd obviously flubbed many phrases. Ammi would have made him repeat them and helped him practice better. If only she'd been in town. Abba hadn't even come to watch his first public recitation, only Amina had.

Arshad follows his father upstairs to check on Amina, and then downstairs to the kitchen. Ismail pours a glass of milk for Arshad and orange juice for himself. Son and father stand in the dark in mostly companionable silence, sipping from their glasses. Through the window they can see the deserted street and the lit fronts of their neighbors' houses, the purple glow of the skies beyond. Everything is peaceful, as though the calm and quiet in their neighborhood extended everywhere.

"Everything went well, Abba?" Arshad asks.

"Masha'Allah, everything went smoothly," Ismail replies. "We raised more money than we expected. And Imam Zia told me what a big help you were all evening. Your Ammi will be very proud."

"Nothing bad happened," Arshad says. But it's more of a question.

"What bad could happen?" Ismail says. "When there's Allah to guide and protect us?"

Arshad knows why his father spent the evening outside, monitoring the parking lot. The world he's seen on TV and on the internet is hostile. The nation is at war with them. Even their president, who claims to support them, thinks nothing of ordering drones to drop bombs and kill their people all over the world, under the excuse of fighting terrorism. Arshad has read on various internet sites—at his school library, since browsing is not permitted at home—that President Obama has sent more drones than any previous president, including George W. Bush, and has increased the size of American troops in Iraq and Afghanistan. Arshad imagines with a shudder a missile tearing through the air and their mosque exploding in a blast of light and fire.

"What would we have done if people had gathered outside the mosque?"

"What people?"

"Christians. White people."

"Why should they gather outside our mosque?"

"They've been protesting outside other mosques. They don't want us to build more mosques."

"We're not building another mosque. And even if they'd protested, we would have handled it."

"How? What if they'd brought guns? Bombs?"

"Don't be silly—nobody's bringing guns or bombs." Ismail gulps down the rest of his orange juice in one long swallow. "Finish your milk. You don't need to be worrying about these things."

Afterward, the two of them go upstairs, change into their pajamas, then end up in the bathroom brushing their teeth together. This doesn't usually happen, except when Tahera is away. This fellowship is gratifying, yet Arshad feels a pang of discontent. Imam Zia's praise has made the day, but the wish lingers that there had been a protest outside the mosque. Then he could have shown them how *he* would have handled it.

He falls asleep, gazing at the projected ayats and the glowing galaxies on his ceiling, willing himself to dream his favorite story about the Prophet. Riding a mare with wings of lightning, the Prophet follows the angel Jibreel from Mecca to Jerusalem, where he leads all the other prophets in namaz, and there in the seventh heaven, he confers with Allah in front of the radiant Sidra tree, which seethes and shimmers like a supernova.

31

Tahera is settled on the futon, wrapped in a comforter, ready to sleep. She has left the shades up so she can watch the fog descend upon the city. The lights smear, the contours of the city shift. Her thoughts pool and eddy in concert with the encroaching fog.

Her answer to Seema should have been simple. How could Tahera even think of not accepting her child? Isn't it sunnah to raise her sister's child—Prophet Muhammad, sallallahu alaihi wasallam, was an orphan and has promised Jannat to anyone who raises one. Surely, Ismail would agree.

Except that the child wouldn't really be an orphan. (How horrible that she can contemplate her sister's death so objectively.) Wouldn't the child's father be the best person to take care of him? But then Tahera can't abandon her nephew to be brought up by Bill, in ignorance of Islam.

More tortuous thoughts: the child might be out of place in Tahera's household.

He may look more like his father than Seema, perhaps bigger and darker than her own children, and she knows it shouldn't matter, but will she be able to ignore the differences? Also, he would complicate their lives, for he wouldn't be mahram to Amina, forcing the girl to wear a hijab at home, unless Tahera were to breastfeed him before the age of two. And what if Bill were to seek custody? Is Tahera expected to fight a custody battle? She doesn't need additional struggles in her life.

Tahera is roused from her thoughts by a prolonged bout of timorous coughs from Seema's bedroom. All evening her mother has been trying to suppress her coughs to clear her irritated throat, to avoid bothering her daughters, and now in her sleep, she seems to have lost her struggle.

Glad for any interruption, Tahera checks on her mother. But by the time she peers into the bedroom, the coughing has ceased. She sees, in the vague half light, her mother motionless, her hands on her chest, her body straight, a blanket neatly smoothed over her legs, as though laid out. Nafeesa's mouth is slightly open, her head tilted back over the pillow. She doesn't appear to be breathing.

Tahera freezes, waiting for some sign of life from her mother.

On the other side of the bed, Seema's face is within an inch of Nafeesa's neck, a hand resting on Nafeesa's hip. Seema twitches suddenly, her fingers clutching at their mother's sweater, causing Nafeesa to stir and, with eyes still closed, take Seema's hand in hers, as though it were the most natural thing to do. She straightens Seema's fingers, massages them, then draws Seema's hand into a clasp by her chest. Seema whimpers, snuggling closer.

But instead of relief, say it is heartache and jealousy Tahera feels at this exchange. She would have liked to rush to her mother's side, to hold her, to take Nafeesa's hands in hers, to kiss each finger as she'd kiss Amina's. But Nafeesa is holding Seema, and it's Seema's forehead she turns to kiss in her sleep. Tahera is merely an observer in the doorway.

Words come to Tahera unbidden: *So she stood in her shoes and she wondered, she wondered, she stood in her shoes and she wondered.*

The words from the past swell in chorus and spin around her. She shuts the door. *That a door was as wooden.* She heads back to the futon. *That the ground was as hard, that a yard was as long.* But how far it seems, as though with every step the distance grows larger. Or is she growing smaller?

It's a nine-year-old who returns to the futon.

Is it too much to ask to be held, to be consoled, to be loved? Is it too much to ask that she not end up where she started—on the outside looking in?

32

Consider Tahera when she's nine years old: standing outside her father's study, peering in, as her father coaches Seema for her first competition in poetry recitation.

Tahera isn't familiar with the poem Seema has chosen: Wordsworth's "The Solitary Reaper." But here is their father, declaiming the poem, filling the study with its lush hills and shimmering valleys. His voice echoes off the walls and the shelves of books. He recites the poem in its entirety, then line by line, and Seema scrambles after him, trying to match his intonation and his pauses. He works on her enunciation, demonstrating the shape of the mouth, the position of the tongue, the force with which to articulate the consonants, how to linger on vowels and glide over diphthongs. Like so, he says, his hands molding Seema's lips and cheeks. He patiently corrects her, making her repeat phrases, over and over, then lines, then whole stanzas.

Next, he shows her how to present herself: neck elongated, shoulders pulled down and back, hands held at the diaphragm, fingers hooked. He bends his knees to better match her height. Standing this way, they recite the poem together, and Tahera is transfixed by two voices that sound as one, word for word, pause for pause. And the words themselves—*melancholy, chaunt, nightingale, Hebrides*—so much mystery, so much magic! She silently mouths the words along with them, her voice tiny in her throat, her eyes fixed on their moving lips.

I listened motionless and still—

Until Seema, catching sight of her outside the study, says, "Abba, tell Tahera to stop making funny faces at me." She shuts the study door in Tahera's face, ignoring Tahera's pleas: "I wasn't making fun, I was just watching."

—The music in my heart I bore, long after it was heard no more.

33

The day of the competition, the auditorium floor is a pool of blue pinafores, fluffy white blouses, and glossy black plaits of hair. At the back, in a row of cream wicker chairs, sit the Sisters of the Convent, in gray wimples and white habits. And sitting beside the headmistress, Sister Josephine, in the seat of honor in the center, in a brown suit and a peacock-green tie, is my grandfather, Dr. Naeemullah Hussein, benefactor of the school and personal friend to the headmistress. He's presiding over the event.

When Seema gets up on stage, it's him Tahera watches, turning around and straining to catch the expressions on his face—encouragement, attention, exultation. When all the contestants are through, he takes the podium for his address while the judges finalize the winners.

"Why poetry?" he begins, then pauses. "We may as well ask, why life?"

Now his voice resounds in the auditorium, much as it had in his study while coaching Seema. This is Tahera's first time listening to Naeemullah speak in public. There is a power to his voice, an authority that spellbinds her. But though she's entirely focused on his words, her eyes fixed on him, much of what he says escapes her.

This is a father she doesn't quite know, or recognize. A father who doesn't seem to recognize her either, even when glancing in her direction, as if seeing through her, beyond her. She listens in feverish anxiety for elements she can identify, the parts of his life she's familiar with: his family, his practice, their house and household. Instead, he speaks of Joy and Beauty and Truth, as though these were his family. He quotes many poets, but few she knows; nobody from her textbooks—no Walter de la Mare, no Christina Rossetti.

Even his quotation from William Wordsworth is from a poem she hasn't heard before: *My heart leaps up when I behold a rainbow in the sky . . .*

This is the most accessible of the poems he recites. Tahera has seen rainbows before and thinks them lovely, but she can't remember now whether her heart has ever leapt at their sight. She'd like to believe her heart capable of this. For there's little doubt that her father isn't merely reciting Wordsworth's words but living them, reliving them.

"Or—let—me—*die!*" he proclaims, punctuating the line with pauses.

And Tahera shudders, ambushed by the dying tremor he imparts to that last word. A shiver of recognition runs through her body—the thrill and promise of dying—but until now she's never found words to capture that feeling. Her heart executes a neat little leap, even as she despairs she'll never be sufficiently moved that her heart would leap. Even now she's unaware that her skipping heart is doing precisely that.

The winners have been decided, and Naeemullah brings his speech to a close. Old Sister Camilla, their English teacher, reads out the names. He shakes hands with each, before handing their prizes over—books he has selected himself—remarking on the titles and what delights await the winners. The school photographer's flash freezes the smirking girls beside a benevolent Naeemullah.

Now Sister Camilla calls out the winners in Seema's grade, third place to first. Seema is not named for the lesser two prizes. "And the first prize goes to—" Sister Camilla pauses, her leathery walnut face cracking in a wide grin.

Tahera closes her eyes and prays, the suspense unbearable.

What does she pray for? Of course, she wants Seema to win. No other thought occurs to her.

"—Seema Hussein, daughter of our own respected chief guest, Dr. Naeemullah Hussein!"

Tahera claps hard, as though single-handedly she must ensure the auditorium echoes with the sound. But tears prickle her eyes as Seema walks up to the stage and shakes hands with Naeemullah. He draws Seema to his side, and the two smile widely, posing for all the world to see, as the photographer clicks a second photo. If only it were she on the stage with their father.

Afterward, a proud Naeemullah leads both daughters by the hand, stopping many times along the way to accept congratulations. Sister Camilla detains them at the school entrance.

"Child, if you hadn't been so much better than that second-place Anjali girl, we couldn't have awarded you the first prize, lest people think we're playing favorites!" Sister Camilla laughs, a rich bray that along with her protuberant eyes and permanently surprised eyebrows has earned her the nickname Sister Camel. Normally Tahera would join in Seema's barely suppressed mirth, but today she looks away.

At the ice-cream parlor around the corner from their home—Naeemullah has promised Seema two scoops if she wins—Tahera holds back. She doesn't want any ice cream today, she says. "I too will take part next year and win."

"Yes, but we're celebrating your sister's performance," Naeemullah replies, pulling gently at her plaited hair. "And you can have two scoops as well."

Seema already has her heaped cone—two moons of peach tutti-frutti!—and makes slurping sounds to tempt her. Tahera succumbs. But she limits herself to one scoop. And, even as she frantically licks the cone to keep the melting ice cream off her pinafore, she repeats her vow: She will take part next year and win.

She pesters her father almost immediately for a poem to begin practicing. He's delighted: He has just the right poem for her! He needs to change a few words, but he's sure she'll like it. He sets up his electronic Remington typewriter, and pounds away at it, consulting a book. He doesn't allow her a peek until he's done. The poem is skinny but long, covering two full sheets. A poem by John Keats written especially for her! *There was a naughty girl, a naughty girl was she—*

("But I'm not naughty." "Yes, you are, look how you pestered me all week.")

She must learn it by heart first. In a week she can even recite it halfasleep. The evening she's ready, the door of the study shut behind them, his eyes fixed on her as they've never been before, he says, "Show me what you've learned."

What comes over her? It's a slight poem—Seema derides it as childish, with silly rhymes and a sing-song rhythm. Seema's mockery is still strong in her mind. But there are other impressions too: her father coaching Seema, patiently coaxing sounds out of her, their lips and mouths in articulated synchrony.

Or—let—me—die!

Tahera recites the poem as she never will again, no matter how hard she tries, no matter how many times her father makes her repeat it, each time with different instructions. That first time, the poem is both old and new, she is swamped with both fear and excitement, she feels the pull of both the ridiculous and the heartbreaking. Her voice contorts to include her sister's derision, her father's control, her own desperate yearning. By the end, she has briefly intuited the poem's secret heart that her sister has been blind to: That the naughty girl in the poem runs away with her knapsack only to find little difference between her origin and destination, between where she started and where she ends up. That the ground is as hard, that a yard is as long, in both places.

She stood in her shoes and she wondered—

When Tahera finishes, she notices the surprised elation in her father's eyes, which she'll search for in every subsequent attempt, during every competition, no matter how many prizes she wins.

34

Nearly thirty years later, Tahera is propelled from Seema's bedroom doorway by the very same lines ringing in her ears, threatening to remake her into the girl her nine-year-old self had been. She knows she should simply banish the poem from her mind, as she'd done the previous day when Seema brought it up, to keep the past safely locked away, as she's so far managed to do. But some elusive lines nag like gaps created by fallen teeth.

The Keats book lies where Seema had discarded it, on the floor, under the chair. Tahera flips through and finds the poem, reads it standing, once through. Her father had chosen well—it's exactly the poem to lure a nine-year-old deeper into his thicket of poetry.

And the book has so many poems she'd fallen in love with, the ones memorized and recited repeatedly, sometimes under her breath while walking to school and back, sometimes sitting on the veranda watching vendors push their carts by on holidays, or treading her bicycle around the compound outside their house. She skips from poem to poem, here a line, there a stanza, each triggering a memory of the circumstances surrounding its discovery. Racing to the lighthouse on the beach. Reading by candlelight during power cuts. Crushing on her neighbor with the curly hair and white teeth. Watching Ammi tie Seema's first saree. Standing in Abba's study.

"Land of milk and honey, halfway across the world. What an adventure! I'd have sacrificed anything for the chance when I was younger. They have your favorite season, too, only they call it 'fall.' *Season of mists and mellow fruitfulness*—" That's how Abba put it, as she stood before him in his study, summoned there as though she were still nine years old.

But she'd neither asked for the chance nor wanted to marry someone halfway across the world. Abba must have known Seema had moved to California, from the cards and letters Seema kept sending—addressed to him only—all those years. He'd opened none—they still remained unopened, Tahera knew, for she'd found them the last time she visited Chennai, the envelopes faded and fraying, stashed in the overstuffed drawers of the walnut table in his study, under clippings of his letters to editors published over the years—and their postmarks surely told Seema's story. Yes, he'd known where Seema had moved to, and in his continuing duel with her, best-loved daughter now fallen out of favor, he'd determined to send his secondary daughter there. Not as an ambassador but merely to proclaim his dominion, much like emperors established outposts. As though he'd no use for Tahera by his side.

She forces herself to take deep breaths, to curb the dizzying rush that is overpowering her. For a moment she's not sure where she's standing—neither Chennai nor Irvine, but in some foreign land, barren, shadowy, and chilly. There's little in this apartment to secure Tahera to the woman she is now: beloved wife, loving mother, skilled doctor, respected member of her community. She senses the weight of her entire past pressing, the floodgates buckling.

She flings aside the book, the poems that have brought her to this brink of fracture, and seizes and unfurls the janamaz in the middle of the living room. This is what she should have done earlier. The past, the poetry—beauty and love, joy and despair, anger and sorrow—what place do they have in her life anymore?

In the bathroom, she affirms her intention to perform wadu. Merely washing her hands before touching the Quran seems insufficient today. The cold water stings as she splashes her face. She runs wet fingers over her hair, keeping her head down. It feels important to avoid looking at herself in the mirror, as though she's a portal for everything unclean and needs to keep herself at a distance. Finished with the wadu, she places her wooden rehal on the janamaz. She unwraps the quilted maroon cover that protects her Quran and takes it out. The book opens at the marker, where she'd left off reading the previous time. She lowers it gently onto the rehal.

Seated on her knees, her covered head bent over the book, she reads without pausing to think, her marker tracing each line, skimming the surface of the text. She has read the Quran many times, has memorized many surahs and ayats, though she understands only a fraction of what she can recite. Through familiarity and practice she scurries through verse after verse, pausing only to turn a page before hurrying on. She purses her lips, so the words may be contained within her—outside, just a mumble, like the buzz of a bee, but inside the poetry resonating in her body, reverberating in her bones and organs and flesh. She has always found this sensation hypnotic and soothing.

But why is she slowing down? Why does she feel as though her lungs are about to burst, as if she's been breathing in verses instead of air? Her body is trembling again. She presses on despite her confusion—what's happening to her?—but the words lift off the page, the black print and white paper fusing to a foggy gray. Something strikes the open page and lies there perfect as a raindrop on a leaf, its surface quivering. Through it, the blurred outline of a letter shimmers, refracted beyond recognition.

It takes Tahera a few moments to understand she's crying.

Forgive me, she prays, cupping her eyes to prevent the drops from further defiling the Quran. Her shaking hands struggle to wrap the Quran back in the cover. But she continues to sit, still on her knees, head bent before the wrapped Quran on the rehal, as her tears now strike the janamaz, in splotches growing darker.

This isn't the release she'd hoarded her tears for—the tears she's refused to shed since seeing the ones clinging to her sister's eyelashes, the tears she's been unable to shed since learning of her mother's diagnosis. Every time she's seen her mother's eyes sparkling the last two days, she has willed her mother to let the tears flow. She would be redeemed if only Ammi would shed a few tears, showing Tahera she cared, showing she knew Tahera was a good daughter doing the best she can. Then Tahera too could join in. Their tears would reunite them in ways words and actions could not, washing away the guilt and resentment built up over the years.

She tries to stifle her sobs, so she won't wake her sister and mother, sleeping heedless in the adjacent room, hands clasped in each other's. But she also can't stop wishing that they were roused to check on her, to find her distraught and destroyed, to join her in consolation, even Seema, so they could grieve together for everything they've lost, for everything they're about to lose.

She rises, eventually, as if from under anesthesia. In the bathroom, she examines her face. It's puffy, her nose runs, eyelids droop over reddened eyes. She massages her cheeks, then presses fingertips against her eyelids, pushing the offending eyeballs deep into their sockets—as she's seen Arshad sometimes do—some physical sensation to prod her out of stupor. She has admonished Arshad many times against the practice of inflicting pain on himself, but she understands now why he persists—the pressure steadies her, and as she continues to press deeper, a universe explodes into existence, a kaleidoscope of glow and shadow that comforts, delights, mesmerizes. When she finally lets go, the bathroom rocks back into place in a brief disorienting burst of light, her face in the mirror staring back at her—grave, like the face Arshad shows her when she yanks his fingers off his eyes—the pain quickly fading.

How resilient the body is, she thinks. How much pain the body can handle, how well it repairs itself, by Allah's design. Such must be Allah's grace and mercy. Allah wouldn't impose on His followers more than their bodies or minds can bear.

She washes her face, rinsing her mind of its haze. The living room is as she left it, the Quran on the rehal on the janamaz. She puts away the Quran and the rehal. The Keats book lies on the futon, benign now, spent. She flips through its pages for the second time, feeling stronger for the cleansing she's just been through. The words have indeed lost their potency. These are merely words—even if beautiful—words and phrases concocted by mortal men aggrandizing themselves, seeking to lighten their own insignificance.

She shuts the blinds, and the city outside disappears. Rearranging the floor lamp, she settles herself to read, surrounded by the half gleam and shadows of the room.

She reads critically at first, dispassionately evaluating each line for accuracy and truth. Some of it now seems ridiculous—Keats's obsession with ancient Greek mythology, for example, with its drunken, depraved gods and goddesses. And hyperbolic—that comparison to sighting a new planet or ocean on reading Homer! How could anything composed by a human compare to the glories of Allah's creation? And Keats claims to be overcome by a mere translation. No translation of the Quran could affect her the way reading the original does. The mystery, the awe, is lost without the sonority of the Quran in Arabic, the way the words flutter in her throat—how could the flapping of the crow's stubby wings compare to the blur of the hummingbird's? She smiles to herself: now she's imitating Keats, fabricating her own poetic conceits. She regrets she has little time to learn to recite the Quran like Arshad.

As she continues to read, she relaxes. These poems had supported her once, provided her with a metaphoric shoulder to lean on, and yes, to cry on as well—it surprises her now how dark her favorite poems really were, never joyous paeans, but the odes and elegies on loss and death and yearning. There could be no harm in these. Why had she felt the need to renounce them? Perhaps she'd simply been too busy, as mother, wife, and doctor. When had she performed this particular ode, which competition? She'll have to ask Ammi or Seema tomorrow.

An hour passes, and her eyes glaze over. There's no sound from the bedroom; Ammi and Seema must be in deep slumber. How excessive her reaction to the sight of them huddled together. But it had led to the rediscovery of these poems. For that she must be grateful. Allah knows best, and everything serves a purpose. Allah will help her survive the coming days. Allah will help her decide how to respond to Seema's request. She will perform istikhara later to ask for His guidance.

She's moved by a sudden urge to be outside, to feel the sky above her, the city around her, to feel small. She throws a shawl about her head and shoulders and, climbing through the window, lets herself out onto the fire escape. There is no sky though—clouds cover all of it, and a fine mist has descended on the city. She stands cocooned, disturbed only by the sirens and flashing lights of the sporadic ambulance or fire engine. A faint smell of rust and smoke envelops her. A chill wind grazes, and she laughs as she shivers, welcoming the tingling sensation of gooseflesh, as though the wind were scouring her skin of the layers the years have deposited. She lets herself enjoy the half-white darkness like her younger self would have. Her thoughts briefly wander toward Irvine. The fundraiser must be long over, her children must be sleeping. She should have called Ismail to find out how it went. Auzubillahi minashaitan irrajeem, nothing untoward should have happened. But she won't think about it now, she'd like to savor a little longer this Tahera of old.

When she returns to the living room, she hides the book of poems away, out of sight, in the bookshelf, behind the Quran.

35

Sunday morning, Irvine: Ismail wakes up for fajr to the shrill cry of the alarm clock. But today he's not as irritable, even without Tahera's gentle hands to shake him awake. He lies in bed basking in the memory of the fundraiser—Masha'Allah, they had raised more than they thought they would.

A bleary-eyed Arshad joins him in the living room, and they pray fajr together. After the namaz, Ismail is too energized to go back to bed, and he busies himself with spreadsheets on his computer, tabulating donations and expenses, starting the report he'll share with the committee.

It's not yet seven when he receives a call from Imam Zia. He answers eagerly.

"I'm sorry to bother you so early, Brother Ismail," Imam Zia interrupts. "Especially after all your great work. But can you come over? There's some trouble at the mosque."

"What trouble?" Ismail asks.

"Some stuff on the walls. Not very nice. We should do something about it."

At the moment, Ismail is still floating high, and despite knowing Imam Zia's tendency toward understatement, he assumes the matter is trivial, perhaps some child who'd splattered paint on the walls during the calligraphy competition. "Sure. I'll be there as soon as I can."

He gives the children another half hour of their Sunday sleep, then wakes them and tells them to get ready. They'll be back soon enough from the mosque, so no breakfast for now, and the kids only get their morning milk, strawberry or chocolate.

The mosque is aglow in the golden morning light, the blazing green of the dome, the shimmering ivory of the stucco walls. A group of men stands on the steps of the main entrance, silhouetted against the lit walls, Imam Zia recognizable by his taller figure and turban. Ismail parks, and encourages the children to run toward the mosque. Striding toward the men, he feels elated and raises his hand in greeting. The sun is behind him, his long shadow ahead, waving in its turn. But the men don't seem to notice him.

He's still some distance away when Arshad shouts, "Abba, look!"

Arshad is pointing toward Imam Zia, who is rubbing at the wall of the mosque with the edge of his robe, and only as Ismail draws nearer does he notice the virulent red scrawl. From that detail his eyes pan to take in the entire red-stroked front wall of the mosque, which had until then been hidden by the red-blue-green striped canvas sides of the not-yet dismantled shamiana set up the previous day. It takes him many more seconds before he's able to put the strokes together to form letters, then words.

"Arshad, Amina, come back," he yells, breaking into a run toward them, not knowing why he's running, only that he must stop them before they get closer to the walls. Does he imagine the paint is blood? He recalls reading about the blood of pigs used on mosques, recalls images of blood streaming down victims of bomb blasts. He pounds the gravel of the parking lot, as if he were trying to crush the pebbles into the ground. Amina freezes where she is, and he picks her up, then increases his stride until he catches up with Arshad and yanks him around.

"Abba," Arshad whimpers, and Ismail is not sure whether it's in reaction to the desecration of the mosque or if he's hurting his son's arm.

"Close your eyes." He almost snarls, harsher than he's ever been with his children. Amina squirms in his hold, and he presses her face against his chest. With the other hand, he drags Arshad up the steps of the mosque, ignoring the men calling out to him, until they're in the foyer. "Stay here," he orders. "I don't want you coming out."

When he joins the others, he cannot bring himself to look at them or at the wall. It's his fault—his hubris caused this. He should have heeded their warnings to keep the fundraiser modest, discreet. How proud he'd been about the write-up in the *Sentinel* earlier that week, in which he and Imam Zia had been quoted extensively. How proud of cultivating a reputation as an unflinching advocate of the Prophet's forthright ways, scoffing at suggestions to minimize the expansion plans. And what devilry had made him expose his children to this profanity, bringing them along so they'd be witness to the accolades he'd hungered for? Had he thought he'd face no punishment for his sinful pride, his self-glorifying desires?

He turns to the wall, ignoring Imam Zia's hand on his shoulder, pretending to study the graffiti, tracing the surface of the paint—thankfully, not blood—still a little sticky, the red rubbing off lightly on his fingers. This close to the wall, he cannot make out the letters or the words or the images, only the violence of the crimson strokes, like bloody gashes in the skin of the mosque. He murmurs ayats from the Quran under his breath, in repentance for his sins.

36

On my mother's mind as she wakes up Sunday morning: Leigh. Nafeesa's side of the bed is empty but still retains her warmth, and Seema slips into reveries of other Sunday mornings waking up beside Leigh, to her sleepy-wide smile and languorous embrace. Then the leisurely entangling of lips and limbs, the pleasures and promise of the day unfolding in slow motion as though to ensure no moment is wasted without being intimately savored.

But the reveries are too soon marred by memories of the previous day: her abject appeal to Tahera, Tahera's pitying deferral, her tears that had visibly burned through the air before she'd excused herself to the bathroom. Had she expected Tahera to throw herself at her in remorse or reconciliation? Why had she worked herself into such desperation, and hope? Now she has ceded power and is forced to wait on Tahera's answer and to pretend not to care while her sister deliberates.

Nafeesa sits down beside her. "Are you all right? You tossed and turned all night."

My mother blames me. "The baby was up all night, kicking."

"I'll ask Tahera to take a look at you. You don't look well."

Nafeesa is unexpectedly persistent, but Seema remains firm. She cannot give Tahera any more reason to patronize her. "Ammi, I have a checkup tomorrow. I'd rather wait for my own doctor."

Leigh's call is no relief either, with her plaintive "I miss you, why don't you slip away and meet me at our spot?" Every Sunday since they've been together, after a lazy morning in bed, they amble on a pilgrimage to that spot in Dolores Park where they first kissed. They missed last Sunday because of Nafeesa. And Seema feels guilty because she has made plans with Divya today.

"You can say you want to get some exercise." Leigh offers various excuses, and as Seema counters each one, Leigh's voice turns forlorn. "I won't force a discussion about you-know-what, I promise."

Seema's guilt is compounded: it's mostly her fault that Leigh has come to place so much significance on being present at the delivery. The two of them have rarely spoken about their future together beyond that horizon; Seema has been careful not to. But she has never stopped Leigh from visualizing her involvement in the baby's future. Leigh talks about diaper changes, about pushing the stroller down to Dolores Park and up the hill to "our spot" so baby Ishraaq can take in the panorama of the city and its skyline—and Seema has welcomed it, even encouraged it. As if she's readier to accept a partner-caretaker, to make less frightening the responsibility of the baby than a partner for herself. She's secretly glad that the question of marriage couldn't arise in the near future, since same-sex marriages in California were overturned two years ago by Proposition 8.

Seema can picture Leigh's lanky frame sagging at her refusal. "But I'll see you tomorrow at the doctor's, right?" Seema presents it as previously decided, though it's an atonement.

But maybe it's the right opportunity after all to introduce her lover to her family—as a friend, of course, so it isn't an irrevocable step. Perhaps meeting her family will be sufficient to satisfy Leigh for some time, perhaps being able to assign a face and a name to the idea of a lover would soften their reaction if and when she tells them about Leigh.

Leigh gives an excited whoop—she can't wait!—and placated, hangs up.

At least Leigh's call has given Seema a plethora of excuses to get out of the house to meet Divya. But, unfortunately, the excuse she settles on—exercise—runs into trouble.

"Why more exercise, Seema? Didn't you say you were exhausted from all that walking yesterday? And you have back pain. You must take some rest today." Nafeesa holds on to Seema's hand, even as she prepares to leave the apartment. "Tell her, Tahera, tell her to stay home and rest."

Tahera looks up from the book she's reading. "Ammi says you're not feeling well?"

"I'm fine. Ammi is needlessly worried."

"She shouldn't go alone. Go with her, Tahera," Nafeesa entreats.

"I can take care of myself," Seema says, exasperated. "Why don't you understand I just want some time by myself? It's not easy having the two of you here all the time."

She regrets the words as soon as she speaks them. Her mother lets go of her hand, her sister compresses her lips. Seema lets herself out of the apartment without looking back. The message in her mother's stricken eyes pursues her through the darkened staircase. *But I came all this distance for you. You'll have all the time in the world for that—later!* What is she doing, alienating the only person who has cared for her all these years? And for what reason—what could come of this meeting with Divya, other than complications, and a sense of betraying Leigh? Divya has been asking for a few months to get together to process what they once had—no doubt to also press again for getting back together.

Seema lumbers back up the stairs. As she fumbles with her keys, the dead bolt flicks back, and the door swings open to reveal Nafeesa, poised as if expecting her return, and behind her, Tahera. Seema throws up her hands. "All right."

Nafeesa hurriedly gets out of the way, but it looks for a moment that Tahera will balk. But she merely shrugs, puts down the book in her hand—the Keats book she'd rejected two nights ago!—and puts on her jilbab and hijab.

"I'm sorry for what I said," Seema says. To her shame, Nafeesa clasps her hand with an expression that feels like gratitude.

37

The buzzer blares in the apartment, and you, Grandmother, are alarmed by its sudden screech. You can't imagine your children are back from their walk so soon, unless they've quarreled already and Tahera has returned alone. You've been congratulating yourself on throwing your daughters together again.

That impatient screech once more, held longer, and you nervously stab at the intercom panel, unsure which button to respond with. "Yes, who is it?" you say into the speaker. But instead of a reply, you hear an answering buzz from the entrance and the door clicking open, then footsteps up the stairs. You panic, casting about in your memory for anything Seema has told you regarding safety in this neighborhood.

There's a knock on the door. "Tahera, is it you?" you ask. You're too short to even look out the peephole.

"It's me, Bill Miles."

A muffled voice, but the pitter-patter of your heart slows down. You recognize it, though you've only heard it a few times, and only once in person, when Seema brought her husband to Chennai, at your sister Halima's house. "Seema's not home," you say.

"I know. Can I speak to you, Mrs. Hussein? Please."

You're relieved that the anxiety of the past moments was unnecessary, and curious, too, about what he wants. Though Seema may disapprove, you open the door.

He appears a little older, more gray flecking the sides of his springy hair, even the goatee on his chin. He used to be clean-shaven. His goatee reminds you of your husband's, except that my grandfather's is completely white.

You're unsure what to do next. Do you invite him in? Seema has said nothing against him, and you believe her assertion that the divorce was a mutual decision. Though that doesn't absolve him of abandoning his son.

Bill is shy, even a little sheepish. "Can I come in?"

You stand aside. He enters, and you shut the door. He wheels around the living room once, as though searching for signs of Seema. There's nothing—no photos, no wall hangings, no personal belongings—to indicate Seema's presence here, only Tahera's: suitcase, janamaz, Quran on the rehal. You were quite shocked at how bare Seema's home is, but he doesn't seem surprised.

"Thank you for being here for Seema," he says.

You don't respond but wait for him to continue.

He sits down on the futon, less of a giant now. "I was jogging past when I saw Seema and her sister leave."

"They went for a walk. They should be back soon."

"Actually—I wanted to speak to you. About Seema." He hesitates. "She will not talk to me." He looks up at you, eyes crinkling into a question, as though asking how much you know, how much Seema has told you.

The man in your daughter's living room is a stranger. But he clearly wants something from you, and that gives you courage to ask him the questions you cannot ask your own daughter. "Why—?"

"Why she'll not speak to me? Why I want to speak to you?"

You shake your head. "Why did you leave Seema alone when she's carrying a baby?"

Bill is taken aback by your directness. "I didn't," he stammers. "At least, I did, but I wanted us to get back together. I still want us to get back together."

This startles you. When Seema told you she was pregnant, that she meant to bring up the child by herself, she'd led you to believe there was no hope of reconciliation, that Bill didn't want to be involved with the child. Had she lied? You can't put it past her. Seema, you've always known, is quite capable of stretching the truth, especially when it concerns decisions she thinks you'll not understand. But whose fault is that? You've never made an attempt to understand her, or Tahera, for that matter.

Bill mistakes your confusion for disbelief. He continues to stammer an explanation: There had been problems, he'd been too hasty, he hadn't been sure what Seema wanted. Seema herself had doubts. He still loves Seema. He breaks off, then repeats himself, catches himself short, then starts again.

You only half listen. There are always problems between husbands and wives, and living with Seema must surely present challenges. You gaze instead at his face, seeking in his eyes expressions of sincerity.

But he's never still enough for you to gauge that. He fiddles constantly with the zip of his jogging suit, he turns frequently to check the door. He can't hold your gaze before glancing away. His eyes dart from floor to corner to ceiling until, as if tired from all this motion, he stops speaking, fixing his attention on the Quran in the bookshelf.

"Is that a Quran? I've never known Seema to have one."

"That's Tahera's," you say. "Seema's sister."

He walks over to the bookshelf, as if drawn to the Quran. He reaches to pick it up—

"No." You move to intercept. "You're not supposed to touch the Quran with unwashed hands."

With those words, something shifts. Until a moment ago you'd been pondering whether Seema's best interests lay in getting back together with him, but now—perhaps Seema already realized how distant, how different their worlds are. Fiaz's pleasing Urdu echoes in your ears. You can't help but compare the virtues of these two men as spouses, sons-in-law.

"I'm sorry. I didn't mean any disrespect." Bill is clearly unsettled by the force of your curtness. He smiles awkwardly. "My father converted to Islam."

The day seems full of surprises. Seema never mentioned this to you, and neither did he. You'd assumed Bill and his family were Christians, like most Blacks, though you know of Muhammad Ali, of course. Why would his father convert? You wait for Bill to clarify, but he has become quiet, standing with hands folded, and doesn't seem to want to say more.

"When?" you ask, because you can't ask why. "And you?" Perhaps, if Bill had converted to Islam, Seema's father might have come around.

"No, not me. I didn't see my father, growing up. I was brought up by my grandparents. That's why, Mrs. Hussein—" He takes a deep breath and reaches a hand out to you. "I know from personal experience how difficult it is growing up without a father. I don't want my child to go through that. Please, Mrs. Hussein, I just want Seema to hear me out. I'd like to remain a part of my child's life. Will you speak to her? For your grandchild's sake?"

This time, there's no doubting the sincerity in his voice. Surely Seema wouldn't want to deprive her child of his father? If there's a chance you could unite them, you must act. Isn't one of your aims in coming here to somehow reconcile a father and his child?

It's beyond midnight in Chennai now. You imagine your husband in bed, sleeping the way he does, unstirring, as if no worldly worries could keep him awake. He hasn't called you here. He said he wouldn't, and he's stuck to his word. You called him once to let him know you arrived safely. You've been hoping he'll call, though you know how stubborn he is. Your daughter is stubborn too, but you'll make her listen this time.

You agree to talk to Seema. Bill thanks you profusely, pressing your hands between his saucer-sized palms. He gives you his phone number, asks you to call him if you have any news, or need any help, anything at all.

Now that you've agreed, he's in a hurry to leave, gone with a clatter of footsteps.

38

On the day, seven months ago, when my to-be father Bill is to learn of the possibility of me, he wakes to blue skies, the light lithe and lively. It is the first day of April. Each hue sparkles, scrubbed of its winter grime.

It's a few weeks since he and Seema filed to have their marriage summarily dissolved, their issues amicably settled. Just the previous week, Obama had finally signed the Affordable Care Act into law, reassuring Bill that Obama's tenure would have a legacy rivaling that of almost all other presidents, even if Obama achieved nothing else. The teabaggers hell-bent on thwarting Obama's agenda have been outwitted and outplayed, as Bill had predicted.

It is spring in San Francisco, blithely expectant. The divorce would not take effect for a half year, but already Bill meets the day as though impatient after a long dormancy. Even hearing from Seema—she calls him at work, asking to meet for lunch—only checks his spirits a little: there are a few matters remaining to be discussed.

They meet at a restaurant close to his office. In the half gloom of the fluorescent interior, he can persuade himself she's from a past life, already fading. He has prepared for much, but not for what she says: "Bill, I'm pregnant."

At first, he doesn't believe her—it's April Fool's Day, after all. Next, he's puzzled: What game is she playing? Is she setting the stage to revoke the dissolution, to get back together, or seek some kind of spousal support? And how could she be pregnant?

"That night we decided to separate—" Seema says, "I'd had my IUD removed a few weeks earlier."

The memory comes back to him—the morning fog, the ferocious coupling, its urgency heightened by the knowledge of the impending parting, the thrill of one final possession. Later, the relief and regret, at the ease of his reprieve the night before, her ready acceptance.

He's confused: Had Seema come that night prepared to agree to a child? But by then his insistence on a child had become a face-saving way of letting her go. And having experienced the potential of a reawakened life, does he really desire to return to the depression of his previous existence? His chest compresses. He says, "This will invalidate the summary dissolution. When did you find out?"

"A week after we signed."

"And you're telling me now? After more than two weeks?"

"I had to decide what to do."

"What were you deciding?"

"I want to keep the baby."

"So I am to have no say." In either decision—removing the IUD, keeping the baby. It's just like Seema to make decisions for the two of them, as though his opinion doesn't matter, as though she can always count on him to come around. He must make it clear he's no longer willing to follow wherever she leads, no longer willing to let her govern his life. "I don't want a baby now. I don't want to get back together."

"I don't want to get back together either."

He sees it clearly then, her stratagem. He leaps up, enraged. "This is what you planned, you and Divya? First you screw me, then you screw me over, so you and Divya can play mommies together? Don't give me that face—I know about you two. Fuck you, Seema. You won't get one cent out of me for this."

They haven't ordered yet. He flicks his menu toward her and, ignoring her cries, strides out of the restaurant. "Fucking lesbians." The dazzle of the day outside blinds him.

Seema leaves messages, which he deletes without listening. She emails him insisting he's wrong, she means to bring up the baby alone if he doesn't want to be involved. She doesn't mean to impose the baby on him, she doesn't need his money. But meanwhile he has found out he has very little power in the matter: by California law, he will be held responsible for child support, no matter what. He is the sucker chosen to subsidize Seema and Divya playing house. Abort the baby, he replies, tersely.

When he finally agrees to meet again, he demands they draw up papers to absolve him of any commitment to me; the marriage dissolution can proceed then. This is really a symbolic gesture, since no court of law in California will recognize the document if it's against the child's best interests. But this is the best he can hope for. In return, Seema requires him to sign away his parental rights. That he can do: sign away his rights but not his responsibilities. He draws up an affidavit, and they both sign.

But later, he finds that a legal document has not obliterated those instincts of fathers-to-be that well up in the cracks in his mind and heart as the day of my birth approaches. The idea of me begins to tug at him.

He has no clear picture of me—my mother has let slip my gender, and he'd wanted a daughter earlier. His conception of me is fed by photos of his own infancy, by movies and television, advertisements. But for all the borrowed imagery with which he gives me skin and flesh, for all the similarly counterfeit visions he creates of our shared future—playing catch, fishing, watching football, grilling (counterfeit because he's never experienced these with his own father)—there is a core that cannot be denied: he is moved by some instinct that does not owe its existence to his received ideas of fatherhood. A son with part of his genetic code is being brought into the world, and this knowledge is sufficient to trigger an inborn desire to protect me, to ensure my passage to manhood. He can't be one of the fathers Obama decries—the ones MIA or AWOL, having abandoned their responsibilities.

He wants, then, to reassume the title of father he so cavalierly renounced and become the father he never had. But Seema's number comes up disconnected, and his emails go unanswered. He calls her office, but she always manages to elude him. Her friends refuse to give away her address. He finds out, too, that Seema was right in one regard—she and Divya are not together. He considers revoking the summary dissolution himself, but he dithers too long—it's September by then—and the divorce goes into effect.

Earlier this month, October, he unexpectedly catches sight of my very pregnant mother near Dolores Park, walking beside a tall youth in a hat. He runs after them, wondering who the youth is. He checks himself when he realizes that it's a girl, and by the way she looks at Seema, she's clearly in love with his now ex-wife. He watches through the glass from outside the café, taking in the softer, more rounded figure Seema now presents, full with his child, smiling at the girl—how many times had that same smile been bestowed on him. It's inviting and enveloping, reveling in its own power, with just a hint of affectionate detachment. He'd forgotten how hard it was to resist it, how weak and worshipping it made him feel.

As he jogs away from my mother's apartment this morning, after asking my grandmother to intercede on his behalf, he vows: he'll fight to keep his family, the way his incarcerated father was unable to.

39

As Seema and Tahera set out, the late October sky is a washed-out blue. A bleary-eyed sun shines down on the empty streets of the Sunday morning. Seema has made this trip to the park many times before with Leigh, the two of them ambling through the Mission holding hands. Today she walks faster, knowing Divya will be waiting at the café at the base of the park. She's decided to pretend to encounter Divya by accident. But Tahera, in a maddeningly expansive mood, is refusing to be rushed. She smiles at passersby, oblivious to the hem of her black jilbab sweeping the ground—crying to be stepped on!—or their curious glances in her direction, and stops to examine storefront displays and murals scattered throughout the Mission.

"Doesn't that woman remind you of Halima Aunty?" Tahera says, in front of a psychedelic mural on one wall of an open parking lot, three stories tall. A plump large-breasted brown woman is seated, in a purple dress and green sash, her knees up, her legs apart. In her hands she holds a naked brown baby, who in turn holds a glowing globe, a bright yellow sun. The woman laughs at the baby, who smirks down at the passersby. Bees hover in the blue air above the overflowing platter of multihued fruits by her feet.

Seema has never noticed the resemblance to their Halima Aunty before, though the moment Tahera mentions it, the likeness leaps at her—the laugh lines around the eyes and the mouth, the double chins, the mole on the cheek, where a bee rests. How had she missed this until now? "I saw her last year," she says. "She was as jolly as ever."

Halima is their mother's sister, so unlike their mother in every way. Where Nafeesa is small and compact, Halima bulges good-naturedly in all directions. Where Nafeesa's voice is soft, Halima can be heard across a boisterous wedding hall, her generous laughter immediately recognizable. When your Halima Aunty laughs, their father would joke to her face, even Allah has to cover His ears.

"Wait, you saw her so recently?" Tahera asks.

What no one has shared with Tahera is that Seema and Bill were in Chennai a year and a half ago. Seema had joined Bill on a work trip to Singapore, and they flew to Chennai for the weekend. They met her mother at her aunt's place one evening, Seema forbidden to enter her old home. Only after I'm dead, her father had said, a commandment neither daughter nor mother could bring herself to violate. Halima talked about compelling Naeemullah to receive the couple, but that didn't happen. Halima has always been Seema's most vocal supporter, least cowed by Naeemullah and most willing to stand up to him, but none of her entreaties over the years have had any effect. Tahera was kept in the dark about the trip in case word got back to Naeemullah.

"A laddoo for each cheek," Seema says, deflecting Tahera's query, pointing to the stippled oranges in the platter of fruits in the mural, which resemble sweet golden laddoos. Their aunt had a habit of thrusting sweets into their mouths whenever they visited her—besieged by her overflowing body, squished to her ample belly and breasts, soaked by the wet kisses she showered on their cheeks and foreheads, and always with the box of sweets she rushed toward them, forcing them to open their mouths, refusing to take no for an answer. Their mother is never as demonstrative. "It's sad. She spoiled us as if—"

Seema breaks off, her eyes fixed on the baby's smug face and the burning sun clasped in his hands. A memory from her visit: Halima Aunty greeting them both with laddoos, stuffing one into Bill's mouth as well, ignoring his protests. Her mother had mostly been quiet that evening, smiling frequently, but not saying much, as if her tongue were even here controlled by the absent husband and master. What a difference it would have made to have had Halima Aunty as mother instead.

Another difference: their aunt is childless. She couldn't conceive due to some hormonal imbalance, which accounted for her constantly expanding girth. Their aunt had undertaken many pilgrimages to various durgahs around India—Nagore, Haji Ali, Ajmer, Nizamuddin—as well as umrah to Medina a few times, with the sole purpose of praying for a child, prayers that had gone unheeded.

Looking at the laughing woman holding the baby, Seema recalls with remorse that she hadn't informed her aunt about her pregnancy, or the divorce. Instead her aunt learned of them from her mother and called in support: "Don't worry, Seema, you'll be a good mother. I'm very proud of you, what a brave step you've taken."

"Yes, it's a pity she never had children," Tahera says. "But everything is by Allah's plan. Shall we turn back? Ammi's alone at home."

"Everything?" A swift anger seizes Seema. "Halima Aunty's condition? Ammi's illness? Everything?" What she wants to add but doesn't: My entire life? Another memory of her aunt consoling her, years earlier, when she'd forsaken her father's house: "I'm not sure I understand, Seema, but I know you wouldn't do something simply to cause your family pain."

Tahera purses her lips, and Seema turns away before she says something she cannot unsay. "Once around the park, and we'll go home."

They continue in silence, Tahera's earlier affability torched, Seema wishing she'd held her tongue. Thankfully, Divya is waiting outside the café, and Seema doesn't have to find a pretense to linger till Divya gets there. But just as she'd feared, Divya is dressed as if on a date: a ruffled midi in mauve and dull-gold peep-toe flats. "I see a friend, I'll have to say hello."

She's already warned Divya that Tahera is accompanying her. "Oh my God, Divya, three days in a row! What are you doing here?"

"What can I say, it's my good karma." Divya's eyes flick toward Tahera before she smiles, and Seema hopes Tahera didn't notice the quick pout or the sulk in the voice.

"We were out for a walk around the park. You can join us if you're free."

"You won't mind?" Divya trains her dazzling smile on Tahera.

To Seema's surprise, Tahera is far more welcoming than she'd been with Fiaz. "I'm Tahera. Please join us. And"—she holds out a hand in greeting—"you can tell me all about Seema's life in San Francisco."

"And I've always wanted to know how Seema turned out the way she is." Divya smirks at Seema. "Isn't this your worst nightmare? Your *best friend* and your sister exchanging stories about you?"

Divya's sly emphasis is unsettling. "Hey, no tattling!" Seema warns, as Divya falls in with them, but on Tahera's side.

Divya directs the conversation, her first questions innocuous enough—about home and school—but Tahera's replies grow involved in response to Divya's show of interest. They pull ahead, heads bent toward each other, as though intimate confidants. Any other time Seema would have found the odd picture they present hilarious, the sexy and the dowdy, the worldly and the unworldly, poster children for acceptance and diversity in mauve and black. "You're walking too fast," she cries, annoyed.

But they don't heed her, glancing back only occasionally as they make their way up the hill on the western side of the park. They're punishing her, clearly. Divya must have assumed she invited Tahera along to act as a safeguard, to thwart the talk Divya wanted. Seema grits her teeth and strains after them, afraid now what Divya may choose to disclose.

They stop at the top of the hill to wait for her at the spot Leigh calls theirs. She struggles up the steep climb, maneuvering her way past strollers, and dogs on leashes, and couples carrying picnic hampers and blankets, all moving in the opposite direction. There's some event happening: a stage has been set up in the natural amphitheater formed by the bowl of the park, the lawn in front of it already dotted with groups of people.

When she finally reaches them, Tahera exclaims, all innocence, "The view from here is beautiful, isn't it? Season of mists and mellow fruitfulness—"

Seema strains to regain her breath. The city glimmers, unreal and unfocused, its colors and lines blurred by the thin scrim of mist still hovering over it. Or are tears—of frustration—clouding her eyes? She'd given up a tryst with Leigh for this.

"I'm sorry we left you behind," Divya says. "We were so engrossed."

"I hope you both learned what you wanted to know." Seema swallows her anger. Serves her right for even agreeing to this assignation, knowing how volatile Divya could be. But Divya couldn't have revealed anything disastrous: Tahera seems fine.

"I learned how sneaky you were, even as a child." Divya smiles vaguely. "But what I want to know is—" She bends down to inspect the ground, and picking up a pebble, tosses it toward a group of unkempt young men reclining on the dewy grass some distance down the slope, passing around a joint. The pebble hits a man with shaggy blond hair. "Hey, what's going on down there?" Divya calls out, when he turns.

"Dunno. I think candidates for something, the board of supervisors maybe. There'll be lots of yapping."

"But picnic baskets?" Divya turns to Seema and Tahera. "I need to find out what's going on. Tahera, it was lovely talking to you, I hope to meet you again. Seema, we'll catch up soon."

She blows kisses at them, slips off her shoes, and skips lightly down the green slope, her mauve dress fluttering like an overblown flower.

40

Season of mists and mellow fruitfulness! Close bosom-friend of the maturing sun— Tahera finds the pleasure of Keats's odes distinct and transporting, like biting into one of the crisp golden apples a Kashmiri patient used to gift her father every year. There is of course no autumn in Chennai, only the onset of the northeast monsoons; nevertheless, she always claimed it as her favorite season, based on the ode and postcards her father used to receive from his friends in England, of trees with leaves the red-gold of the gulmohar reflected in the drowsy waters of brooks. *Autumn!* Living all these years in Irvine, she'd even forgotten how the word sounded, like an incantation, having come to think of this time of the year as fall.

Earlier that morning she was tempted to see how much of the poem she recalled, and whether she could memorize the lines again. Surely there was no harm in this: after all, the ode is a celebration of Allah's creation and His munificence. She found it surprisingly easy—as if it were meant to be. In less than half an hour, while her mother showered, she relearned the entire poem. On the walk to the park, its lines and phrases keep her company. How mellow San Francisco is this autumn Sunday morning! How sweet seem the stores of apples and peaches and pears, filled with ripeness to the core. The swollen pumpkins, lying plump by the door. The clumps of chrysanthemum, and sunflower, and marigold. And surely in the mural, it must be Autumn herself seated on the granary floor, her harvest spread carelessly at her feet, while bees buzz ceaselessly about!

Seema's secrecy regarding meeting Halima Aunty pricks this Keats-induced bubble, and Seema's question—*everything* is by Allah's plan?—bursts Tahera out of it. Inclined now to resentment, Tahera recognizes Seema's subterfuge: the walk is an excuse, Seema as usual camouflaging her true intentions. No doubt Seema planned to meet Divya at the park, which explains her initial reluctance to bring Tahera along, expecting to draw comfort from her friend, perhaps even complain about her sister and mother. The attention Divya pays Tahera must have been unwelcome to Seema, and this disposes Tahera to like Divya, despite her modern leanings and attire. Divya, it also turns out, is an excellent conversationalist, interesting, and interested, not only in their childhood in Chennai but also in Tahera's life in Irvine.

The pleasure of Divya's company soon overshadows the irritation at Seema's deviousness. The day regains its benevolent autumn haze. *Where are the songs of Spring? Ay, where are they? Think not of them, thou hast thy music too—*

Passing the mural on their way back home reminds Tahera of her aunt again. A regular occurrence at their kitchen table in Chennai: Ammi and Halima Aunty whispering to each other as they dip biscuits in chai, their private conversation stalling whenever the girls draw near. Tahera can picture them at the same table, their gray heads even now bent in confidences. And it will be Halima Aunty tending to Ammi during her last days. Growing up, Tahera had always thought she and Seema were each other's best friends, just like that older pair of sisters, had thrilled whenever someone commented, seeing them walking hand in hand: See how close they are! They were the Hussein sisters. But that was before she'd discovered the extent of the secrets kept from her.

Tahera slows down. "Do you want to know what your friend Divya told me?"

But Seema doesn't hear her and continues walking. A cloud moves over the sun. Seema turns to look back only after some length. "Why have you stopped? I thought you wanted to get back home quickly because Ammi's alone."

"Now you're worried about Ammi."

"What does that mean?"

"Nothing. It means nothing. We mean nothing to you, Seema."

"What?" Seema finally stops to face Tahera, hands up in confused exasperation. "What did I do?"

Tahera cuffs herself on her forehead, a spontaneous revival of a girlhood gesture. "How stupid of me to think you'd remember the way you left. Why would you? You've not spent years trying to forget that time like I have."

The sun masked, the street dimmed, Tahera is back in their home in Chennai, just returned from her daylong clinical rotation, and the house is dark. Her mother usually leaves a lamp on after dusk, even if she's not at home. But it's not a power cut or a blown fuse, for there's a streak of light under the closed door to her father's study. Tahera calls out to him. When he opens his door, the light from the study reveals an apparition—Ammi!—sitting statue-like at the other end of the living room.

Tahera recoils. "Why are you sitting in the dark, Ammi? You gave me such a scare. Where's Seema?"

Her mother makes no reply, but Abba says, "She's dead to us. I don't want to hear her name spoken in this house ever again." He turns back to his study, plunging the living room into darkness again.

The sun peeps out briefly, the sidewalks blaze, and Seema flickers in what seems a distance away. "You know what hurt me most? That I had no idea at all," Tahera says. "Remember the evening before you left? You took me to our favorite chaat stall, the one in Fountain Plaza. Your treat, you said. You ordered everything—samosa chole, bhel puri, pav bhaji, Thums Up, Limca, masala chai—even though we couldn't possibly finish it all. But you insisted we stay till we did. We sat there for two hours while we stuffed ourselves silly. You said you couldn't eat enough, because you'd get nothing like this at Oxford. You must have known then what you were planning to do. But you didn't say a word to me. I was the last to find out. I didn't even learn the real reason until a year later."

The days and months after Seema's departure she'd obsessed over every detail of that last evening together, sifting for any hint that would explain Seema's expulsion. She'd asked Seema: What's up between you and Abba? Seema had replied, shrugging as she scraped the straggling chole off the plate: He wants me to get married now, and I refused, but he'll come around. Tahera had overheard snatches of discussions between her parents, so Seema's account hadn't come as a surprise. And she'd accepted Seema's easy dismissal of their father's authority. After all, there was nothing his golden daughter could want that Abba would deny.

But, of course, she hadn't understood then why he didn't relent about Seema's marriage after her disappearance, brooking no discussion, locking himself up in his office whenever Tahera persisted. Or why Ammi seemed so unwilling to challenge him, barely dragging herself through long days, haggard and woebegone. Tahera uncovered the real reason months later, when she recognized Seema's handwriting on unopened envelopes while rummaging through her father's desk for a sheet of paper. She'd snuck out the most recent one, tearing it open in her bedroom, her entire body trembling. That's how she came to learn what Seema was, what Seema claimed to be.

"You didn't reply to any of my letters. I'd cry on Ammi's lap after checking the post every day, waiting for your reply. I fought tooth and nail with Abba, accusing him of hiding your letters to me. But you didn't ever write to me, even though you continued to write to Abba, who wouldn't even open any of your letters. You couldn't be bothered with me, Seema. I wasn't worth your time." Tahera swallows an angry breath and steps off the pavement. A stream of cars prevents her from crossing the road.

"Tahera, stop." Seema hurries toward her, grabbing Tahera's arm as she waits for the last car to pass. "I was trying to figure out some things myself. I thought you wouldn't understand. And wasn't I right? Remember that letter you sent me from Irvine?"

But Tahera cannot stop. "Do you know what you put us through? Did you ever wonder what happened after you left?" She unclasps Seema's hand from her elbow. "And you expect me to disrupt my family and take on additional burdens for your child simply because you asked. That too without apologizing, or even acknowledging what you did. It seems like you haven't figured anything out after all. You're still the same Seema you always were. Only concerned about yourself and what you want. Never caring how it will affect others."

Tahera takes a step forward but is tugged back—Seema is standing on the hem of her jilbab trailing on the pavement. Tahera gives it a yank, whipping around to thrust Seema aside.

Had she jostled Seema too abruptly, too roughly? With a groan, Seema clutches at her belly and lurches. Tahera instinctively throws out a steadying hand, for the second time on that trip, but Seema is already sinking to the pavement, twisting at her knees, grasping at Tahera's jilbab to lower herself. She drags Tahera down with her.

Tahera has barely caught her breath to murmur, "Ashukrulillah! Seema, are you okay?" when with another shudder and a piercing cry—"Allah!"— Seema pitches forward on her haunches, forehead dropping to the pavement, as though in sajda.

Tahera crouches by her sister, fear clenching her chest tight where moments ago there had been fury. Surely this can't be more than a contraction? But it isn't the time for panic or self-recrimination, and she lets experience take over, keeping her voice steady: "Seema, are you in pain? Can you sit up?"

Seema's back moves in prolonged judders. Tahera places a soothing palm on it, urging: "Take slow, deep breaths. Relax, breathe in through your nose and out your mouth." She calls out each breath—"in, out, in, out"—for what seems an eternity, practicing it herself for the calm it brings her too. Seema's body gradually stops trembling.

A shadow falls on her. A straggle of pedestrians have gathered around. "Is she okay, do you need help?"

"She's fine, I'm a doctor, please stand away, she needs air." She ignores the crowd, bends over Seema, whispers into her ear—"I'm going to raise you up"—and helps Seema to sitting.

Seema's eyes are tightly shut. With the fabric of her jilbab Tahera wipes Seema's face, and Seema submits to it mutely, tilting her face up as Amina would, letting Tahera wipe the tears from the corners of her eyes. Only then does Seema open them.

There's distracting chatter from the crowd. Questions and suggestions: 911, ambulance, ER. "No, can you get us a cab please?" Tahera has decided to take Seema home, where she can examine Seema immediately, rather than go to the ER. "Seema, don't try to get up yet."

Seema nods and sits still, head bowed, hands on her stomach, while Tahera occupies herself straightening Seema's clothes and brushing away dust, glad for something to do, all the while maintaining a firm grip on Seema's arm. "It's okay, you'll be fine, I'm here."

Only after she's assisted Seema into the cab does she allow herself the torment of the deferred guilt and apprehension. Ammi had charged her with protecting Seema and the baby. Instead, she may have endangered their lives. Is she making the right decision taking Seema back home instead of to a hospital? And how to explain to their mother the need for a checkup?

But there's gratitude also. Toward Allah, subhanahu wa ta'ala, for not permitting some harm to befall Seema and for keeping away the monstrous wish of the first evening. Gratitude toward Seema too, for accepting her ministrations without recriminations. She's grateful again when Seema whispers, just outside the apartment door, "Let's not say anything to Ammi."

41

Grandmother, when Seema struggles to kick off her shoes, and Tahera bends down to remove them, you're immediately aware something has happened. Seema holds on to Tahera's shoulders for support, even as she says they've had a good walk.

She heads to her bedroom, while Tahera removes her hijab and folds it unhurriedly, with her usual meticulousness. But you're not taken in. Not for nothing are you their mother, even if you haven't seen them much the last ten years. You'd been pondering how to get Seema alone so you could speak to her about Bill's visit, but that thought flees your mind. "What happened?" you ask Tahera.

"Contractions." Tahera pulls out a small black bag from her suitcase. "I don't think it's labor, but I need to examine her." When you follow her to Seema's bedroom, she stalls you: "Ammi, can you make us some chai, please?"

You nod through your anxiety. Why would Seema agree to have her sister look at her now, after refusing so forcefully that morning? You busy yourself at the stove, while straining your ears to what's going on in the bedroom. But Tahera has shut the door, and you can't make out much. So you concentrate on making your special chai instead, crushing a cardamom pod and slicing slivers of ginger and adding them along with a couple of cloves to the tea in the bubbling pot. You set out cups on a platter—not the regular mugs but three cups from a fluted porcelain set you'd found while rearranging Seema's kitchen cabinets that morning—and when you've sweetened the chai with an extra spoonful of sugar, you carefully strain it and ladle it into the teacups and carry the platter to Seema's bedroom. It seems ages before Tahera responds to your knock. She takes the platter from you, and you worry for a moment that you're not to be admitted in yet.

Seema is sitting up in bed, her stomach exposed. She listens through a stethoscope, moving a hornlike attachment across her stomach. "Ammi, listen—you can hear Ishraaq's heart."

She holds out the stethoscope. But first you look to Tahera—for reassurance—and only after the slightest inclination of her head do you go to Seema's side. Still, you fumble with the earpieces.

Tahera adjusts the placement of the horn. "Can you hear him?"

You can't—your own heart is beating too rapidly, your relief is a daze of weakness—but you nod and smile, consoling yourself that all that matters is that the baby is fine.

Afterward, for the first—and only—time, all three women, my grandmother, my mother, and my could-be mother, speak to me directly.

Grandmother, you go first, your face inches from Seema's stomach, cooing, "Ishraaq, darling grandson, I can't wait to hold you in my arms, to call you my calfling, my sugar dumpling, to sing you a lullaby." You apply your ear directly to Seema's stomach and pretend you can hear me, amid all the other noises the body makes. "He says he can't wait to meet his Nani either," you announce. "Tahera, say something to your nephew."

Tahera sits down beside Seema, and in a voice that is unexpectedly tender, she whispers, "Sweetest nephew, this is your Tara Aunty. Can you hear me?"

In answer, Seema's body rumbles. The three of you laugh.

"What a majestic voice he has," you say. "Like Akbar in *Mughal-E-Azam*." The rumble reminds you of the deep baritone of the actor Prithviraj Kapoor, who plays the Mughal emperor Akbar in your family's favorite movie. Your family never missed a chance to watch it, either on TV or in a local theater. You rub the tip of your nose on Seema's stomach as though to nuzzle me. "You'll grow up to have a voice just like that, and you'll be brave, and strong, and wise, and famous, won't you? You'll make your Nani proud."

This time your daughters' laughter sounds strained, especially Seema's. Your reference is a misstep. It's their father's enthusiasm for the movie that your daughters embraced, about the doomed love between the beautiful servant girl Anarkali and Prince Salim, which brings down the wrath of his emperor father on both of them. It's impossible to recall the movie without also remembering the way their father would declaim, in his performing voice, the more poetic of Akbar's dialogues. "Your voice should ring like that," he'd exhort, whenever he coached them for their contests, brushing aside their objections that Prithviraj Kapoor, with his quivering jowls and flashing eyes, was given to overacting.

"Ammi, don't put so much pressure on my son, he's not even born yet," Seema responds. "I'll be happy if he grows up strong enough to follow his heart, as long as he doesn't forget his mother." She caresses her stomach. "Ishraaq, you'll always love your mother, right?"

The three of you stare at Seema's stomach, as if expecting it—me—to reply, and when I'm silent, you three burst into laughter again.

"He's going to grow up stubborn, just like his mother and aunt, wait and see," you say. You shuffle over to the chest of drawers where Tahera has placed the chai and carry the platter back. The three of you sip your chai from the dainty white cups.

"Mmm, your masala chai!" Tahera says. "And these cups are so pretty. Just like the cups at home, Ammi."

"They *are* from Chennai," Seema says.

Cups from Chennai—there's so little in Seema's apartment with any connection to her past. And you know that it's Chennai Tahera's referring to as home, not Irvine. Something happened on the walk, but you decide not to probe. This is the most relaxed you've seen your daughters together; Tahera has even casually placed her free hand on Seema's. You're reminded of all the times you've seen them like this, Tahera sitting by Seema's sickbed and reading her a book or bending over her with a glass of water or milk to soothe her parched throat.

There's only this to mar the illusion you're back in Chennai, sitting in your own home, sipping chai from your own teacups with your daughters: the knowledge that their father is nowhere nearby, with no intention of joining you, of fixing back together your fractured family.

42

Grandmother, do you remember the night sixteen-year-old Seema played Anarkali in her class production, at her girls-only convent school?

It's Annual Day, and the auditorium is packed with parents and hot with the dusty March heat. You're squeezed in the middle of a long row of chairs, but close to the front, a special recognition accorded to you and your husband.

Your daughters have been called repeatedly to the stage to accept awards, for their proficiency in various subjects, for their leadership qualities and accomplishments. Seema comes to the stage already half made up as Anarkali, in the glittering apricot-orange ghagra-choli that you altered for her on your

Singer sewing machine. Tahera is iron-sharp in her captain's uniform, all white, the pleats of her tunic starch-pressed; she takes part in her class play too, but as narrator. Your husband is in a Prussian blue suit, white shirt, and checked green tie. Your saree is a bottle-green organza selected by your daughters to match his tie; your hair is in a low bun, adorned with a single strand of jasmine, your style for formal occasions.

The play to be performed by Seema's eleventh grade is last on the program. This is the piece the audience always awaits eagerly—an Annual Day will stick or fade in the memory of the school based on this performance, and you and your husband are doubly keen, as it was adapted from the movie by Seema herself.

Hidden hands pull on cords to twitch the curtains aside, and the stage is revealed: The backdrop is a landscaped garden with fountains encircled by rose bushes, the lawns a bright chartreuse, the sky a fake cerulean blue. On a bench center stage sit two figures. In a cream-and-maroon sherwani is the prince, his status signaled by the gold plume pinned to his crimson turban—played by Seema's best friend, Reshmi, in make-believe sideburns and a mustache—and beside him, Seema as Anarkali with her head bowed, veiled in a transparent pale-peach dupatta that you yourself trimmed with silver ribbon and decorated with clusters of sequins.

The prince reaches to lift her veil but is stopped by Seema's hand.

"Anarkali, why do you hide your light from me?" he asks, his voice buckling with nervous compensation.

"I'm only the moon—" Anarkali replies, slowly raising the veil herself.

And you, Grandmother, for whom Seema's beauty has become commonplace, clutch at your husband's hand, surprised by this vision Seema has transformed into, with expert application of lipstick, eyeshadow, and kohl. For an instant you perceive the woman her sixteen-year-old self will become, gloriously beautiful and bold in her allure.

"Don't look at me this way. You're the sun, you'll burn me with the sun's burning rays." Anarkali turns away from the prince, but there's no doubt she's aware of her effect on him. Seema's voice, pitched lower than normal, burns your ears with its sultriness.

The prince's hand shakes a little as he tilts Anarkali's chin toward him. This time his voice is stronger, as though taking courage from her confidence. "Let Salim see in your eyes what your tongue cannot say."

But really, there's nothing this Anarkali's tongue seems incapable of saying. As the play progresses, Anarkali sheds all pretense of timidity and the submissiveness of a servant girl. It's the prince who is rendered mute in Seema's adaptation and Anarkali who rebels against Akbar's autocratic insistence on conformity to the worth he assigns his world. In fiery exchanges, a disdainful Anarkali declares herself willing to accept death to prove her love's invincibility. As pink-brown cardboard bricks are stacked around her to form a tomb under Akbar's unrelenting gaze, and a hapless Salim struggles in the restraining grasp of soldiers, she swears: "You cannot erase my love from the world's face. Death will only cement it, this tomb will forever bear its tale."

The standing ovation begins even before the curtains reopen for the actors' bows. Everybody is up on their feet, including your husband. How he claps and cheers, his hands high up in the air over his head!

But though you join him, you don't feel like celebrating. A new aspect of Seema has been revealed to you: a daughter older than her years, a daughter whose voice and words and poise are already signaling a departure from you, from everything you've imagined for her. You don't know what to make of these misgivings. You're ashamed of the small-minded suspicions sprouting in you—some disastrous attachment, some unsavory weakness—but you'll be slipping up in your duties as a mother if you ignore them. Yet, despite your newly awakened fears—you go over in your mind all the boys and bachelors in Seema's various circles—it doesn't occur to you to look closely at Seema and Reshmi as the two girls take their bows.

Why should it? After all there's little precedent to alert you to a connection of that sort. With Reshmi's arm clasped around her waist, Seema inclines a graceful salaam toward the audience, then bestows a dazzling smile on her partner—and you have no inkling of the messages exchanged between them. After the show, an exultant Seema, leading an unresisting Reshmi by the hand, does the rounds, mingling with her adoring audience and accepting congratulations. The two of them, still in their costumes, the beautiful servant girl and her bearded and mustached paramour, pose variously—hand in hand, gazing into each other's eyes, embracing—as cameras click.

You have a photo from that evening: You and your husband standing in the center, Seema and Reshmi on either side. You're all smiling, but formally, as though posing for a wedding photo, like the one you'll take with Tahera and Ismail on their wedding night.

Later, alone with your husband, you'll take him to task. "Why are you encouraging your daughters with all this love business? Can't you see how mature Seema has become?"

"What nonsense, it's just a play," he'll reply. "My daughters are too brilliant to waste their time on such matters."

Grandmother, years later when you learned of the gender of Seema's first lover, did you think back to that evening and uncover the identity of Seema's first love and decode the messages that passed between them?

No—you want to believe then that Seema is afflicted by no more than an assumed affectation, acquired along with her Oxford education, a rebellion for rebellion's sake. Even when she chooses banishment over submitting to her father's decree, you still cling to that hope, keeping it alive all those long years of her straying, heaving a sigh of relief when she finally returns to her senses and gets married.

And even today, on this afternoon in San Francisco, when you've just invoked Akbar's name and have spent the morning grieving over a father who will not relent in the face of his child's happiness, you choose not to dwell on that painful part of your daughter's past. You will not speak to Seema today about Bill, or Fiaz, while she's recovering from whatever scare she had, but you are biding your time.

43

Tahera has told herself she'll call Irvine after the asr namaz. She wanted the morning to herself, to reflect on the events of the last twenty-four hours, unprepared and unwilling to discuss them yet with Ismail. She even felt little urge that morning, unusual for her, to speak to her children, especially Amina. Now, right on cue, just as she's finished her asr namaz, as though she can't be trusted to follow up on her word, Ismail is on the phone.

"Sorry, I couldn't call earlier," he says. "I've been busy all day at the mosque."

It's late afternoon in San Francisco, evening in Irvine.

"Was nobody else helping clean up after the fundraiser?" she asks. Ismail can go on for ages about the fundraiser. She's glad for it today, preoccupied with deciding whether to relay Seema's request to him.

She doesn't like keeping secrets from Ismail. But she can't broach certain matters unless she's prepared. If she appears muddled, Ismail will be dismissive of her concerns or, worse, will make up his mind too quickly, and then it will take a confrontation to change his views.

She'd prayed the istikhara dua over Seema's request after fajr this morning. *Allah, who possesses the power and the knowledge that I do not, if accepting guardianship of Seema's child is good for my faith and for my life here on this earth and in the hereafter, ordain it for me and make it easy for me to accept it. If not, keep it away from me and help me reject it.* But she's no closer to making sense of the conflicting emotions and thoughts Seema triggers in her. The dua's effect, of course, may not be direct and immediate, and she may have to repeat the istikhara a few times and be patient.

Only half listening to Ismail, her thoughts are interrupted by the word *police*.

"Police?" she asks, immediately alert. "Forgive me, jaanu. My mind was elsewhere. Please tell me again, what happened?"

Ismail takes a deep breath. "Someone painted graffiti on the mosque walls last night. We spent the morning painting over it."

"Who did it?"

"We don't know yet. We filed a complaint with the police. The entire front wall was defiled."

She can't quite comprehend the extent of the violation, unable to picture the walls. But she knows when Ismail is keeping a tight rein on his emotions— by the swear words he bites off at the first syllables, before they sully his mouth, as he does now. She's never heard him complete a single profanity, ever. "Whoever did it will surely burn in Jahannam," she says.

"We're holding a meeting this evening to decide how to respond. Imam Zia wants to keep it quiet for now."

Tahera asks for more details, partly to stop herself from making any comments—hadn't she privately feared something like this, that Ismail and Imam Zia were perhaps overreaching in their efforts to expand the mosque?— and partly to atone for her morning's omissions, for having been so remiss as to ignore the circumstances surrounding her real life in Irvine. This is clearly not the time to bring up Seema's affairs.

"I took photos, I'll email them to you later," Ismail says. "The children are eager to talk to you."

Thankfully, Amina seems unaffected by the morning's incident. She doesn't even mention the mosque, excited at having spent the entire day with Taghrid Didi at her Najiba Aunty's house. She and Taghrid Didi played with dolls, then helped Najiba Aunty in the kitchen. In the afternoon they baked cookies. "With cashews, and raisins, and pistachios, and rose essence." Amina pronounces the list of ingredients carefully, proudly. "And I prayed namaz with Taghrid Didi and Najiba Aunty. I didn't make any mistakes."

"Good girl! Soon you'll be praying perfectly." Ever since her seventh birthday, Amina has wanted to learn to pray like her Taghrid Didi. The two girls are inseparable, though Taghrid is closer in age to Arshad. Taghrid is a good role model for Amina for the most part, though Tahera sometimes worries when Amina copies everything Taghrid does without questioning, like when Amina insisted on donning the hijab at such an innocent age. Amina's stories contain everything Taghrid did and said today, and Tahera is almost driven to ask if she hadn't missed her mother at all.

Arshad, on the other hand, is more tight-lipped than usual. "Did you have a good time with Najiba Aunty?" He's ordinarily talkative when he returns from his Najiba Aunty's house. Najiba is a substitute science teacher, and she has various science kits in her home that she lets Arshad tinker with during his visits. Today, however, he returns monosyllabic answers to every question.

Tahera, confronted with his remoteness, says, almost petulantly, "Go then, don't tell your Ammi anything."

"I'd rather have been with Abba painting the mosque." Arshad is aggrieved. "Why didn't Abba let me stay and help?"

"Abba has his reasons," Tahera says. "He probably thought you're not big enough and would get too tired."

"I could have done it. He didn't want us to see what was painted on the walls. Like that stopped me from finding out—" He pauses, as though deciding whether to tell her what he's seen.

She can't remember when she's heard her son be this upset or speak this openly. She's both dismayed at his distress and gratified at her new role as his confidant, though this last is surely only motivated by discontent with his father. She urges him on: "What did you find out?"

"They called Prophet Muhammad a terrorist." His voice trembles with anger, slurring the *r*'s. "They called him—" And here he hesitates, unsure of himself, pronouncing the word as carefully as Amina had pronounced *pistachios*. "They said Muslims are not welcome here. Why do they hate us so much, Ammi?"

It's an anguished cry, one that she's never heard from him before. It causes her heart to leap up with the kind of tremor she associates only with Amina.

But what should she say, what could she say? Later, she will rue that she didn't know how to react to it, the years of reserved attention toward Arshad providing her no map.

"Only Allah knows," she says, aware that she's encouraged him to open up only to forsake him. "Remember to say all your kalimas tonight."

She conscientiously narrates the exchange to Ismail, urging him to have a conversation with Arshad. She consoles herself with the thought that his father is the right person to talk to him—after all, she's not even at hand.

44

Evening, Irvine: Arshad is alone in his parents' bedroom, browsing search results on his father's desktop. He's engrossed in his task and becomes aware of his father's presence only when Ismail coughs. Startled, Arshad attempts to kill the browser window—he's only allowed to use the computer for homework, and only under supervision.

Ismail stalls him. "What were you doing?"

"Nothing. I was just searching for something for a class project."

"Did you ask my permission?"

"You were busy talking with Ammi," Arshad whines, mentally chiding himself for neglecting to keep an ear out for his father's return. Usually Abba supervises him less strictly than Ammi as long as he believes Arshad is meaningfully occupied, but after this morning, Arshad shouldn't have counted on it.

Ismail scrolls through the search results. They're on lies about the Prophet. "I told you this morning"—Ismail wags his finger in Arshad's face—"this is not a matter for children. You're not old enough to understand."

Ismail closes the browser window with a decisive click. But Arhsad's not out of trouble yet. Ismail, eyes drilling into him, continues, "Your Ammi tells me you've been using words you're not supposed to know."

Arshad feels betrayed by Ammi. Why did she have to repeat what he told her? "She asked me, Abba," he tries to explain. "I was just repeating what I saw on the wall."

"What do you know of such words anyway?" Ismail asks.

"I looked it up in the dictionary." He hangs his head in embarrassment hoping his father won't ask him what it means. His understanding is still hazy, from the websites he visited today, sickeningly littered with insults and abuses, clearly written by enemies of the Prophet and Islam.

"I don't want you to think about such things," Ismail says, leading him out of the room, gripping Arshad's shoulders. "And don't go looking again on the internet. I want you to forget all about this. Do you understand?"

Ismail's fingers dig into his shoulder blades so deeply that Arshad winces. His father's tone is angrier than ever before.

"Why are you angry with me? Why aren't you angry with whoever wrote those words?" Abba is behaving so unfairly toward him, like when he rebuffed his offer to help paint over the filth. "I did nothing wrong. They're the ones who are abusing the Prophet, who are making up lies about him."

He shakes his father's hands off his shoulders. "They should be killed like pigs." Arshad spits the last word out.

The smack, lightning quick, stuns the boy. But more than the impact, it's the shock that hurts: Abba has never hit him before. He lifts a hand to his cheek, where his father's palm struck, tears of shame searing his eyes. He shudders, his breath sticking in his nostrils and throat. The landing, and his father, tremble in a blurred haze.

Ismail says, "You will not speak like that in this house. Go to your room."

Ismail gives Arshad a push, and he stumbles. Abba, he wants to scream, why did you hit me? Isn't it every Muslim's duty to protect the Prophet's name, to fight those who abuse the Prophet? He kicks the door shut behind him, and the resounding thud that he can feel in his bones fills him with a fierce pleasure. He throws himself on his bed and lies there, sobbing.

Presently a timid fluttering knock on the door: Amina. He half wipes his tears and opens the door. "What is it?"

He sees her shrink at the sight of his tear-stained face, hugging her Asma doll tightly. "Bhaiya, Abba says come down," she says in a loud voice designed to carry downstairs. "He has to go to the mosque for namaz and a meeting." Then in a whisper, reaching a hand out to touch his face, "Why are you crying, Bhaiya?"

"Go away." He swats her hand away. "I'll come down when I want to."

Amina lingers by the door, her eyes turning moist, and he thrusts her out and shuts the door. It's because of her that he has to stay behind.

When he's sure she's gone, he creeps down the stairs—his father is in the bedroom getting ready—and picks up his shoes, then slips down to the garage. He gets into his father's car and waits, seat belt fastened.

Upstairs, Ismail and Amina wander around the house, calling to him. Their voices reach him, thin and disembodied, first Ismail's, irritated—"Arshad, where are you?"—and then, a moment later, Amina's weak and anxious echo.

Minutes pass, and his father's voice gets louder and louder, the annoyance more pronounced. "Arshad! I have to leave for isha namaz. Don't make me late."

He begins counting, calculating he'll need to count to five thousand to remain there for an hour—if he can't go, then neither can his father.

Five hundred later the basement door opens, and Ismail enters. He turns the lights on, then winches up the main garage door. He walks out into the driveway, and Arshad watches him through the rear window, silhouetted against the indigo evening sky, scanning the front lot and the sidewalks for him. At times his father freezes in attention, as if suddenly hopeful. But his shoulders sag as he continues to stand there, as though air were leaking out of him. Arshad has never seen his father look so defeated.

A few stars are visible in the sky, above the glow of the neighbor's house opposite. Arshad is reminded of how they'd stood in the dark—was it only last night?—looking out the kitchen window, sipping their drinks in friendly silence, basking in the success of the fundraiser.

"Abba—" he croaks out, opening the car door. "I want to come too."

Ismail catches sight of him and hurries to the car. "You've been here all along. I was worried."

"I'm sorry, Abba. But I want to come to the meeting."

Ismail looks at him with an expression Arshad can't decipher. He braces himself for another reprimand. He clutches at the door handle to resist efforts to remove him from the car.

But Ismail says, "Go get your sister."

Arshad doesn't move. Has Abba really changed his mind, or is this some kind of ploy? His father repeats his command, and he climbs down from the car hesitantly and backs his way to the house. Once inside, he races to find Amina, keeping an ear out for the engine starting and the car pulling out of the driveway.

He finds Amina combing Asma doll's hair at the dining table. "Hurry, get your shoes, we're going out."

He helps her into her shoes, tying the laces for her, then practically hauls her down to the garage. His father hasn't left yet.

"Get in," Ismail says. "But this is the last time you'll behave this way."

Arshad nods, buckles Amina into her booster seat in the back, then sits up in the front with his father. Ismail says nothing during the drive to the mosque, but Arshad exults: he's finally been admitted into the adult circle. He rolls down the window to feel on his cheeks the slap of the evening air.

45

When they turn into the parking lot, all the lights are on, and the mosque glows from within with a purple-white light escaping through the frosted windowpanes. The newly applied paint has not fully dried yet but shimmers faintly, giving the mosque the air of a mirage. The mosque projects a serene but fragile grace, marred by the blotches of red on the ground, the only remaining witness to the previous night's defacing.

They are late for isha namaz. "Did you do wadu?" Ismail asks, and Arshad shakes his head, embarrassed.

The entrance hallway is packed, as during Eid prayers: the mosque is overflowing today. Ismail leads Amina and Arshad along the walls to the washroom, skirting the praying men, who take half steps without breaking their namaz to let them through. When Amina and Arshad are done with wadu—Amina copies her brother's actions, following whispered instructions from Ismail—they head back the way they came, and the men quietly make room for them, squeezing in slightly, so that Arshad joins one row and Ismail and Amina the row behind him.

Lo: as one, the congregation stands in qiyam, hands folded, and as one, bends in ruku, palms on knees, and as one, stands erect in qawma, hands by the sides, and as one, prostrates in sajda, head to floor, and then sits up in jalsa, hands on thighs.

There is a different energy in the mosque this evening from the other times Arshad has prayed here, as though the worshippers gathered today have altered gravity, so that the very air seems heavier, every action more deliberate to counteract it. Arshad and Amina, their eyes half open to make sure they are in sync with the congregation, murmur their prayers earnestly (with Amina whispering the little she knows, mumbling through the rest). They recite the takbir in unison with the congregation—Allahu Akbar, Allahu Akbar, Allahu Akbar.

Allah is great. Allah is greater. Allah is the greatest.

After the final thashahud and the salaams to the left and right, the congregation is on its feet, milling around, turning to neighbors and clasping hands, embracing, but with none of the gaiety of Eid or the other occasions Arshad has seen here. Instead there is the somber meeting of eyes, of hands, of necks and chests, as at a funeral.

46

All the seats in the conference room are taken. More men throng the back and sides, standing. Yet there's little sound in the room except for Imam Zia reciting from the Quran.

He's seated on the dais, a Quran open on the rehal before him. Though his eyes appear focused on the book, he doesn't turn the pages, reciting instead from memory, as he always does. He glides over the words, swoops at them, hovers, drops. His entire body appears to recite. His chest lifts as he takes a breath before plunging into the cadence of the next ayat; the hull of his body rides each nasal ghunnah, vibrates with each quivering qalqala, with each ululating vowel. It freezes, motionless, at the crest of each soaring note.

Ismail recognizes the surah: Al-An'am. The Cattle. *Say: Travel through the earth and see what was the end of those who rejected truth.* He lifts Amina into his arms and beckons Arshad closer. This is Ismail's favorite—everything essential to Islam, he feels, is captured in this one surah. Don't conjoin anyone as equal with Allah. Establish regular prayers. Be good to your parents and take care of your children. Don't be tempted by illegitimate intimacy and promiscuity. Don't take life, except by way of justice and law. Measure and weigh your actions with fairness. Speak justly, even if a near relative is involved.

Also, doesn't the surah say, Don't revile those that call upon others besides Allah, lest they, out of spite, revile Allah in their ignorance? For Allah has made their actions seem fair to them, and when they return to Him, He will show them what they have done.

Allah knows best who strays from His path. He knows best who is open to His guidance.

How appropriate that Imam Zia has chosen this surah for this evening. Ismail's anger, bottled within him since morning, dissipates, vaporized by Imam Zia's cleansing voice. Even the burden of his guilt—at precipitating the vandalism—is lightened by the recognition that Allah has not set him as keeper over those who stray. Ismail is not responsible for their actions. And as for his supposed vanity—wasn't it merely misguided exuberance? As the surah says, Allah is most merciful, and oft-forgiving.

The surah could easily take an hour to recite, and they're twenty minutes in. Ismail worries that the congregation may lose patience. Thankfully, Imam Zia stops as soon as there are growing signs of restlessness.

Released, the entire congregation erupts in a cacophony of suppressed noises and deferred movements, men clearing throats, cracking necks and knuckles, shifting noisily in their seats. Amina stirs in Ismail's arms—bored, she'd fallen asleep, turning her body sideways and resting her head on his shoulder. She now opens her eyes, wondering where she is that the lights are so bright and the noises so loud, but her father is here, his comforting smell—the cucumber soap he uses, tinged with something that is peculiarly him—engulfs her, and she smiles up at him through sleep-heavy eyelids, then settles back and shuts her eyes again.

Looking around the crowd, Imam Zia prepares to address the assembled. Arshad has waited eagerly for this moment. He'd managed to remain patient through the recitation—which he would have at other times enjoyed—afraid that were he to fidget or complain, his father would regret bringing him. There are few children here tonight.

Imam Zia first speaks about the vandalism. But emotionlessly, with very few details, without quoting anything scrawled on the walls. He then describes meeting with the police, who he declares have promised to investigate the matter and apprehend the vandals. Meanwhile, he will contact the pastors and ministers from the surrounding churches to release a joint statement condemning the act. The community must remain calm. Arshad is disappointed. Isn't Imam Zia going to rebut the accusations and call down the wrath of Allah for the blasphemy against the Prophet?

The congregation appears dissatisfied too. At first the questions are hesitant, logistical. Should they deploy security cameras? And what about the expansion? Should the fundraising continue? Will they still be applying for approval from the city planning commission by the end of the month?

A contingent advocates restraint. Maybe they should wait until the furor around the country dies down, as it's bound to once the midterm elections are over and the hostility subsides. But what starts with only a faint whiff of finger-pointing—perhaps this wasn't the most well-advised time to initiate the expansion project?—soon becomes heated: Why court so much trouble simply over soccer practice? Hadn't the mosque functioned so many years without any problems until these newfangled schemes were instituted? What else could lie behind the decision to publish interviews in the *Sentinel,* if not publicity-seeking and self-aggrandizing?

Arshad squirms, his fists clenched: Why are they squabbling among themselves when the enemies are outside? He senses his father tense up. He looks around the room for signs of support from his father's friends. Won't someone respond? Won't Imam Zia say something? And why won't Abba defend himself? He fantasizes leaping to his feet and shouting down the men attacking his father and Imam Zia. He's puzzled by their passivity. His father continues stroking Amina's hair as though it were the most important task in the world.

An anger mixed with pity illuminates Arshad. He's always cherished that his father is named after the forefather of all Muslims, Prophet Ismail, who'd submitted without demur to being sacrificed on Allah's behest, awaiting patiently his father's knife until Allah intervened. But how powerless Abba must feel if the only person he's willing to show any anger toward is his own son.

Fortunately, the tide begins to change. At first one voice protests: They're doing nothing wrong, why should they be the ones to restrain themselves? Doesn't the Constitution give them the right to practice their religion? Then another voice joins, and then a third. There are dissenting voices too, but in agreement: What has the Constitution got to do with it, when Allah has already granted them rights?

Someone makes an impassioned speech, in Arabic, and Arshad can't fully understand it, and neither can half the assembled, yet the room responds with a standing ovation when the man finishes, along with chants of "Allahu Akbar." These grow louder, despite Imam Zia's admonitions to keep their enthusiasm in check. The chant soon moves to a call-and-response format: three calls of the takbir to which the congregation responds once, in one thundering voice.

Arshad joins in. At first softly, imitating his father, who murmurs the takbir while covering Amina's ears. But the pent-up grievances of the day aren't contained so easily. He feels the words outside him, their crash and ebb rocking everything in the room like a frenzied sea, and they stir up a storm inside. The takbir fills his lungs to overflowing. A feeling of elation courses through him, and the room and the congregation merge in a handful of joyously roared syllables.

During the relative lull of a call, a whimpering cry is heard. It's Amina, rubbing her eyes, waking up from a nightmare. Ismail hurries out of the room, her face pressed against his chest to muffle her sobs.

The congregation returns to its call-and-response takbir, but the rhythm has been broken.

Arshad hesitates: Should he follow? He wriggles his way out through the crowd, sulking. This is why girls, especially seven-year-old girls, should not be allowed into the mosque.

He pauses at the door to listen one last time. Imam Zia is finally able to regain control over the congregation and the room slowly subsides into silence.

47

Grandmother, you are playing a role tonight. You and your daughters are gathered in the living room watching TV—an Indian reality show, a competition modeled on *American Idol*, but for kids, none of them over twelve. Like old times, Seema, beside you on the futon, claims space and center stage, commenting animatedly about the show, its judges, its competitors, while Tahera sits in a chair, reading Keats and only occasionally looking up to see what's exciting your attention. But you, who like Tahera were usually a silent participant too, allowing your husband and eldest daughter to dominate family gatherings, feel compelled to assume the role of your husband tonight. The exuberance you assume now—joining Seema in remarking, exclaiming, laughing—as mild as it is, is alien to your nature.

The next competitor is a girl, no older than seven or eight, dressed in a frilly purple frock. "How beautifully she sings, just like Amina!" Seema exclaims. "She looks just like Amina, too."

Tahera glances up from her book, and the three of you watch, and listen, entranced. The girl never takes her eyes off her mother the entire time she's singing, the camera panning back and forth between them.

"Oh, it's her, what's her name?" you say, recognizing the mother as an aspiring playback singer from yesteryear, who'd disappeared from the music scene as suddenly as she'd entered it.

When the song is done, the audience roars in applause, the judges stand up and clap, and the host runs to the girl and lifts her up to his shoulders and invites the mother to join them on stage.

"She does look like our Amina. Does Amina sing too?" You haven't heard your granddaughter sing, you didn't even know she sings. Yet Seema seems to know.

"Amina sings wonderfully! She could take part in this competition with a little training."

And like the mother on TV, a lovely smile transforms Tahera's face. It's like witnessing a full moon break out from behind clouds. Very rarely does she smile. Even as a child she refrained, as though smiles were some currency she needed to hoard. How pretty she looks when she's smiling like this, how aged and careworn when she's not. You wish you could smooth away the creases that will soon return to her face and shoulder some of her worries. But you don't really know the extent of them. She withdrew from you after Seema left and, over the years, became estranged. She even adopted Seema's habits of secrecy and defiance, as if with Seema absent she had chosen to take her sister's place.

"Amina loves to sing," Tahera affirms, still beaming. "Seema, how do you know?"

"The day I spent with them, she sang that song we used to like as children, the one about the runaway horse. Do you remember, Ammi?"

Of course, you do! The tape recorder blaring, the two girls rewinding and playing the song over and over again, singing along, clopping all over the house, or twirling in tight circles to it, their twin plaits and dupattas flying horizontally. You were afraid your daughters would hurt themselves by crashing into furniture as they collapsed from dizziness. When the tape caught in the spool, the house was quiet again until, giving in to their pestering, their father bought them another copy. You scolded him for spoiling his daughters, and he laughed at you, chucking your chin, saying, "Should I spoil you instead, my beautiful unsmiling wife?"

The phone rings and Seema answers it, and Grandmother, by her face you know this is him: your husband. You've been missing him all evening. Your husband has called, finally, and right when you were thinking about him. Perhaps the timing is a good omen, presaging a reconciliation.

My grandfather's voice floats thinly into the room: "Nafeesa?"

Without saying a word, Seema holds out the phone, the liveliness from moments ago erased. You want to shake her: Say something to your father.

He's querulous. "Why didn't you call me? I was worried about you."

He's never called Seema's number before; he'd vowed never to use it. What made him change his mind, when he could so easily have called Tahera on her cell phone? You want to scold him: Why call here if you're not even going to address your daughter?

You're not going to apologize for not calling, you're not going to say anything unsolicited, even though fifteen minutes earlier you'd yearned to speak to him. Instead you answer to the point: you're fine; you're eating well, sleeping well; yes, you're taking your tablets; yes, Tahera is here, she's reading Keats.

Unsought, he volunteers information about himself: the monsoons have started, and he got drenched in a downpour; the street outside is flooded; the maidservant hasn't come for the past two days, citing the rains as an excuse; your sister, Halima, has been bringing him food.

There's a whiny quality to his voice. You're aware of the others in the room listening to your conversation, and you keep your responses short and impassive.

Hesitantly, he asks when you are likely to return.

"I don't know. Seema is due anytime." You mention Seema's name casually to him, something you wouldn't have dared a week ago. His timidity bolsters your courage. "Do you want to speak to your *daughter*?"

Tahera rises to take the phone from you, and Seema has stiffened. You set a trap for him with that word—he has sworn many times he has only one daughter now—but he doesn't fall for it. "Not now, I'm heading out. I'll speak to Tahera later, it's been years since we discussed Keats."

He prepares to end the call, but Tahera takes the phone and disappears into the kitchen.

You strain to hear Tahera's conversation, but her voice is too low. Now that you can breathe freely again, the extent of your transgression begins to sink in. You wouldn't have dared speak this way in Chennai. Being away from him seems to have loosened his hold on you. You're glad that you undertook this journey. But why did you wait until the final months of your life before taking this step?

Seema's eyes are still glued to the TV, avoiding you, though she too seems to have relaxed. "Seema, when shall we ask Fiaz for dinner?" you say. "Can we do it this week?"

Your sudden switch of topic catching her by surprise, Seema is less resistant, as you hoped. She says, with only a slight frown, "It's not necessary."

"He's so good to us. I promised him."

"He'll understand, Ammi. I'm having a baby after all."

"It's not a question of understanding. I want to. You should call your other friend too. What's her name, Divya?"

"Why? You're sick, you can't stand in the kitchen without coughing. I can't help you cook. Are you going to ask Tahera to cook for my friends?"

"What's wrong with that? Can't your sister do this for you?" You've tasted your first victory, against your husband no less, and you won't let your daughter(s) defeat you. Tahera has finished her conversation, and you call out, "What do you say, Tahera? You'll help me with the dinner for Fiaz?"

"I'll be there in a minute, Ammi."

Seema grows restive. When Tahera returns you notice her fraught face—what could father and this daughter have clashed over now? You regret your peremptory tone.

One glance at Tahera and Seema struggles up from the futon. "What did I tell you? There's no need for all this."

A subdued Tahera registers the scene unfolding. She eventually answers, "Of course, Ammi. If that's what you want."

"What about what I want?" Seema glares at the two of you, then before you can react, turns to retreat to her bedroom. "Fine. Let's not make a big deal of this. I'll ask Fiaz when he's available."

"Ask Divya too," you say.

"No Divya." She yanks the bedroom door shut behind her.

Tahera sits by your side. "Why do you force her, Ammi, when she doesn't want to?"

But it's to be a celebration: You want to cook for your daughter's friends, to throw them a feast. It's to be a thanksgiving, for all the years they were there for your daughter, and atonement, for the years you were not. You recall the chilha, the celebration on the fortieth day after the child is born. But you can't leave it for so far into the future—who knows anymore what the future holds? And besides, you need Tahera's help.

You can't explain all this. You switch the TV off and take Tahera's hand in yours, squeezing, in gratitude for her acquiescence to your plans. Despite the confidence you've shown, you fear that she might still be resentful of your decision to come to San Francisco, to Seema's side, instead of Irvine, to hers.

48

Tahera takes the phone into the kitchen, determined to speak with her father. Refusing to speak to Seema is understandable, but declining to speak with her—how like Abba to cast out all of them when one displeases him, holding them all accountable for each other's lapses.

Naeemullah gives in to Tahera's insistence and desultorily inquires about Nafeesa. Their conversation, like it has the past months, takes on a professional tone—prognosis, progression, pathophysiology. As their discussion tapers off, he clears his throat, signaling he's ready to hang up.

Desperately Tahera casts her mind for something further to interest him. "I've been reading Keats's poems again, Abba," she says, in a rush. "After so many years."

"Wonderful!" His attention is temporarily held. "And what do you think now?"

It's their old debate, one she'd lost to him many times. Naeemullah prefers Wordsworth, pooh-poohing Keats as immature and mawkish, idolized only by young girls with romance on their brains. He would accept grudgingly that Keats's later odes had some merit but was scathing regarding the narrative poems, especially the long *Endymion*: "All sighs and pretty words."

But *Endymion* had been her best-loved. She'd wandered through her youth likening herself to Endymion roving doggedly through earth and heavens seeking his love, the moon. She'd spent countless evenings alone on their rooftop terrace after dinner, pacing back and forth, with only the clouds and the moon for company, futilely trying to memorize the almost thousand lines of the poem. Eventually she'd settled for learning only her most treasured sections.

"I haven't gotten to *Endymion* yet," she lies, slipping once again into her childhood habit of protecting Keats (and herself) from her father (and sister). She'd started on *Endymion* earlier that evening, the poem appearing as strange and otherworldly now as it had years ago, with its descriptions of miraculous natural beauties and its mysterious and mystifying allusions—Phoebus, Dryope, Hyacinthus, Zephyr—names once again unfamiliar and intriguing.

"Ah, your rambling lovesick shepherd—" Naeemullah chuckles. "We'll talk when you've reread it. You're definitely older, but are you any wiser?"

"No one can hope to be as wise as you, Abba." Her bitterness overflows. "Seriously, why do you still treat me like a child?"

An exaggerated surprise, his usual tactic. "Haven't we been discussing your mother like two equals?"

"Like doctors, not father and adult daughter."

"What else do you want me to say?" His voice turns harsh. "That I'm un-happy your mother is there, when her place is here?"

"I would have come to Chennai to look after her."

"I'm fully capable of taking care of her. My only request to you is that you see that she returns soon."

"She's not only your wife, Abba—she's my mother, too. Why do you insist on keeping me at a distance?" From holding her tongue for months—years—she's gone to confronting everyone in a few days: first Ammi, then Seema, now Abba. But the words don't produce relief, they merely serve to reinforce a feeling of wretchedness.

After Seema had left, after he started cutting her off for even mention-ing Seema's name, she'd hoped—despicably, for didn't she still miss Seema then?—that her presence would make up for his beloved's absence, that she would in time come to replace her sister. But he'd distanced himself from her as well. Did he expect her too to fail him, or was she just too poor a substitute?

"But, Tahera, you're in America." The jocular edge to his voice is back. "The last time I checked it's still thirteen thousand kilometers away."

And before she can respond—*It was you who sent me here, Abba!*—he at-tacks: "And why have you started reading poetry again, anyway? I thought you had no use for anything other than the Quran."

"I can read whatever I want. But how are *you* doing, Abba?" She lowers her voice to a careful whisper. "Are you scared that Ammi will choose to remain here with her daughters—even Seema—rather than return to you?" She can feel her spiteful laugh sting, trilling its way across oceans and continents.

If it's revenge, its sweetness is short-lived: a click, and he's hung up. Tahera stands trembling, the phone clenched in her hand.

Heart! Thou and I are here sad and alone. Say, wherefore did I laugh? O mortal pain! O Darkness! Darkness! The childhood balm of murmured lines from her favorite anguished Keats sonnet. How ironic it is that Abba had used Keats to persuade her to give up her initial college plans of following in Seema's footsteps in literature, to choose instead a career in medicine, trailing him. Keats had apprenticed to a surgeon, believing it a fit trade for a to-be poet; Keats had nursed his dying mother and brother before himself succumbing to their tuberculosis. She'd allowed herself to be manipulated, believing Abba wanted her by his side. *Verse, Fame, and Beauty are intense indeed, but Death intenser—Death is Life's high meed.*

A sudden swift urge: Let—me—*die!*

Back in the living room, after Seema's exit, Nafeesa takes hold of Tahera's hand. "What did Abba say? You looked upset."

"Just Abba being Abba." The squeeze of her hand shows that her mother understands. Some sense of their old communion still exists. They'd been a family within a family, depending on each other to withstand the force of Abba's and Seema's personalities.

She feels an urge to lay the weight of her world in her mother's lap again, to seek comfort if not counsel, as she'd done all her childhood, to have Ammi stroke her hair—like when she'd laid her head in Ammi's lap three mornings ago. After Seema's exile, she'd begun to reject Ammi's efforts on her behalf, as if she could no longer risk relying on her. She wants to reach over and touch Ammi's face, to smooth out the lines etched by disease that has added to the distance between them.

What has bothered her since learning Ammi's condition: her easy acceptance of Ammi's impending death. She's tried to tell herself that as a doctor she's become accustomed, if not inured, to death. But this can't be totally true, for she could never, not for a moment, imagine Amina dying without dying a thousand deaths herself.

Over the many years of her medical practice, she has encountered death many times. Patients die—parents, brothers, and sisters, even children. And she's always been perplexed and ashamed at wanting—no, *needing*—to be present when the relatives gathered around the body, envious of both the dead and the surviving.

She understands that envy now. She's always been moved by the portrait of Keats on his deathbed in Rome, ever since she found it in a biography in her father's library years ago. It was painted by Keats's friend and caregiver. Eyes closed, head sunk in a pillow, eyelashes resting on his gaunt cheeks, Keats looks peaceful, a tender curve to the line of his lips. The portrait radiates love. Only someone who loved him could have painted such a portrait; only someone who was loved could be its subject. So would she like to be watching, so would she like to be watched over.

For how can one know the extent of one's love until confronted with its loss? How can one know the extent to which one is loved without witnessing the grief of those who profess it?

This must be why she almost welcomes her mother's death; this is why she's vexed by her mother's stoicism, her steadfast refusal to shed tears. A wordless, nameless sorrow seizes Tahera. Not for anything in the world would she want her relationship with her children, especially Amina, to end up this way.

Her mother still holds her hand, though she's returned to her previous concern. "So you'll help me cook for Seema's friends?"

"Yes, Ammu, of course I'll help." *Ammu*—as she calls Amina at times, as she used to call Ammi at times, something only she did, never Seema. Tahera pats her mother's hand.

Her mother still seems unconvinced, her smile brittle and uncertain. "Tara, it's not what you think. I had to come here, to San Francisco—to make amends, before—" Nafeesa's lips move as though rehearsing what to say next.

Tahera touches her fingers to Nafeesa's lips, silencing her. "Poor Ammu. Why are we always so hard on ourselves?"

Ammi needs her: surely that's enough. Why does she need any other sign of her mother's love?

49

Monday morning, it's raining in San Francisco, a rain that gives the impression that it has not descended from the sky—one can't see the sky for the fog—but that the city itself, its buildings, its trees, its very air, is made out of water. Every surface, budded with tiny droplets, catches whatever gleams of light there are—headlights and brake lights, traffic lights, lights in storefronts and offices and apartments—and reflects them back in a ghostly glimmer. San Francisco is a dream city in this rain. The three women in the car, on their way to what could be Seema's last appointment with her obstetrician before her delivery, are drawn into its lulling embrace.

Fiaz offered to drive when Seema called to ask if he was free for dinner—Wednesday, it was decided. Seema gladly accepted, for though she's only introducing Leigh to her family as a friend, she's still beset with fears about the meeting, and Fiaz would be a welcome buffer. She can count on him to avert any awkward or unpleasant incidents. Besides, it was Fiaz who accompanied her on her earlier visits, until Leigh took over, and there's satisfaction in his attending the last, a reassuring presence in her life. Cocooned in a car whose small windows have misted from the warm breath of the four people inside, Seema sits heavy in a cloud of regret and fantasy, deploring the choice forced on her between family and lover, dreaming about breaking free by greeting Leigh with a kiss on the lips—but only if it wouldn't send Leigh the wrong signal.

Nafeesa, peering out from the back seat, cannot help comparing the rain to the downpours in Chennai during the monsoon. Here it is muted, apologetic, even refined, like everything else, and leaves no trace, drained instantaneously by some hidden system of sewers. In Chennai, it pellets the city, aggressive and unrelenting, intent on scarring; it puddles the surface within minutes and swamps the streets, churned to a muddy froth by pedestrians and charging scooters and automobiles. The rain here is soothing—even the numbing pain Nafeesa woke up to this morning eased a little as she waited for the car. She did not mention the pain to her daughters, fearing they might insist she stay home and rest. Now in the car, the world securely blurred into a restful loveliness by the scrim of water, the pain seems almost bearable, something she could learn to live with.

Tahera, too, finds the drive comforting. The city with its half-visible hills and vistas is so different from Irvine, and even from the San Francisco she's seen so far, that she feels transported to some other world, different from the one she went to bed in yesterday. The photos Ismail sent her last night, documenting the desecration of the mosque, seem too ugly to belong to the place revealing itself to her now through the speckled window and the wavering mist: the gorse-strewn crest of a hill, studded with crags and capped by a clump of trees, their leaves turning gold, silhouetted against the pearl-gray sky. It's an elusive and elegiac landscape, one she can picture Keats wandering in. It reminds her of the painting of Keats seated in the heath, listening to a nightingale, before he'd been forced to leave for Rome in a desperate pursuit of recovery from his tuberculosis. She'd clandestinely cut the two pictures out—that painting and the portrait of Keats on his deathbed—from her father's book and pasted them in a diary she carried with her. She wonders if the diary still lies somewhere safe in her old room in Chennai.

50

Leigh waits at the doctor's office, unsure what to expect. For Seema, she's brought three long-stemmed calla lilies, the classic creamy white spiked with golden yellow, their flower. For Seema's family, she has dressed carefully, her trimmed jacket instead of her usual geometric waistcoats, her Wellingtons instead of her combat boots, and no hat, her hair brushed rather than tousled.

Fiaz peeps into the reception. "Look at you, all suited and booted!" he announces loudly, as if alerting someone.

"I didn't expect *you*, Fiaz." She's a little aggrieved at his inclusion. Did Seema ask him along to counterbalance her? She's miffed, too, at his description of her outfit, after all the trouble she'd taken to appear less androgynous.

He holds the door open for the women following. Her first sight of the sister shocks Leigh. She has Muslim friends, some who wear the hijab, but she's never met a Muslim this severely attired. A gray hijab wound tight around the face barely exposes the cheeks and chin and forehead, and loose lines of a black full-sleeved gown conceal the rest, only hands visible. A nun, in cloak and habit, would appear fashion-conscious next to her. And Seema's mother, so different—small and unthreatening, like a kohl-eyed doll in the pink sweater and blue shawl that envelop her. Then Leigh notices the grave lines of her face, and its features, very like the sister's. No one would mistake them for anything but mother and daughter.

"Ammi, Tahera—my friend Leigh," Seema says. "She's been coming with me to all my checkups. Leigh, this is my mother, Nafeesa, and my sister, Tahera." She accepts the lilies Leigh holds out at arm's length. "Are these for me?"

Leigh places a friend-like kiss on Seema's proffered cheek and exchanges awkward handshakes with Nafeesa and Tahera. They look at her with unguarded curiosity, while she tries hard not to stare at them resentfully. Leigh has never had to worry about her family's acceptance. Her Irish father is a very lapsed Catholic and her Chinese mother an indifferent Presbyterian, both professors at Berkeley and both supportive of her decision to come out in high school. Seema has always maintained she's not bothered by Islam's strictures against their relationship: *Those crazy mullahs, they've nothing better to do.* But these two women still seem to control Seema after all these years out.

"Oh my!" The plump gray-haired receptionist exclaims, opening her eyes wide at the odd foursome accompanying Seema. "So many new faces today. Isn't that nice, having so many people to take care of you?"

Fiaz says, "I'm just here for the candy. They'll do all the work." He banters with the receptionist, making an elaborate act out of choosing from the bowl she offers—Nafeesa must have strawberry, while Tahera gets mango—and Leigh uses the diversion to sidle over to Seema.

"I'm glad you're here," Seema whispers. She strokes Leigh's arm with the lilies, keeping one eye on her mother and sister.

"What shall I say when they ask how I know you?" Leigh whispers back. "Do I look okay?"

"You still look like a schoolboy. They'll wonder what I'm doing hanging out with you."

"But *you* love me."

"Shh—go chat with my mother and sister."

"Your sister frightens me." Tahera seems so closed off. Her reaction to Tahera suggests some deep-rooted ambivalence she's never acknowledged to herself before. She feels unsafe, threatened.

The receptionist hands Seema a urine container, and Seema leaves for the bathroom, handing the lilies back to Leigh. Nafeesa has sat down with Fiaz, and they're both engaged in a conversation—in Urdu, Leigh assumes, envying the intimacy that seems to have developed between them. She wishes she hadn't looked in Tahera's direction, because now Tahera makes her way toward her.

"You're Seema's friend." Tahera flashes a smile that surprises Leigh with its welcome. "I met another of Seema's friends yesterday. Divya—do you know her?"

"I do." Leigh is chagrined: even Divya has met Seema's family before her. "Where did you meet?"

"Near the park, with that panoramic view. When Seema and I went walking. Divya is very nice."

"She can be." Leigh struggles to keep her voice even. "I'm sorry, but—when? I mean, what time?"

"Around noon. Why do you ask?"

Leigh shouldn't have asked, but she did, and now the day loses it bright edge, flattens to match the gray outside. Not only did Seema turn her down yesterday, but she took her sister and Divya to their spot. And as the park is not Divya's scene, her presence couldn't merely be a coincidence.

The lilies in Leigh's arms become a mocking reminder of the day she first whispered her love. Seema hadn't responded but had arrived the next time with these lilies and an apology that she wasn't ready yet to make such a declaration. And Leigh, who'd been expecting it to be their last time together, was relieved. Calla lilies would be their flower, she'd declared, the first flowers either had given the other. But if Divya is back in the picture, she wishes she hadn't brought them today.

She would be foolish to confront Seema here, so she opts to engage with Tahera, discussing her journalism and Tahera's practice in a pleasant exchange. Her initial response to Tahera now seems absurd: it's not Tahera who's the threat. When Seema returns, she's immediately called in. Seema's obstetrician, Dr. Jennifer Connelly, doesn't object to having a partner or a friend present while examining her pregnant patients, and having accompanied Seema on previous visits, Leigh has been looking forward to this—until now.

She straightens to go with Seema. But so does Tahera. They both stop short, confused, looking to Seema for direction.

"Would you rather have your sister with you today, Seema?" Leigh asks, her voice small, both wanting to be the one chosen and fearing the moment when they're alone together in the examining room, waiting for the doctor.

"You two decide," Seema says, as she follows the nurse out. "Or maybe you could both come."

Tahera shrugs, and leads, and Leigh trails behind, stopping to hand over the lilies to Nafeesa.

"Come get us when you're doing the scan," Fiaz says, "so we can get a peek at little Ishraaq."

In the examining room, Seema turns to Tahera to help her undress, while Leigh looks on, her role usurped. She knows why, of course, but she has to fight a rebellious urge to take Seema in her arms, to kiss the engorged curves of Seema's body, to stroke her thickened aureoles and massage the swell of her labia until Seema cries for mercy, for forgiveness. She averts her gaze and has to be content with their fingers brushing when Seema hands Leigh her under-garments, as Tahera knots the back of her gown.

51

Seema arranges herself on the table, exposing her belly, while Dr. Connelly and Tahera discuss Tahera's background. If Tahera's hijab and jilbab make Dr. Connelly uneasy, she doesn't show it. Besides, speaking about her practice, Tahera is transformed into a professional, her manner assuming authority.

Dr. Connelly begins by palpating Seema's belly, her pressure firm and in-sistent. My mother feels me kick as the prodding fingers awaken me. Usually Dr. Connelly conducts her examination in silence. But today she repeats aloud to Tahera the notes she's jotting down, and Tahera explains to Seema the more technical observations. Her explanations are lucid, and her professional voice is reassuring. Dr. Connelly remarks that Tahera's patients in Irvine are very lucky, and Seema is absurdly gratified, proud of the doctor her sister has be-come. Even Leigh, initially resentful, seems mollified, her questions answered comprehensively between the two doctors.

Though declaring everything normal, today Dr. Connelly wishes to also conduct a pelvic exam, wanting to take no risks this close to term, given Seema's advanced age and risk profile, which includes a history of irregular and heavy menstrual bleeding. Seema dreads these. With her legs thrust open, and fingers and speculum intruding into her body, she feels defenseless and exposed. But Tahera concurs with Dr. Connelly, so she reluctantly agrees.

She steels herself, biting her lips and holding her breath against the waves of discomfort, even pain, as Dr. Connelly probes inside her. The reminder that what she'll actually have to go through will be a thousand times more harrowing sets her heart palpitating, and I react to her panic, twisting and squirming as I never have before. Sensing my distress, my mother forces herself to relax, glad for Leigh's hand to grip, grateful for the security Leigh's hand returns. And with Tahera here, she doesn't need to try to make sense of the terms, even those new and unfamiliar—*consistency, effacement, softness, station*—that Dr. Connelly calls out in her crisp clinical way along with measurements.

Seema closes her eyes and lets Leigh's clasp and Tahera's voice—still continuing her reassuring commentary—carry her away from the room, beyond the rain pattering against the windowpanes.

Unexpectedly, she is recalled to the room by another voice that once had a similar calming effect on her. He'd spoken just one word to her last night, after more than fifteen years of silence, and yet he sounds so clearly in her mind. Momentarily, it's her father's voice in the room lulling her with explanations and assurances, his grasp carrying her to safety.

52

Finally, here I am, a glow on the monitor. The sonologist is using the latest imaging technology to peer into the darkness of my mother's womb. Various parts of me flicker on the screen as he moves the probe, sepia-toned close-ups that you, Grandmother, never thought possible.

Here is the umbilical cord snaking across the screen. And those are my fingers, and the curve of my bottom, and my distended belly. The protuberance there is my penis and the empty bag of my scrotum—Dr. Connelly clarifies that my testicles could take up to a year after birth to descend. And here's my foot with my tiny flexed toes.

Even though you cannot see my face—my head has already descended into my mother's cervix—you're enchanted, your visions already excited by these odds and ends of me. You clutch Fiaz's hand, for he's closest to you, and lean against him, for the moment portals to some future that is haloed and more lovely, your faith in the persistent regeneration of life reinforced.

But at the very moment when you're gazing with tenderness at me, you become aware of everyone gathered around, and rue: there are two people missing, two fathers. Your husband and Bill should have been here. What kind of world would deprive two children of their fathers while they are still alive?

It seems a cruel travesty that the only man here is Fiaz—and who is he to Seema, anyway? The gratitude that you felt toward him just a little while ago turns into resentment, as though he has usurped a place in your daughter's life that rightfully belongs to someone else.

Meanwhile, the sonologist moves the probe around to locate my heart, and the image of my chest on the screen pulses with my heartbeat. He announces that my heart rate is exactly what it should be, twice my mother's. More readings from various points on the globe of my mother's belly help him estimate my weight, my volume, and the volume of the liquid I'm enclosed in.

"He's a big baby, bigger than your average South Asian baby. But everything looks fine," Dr. Connelly says. "The amniotic fluid seems adequate. The baby is in position and shows no signs of distress. All we can do now is wait."

Seema struggles off the table awkwardly, triggering your natural instinct to go to her aid, but you're paralyzed by spasms of censure cramping through you: This is surely Seema's fault. It's her fault that there's only this motley group to depend on—a couple of friends, inexperienced and uncommitted, a distant sister, a dying mother—and no husband, no father. It's her fault that your grandson is to be robbed of a father, a grandfather, and a full and fulfilling childhood. It's her fault that you too were robbed of your full family and a fulfilled past.

And, as though your heart and mind—revolting against being asked to withstand the extremes you've swung through the last few minutes, from boundless affection toward Seema to censure—have released some check on your body, the pain from earlier this morning comes surging back. You begin to shake uncontrollably.

Seema has left the room with her friend and the doctor before your distress is noticeable. Tahera and Fiaz surround you.

Ammi? Aunty? What's happening? Are you okay?

You clench your jaw and breathe out—I'm fine, I'm fine. You don't want to make a scene. Already the sonologist is gaping at you, unease on his face. You grasp Tahera's hand to steady yourself and ask her to lead you out of the room. Fiaz and Tahera assist you back to reception, the pain pulsing every step of the way. Fiaz eases you onto a seat, and Tahera sits beside you, stroking your still-shuddering shoulders and chest.

Fiaz hovers about with questions: Shall I get her some water? Should we call someone?

The receptionist makes as if to hurry toward you, and you wave her back. "Where's Seema?" you pant. "I don't want her to see me like this."

"Don't worry about Seema," Tahera says. She rubs your palms and blows into them, as you'd done to her many times when she was a child, in a futile attempt to ease the pain.

You'd been caught off guard by the suddenness with which it returned. You know its course, its peak and gradual ebb—you'd like to be alone with it. "I want to leave. Everybody is staring at me."

You try to push yourself off your seat. Fiaz lends you his arm.

"Ammi, stay here till you feel better. It's raining," Tahera says.

Yes, outside everything is a blur, only smudged shapes visible through the raindrops that break against the glass and speckle the window.

"We can wait in the car," Fiaz says, responding to your tightening grip on his arm. "Leigh is with Seema. She'll take care of her."

You hobble past the receptionist, holding tightly on to Fiaz's arm. Downstairs, you wait on the steps under the glass canopy for Fiaz to drive his car up to the entrance of the hospital. You ignore Tahera's pleas to take a seat in the lobby inside or to at least take her arm for support.

She is distraught. "Ammi, why won't you listen to me?"

Because: this pain is an appropriate punishment for your unforgivable anger toward Seema. How could you start blaming her, like her father and sister? Instead of making amends, your visit to San Francisco is now tainted. Clutching the ends of your shawl to your chest, you huddle in your misery and your suffering. "Leave me be, Tahera. Nothing can be done."

The spasms in your legs make it painful to stand, and you know you should take the arm Tahera has offered, but you can't ask for it now. "You can't help me, Tahera. If you want to help me, there's only one thing you can do. Help your sister."

You lean back on the front glass wall of the lobby. Tahera begins pacing the length of the shelter, her jilbab swirling. But you have nothing to offer her, you know only what you need from her.

"Ammi, why do you say such things? Is my presence here no help to you? And am I not helping Seema already?"

"Promise me you'll continue to help her after I'm gone."

"Why do you only think about Seema, Ammi? You never think about me."

One side of Tahera's hijab and jilbab is wet from the sudden downpour curtaining the canopy, but she's oblivious to it, merely dashing away the drops of water dripping down her face. The rain has become as vehement as in Chennai during the monsoons. You remember how Tahera would run up to the rooftop to catch the first shower every year, despite your admonitions, returning drenched and shivering but elated. You would wait with a towel and, if you'd made some that day, a hot glass of the peppery rasam she liked.

"Tahera, you know that's not true. I think about you all the time. I worry about Seema—" If there is a question, it's only which daughter you have failed more.

Fiaz's car pulls up and he jumps out. "You're getting wet, Aunty. Please get in." He looks at you both, perplexed. Tahera's standing at the other end of the steps, her face papery pale in the dark silhouette of her attire. "Tahera, you're shivering. Why didn't you wait inside?"

53

Fiaz texts that her mother and sister are with him in the car. Seema assumes this is to give her time alone with Leigh, who reports that she finally understands Seema's reluctance to introduce her to her family.

"They're both so intense. Like they have tempests bottled up inside them. Your mother was literally shaking after seeing the baby pictures. But I'm glad to have met them. And I'm so happy to see baby Ishraaq curled up inside you."

Leigh's previous resentment seems to have evaporated, and Seema is relieved. "Thank *you*, for being here today. The pelvic exam would have been an ordeal."

Should she say it now? *I can't imagine going through the delivery without you!* She wants them both there, Leigh and Tahera.

She pivots instead to the dinner party, thankful that her mother had insisted on it. "Just you and Fiaz. I thought, you know, a good opportunity—"

"No Divya?"

"Divya? No! Why?"

Leigh shrugs, and although they continue to hold hands as they leave the clinic, and even manage to steal a few kisses in the elevator, some of Leigh's earlier restraint has returned.

There's a light drizzle outside, and Fiaz offers to drop Leigh off at her office, so Leigh squeezes into the back of the car with Nafeesa and Tahera. Both mother and sister appear withdrawn, Tahera especially, staring out at the rain through the window, barely acknowledging the others, while their mother sits rigid, as if to not impose on Leigh either in space or in spirit. Even Fiaz is curiously quiet.

Seema feels the need to fill the silence with chatter, launching into a description of her first view of me three months earlier, with the same 3D ultrasound technology, my face visible then. "I wish you could have seen his face today, Ammi."

"I can wait," Nafeesa replies, still stiffly. "It's only a few more days."

"Leigh was there, too," Seema makes it a point to mention. "You thought he looked adorable, didn't you, Leigh?"

Leigh merely nods, and Seema has to shift around to read her response. She notes the three women sitting remote like Easter Island statues, something vital missing. "Hey, where are my lilies?"

"I gave them to your mother to hold." Leigh looks for them in the back seat.

Finally shaken out of her inertness, Nafeesa rushes to apologize. "Oh, I forgot them when we left. I'm so sorry. It was my fault. They were so lovely."

Her mother is visibly upset, her face almost crumpling in remorse—much more than the lapse warrants. Leigh's disappointment is palpable too, even as she turns down Fiaz's offer to drive back to the hospital to pick them up.

But Fiaz does anyway, making a swift U-turn. When he pulls again under the canopied entrance, Leigh dashes out and returns a few minutes later with the lilies, panting. She hadn't waited for the elevators.

"What good friends you are to Seema," Nafeesa exclaims. "You both take such good care of her. I hope you'll always do that."

Her mother's gratitude toward her friends is encouraging. Her mother has accepted Leigh as important to Seema's well-being, even if not yet as a girl-friend, and Seema is touched. She's touched, too, by the solemnity with which Leigh presents her the lilies the second time, as if responding to her mother's stated hope with a promise—of forgiveness, of faithfulness.

Back at home, Seema places the flowers by her bed, adjusting the stems so the cupped openings would curve toward her sleeping self, the three lilies arcing gracefully over the vase's tear-shaped rim.

54

It is afternoon in San Francisco, and the two sisters are confined to the living room. Their mother rests in the bedroom after the morning's exertion. A soft mantle of rain cloaks the city, insulating them from everything outside. Not only has their sense of place been blotted out but also their sense of time, for the drizzly day appears at a standstill. Seema complains of aching feet—swollen these last weeks of pregnancy—and Tahera offers to massage them.

A surprised Seema accepts, and Tahera starts self-consciously, seated on the floor with Seema's feet in her lap, the massage at first perfunctory. But as she presses her knuckles into Seema's feet, Tahera adopts the fervor of her seven-year-old daughter, kneading her sister's skin and flesh to the very bones inside.

Then, time doubling back on itself, she slips into an old ritual from their childhood: cracking toes, tugging on them with a quick jerk and snapping them up or down, to the satisfying accompaniment of a pop.

"I can't remember the last time we did that." Seema winces in enjoyment. "It must have been a day like this." A holiday spent indoors, sitting on a damp windowsill with Tahera, cracking each other's toes to pass time, watching the rain and praying it would stop or at least lessen by the evening so she could persuade their father to take them out, perhaps to the bakery or a movie. She detested the monsoon season, for the claustrophobic powerlessness it stirred up in her, with its cloaked skies and smothering rain. "But, Tahera, you liked rainy days."

"I still do. I miss the monsoons. It never rains like that in Irvine." Tahera recalls with a pang what she liked most about them: the long weekends forced to stay indoors, she and Seema lying side by side in bed, heads on the same clammy pillow, reading aloud to each other, and nights spent huddling under blankets against the nippy tentacles of the monsoon chill. "But I hated that moldy smell in our clothes from drying inside. And our shoes and socks would be caked with mud."

"Remember how Ammi would scold you for getting wet? You kept losing your raincoat at school until she—"

"Let's not talk about Ammi." The morning's wretchedness is too fresh. There's clearly not much time left for their mother, and much of what's left is to be consumed by pain. The worst of the morning is the memory of her trying to force her mother to apologize for wanting to ease her heart's worries about her other child. Why fault Ammi, when she herself cares for Arshad and Amina so differently? And as for Ammi's behest: *If you want to help me, help Seema . . .*

Seema senses Tahera's ache. Unlike the previous times when Tahera rebuffed conversation involving their mother, her current tone doesn't signal a rebuke. Soon, when only reminiscences will have the power to bring their mother back to some semblance of life, who can they talk to about their mother but each other? And how are they to do that, without reopening old wounds, reliving old griefs?

As if not knowing what to do next, Tahera starts massaging her feet all over again. "Stop, Tahera. My feet have had enough, thank you."

How to comfort a sister she hasn't comforted in so many years, or perhaps never? She'd like to touch Tahera's bent head, to stroke her hair, but though she has accepted Tahera's attentions of the past twenty-four hours, she's unsure how Tahera might react to her overtures. *You couldn't be bothered with me, Seema,* Tahera said only yesterday. Reclaiming her feet from Tahera's lap, Seema manages to find her voice. "Tahera, can I ask you something?"

Tahera stirs, but she doesn't look up. "Is it about the guardianship? I haven't spoken to Ismail yet."

"No. Can I ask—what happened? After I left?"

"What happened?" Tahera rises abruptly. "You really want to know?"

Seema nods, unsure if Tahera's question is merely rhetorical. Her sister is a hazy vision standing by her side, her face a blur Seema is glad she cannot read.

"Here, let me give your shoulders a massage too," Tahera responds gruffly. "Ammi says you were complaining about a backache."

Seema doesn't demur. Standing behind Seema, Tahera sinks her fingers into muscles tense from holding extra weight, growing pliable in her hands as she digs into them. Her posture, the pressure, the concentration, is familiar to Tahera from childhood massages practiced on her parents and occasionally even her sister. From there, it's a small step to another more frequent childhood ritual. "Your hair's all tangled, let me fetch a comb. Single or double?"

A single plait, like when they'd do their hair in college, twin plaits like they remade for each other every morning before school.

"You choose."

Tahera passes the comb repeatedly through Seema's hair, her sister pliant, not protesting even when her head is yanked back at a particularly difficult tangle. It's only then that Tahera is able to speak. The act of disentangling Seema's hair has freed something knotted inside her as well, the act of gathering tresses and weaving them together has brought some order and calm to the snarl of memory.

"I missed you, Seema. I would lie in bed and wonder what you were doing. How you were spending your days, who you spent them with. It was very lonely after you left. Ammi became quieter, speaking only when she had to—a shadow of herself, slinking through the house. Abba remained Abba, of course. Only now he bullied us more often. He became very upset if we so much as mentioned your name. He'd stop speaking to us for days at a time."

Tahera's fingers are nimble. Their rhythm lends a cadence to her speaking, easing her hesitation when seeking words or phrases, their assurance lending her self-control. It helps that Seema can't look at her, that Seema remains silent, that Tahera can pause as long as she wants to, pretending she needs to run the comb through Seema's hair again.

"We went out less, afraid of having to face questions about you. If someone inquired, Abba would say you're doing fine. But he'd lock himself in his study after. We stopped visiting relatives. Our world shrunk around us. Only Halima Aunty called. She never cared what Abba did."

What Tahera remembers, but cannot speak about: How it was then, when she'd been searching for some escape from a life that seemed to be closing in upon her, when even the poetry she turned to for solace seemed tainted, bearing the imprint of a father who'd promised the world to his daughters yet sought to impose his will on them, she'd discovered the comforts of prayer, Halima Aunty's quiet faith and rituals providing a refuge she could lose herself in. And the more her father mocked her transformation, the tighter she pulled its protection around her.

Seema focuses on the steady tug as Tahera pulls her hair tight, even welcoming the sudden jerks and the attendant snap of pain. These allow her to momentarily forget the hurt in Tahera's voice, to believe that she's experiencing Tahera's pain herself. Her mother has never mentioned any of this, and she has not thought to ask. *Never caring how it will affect others*—Tahera's charge from yesterday stings, for there's truth in it.

Tahera finishes with the braiding and, with that, her account. Seema examines Tahera's handiwork: two plaits, expertly braided, exactly the way Tahera used to do them years ago. Daily gestures of sisterly affection that Seema had taken for granted, then completely forgot. She can't trust herself to say anything.

Thankfully, Tahera too seems anxious to forestall a response. "Do you have any hair bands?" she asks, already halfway to Seema's bedroom.

"In the dresser. Top drawer."

Tahera must flee the living room immediately, for she sees not Seema of the last week, nor the sister who abandoned her years ago, but the sister who held her hand as they walked to school, taught her to climb trees and ride a bicycle, whose capers charmed the most dreary days into promise and delight.

She fumbles in the drawer for the bands. The bedroom is dark, and she needs light, but her mother is sleeping. She pulls out a handful of elastics to select a pair by the window. Her mother is curled up on her side, legs drawn in, face calm in the soft curtained light, no traces showing of the morning's suffering. Some afternoons, finding their mother napping like this, Tahera and Seema would unbraid her single plait and rebraid her hair into twin plaits, like the ones they sported. Ammi would scold them when she woke up, though she wouldn't undo their work. How young the twin plaits made Ammi look then, just like how young Seema looks now and how Amina will look in a few years.

A mother for whom time will soon cease, a sister recovered from the mists of time, a daughter whom time is changing too rapidly.

Yet, do not grieve. She cannot fade, though thou has not thy bliss, for ever wilt thou love and she be fair—

"Did you find one?" Seema asks as Tahera hurries back to the living room with the clutch of bands.

"I just remembered," Tahera's voice is unsteady, "how we used to do Ammi's hair. If only—" But she can't continue, instead holding out the muddle of bands to Seema in a trembling palm.

Seema takes the bands and gestures to the chair in front of her. "Sit."

Tahera sinks instead to the floor. She looks at Seema for an instant, then buries her face in Seema's lap, even though there's little space there, the swell of Seema's belly obstructing most of it. Her entire body shakes, her shoulders shuddering.

This is unexpected. Seema has seldom seen Tahera cry. She's always envied her sister's strength, her capacity to contain her pain, her refusal to seek solace from anyone, her stubborn rejection of any offered.

"Tahera, don't cry." Tahera's head lies in her lap. Is she even allowed to comfort Tahera, in light of having abandoned her, the anguish she'd caused her?

"Tara, don't cry," she repeats helplessly, as Tahera struggles to regain composure, smothering her sobs in Seema's pants.

Seema begins, hesitantly, to stroke Tahera's head. Her sister's hair is in a loose, untidy bun. As girls, her sister had the longer hair, thick and luxurious like their mother's. But now her hair is much diminished, much streaked with premature gray. Feeling like a trespasser, Seema undoes the knot of the bun. Then, since Tahera still doesn't stir, she shakes out the tresses, running her fingers through them to straighten and untangle.

Tahera's face lies against Seema's belly. Seema's fingers passing through her hair, and the warmth of Seema's body, are too comforting for Tahera to let go of. She reaches her arms around us both.

She tightens her grasp. I feel the pressure, and Tahera can feel me shift as I respond to it, my slightest movements magnified by the proximity. The heat of me dries the wet from her tears, and the moving life of me calms and soothes.

She says, voice muffled by her mouth against the sky of my world, "Seema, you can name me as Ishraaq's guardian."

Seema cups Tahera's face to study it. "Do you mean it?"

"Yes."

Tahera's face is blotched with tears, the loosened hair disheveled and straggly. "Turn around," Seema says. "Let me fix your hair."

As Tahera sits cross-legged on the floor, like all those years ago in Chennai, my to-be mother combs my could-be mother's hair and gathers her tresses into the twin plaits of their girlhood, both silent now—for what more can be said?—while rain patters against the windowpanes.

Two

2003–2008

I

My to-be father Bill, seven years ago, at thirty-four: He's marching down San Francisco's Market Street, carried along by the largest crowd he's ever seen. There are people swarming around him, thronging pavements, filling windows of buildings above, even swinging from lampposts. There are flags and banners and placards everywhere: *Not In My Name. Drop Bush Not Bombs. No Blood For Oil.* The air is feverish with the sound of chants, throbbing with the sound of drums.

It is February 2003. Earlier that weekend, millions had poured out onto the streets in other cities across the world—London, Madrid, Rome, Paris, New York, Baghdad, Sydney, Tokyo, Calcutta—to protest the proposed U.S. invasion of Iraq.

Bill, at that time, heads a Bay Area start-up with his friend Josh, developing software to make medical records available across hospital networks. The work has been especially demanding the last year, after the tech bubble collapsed and investor funding dried up. In its struggle to remain afloat, the company needed to downsize, and Bill is now its entire legal team, as well as its chief operating officer. He should be working today, to put together a presentation for a prospective client that could underwrite the costs of future development. Instead he's here, chanting with the group he's fallen in with, shouting his throat hoarse.

Bill has never taken part in such demonstrations before. There are blue-uniformed riot police everywhere—on foot, mounted on horseback, seated on motorbikes—all armed with lethal-looking batons, geared in shields and helmets. Placing himself in any situation that invited the attention of the police was high on the list of activities that displeased his grandmother. He can almost feel Mame's fingernails pinching into his earlobes, showing her disapproval.

But he'd chosen to march after all.

Bill doesn't consider himself a pacifist—he supported the first Gulf War, the rooting out of the Taliban from Afghanistan, and the broad outlines of "The War on Terror"—or an activist. Until now, he's never joined any political or politically inclined organization, not even the Black Student Union at Stanford, where he got his undergraduate and law degrees.

Bill has always believed what his grandparents spent their life impressing on him—that his life is what he makes of it. That if he stays out of trouble and works hard, he's bound to succeed. That there's nothing stopping him, not the color of his skin, not his race, not his background, only the powers he lets control him.

His life has borne this out. Years of hard work in a mostly White and Asian high school pay off. He graduates from Stanford with distinction, and without debt, cobbling together a slew of scholarships. A phenomenal LSAT score enables him to enroll in Stanford Law School, allowing him to remain close to Mame after his grandfather's death during his sophomore year. His success at his first job, at a large firm in San Francisco, allows him to quickly clear his law school loans. This positions him well to make the switch when the dot-com boom takes off, joining his best friend, Josh, also from Stanford, to start a company that angel investors salivate over as a probable emerging market leader in healthcare software.

But when the dot-com bubble bursts, it also unfairly devastates their start-up. The last two years have been a series of setbacks, with their VCs pulling out and their flagship product floundering, despite all their efforts to turn the tide.

Bill, for the first time in his life, is facing the certainty of failure, of all his hard work of the past few years coming to nought. Many of his friends cashed out before the bust, selling their half-baked start-ups at the first opportunity, as though they understood something he didn't—that knowing how to ride the wave and knowing when to get off was more important than hard work.

Now the purveyors of the war are setting in motion another wave, one they intend to ride to wealth and fortune, a wave that will destroy another country in its wake. Even to someone as politically uninclined as Bill, it seems obvious that the proposed war is a cynical misuse of 9/11, initiated by oil companies and their Washington enablers seeking access to Iraq's oil fields. The ever-changing rationales for the war—Saddam Hussein's purported links to 9/11; next, his arsenal of weapons of mass destruction; finally, freedom and democracy in the Middle East—strike Bill as similar to the ever-changing explanations that Wall Street had spouted to justify its exuberant evaluations of the dot-com start-ups before the bust. Wall Street had claimed that the market was no longer constrained by outdated laws or history, just like the proponents of the war are now claiming the right to preemptive strikes and expressing an optimism not supported by past misadventures.

There seems to be hope in the air, though, as Bill marches down Market Street. Surely such a massive demonstration of the people's will cannot be ignored. The moment is pregnant with possibility, as if this march were not only about preventing a war but also about reclaiming strengths left unused, about rediscovering kinship long forgotten. Bill, whose only experiences of comparable crowds were football matches in Stanford's stadium, is jolted awake to a boisterous, almost joyous new world bursting all around him.

Someone hands him a placard. *Peace*, it says simply, a sentiment he can get behind wholeheartedly, something Mame could have no objection to. He thrusts it in the air in time to the drumming and the ringing of a temple bell somewhere ahead, as do the others marching beside him.

By Powell Street, near the cable-car turntable, there's a sudden commotion. A minute ago the march was proceeding peacefully, but now a section in front charges to the left into the Nordstrom mall. Bill stands rooted as he sees figures dressed in black jeans and black long-sleeved T-shirts emerge from the group ahead. They have black ski masks pulled down to cover their faces, and armed with skateboards, they pound away at the display windows. Chants turn to hoots and shouts; the sound of breaking glass replaces the drumming.

Soon the air is rent with screams as the riot police swoop in from both sides of the road, their batons raised, their bikes careening toward the mall to seal off the entrance. Bill's section of the march is in disarray. The street flashes with the chaos of batons, placards, and banners caught in sunlight, the black of the vandals, the blue of the riot police, the gleam of motorbikes, the glitter of glass shields.

A policeman on a motorbike chases a vandal running in Bill's direction. Bill is convinced that underneath the black attire the vandal is black-skinned like him, despite glimpses of fair hands and fair rings around the eyes visible through the ski mask. Mame was right, he should have listened. He backs away, fearful now, without looking behind him, and stumbles against someone, bringing them both down, even as the vandal veers away and the motorbike follows.

He's unhurt, but he has landed on a woman, who has twisted her ankle.

2

Bill, as a fifteen-year-old: he's in his room in Oakland, the sheets pulled around him, shielding him from the lonely dark of the attic and the darkness beyond, the night sounds of the world muted, the city silenced.

He hears Mame and Grandpa in muffled conversation downstairs—Mame moving from room to room, Grandpa following her around in his creaking wheelchair, asking her what she's looking for, growing crosser as she continues to ignore him. His chest clenching, Bill slips out of his room to the staircase landing to keep watch.

He hadn't expected Mame to discover the loss so quickly. It's too late now to slip downstairs and replace the note where he found it. Mame wouldn't believe she hadn't looked there already.

Her face grim, her glasses high on the bridge of her nose, she's done looking. She finally says to Grandpa: She's missing a hundred-dollar bill. She dropped it while counting money she withdrew from the bank, had found it later and placed it—where? she's losing her memory—intending to return it to her purse. And Grandpa says he'd have saved her the trouble if she'd told him earlier. He came across it and put it away but forgot to tell her about it—he's growing old too. A minute later he returns from the bedroom with a bill.

Mame must know, or at least suspect—even if Grandpa has handed her a spanking new bill—but she accepts it without demur. Bill spends a sorry sleepless night, dreading the inevitable interrogation in the morning. Why had he so easily succumbed to temptation, with no clear idea what to do with the money? And Mame was never one to overlook his misdeeds—*This is for your own good!*—even the ones Grandpa sometimes took the fall for, like pilfering cookies from the pantry.

And yet, the next morning Mame says nothing, handing him his lunch with only a soft look of reproach. Still he cannot work up the courage to confess. He must seek out his grandfather and return the money to him.

It's not much easier confessing to Grandpa. I can't believe you would let her down this way, Grandpa says. How hard Mame worked, two jobs, and sometimes weekends too, to keep this house running, to make sure Bill would have a future. She's beyond sad, and discouraged.

Bill hangs his head and promises then, the weight of the world on his tongue, never again to let Mame down, never again to take for himself the fruits of someone else's labor.

3

That February morning at the protest, Bill is smitten. The woman is dressed to draw eyes—a spaghetti-strap scarlet dress, matched with scarlet lipstick, shocking like freshly spilled blood—and he is indeed transfixed. He gives her a ride to an urgent care center and waits with her, solicitous and apologetic, his face an echo of empathy at her grimaces of pain. Afterward, her foot braced and bound, he procures a crutch for her, and when she expresses a desire to return to the rally, he offers to accompany her.

Seema is thirty-three and by now used to such attention from men. She's amused by Bill's bashful solicitude, and since her current plight is his fault, she doesn't think twice about making use of him.

The march has emptied out in the Civic Center Plaza, and they stand under a tree at the back, Seema leaning against him for support, the lawn in front of them rippling with shoulders and heads, banners and placards.

Beside them stands a group of protestors dressed like Iraqi mothers, in black hijabs and abayas, wearing mournful masks and holding rag dolls that resemble dead children. They mime grief, raising hands to lips in slow motion as though to stifle a cry or beg for a reprieve. Seema notes that Bill is shaken. He can't take his eyes off the group of mourning mothers, as if only now becoming conscious of the human toll of the war.

"The imagery is very effective," she comments, to which he nods mutely.

He's also clearly discomfited by the speeches—standard vehement denunciations of the war, peppered with words like *hegemony, subjugation, colonialism, racism*—and squirms at the violent invective directed against Bush and Cheney, Wall Street, Israel, America. He tries to hide his discomfort from her, though, by cheering and clapping with the crowd, especially during the songs.

"That's Joan Baez singing," she points out.

"Who's Joan Baez?"

She opens her eyes wide at him. "She marched with Martin Luther King Jr.? She sang 'We Shall Overcome' at the March on Washington, the one where he delivered his 'I Have a Dream' speech?"

Seema is a veteran of such protests, a little disillusioned. She knows what to expect: a parade of minority speakers before a self-congratulatory liberal White crowd that will afterward return to its safe White slice of the world, while the rest of them will still have to deal with whatever is transpiring.

Seema is also a little bitter. She'd moved to Boston two years ago to join her girlfriend Ann after four years of a long-distance relationship. Just months later, Al-Qaeda strikes on 9/11, and what starts as heated arguments—in response to Seema calling Ann's and America's reaction to the collapse of the Twin Towers "White hysteria at the loss of its privileged security"—ends in acrimonious fights and a breakup a year later. Seema had returned to San

Francisco earlier this month, while Ann was now moving to a safe White sub-
urb with her new, more suitable White lover.

An Iraqi duo begins an Arabic version of John Lennon's "Imagine," and
the crowd accompanies the refrain lustily in English. Bill has a comforting
baritone, and he sings with sweet conviction, swaying to the music, clearly a
ploy to have their bodies touch. But she sways along with him, eyes closed,
her head now and then resting on his chest as she leans back for support—
she's a foot shorter, barely making it to his shoulders. It's a new experience,
having a man stand this close to her.

It's also weirdly exciting. Bill reminds her of her first girlfriend, Chloe,
with the same tawny skin, the same frizzy close-cut hair, even the same lips,
and only a little taller. With his glasses he looks more like an academic than
the lawyer he claims to be.

What would her old friends think if they saw her like this? Few even
know she's returned to San Francisco, for that would be admitting failure. She
should claim Ann made her straight! At least that is worth a laugh.

After the rally, Bill insists on dropping her off at her apartment in Bernal
Heights.

"Can I see you again?" he stammers, as he helps her up the stairs.

"There should be another protest soon," she replies, smiling.

"Well, call me if you need any help before then. I feel awful about your
ankle."

They exchange numbers, though she expects never to see him again.

4

My to-be mother Seema at twenty-one, twelve years earlier: Riding through
the streets of London in a red double-decker bus, a banner emblazoned on
its sides, *Visibly Lesbian*. The bus is packed with women, all dressed in black
T-shirts, a bomb with a lit fuse printed on the front, with the name of their
group inscribed around it: *The Lesbian Avengers*.

It's a raucous bus, the women are whistling, clapping, stomping, hanging out of windows, flashing breasts, snogging, calling out through megaphones to pedestrians and drivers, to shoppers and tourists, even to the traffic police and bobbies: Hey you, in the brown coat, in the blue jacket, in the high heels, in the uniform, in that absurd hat, yes, you, we're talking to you, hello, we're lesbians, we're dykes, we're butch, we're femme, we can smell your homophobia.

And though it's a gray day in London, with clouds threatening to rain on their parade, nothing can bring Seema down, for standing next to her in the bus, her hand threaded around Seema's waist, her chin resting on Seema's head, is Chloe, lithe muscular Chloe, buzz-cut Chloe, Chloe whose smile can burn through Seema, whose whisper can make Seema tremble at her knees, whose touch can make the hair on Seema's skin stand on end, whose hands and lips can reduce Seema's body to feeble quivering flesh. Chloe, Seema's first lover, if not her first love.

What a day it is! They hoot and toot their way around early 1990s London. They scatter leaflets over bewildered disapproving crowds. They descend on Marks & Spencer on Oxford Street and pose with mannequins clad in lacy underwear in the lingerie department. They take over squares and circle fountains chanting, "We're here, we're lesbians, get used to it."

For the pièce de résistance, they head to the Tate, and in front of Rodin's *The Kiss*, they stage a kiss-in.

"Babe, shall we?" Chloe murmurs, her tongue in Seema's ear.

Seema hesitates only for a moment. She's come a long way in the few months since she's been recruited—*We recruit!* screams the Lesbian Avengers' tagline—and taken under Chloe's wing.

Chloe is twenty-five, a graduate student in women's studies at Oxford, a core member of the Avengers. It's with her that Seema attended her first Avenger meetings and her first protests: for the immigration rights of gay partners and against Clause 28, which declared illegal actions that could be considered as *promoting* homosexuality in schools. It's with Chloe that she shared her first kiss, in Chloe's darkened flat, after returning from one of those events.

And it's with Chloe that she will now kiss for the first time in public. Look at them as they pose on a stool in front of Rodin's sculpture of Dante's embracing errant couple! Chloe has rolled her sleeves up to expose her sculpted arms.

Seema sits in Chloe's lap, their legs entwined. Chloe's hand rests on Seema's thigh, Seema's hand is around Chloe's neck.

They make a passable imitation of Rodin's sculpture, but there's one major difference: whereas the marble lovers are frozen with their lips apart, as if punished for eternity, the lips of these flesh-and-blood lovers are locked, their supple tongues free to seek each other.

5

Bill calls Seema twice over the next few days to check on her foot. She politely declines his renewed offers of help. The following weeks go by in a desperate haze of meetings, presentations, and strategy sessions, work made all the more dissatisfying now because Seema keeps intruding in his thoughts. The few hours he spends every night at his apartment feel even more desolate than before. He moved to San Francisco after Mame's death last summer, from the condo in Oakland where they'd lived together. He misses Mame all the more now.

He broods over Seema and begins to follow the news on Iraq closely, reading everything he can lay his hands on. He fantasizes about wowing Seema with his newly acquired knowledge at some anti-war meeting in the city. Josh urges him to call her, even threatens to call her on Bill's behalf.

In mid-March, Bush issues an ultimatum: Saddam and his family have two days to leave Iraq. And two days later, as promised, missiles rain over Baghdad. Bill watches the coverage on TV as the assault begins. As predawn skies flare into light, and cloud clusters bloom soft and pink, like roses, he plucks up the courage to call Seema.

She's surprised to hear from him but not displeased to have someone to rant to. She savages Bush's announcement—*We come to Iraq with respect for its citizens, for their great civilization, and their religious faiths. We have no ambitions in Iraq!*—and speaks of herself ravaging Bush: "I'd like to tear his eyes out from his dumb face and scratch more furrows into his forehead."

He's both startled and bemused by the intensity of her anger, as if the assault on Iraq were somehow personal. Mame has drilled into him that anger is never the answer: you kept your head down, you worked hard till you reached a place where you couldn't be touched.

He suggests meeting up for drinks, to help take her mind off the matter.

She makes a counterproposal. There are to be protests downtown in the morning, in front of businesses profiting from the war—does he want to join her? "We have to do something, even if it will have no effect. They want us to feel too powerless to even protest."

He hesitates. The run-in with the police during the march unnerved him, and tomorrow will surely be worse; besides, he has work. But he can't let this opportunity to meet Seema slip away. He agrees to pick her up at eight in the morning.

Josh gives his blessings: "You don't believe all that leftist crap, do you? But if it's for a girl—what the hell. The company is going down the drain anyway. Just don't get arrested."

Bill is at her doorstep at eight sharp, nervous from the sleepless night, not knowing what to expect. She comes out wearing a khaki trenchcoat and knee-high black boots. Her hair is pulled back tightly, not a single strand straying, and she's lined her eyelids black, so her eyes appear to flash. There's a hard glitter about her—buttons, belt, zippers—as if she's armored.

"Yowza!" he says. "Are you planning to take the city hostage?"

"That's the idea," she replies, climbing into the car.

An intoxicating joy wells in him as they drive downtown. Already the city feels different—with Seema beside him—burgeoning in its chaos. Some streets appear cordoned off, and side streets are jammed with cars nosing their way around blindly, diverted from the main thoroughfares. A few intersections are blocked by crowds seizing the center, with no one to stop them, as if the police have abandoned the city. Bill and Seema park and make the rest of their way on foot.

Downtown clamors with the honks of cars and the din of protestors. The mystery of the missing police is soon solved. The crowd at Embarcadero is much smaller than on the Sunday of the march, but the city's entire police force seems to have gathered here. At one intersection, a group of eight protestors, in orange overalls, have chained themselves together to newspaper racks dragged to the center. To prevent their circle from being broken, they hold hands through thick pipes, and iron chains run between bicycle locks around their necks. Almost two dozen policemen surround them, with glass shields and three-foot wooden clubs. The sidewalks are lined with more police, preventing supporters on the pavements from breaking free and going to the aid of the group in the center. An officer with a bullhorn screams, "If you don't disperse we'll arrest all of you."

The supporters don't obey but instead chant, "Stay strong, this war is long."

Seema pushes her way through the crowd toward the front, beckoning Bill to follow with one backward glance. This is more confrontational than he'd expected, but he plunges in behind her. They come face-to-face with an impassive policeman, his arms outstretched and linked to policemen on either side in an attempt to contain the crowd, as firemen in goggles, armed with circular saws and chain cutters, approach the group in the center. The supporters grow louder as it seems more and more likely that the firemen will succeed. They thrust themselves forward trying to break the cordon, only to be shoved back.

Tiny in front of the huge policeman, Seema is a spark of fire—skipping, darting, hissing, throwing herself at the policeman as though she means to bust through. Bill hovers protectively by her, ready at any moment to interpose himself between her and the policeman. He feels compelled to provide a foil for her, shaking his fist and screaming full-throated with the rest.

A cry goes out, "Don't let them be arrested!" The firemen have cut through, and the police are closing in on the eight protestors. The supporters surge in a concerted push, the cordon is broken, and the crowd floods the intersection.

In the confusion Bill loses Seema. He looks around frantically—she's darting toward the center. He races after her and grabs hold of her hand, having no idea what he's doing, or what she or the crowd intends to do now.

The next few minutes are a blur. He follows Seema, running this way, then that, through the disarray of uniforms and batons and shields, forming a ring of protection first around one orange-clad protestor then around another. He doesn't think this will work—how long can the crowd protect the protestors before the police start arresting everybody? But then the strategy becomes clear: to hamper the police enough, giving the protestors time to melt away. Already some of them have shed their overalls and pipes and chains and merged with the others. Before he knows it, another shout goes up: "All clear!"

The crowd disperses rapidly, and he sprints after Seema toward an unguarded stretch of pavement. People lining it pull apart to let them through. He leaps through the opening, over the edge of the sidewalk as though clearing a high hurdle, and the opening closes up again behind him.

He doubles up, gasping for breath. Seema leans against the wall, a hand on his shoulder. She appears to be shaking, her face contorted. Is she hurt?

But she's actually laughing, a silent laughter that wracks her entire body, and he finds himself joining her, his eyes watering. When they both recover sufficiently to totter, supporting each other, to check on the road, there are only policemen and firemen in the intersection, picking up the discarded pipes and chains and orange overalls, dragging away the abandoned newspaper racks.

Bill intended to spend only a couple of hours at the protest, but Seema's company is exhilarating, the excitement addictive. They join crowds blockading the Federal Building on Golden Gate Avenue. They shout chants in front of the Transamerica Pyramid against the military-industrial complex fronted by the Carlyle Group, to the accompaniment of drumming and dancing. They have lunch and spirited discussions with other protestors they've befriended, and their group swells as the day advances. Traffic has been wrestled to a standstill. Cars and buses are abandoned everywhere, and intersections continue to be blocked by sitters and bicyclists. The police arrest protestors where they can, but their group manages to free quite a few by surrounding the officers and harassing them into letting the arrested go.

By afternoon, Bill is inured to the sight of protestors in handcuffs, though still shrinking from encounters with the police himself, Mame's censures continuing to prick. Seema seems unafraid of being arrested, though she celebrates every protestor freed as a small victory.

In the evening, people pour onto Market Street, and an impromptu march wends it way toward the Civic Center Plaza. Darkness descends over the city, and the plaza is lit by the soft halo of candles as the marchers settle into a vigil.

But seated now on the lawn with candles in their hands, Bill is disquieted by Seema's transformation. Wearied lines appear on her face. In the hush of the flickering light, the fire and fury of the day have given way to resignation and despair.

He asks, "Are you okay?"

She says, "None of this matters, of course. We can march all we want, we can fight all we want, it's no better than sitting here kumbayaing with these candles. Nothing will really change. Whatever progress we make will be because they've already figured out how to use it to their advantage. They'll throw scraps at us to distract us from what we're about to lose. Even these protests are just to keep us distracted and occupied. Don't you feel that way too?"

Bill knows what her question alludes to—the color of his skin, his experiences as a Black American. He's avoided such conversations even with friends, and were he to find himself embroiled in one, he has managed to maintain a noncommittal silence before changing the topic. But he's aware of something pressing against the boundaries that had been his self a month ago. And he can't ignore Seema's appeal, although he doesn't know what she expects.

"My father died in prison," he says, the words sticking in his throat. "He'd joined the Black Panther Party while he was in college."

She sits up. "Wow! I wouldn't have guessed."

"He was arrested a few months before I was born. I've only seen photos of him. His parents brought me up. They always used to say you beat them by being better than them. And that's what they brought me up to do."

"Why was he arrested?"

"I don't know. Mame—my grandmother—rarely spoke about him." He regrets now that he didn't pressure her. Mame had always maintained a tight-lipped silence about his father, though his presence hung over Bill all through his childhood in the yellowing photos hanging in her bedroom. What little she told Bill was when he was leaving for college, and then just the bare facts.

"He died of a ruptured appendix—at least that's what they told Mame. He was only twenty-five, and he'd been in prison for four years. Mame didn't want me ending up like him."

"Your grandmother must have been through a lot." Seema's face is gold from the candle flames, softer now if more remote. He's hypnotized by the play of light on her cheeks and lips, eyelids and earlobes. "What about your mother?" she asks.

"Mame spoke even less about her. Maybe she belonged to the party too. I don't think they were married. She stayed with Mame for the delivery. But a few months after I was born she left us and disappeared. No one knew where."

"I'm sorry." Seema strokes his hand.

He hesitates, overcomes his anxiety that perhaps he's moving too fast, and puts an arm around her, drawing her toward him, something he'd wanted to do all day.

She doesn't pull back and even rests her head on his shoulder briefly. "I'd love to see some photos of your father," she says.

"Mame's things are still in boxes. Come home, and you can go through them, while I make us some dinner."

"Are you sure?"

Yes, he's sure, he says. A dinner with Seema would cap a most incredible day, though he feels guilty using his father this way, having forgotten him all these years.

6

Bill decides on a simple shrimp and grits, and collard greens, picking up a few groceries on the way.

The smell of crisping bacon reaches her in his spartan bedroom, where she rummages in the box he's placed on the bed. She doesn't ordinarily eat bacon, a vestigial unease from her Muslim upbringing, but she tells Bill, "I'll have it the way your grandmother made it."

She has found photos of Bill's father—black and white, some framed, some loose, all fading—from toddler to youth. She can see Bill in his father at his oldest, in what seems to be a high school yearbook photo, posed in a white jacket and shirt, with a bow tie, and a rose clipped to his lapel. Bill's father is spectacled too, his eyes through the glass presenting a brooding studiousness.

She's a little disappointed: the photos seem innocuous—tame, almost—not what she expected of someone who joined the Panthers. "Are there any more? Any later photos?"

They sift through the box, through old church circulars and scrapbooks of clippings on gardening tips. They finally find another photo, tucked away in a brown-paper cover in Mame's Bible. Untouched for many years, this one is very well preserved, startling in its clarity.

Bill's father is older here, though he still looks very young. His spectacles glint so fiercely his eyes can barely be made out. But still the brooding mouth. He wears a black jacket and a white turtleneck. On his head—his hair now an Afro—is a black beret. On the jacket's lapel is pinned a white badge, though Seema can't tell what's on it. It takes her a moment longer to notice, in the shadows, the rifle slung across the shoulder.

"He's beautiful," she says, envying the resoluteness stamped on his bearing.

"I never saw this one before." Bill takes the photo from her. "I can see why Mame kept it hidden from me."

He studies the two photos side by side, this and the yearbook photo, one washed out to a placid yellow paleness, the other fierce in its intense black-and-whiteness. "Night and day," he says. "You looked like this in the morning, in your trenchcoat and boots."

She laughs. "He's the real deal. I'm only playacting. I wonder what he went to jail for."

They sip wine, then dine on the creamy grits, the juicy shrimp, the bacon adding a crunch to the collard greens and a smokiness she savors. She's impressed by his culinary skills—she has none—and impressed, too, by his exhaustive knowledge about the events leading up to the war.

When he asks about her family, she says, "I don't like talking about them."

"Why?"

All she needs to say is *My father cut me off when I came out as a lesbian.* The day is beyond date territory now, and she should have clarified earlier. But she'd ignored many openings, reluctant to bring the day to an end. Bill's eager and anxious willingness to please her, to accommodate her wishes while protecting her from their consequences, is a novel experience—a princely masculine courting, almost a revival of the princess days of her girlhood. And his father is the real deal. She takes a deep breath. "I really like you, Bill."

He notes the implicit *but* and freezes, fork-speared shrimp midair. His face falls. "You're married. You have a boyfriend."

She shakes her head.

"Your family wants you to marry an Indian—a Muslim. Or—you don't date Black men."

She snaps her fingers. "You're right on both counts."

He throws down his fork. "You know—Indian women and racism, what's up with that?"

"I don't date any men. Period." She speaks sharply, upset by his accusation of being racist, though it's her fault for making a joke about it.

He stares as if he doesn't understand her, then as if he doesn't believe her. Her continued silence and unflinching gaze must have convinced him, for finally he says, dully, "You don't look like a lesbian."

"I don't know what you think a lesbian looks like. Ever seen the Dyke March? We're all kinds."

"You'd have gotten tired of me soon, anyway. I'm only a boring lawyer, I don't even look interesting, unlike my father." He chuckles resignedly. "And Mame would definitely have not approved of you."

"Bill, I really do like you. I wish we could be friends."

He clears away the dishes. When she's leaving, he swears that he won't hold on to hope of things changing between them. But yes, he doesn't regret the day at the protests, and he'd like to remain friends.

7

Though there's little hope of it happening, Seema thirsts for Saddam Hussein to teach America a humiliating lesson, for supporting him as long as he remained compliant, only to disown him when he asserted his independence. Anything less than humiliation would spur American imperialism, she thinks, becoming another feather in the cap for American exceptionalism.

She remains outspoken about her sentiments, despite alienating many of her American friends—even Fiaz, who, while decrying the Bush Doctrine of preemptive strikes, supports getting rid of the tyrant and, now that the war has been launched, desires a quick, successful end to it.

"Thank God I'm not an American citizen," Seema says. "I wouldn't be able to live with the hypocrisy."

"You are living here and enjoying its freedoms," Fiaz points out.

They're colleagues as well now, since Seema's return from Boston. These discussions have strained their earlier companionship.

"I can always go back to India."

"But will you?"

Yes, she enjoys her freedoms here, including being out and proud, and cannot conceive what her life would be like in Iraq under Saddam or even in India, were she to return to it. But her point is that America cannot be allowed to value the lives of others any less than the lives of its own citizens. For when she watches the TV coverage she sees only rabid cheerleading from the American newscasters—predominantly White men and women, but also a few persons of color, who should know better, given the history of their own oppression and exploitation in America. From the front lines the journalists all report gushingly, from the point of view of the armed forces they've been "embedded" in, inflating victories and slavering over stories of coalition forces saving Iraqi babies and being welcomed as liberators. And liberal America seems to have fallen in line, extolling what seems to be the swift and decisive campaign Bush had promised.

The lone source she holds on to desperately is Al Jazeera reporting from Baghdad, with its pictures of a city in fiery ruins, of bloodied dead and dying, of resistance, of captured coalition servicemen. She even takes solace in its English website's periods of mysterious unavailability, suspecting American censorship of unflattering news. But there's no denying that within three weeks of the start of the war, Baghdad is in American hands, and Saddam Hussein has fled underground. In three more weeks, Bush lands on an aircraft carrier and disembarks in a military-green flight suit and prominent codpiece, cockily proclaiming to the cameras and the world: *Mission Accomplished.*

Seema is depressed. The defeat feels personal. She feels increasingly powerless, increasingly useless, as San Francisco settles back into business as usual, as if the war were a distant memory. Iraq, meanwhile, has descended into an insurgency tending toward civil war. The Bush administration is widely panned for having no plan to secure Iraq in the aftermath of Saddam's expulsion, but the satisfaction of "told you so" is fleeting.

If nothing else, Seema vows, she must at least fight to prevent Bush from being reelected for a second term, to avenge Saddam's ignominious dismissal and defeat.

8

Bill, by then, is one of the few friends still willing to listen as she rants about how pissed off she is that many of the Democratic challengers to Bush supported him in the lead-up to the war. It is he who suggests she look into volunteering for Howard Dean, one of the few Democrats willing to take on his own party for its support of Bush's policies and the Iraq War. He's a fighter, with a wagging finger and beetling eyebrows. The more Seema learns about him the more she likes: he's a doctor, not a politician; he's never lost an election; he's the first governor of any state to sign a same-sex civil-union bill into law. And if he's White, he's partly redeemed by having requested to be roomed with a Black student while at Yale.

She's sold on Dean when she hears him speak: "The great unspoken political lie is *Elect me and I'll solve all your problems.* The great unspoken truth is that the future of the country rests in your hands, not mine. You have the power to rise up and take this country back."

The internet is beginning to make its power felt, providing Dean supporters with new tools to connect online. Seema, fueled by a renewed sense of control, throws herself into organizing meet-ups and fundraisers through the summer and fall of 2003, maintaining a blog highlighting Dean's policy positions, and creating posters and presentations to be shared with other volunteer groups around the country.

In these efforts she finds in Bill a willing assistant. Any hopes of reviving his start-up have been dashed over the summer, and he has plenty of time on his hands now. He helps set up her Dean website, drives her to meetings, takes over planning her events, and even shops for them and cleans up afterward.

"He's in love with you," Fiaz tells her. "Are you sure you know what you're doing?"

They are at a Dean for President meet-up at Bill's apartment. This is Fiaz's first time encountering Bill, though he's heard about him for a couple of months now. Fiaz is the only one from her queer circle who has met Bill.

"Bill knows what we're doing—we're volunteering for the Dean campaign."

"And you're not falling for him?"

"Of course not. He wants to help, and he's super useful."

"He's super sexy, too, in a straight-professor kind of way." Fiaz eyes Bill appreciatively. Bill, talking to a woman volunteer at the other end of the room, glances in their direction. "Don't say I didn't warn you."

She's noticed, of course, the way women at the meet-ups navigate toward Bill. She's joked to Bill about it: he's the draw, not Dean! She's even encouraged him to ask some of the interested women out on dates. But she has to admit—to herself at least—the unexpected pangs of possessiveness whenever Bill returns their interest.

"This is new," Bill says. "They've always ignored me before. Having you by my side has increased my cachet."

What's also new is Seema's experience having Bill around. She hasn't started dating again in San Francisco. She tells herself she can't be preoccupied with love while Iraq is disintegrating—there are more important matters.

Bill's solicitude, of course, goes beyond favors. He's remarkably detail oriented, great at logistics and organization. With his assistance, she gets to concentrate on what she does best—preparing and delivering the message—and the Dean campaign has begun to notice.

And having a man around makes her feel safer, more supported. She derides this as heterosexual conditioning, just as she complains about heterosexual privilege—as a couple she and Bill are taken more seriously, even treated better, like being seated quicker and served faster in restaurants, for example. But she can't avoid pondering the *what if.*

Sometimes she imagines herself sleeping with him. A charge has developed between them, like static electricity. She's never been with a man before, and the idea takes on the thrill of a taboo to be broken. She'll lose her gold-star status, of course—she can already sense her lesbian friends pulling away from her, some rudely and resentfully, as rumors of her "dating" a man begin to invade her queer circles—but fuck them. Isn't true equality about being able to sleep with whomever she wants to?

At least the Dean campaign, working on a shoestring budget, is appreciative of her contributions. Over the summer, the efforts of the snowballing number of volunteers bear fruit, and Howard Dean is catapulted into the front-runner slot for the Democratic nomination. As fall turns to winter Seema is in regular touch with the headquarters in Vermont. Her blog posts are highlighted on the campaign's website, her suggestions are incorporated in press releases, her PowerPoint presentations and posters make their way into the hands of every volunteer group around the country. Come December, she receives an offer to move to Burlington and join the campaign officially.

Seema considers the offer seriously. Accepting it would change the trajectory of her life. Her "activism" until now has been on the fringes, with little chance of having any real effect. Perhaps she could be like her ex Ann, who is now on the brink of what could be victory—the Massachusetts Supreme Court has just decided that it's unconstitutional for only opposite-sex couples to be able to marry in the state. Ann must surely be feeling triumphant—Seema can picture her in a white tuxedo, as though stepping out of a wedding magazine, a white-gowned bride in tow, all lip gloss and blond highlights.

But the ruling would definitely be used by the Republicans in the next elections—declaring it the end of marriage and civil society—to scare conservative America into turning out to reelect Bush. Once again, the need of a privileged few would trump the necessity of protecting the rest of the world from disastrous policies. The world wouldn't be able to survive another four years of Bush, who despite the chaos in Iraq, could claim victory: mid-December, the U.S. forces succeed in capturing a bedraggled Saddam Hussein, hiding in a spider hole on a deserted farm. If Bush smirks occasionally during the news conference announcing Saddam's capture, she can't really fault him, though it does stoke her fire to deny him further successes.

Another reason to accept the Dean offer: it would provide a natural ending point to her relationship with Bill. She's definitely not "in love" with Bill, though in half a year she's let herself become dependent on him like she's never allowed herself to depend on anyone else before, not even lovers.

A part of her regrets that she'd be giving up a chance to experiment being with a man, while another part is relieved: What if she likes it after all? It would give lie to her life until then, making her suffering and sacrifice—the rift with her father, the exile—meaningless. And is she then to sell out and settle down to a complacent conventional life with Bill, housed and hitched like Ann?

There's really nothing conventional about her relationship with Bill, though, and Bill is the opposite of Ann in every way—a Black man, from an underprivileged background, the awakening son of a Black Panther, a rising descendant of an oppressed race. There would always be battles to be fought. And it needn't last forever—nothing lasts forever.

She keeps the offer a secret and decides she doesn't need to decide yet. She could join the campaign after they win Iowa, which will be the first test of Dean's strength for the presidential nomination, kicking off the primary season in less than a month. Meanwhile, there's a lot that needs to be done, and she can't do it without Bill's help.

9

Josh warns Bill: "Be careful, she's a lesbian, and a Hussein. She'll dance on your heart in her boots and stomp it to bits."

But Bill remains hopeful, perhaps because Seema never talks about dating anyone. The two people in his life could, of course, get along better—Seema calls Josh a Zionist, and Josh has labeled Seema a terrorism apologist—but at least they rarely encounter each other. What remained of the company was finally sold in November to a more successful competitor—for pennies on the dollar—and Josh is already on to his next venture. Bill has decided to take a few months off. For the first time in his life, he can devote himself to something other than his school, or job, or career. He's chosen to devote himself to Seema.

And to remedying his ignorance of his past. Discovering the photo of his father in Black Panther uniform has awakened something in him that mere acquaintance with the fact hadn't. When he's not helping Seema with one of her Dean-related projects, he reads with a lawyerly assiduity foundational Black texts he should have read earlier, maintaining careful notes as if doing research. He can't read enough about the Black Panthers, especially autobiographies and writings of its lead members. The world they describe—the hunger, the anger; the intelligence, the hysteria; the resistance, the militancy; the hideouts and shootouts; the fear, the hubris—seems completely removed from his world growing up with Mame and Grandpa, though only a few years apart and on the other side of town. He can't imagine his father in that other world, not the bow-tied student, not even the bereted soldier.

Searching for further clues about his father, he methodically sifts through Mame's unopened boxes. He'd hired movers to pack them, too drained after Mame's death to deal with the remains of her life. He finds a few of his father's yearbooks but little else. Even in death Mame has made sure he wouldn't stumble on anything that could become a distraction. At times he feels he's disrespecting Mame by going through her belongings, like he's raiding her grave. But surely it had to be done.

And it becomes a thing to do with Seema, who is keenly interested. After a meal at his place, they open another of Mame's boxes, sipping a glass of sherry, Mame's favorite. Those nights are rewarding, even if they learn nothing new about his father, even if the night ends as it always does with him driving Seema back to her apartment and then returning to decide what to do with the contents uncovered.

Memories of living with Mame are evoked and shared—first in the blue-shingled house, his room in the attic overlooking the garden with its pride of Mame's roses, and after Grandpa's death, in a small apartment whose only charms were a spacious kitchen and a partial view of Lake Merritt—both spaces fragrant with the after-scent of summer roses all year long, which still persists faintly in many of Mame's belongings. Seema listens eager and rapt as he speaks about his youth, something intimate settling between them. His only regret is that she continues to share little about her own childhood, her own life, even when asked directly.

When they're done with the boxes, they go through Mame's clothes. Seema helps sort them, exclaiming over the dresses and jackets and scarves, holding them up against herself: "Your Mame sure was stylish."

They come across a locked jewel box that Bill can't find the key for, and which Seema pries open with a knife. It doesn't contain any jewelry but does contain what they'd been searching for all along. There's a paperback book, the cover missing, its pages marked with water stains, and a sheaf of yellowing letters, the ink fading but still legible, each dated and addressed *Dear Mother and Father* in a fluid graceful cursive.

Seema is thrilled. "Your father's handwriting is lovely, just like my sister's."

But Bill is torn between sharp guilt and dread. Should he be reading what Mame sought to keep hidden? And what if he finds in them something disquieting or worse?

He hands Seema the letters, unsteady, the way he'd felt months earlier finding the Black Panther photo. "You read them first."

"Are you sure? We don't have to read them now." But she's already scanning through the top letter. She looks up. "This is written in prison."

He nods, having realized that from the dates on the letters. He flips through the warped pages of the book he's still holding. It's a beat-up copy of *The Autobiography of Malcolm X*. His father's name is inscribed on the title page in the same distinct handwriting. Had his father been reading this in prison or earlier? Would his father have even been allowed it in prison? Bill has read it recently but without imagining his father holding the same book in his hands. The second half—after Malcolm X claimed to be saved—has many passages underlined. Bill browses through some of them, passages his father must have returned to more than once, for they bear the marks of various pencils and pens.

Reading his father's notes in the margins, Bill perceives a glimmer of what Mame must have dreaded all the years she was bringing him up. He can sense it again now, his own self constricting in response to Mame's unvoiced anxiety outside home, her hand tight around his wrist even in his teens, as though she were afraid to let him wander away, as though she couldn't be at ease until she'd dragged him back up the stairs of their stoop.

He becomes aware that Seema has stopped reading, the letters in a heap on her lap. She's cracking her knuckles, the sound of popping joints painful to his ears. Her face is pinched with the effort to control herself.

"What do the letters say?" His own distress is overshadowed: What could possibly be in the letters to upset Seema so much?

As if she hasn't heard him, she says, "Bill, can you take me home, please? Now?"

She doesn't wait for him to reply but sweeps the letters off her lap, gathers her jacket and handbag, and heads to the door. He knows she won't reply to his questions in this state. He puts the book back in the jewel box, but the letters must be folded before they can be returned. He picks up his car keys, pulls his shoes on, and follows her out.

They drive in silence to her apartment, a brittleness between them that could shatter if he so much as makes a move toward her. At her doorway she says, "I'm sorry, but I just need some space. I'll call you."

Back at his apartment, Seema's absence is palpable. But Mame's presence is strong in the living room, as if she's there disapproving of the ransacking of her possessions, her clothes in stacks on the sofa and chairs, her jewel box open. And there's another presence—elusive, indeterminate—the specter of his father hovering restively in the room.

Bill first sets about repacking everything but the jewel box and its contents. There are a few letters left unread in the box; the remaining are in Seema's messy pile. He goes through them, identifying the sheets of each letter, and folding them back together as they were. Seema must have been reading the top letter last.

It's an exhortation, echoing Malcolm X. To Mame and Grandpa to renounce Christianity and embrace Islam. To raise his son as a Muslim.

It praises Islam for its inclusion, it condemns Christianity as criminality. The Christian God is a false god, who'd made them believe that everything white is good, to be admired, respected, and loved, and that everything black is ugly, a curse, to be hated and loathed. But there is only one true God, Allah, with Muhammad as His prophet. In Islam, all the colors are united, the White man stands equal with the others before Allah. Only Islam can save the Black man by giving him the dignity he needs to live his life as a whole person, only Islam can save America from the malignancy of its racist cancer. *La ilaha ill'Allah Muhammadur rasulallah.* The letter is signed *Abdul Jabbar.*

Bill picks up the box. It's carved walnut with a crimson velvet lining, dried rose petals from Mame's garden at the bottom. Mame's fragrance is strongest here, stubbornly clinging to the velvet and the petals: the box must have remained locked for years.

One whiff and Bill is enfolded in Mame's embrace, in the pink chiffon of her Sunday dress, a rose pinned to its pleated lapel, the mesh of her matching hat grazing his face, as she gives him a hug before leaving for church—"Be a good boy now, and take care of Grandpa"—the fragrance lingering as he reluctantly waves her goodbye—"Why can't I come with you to church?"—his hand tight in Grandpa's hand. And after that, from Grandpa's colostomy bag the odor of shit returning as Mame's fragrance fades. His resentment grinds: he'd rather have gone with Mame. He wheels Grandpa back to the parlor in the grip of that odor, the dread—he can feel it rising within him, the puke—that he may be called upon to empty the bag before Mame returns. He's almost dizzy with nausea. He takes another deep whiff of the box's crimson interior before he shuts the lid.

Over the next few days he gives in to temptation and reads all the letters. A sense of betrayal unsettles even his sleeping hours. But who has been betrayed—he himself, his father, Grandpa and Mame, or even Seema? And who has betrayed whom?

He thinks he understands now why Mame always left him behind with Grandpa when she went to church, thinks he understands, too, Seema's reaction, knowing her severed relationship with her religion.

He waits for Seema to call, respecting her wish for space but desperately craving her return.

10

Reading Bill Sr.'s letters immediately recalls to Seema's mind Tahera—the same controlled grace in penmanship concealing the same force of passion. But had their handwritings been totally unlike, the contents of his letters would still have triggered a memory of the last letter Seema received from her sister.

It was in response to Seema's overture to Tahera after her marriage. Seema, of course, hadn't been invited to the wedding. In fact, her mother had only informed Seema of the event after the fact. Remembering the weddings of their childhood, the glitter and gold, the frolic and festivities, Seema's sense of loss at the belated news of Tahera's wedding had been acute and unexpected. The much-anticipated biryani cooked by bawarchis in enormous dekshas that could fit both sisters comfortably, with a taste and aroma unmatched by even their mother's most delicious version. Her yearnings as she and Tahera insinuated their way to the bride's side, so they could hold up the translucent gold- or silver-trimmed red maizar and the strings of jasmine and roses that veiled her, a ringside view of the shy bride's face as the nervous groom bent down to take a peek after the nikah and, later, of the bride's tears as her family gave her away during the jalwa.

Still, she accepted the distress and regret in her mother's voice as apology enough. She wasn't entitled to much more, anyway.

When she'd left home without saying anything to her mother or sister, she'd assumed the parting was temporary. Her father's implacability and her ensuing fall from grace shocked her into stunned shame and despair. The star of the family, and her light so swiftly snuffed out.

Her despair was misplaced in Tahera's case at least—her sister's letters clearly showed she wasn't aware of the real reason behind the excommunication. But Seema couldn't bring herself to come out to Tahera, to open herself up to the humiliation of further rejection, from someone who'd looked up to her all her life. Their father, who always supported Seema, had forsaken her. Their mother seemed more interested in having her return to the fold than in supporting her. How could Tahera come to understand? Especially when Tahera was poised to supplant her as their father's favorite.

Seema didn't reply to any of Tahera's letters. In time, Tahera's letters ceased.

A year after Tahera joined her husband in Irvine, their mother gave Seema Tahera's phone number and address, expressing a forlorn wish that the sisters look out for each other, both dwelling apart on a distant continent.

Seema was thrilled: far from their past in Chennai, thousands of miles away from their father, perhaps it was possible to reconnect, to reclaim their past sisterhood. But what was she to say about her precipitous disappearance and silence and the subsequent life she's carved for herself, now with Ann by her side? She knew through her mother that Tahera was no longer in the dark about her sexuality, yet it took Seema weeks to gather the courage to call.

The phone was answered by Tahera's husband, and she was forced to wait, ruing the mischance—she'd counted on the tide of surprise to carry the conversation through. When Tahera finally came on the line, her voice was a studied formal monotone: "Assalamu Alaikum?"

"It's me, Seema."

"I know."

"Ammi gave me your number."

"She gave me yours too."

"You're in Texas. You're married."

"Yes, his name is Ismail. He works for a computer hardware company."

"I heard the nikah was grand."

"Alhamdulillah, it went well."

"Congratulations. And celebrations!"

But not even the reference to the Cliff Richard song they used to sing together at weddings elicited an echo of the sister she knew.

"Thank you. It's as Allah wishes."

The exchange couldn't last much longer. Tahera had transformed into an impassive stranger. Even more shocking, she was now mouthing religious phrases with no apparent irony, phrases they would mock particularly sanctimonious elders with, behind their backs. She wielded these like charms to ward off Seema, to prevent her from even thinking about sharing the details of her scandalous life. Seema ended the call without mentioning Ann.

She'd been more disappointed than she cared to admit. Somewhere in the depths of her consciousness, she'd already picked up the snapped threads of their relationship. But how could Tahera have changed so much? Was it the husband's influence? And why had their father chosen such a husband?

Later, Seema learned from her mother that Tahera had taken to praying five times a day even while living at home in Chennai, and she insisted on marrying a committed practicing Muslim, adamant against their father's wishes. Seema found this hard to believe, even envisioning strategies to rescue her sister, until the day—a few weeks later—she received a letter.

In her sister's elegant handwriting, flowing yet precise: Seema is living in sin and must beg Allah's forgiveness for her dissolute past. Seema has neglected namaz and has pursued illicit desires, and she's bound to Jahannam unless she repents, believes, and practices righteousness. Allah is most merciful, and He would surely forgive and accept Seema back. Tahera is available to help only if Seema acknowledges the error of her ways and with true repentance intends to follow the ways of the Prophet.

Seema read the letter with the shock of betrayal, for there's no mistaking the conviction in the words. Reading Bill's father's letters, the betrayal felt raw again. She'd cheered his unequivocal condemnation of White America, but the letters ultimately recalled the rhetoric her sister had used.

Islam alone can save the Black community, Islam alone can reform their people's morals and protect them from the evils that blight them—lawlessness, drug addiction, alcoholism, fornication, adultery, degeneracy. His parents are misguided in remaining faithful to a religion that keeps them enslaved.

After reading the letters, Seema insisted Bill take her home. It was only afterward that she felt ashamed for not considering the effect of his father's letters on him. But Bill doesn't call, and with each passing day it becomes harder to reach out to him.

Perhaps this is the sign she's been waiting for, about whether to end it with Bill, and when, for she knows she's pretty much set on the offer to join the Dean campaign and move to Vermont. She'd been clinging to fantasies of mutual comfort and support, even a kind of love, concentrating on Bill's many virtues and attractions—including having a revolutionary for a father, except that the father had turned out to be not a martyr but a fundamentalist like her sister.

But later that week, in the run-up to the Iowa caucus, Howard Dean's lead in the polls shrinks considerably. There's a panicked call for an all hands to help stem the bleed. With a relief that she doesn't pause to examine, Seema rings Bill up to ask if he'll fly with her to Des Moines.

II

January 2004, Iowa: Seema, with Bill in tow, is immediately pressed into supervising sundry initiatives—volunteer training, phone-bank shifts, door-to-door canvassing. She's a natural at this. Her allure is immediate, her enthusiasm infectious, and she projects assurance and authority.

From the very first day, they put in long hours—returning at night to the twin room they share at a motel on the outskirts, only to sleep, shower, and change. Bill is familiar with this pace from his long workdays at the start-up, but Seema shows surprising stamina. She's up before him, as fresh as the day before, and he rarely sees her flagging.

He marvels at the effect she has on the other volunteers and campaign workers, reviving their energy and spirits. By the end of the first week she's made herself essential to the Des Moines operations.

This is Bill's first experience of winter and wide white landscapes, and his first time in the heartland, in an overwhelmingly White state. Everywhere they go, he and Seema stand out. They are confronted with looks of surprise, bemusement, and even overt distrust. Bill has never felt more self-conscious, the awareness sharpened by everything he's discovered over the last year. It forces him to question, as he's never done before, every interaction. Is it wariness he encounters, or calculation, forbearance, impatience, evaluation, condescension? The strain is wearying.

Seema has adapted well to this scene, suppressing talk of her usual grievances. "Do you see anyone else around who can defeat Bush? I've got to work with what I have."

And what she has, an exotic glamour, she plays up subtly. Bill can't say exactly what's different about her in Iowa, but whatever it is, it's working. The newer campaign workers, young and barely out of college, vie with each other for her attention, readily submitting to her leadership. Media events and interviews are enlivened, Seema bringing to them the feisty vitality of a hothouse flower. The senior campaign staff, overworked as they are, are grateful, even if they sometimes resent being crowded out of the picture. It usually falls to Bill to soothe their ruffled feelings, a task he's good at.

"Remind me again what's in this for me?" he asks Seema.

A joking voice but a nagging question since he allowed himself to be persuaded to join Seema on this trip. She's taken three weeks off from work, feigning a family emergency. He has no one to answer to, and no job lined up yet, but he's not the driven supporter of Howard Dean she is, nor is unseating George W. Bush his most burning desire. What's he doing here then? To say he's here for Seema, to say he can't abandon Seema: how foolish, how foolhardy.

His last relationship—which ended a year and a half ago—was with Vanessa, a tax attorney, a Black Latina whom Josh had set him up with. And then had come Mame's death, driving out any thoughts of dating, until he'd met Seema. Since then, Bill can count on one hand the number of times he's had sex, each time with women from the neighborhood sports bar that he sometimes visited late Saturday nights when he was too wound up to sleep. And each time he'd felt guilty; whether Seema was sleeping with anyone, he didn't, couldn't, ask.

Just as he can't ask about what he's hearing now from the campaign staff, that Seema is likely to join the national headquarters in Vermont after the Iowa caucus. If that were true, the days of Seema's withdrawal following the discovery of his father's letters will have been a mere taste of the days to come.

But there's little time for repining. If Seema had been pushing herself and Bill hard before, with caucus day approaching they're working almost without rest. The overextended days are a refuge: he has little time to wallow in the guilty hope that a Dean loss in Iowa would somehow secure him Seema. For, in the days immediately before the caucus, Dean's popularity takes a further dive. His opposition to the Iraq War has been turned around to paint him as inexperienced in foreign policy and incapable of keeping America strong. Seema dismisses the polls. Dean will win, if only by the smallest of margins—surely the passionate labor of the thousands who've followed Dean here from all over the country can ensure that. But Bill has his doubts. Iowans appear weary of their pervasive presence, considering them outsiders interfering in their state: the orange beanie that constitutes their uniform has become a target of ridicule in local papers. And the headquarters has become increasingly disorganized and dysfunctional, riven with indecisiveness and internal disputes.

Caucus day whizzes by with the surreality of a time-lapse video. It's morning, it's noon, it's evening, time lurching forward, each new assignment so clamorous in its importance and urgency as to displace all memory of the assignment just completed. Bill and Seema step out only after the caucus commences, and there's nothing more that anyone can do. They're famished, they bolt down an untasted meal, and still bruised from the day's battering, they make their way to the ballroom rented for the after-party to await results.

The ballroom is swarming with a thousand exhausted but exhilarated troopers. But the mood soon turns somber as the results begin to trickle in. Dean has slipped to third place, and a distant third at that. Bill senses the struggle with which Seema controls herself, but he doesn't presume to offer comfort or hope: she has retreated to the remote self he knows to leave alone, though they sit side by side. To have worked so hard, and fallen so short—he aches to console Seema, to assure her that the effort is not all wasted, but of this he's not sure.

He takes her hands in his to massage them to warmth, even as a slow chill steals into him. Had the results been closer, he could have expected Seema to double down, convinced the defeat could be reversed. But with little chance of recovering from this debacle, Dean will be forced to end his campaign, perhaps even tonight. Seema would surely take this as further proof of her—and

Bill's—insignificance. And she could withdraw completely, shunning any-thing that reminds her of today—including him.

When Dean comes out on the podium, the ballroom is still grieving. But Dean knows how to fight: he rolls up his sleeves and gives an impassioned speech, promising his followers that he's not giving up, that he'll lead them to victory through every remaining state primary to the White House.

He ends with a scream—"Yeah!"—from somewhere deep within him and electrifying, his fist smashing through the air as if he were crushing every ob-stacle in his path—opposition, destiny.

The speech revives the entire ballroom, as it does Seema. She's restored to some measure of her customary animation, making plans for the future. Bill, too, is almost persuaded to believe in Dean's continuing viability.

But the flame that Dean has reignited wavers as soon as they leave the ballroom. They crawl back to their motel in silence, undress in silence, get into their respective beds, turn the lights off.

Bill has never been back in the room this early before and with no concrete plans for tomorrow. Despite his exhaustion, he can't sleep, unable to dull the consciousness of some inevitable change that day must bring. He lies staring at the window, at the icy white light leaking in through the curtains, ushering a desolate winter into the room.

"Bill, I can't sleep," Seema whispers. "I'm cold."

"Me too," he says, turning toward her.

"Can I join you?" she asks.

Should he have replied that it isn't a good idea? That she might regret it the next morning? All he knows in that moment is his need. He's able to stutter, "If you want to."

And in reply, Seema slips out of her bed and into his, under his comforter.

How awkward that first coupling is, as if he's never kissed before, never touched a breast, never gone down on a woman. His hands tremble. He's never felt clumsier, all thumbs. His tongue seems swollen, his breathing is a wheeze.

"Relax," she says. "I should be more nervous than you—I've never slept with a man before."

But that only leaves him more shaken, as if he's been given this one chance, and he's squandering it.

"It's okay," she says. "Just hold me."

Despite having desired this for so long, having dreamed of this the three weeks he's spent with her in this room, he can find little comfort in Seema's warm breath on his chest, the length of her body smoldering against his. All night—after she's gone back to her own bed—he rehearses apologies, excuses. He alternates between blaming himself and blaming Seema for succumbing to the folly. He shames himself for performing so inadequately.

He wakes up no closer to knowing what to say to her. He goes for a walk to clear his mind, while she's still asleep. The only sensible solution is to claim that the night was a mistake, that he shouldn't have taken advantage of her vulnerability. Perhaps their friendship would survive it. He returns with coffee and a prepared speech.

She accepts the coffee but, before he can speak, offers, "Maybe I shouldn't have sprung it on you like that last night. Maybe we can give it another try. That is, if you want to—"

And yes, my yet-to-be father wants to, wants to so badly that he suppresses all doubts that would have saved them both so much grief.

12

Here's what happens next: Dean's defiant speech is reduced, by a media gloating at his Iowa drubbing, to the final ten seconds of his roused red-faced scream. Overnight, Dean becomes fodder for late-night TV hosts and comedians—portrayed as too angry and pilloried as unpresidential. The clips go viral on the web, and Dean cannot survive the assault, falling victim to the very internet that had elevated him. Within a month, he drops out of the race.

Seema is furious and dejected; she's back in San Francisco, having lost not only her lone champion against Bush but her ticket out of her current life.

Meanwhile, as if to rub salt into her wounds, San Francisco has erupted in jubilation: its ambitious new mayor, Gavin Newsom, beating Massachusetts to the punch, has ordered the city to issue marriage licenses to same-sex couples, in defiance of Proposition 22. The city cheers as gay and lesbian couples queue in front of the county clerk's office in lines that stretch around the block. Champagne flows on the steps of the city hall as newlyweds exit lip-locked and teary-eyed. The Castro transforms itself into a twenty-four-hour street party.

Seema rants to Bill: How is she to celebrate while America turns a blind eye to the pain and suffering of the Brown peoples it has invaded illegally and is dooming itself to four more years of a war criminal? The CIA had finally admitted, just the week before, that there had been no imminent threat from Saddam's WMDs. How could queer America justify rejoicing at what is simply fuller participation in the imperialistic American Dream, while Iraq is rapidly sinking into further chaos, with car bombs ripping through Baghdad practically every single day?

Bill is the only person she can say this to. Her queer friends are all too ecstatic and will be too defensive: they'll disparage her, insinuating that she's capable of saying this only because she's now dating a man, a fact she can no longer deny, even if her mind still abounds with ambivalences.

She doesn't question the night in Iowa—it had to happen, if only so she can have tried it. If only the experience had been more conclusive. But what had indeed been wonderful was the warm succor of Bill's body after the cold failure of the night. She hadn't been held that intimately by anyone since Ann, and never with that protective embrace. Had she actually been relieved that the sexual act itself hadn't progressed far, so she needn't make a decision that very night? Had a part of her been envisioning their future together in Vermont?

Now with the campaign dead, and with the marriages in San Francisco's "Winter of Love" thrust in her face, she can't help but question: What are she and Bill doing?

The answer is they're "dating." They're taking things slowly, sex can wait; they've advanced to holding hands, to quick kisses on cheeks, to back rubs and shoulder massages, to holding each other in bed. The answer merely raises more questions: of betrayal, of hypocrisy, of fraud. If there is a bright spot, it's that Bill, wary about the effect of the ongoing marriages on her, rarely brings the topic up himself, and at least with him she can ignore the entire hoopla roiling San Francisco.

13

But this, too, happens: A couple of weeks after returning from Iowa, Seema sits up in Bill's bed with a gasp—of terror, a nightmarish vision of her body in the coils of carnivorous tendrils; of pain, as if her insides were being wrenched out. She kicks the comforter out of her way. The hour is just past four in the morning.

It's a damp February, and the air in the room is heavy and clammy around her nightgowned self, like childhood memories of monsoon. Other memories impinge, of the indignities her body is capable of inflicting on her: she still suffers occasionally from her pubescent ailment of traumatic irregular periods, though their frequency and intensity have much reduced over the years. But what's happening now cannot be that, surely not without the usual warning symptoms—she presumes she knows her body well enough by now, although she has been puzzled by a strange tiredness the previous week, which she attributed to depression and despair from Dean's loss.

She scrambles out of bed, evading Bill's pacifying arms, and heads toward the bathroom.

"Seema, are you okay?" he asks.

Even in her urgency she recognizes that his voice is alert, slumber-free, as if he's been lying awake the entire time. She feels both bolstered and badgered.

He turns on the night lamp.

Simultaneously, she feels the floor give way, as if the light has brought the roof and room of her caving inward. She squeezes her thighs and knees tight together, against the knife-edged pain, but the flow is not to be contained: the warm gush streams down her legs to a spreading pool around her feet, to the Berber beige of the bedroom carpeting. Any move to the bathroom now would only leave a trail, and she lowers herself to a clenching squat, hoping to minimize the damage, pressing her nightdress into use as a pad. The fabric soaks and turns crimson.

Bill is beside her, his arms around her, seeking to help her up.

"Don't! Leave me alone—" She pushes him away, too embarrassed to have him looking at her.

Another piercing pang—its ferocity is unfamiliar to her: what exactly is this?—another tingling spurt, almost scouring on its way out, viscous, clotted. She is too faint to fight Bill off now, one hand on her back and another reaching under her, and then a flick upward, and she's in his arms, the length of her curled up by his chest, one palm supporting her *there*, where he's been allowed only recently, a gentle alleviating pressure.

"Where?" Bill asks, his voice still steady, though his arms strain, and he pivots as if to carry her back to the bed, which is closer.

"No, silly—the bathroom." A weak laugh, despite herself; her gown has surely soaked through and soiled his hands.

Bill sets her down on the toilet seat, letting her slip from him a little hastily, clumsily, when she grimaces with the knowledge of another impending attack.

He backs away, turning to wash his hands at the sink as she scrunches down into herself over the bowl. He's careful to avert his gaze.

"I'm okay, I'll be okay, go—" she says.

Although she wouldn't mind Bill staying, for a coiling dread tightens with each additional spasm: what's happening to her, inside her, cannot be the usual disruption. But Bill takes her at her word and leaves, while she continues to strain over the toilet bowl, trying to empty out as quickly as possible whatever is writhing within her, even as she prays it's merely her period, one more vicious than usual.

Bill has left the bathroom door ajar, and she focuses on his movements to still her anxiety. First, his measured footsteps as he goes to the kitchen and returns with a roll of paper towels, then as he blots the blood-soaked areas of the carpet, then as he crisscrosses the bedroom covering up with white squares the trail she has left behind. Now he sits on the edge of the bed, the side closest to the bathroom, elbow on knee, his chin resting on a fisted hand—not Rodin's *Thinker* but *Worrier*—and now he paces up and down the width of the bedroom, between the bed and the wall, the reassuring sliver of him visible each time past the bathroom door. As time stretches, she hears him pause longer and longer by the door, until he's a fixed presence on the other side, a guardian spirit breathing.

A timid knock on the door. "Seema, should we go to the ER?" Bill sounds apologetic about his ignorance, his lack of experience.

She's been in here for the better part of an hour, and the bleeding has nearly stopped, only slight spotting left. "I'll be out soon. Can you get me my handbag, please?"

She wants her menstrual cup, though she's certain now it's not her period. She discards her stained nightgown, washes herself slowly in the shower, the water so abrasively scalding that her body barely registers the softness of the towel afterward. She inserts the cup and wraps the towel around herself but is reluctant to leave the security of the bathroom.

Bill is waiting. "I was worried." He holds out the flannel shirt he's lent her before and his softest corded pajama pants, the ones she has much admired. "Here—you can roll the legs up."

But one further glance at her face, pallid and drooping, and he latches on to her apprehension. "What is it?" he whispers.

She shakes her head—I don't know—as she debates whether to accept the clothes he's offering or to get dressed and leave.

"I can take you to the ER." He's observed her glance in the direction of her dress hanging by the door, and is doubly alarmed now, alarmed on her account and alarmed she might withdraw.

She does not withdraw. She can't be alone. And the prospect of the ER is both daunting and demoralizing, to be subject to the mercy of doctors who don't know her body. Besides, she feels exhausted suddenly, enfeebled, and only wants to crawl back into bed. "The bleeding has stopped. I prefer to be checked by my own doctor."

It's Sunday morning, and that means at least a day, if she manages to get an appointment for Monday. She takes the shirt from him, but her fumbling fingers are stumped by the buttons, and he does them for her, helps her pull on the pajama pants, and crouches by her feet rolling up the bottoms, while she supports herself pressing down on his head. He leads her back to bed.

As she dozes back to sleep, her body curled toward his, her head halfway on his shoulder, she knows he can't be entirely comfortable, but he doesn't complain, and she accepts his offering, too drained even to be grateful, knowing that he's probably going to lie awake next to her the entire time.

When she wakes up later there's been little to no further bleeding. The day passes in a haze of drowsiness and lethargy. She's grown leaden with her anxiety about the outcome of the upcoming appointment, her body somehow grown too weak to bear its own weight, ready to give up its responsibility to something or someone else—the bed, Bill. She lets him help her sit up in bed, fluffing the pillows behind her, lets him spoon her the moong dal and rice ganji he's made from her descriptions of her mother's sickbed recipes, lets him distract her with poems from the collected works of Audre Lorde he's picked up based on a suggestion she once made long ago, his reading voice quite expressive for someone unused to reciting poetry, and wholly earnest, like Tahera's. She naps, soothed by the signals of his presence around her, his sounds from the living room, his shadow in the bedroom. She could almost be home in Chennai.

Bill accompanies her to her appointment the next day. There she learns, to her immense relief, that unlike in the past, her latest episode of bleeding was due to chemical pregnancy and a miscarriage, resulting from their first and only occasion of unprotected sex, frustrated and abbreviated as it was, the night of the caucus. Astonishing to think that Bill's sperm could be so virile and so numerous as to prevail even in his precum, with little penetration. Her doctor's suggestion of birth control with a hormonal IUD has an added benefit: it has been shown to reduce the intensity of menstrual bleeding. Another demon from her Chennai days could simultaneously be laid to rest.

14

Two other things happen in the first six months of my to-be parents getting together—one that stokes their anger and one that offers them hope.

In April, stories of torture and rape of Iraqi detainees by American soldiers are reported by the national media. The photos emerging from the Abu Ghraib prison horrify: of naked Brown men in barred prison cells and dimly lit corridors, some hooded, some shackled, some dragged around on dog leashes, some posed in sexual positions, some heaped like carcasses, while American soldiers—White, and in uniform!—stand around them, over them, straddling them, flashing triumphant smiles and thumbs-ups. Seema is outraged, though not surprised; Bill is especially haunted by one photo: a detainee hooded and robed in black, the lines reminiscent of the white regalia of the Ku Klux Klan, a savage irony, for he's precariously poised on a cardboard box, arms to the sides, wires running from his fingers to electrical connections behind him. It's his father's face Bill imagines under the hood, a father who'd died in prison purportedly of a ruptured appendix.

Seema has never seen Bill this shaken, his anger shining through his attempts to repress it—she welcomes it, even as she comforts him. He is as riled as she that the Democratic nominee to challenge Bush is to be Senator John Kerry, who'd voted to authorize the Iraq War, only lately coming out against it, professing to have been misled about Iraq's WMDs. Kerry's vice-presidential pick is slick-haired senator John Edwards, who had also voted in support of the war.

At the Democratic convention in July, Kerry accepts the nomination with a salute, touting his military credentials and Purple Heart—which Bill and Seema watch with disgust. But at the same convention, a young state senator from Illinois, running for the U.S. senate, gives a keynote speech that electrifies them. He is fresh-faced but confident, he is Black, and his words soar.

He speaks of hope. Not blind optimism, not willful ignorance, but the hope of immigrants setting out for distant shores, the hope of slaves sitting around fires singing freedom songs. What is this audacious hope—a belief in things not seen, a belief that there lie better days ahead—based on?

It's only in America, Barack Obama says, that such things are possible, with its faith in simple dreams and insistence on small miracles, in hard work and perseverance, summed up in a declaration made more than two hundred years ago: *We hold these truths to be self-evident, that all men are created equal, that they are endowed by their Creator with certain inalienable rights, that among these are life, liberty, and the pursuit of happiness.* Isn't his presence on this stage improbable enough that it constitutes proof?

It's the messenger, of course, as much as the message. My to-be father is immediately smitten. A prophet in his own image, living and preaching a message of belonging and flourishing in America. There seems to be no anger in Obama, his face soft, open, solemn, creasing to sweetness whenever he smiles, so different from the man in the photo Mame had kept hidden, with the gun and the hard set to his jawline.

My to-be mother is at first a little skeptical, with the wariness of the recently burned, made uneasy precisely by Obama's lack of anger. But Bill channels Obama with the single-mindedness of an evangelist, and he succeeds in persuading Seema to join him in his faith, her last reservations suspended when he reads to her Obama's speech denouncing the Iraq War from two years earlier, even before Howard Dean.

No sooner does the Kerry-Edwards ticket lose in November than a buzz begins to build around Obama, even though he has just won his first term to the U.S. Senate and has denied any presidential ambitions. Bill and Seema become early acolytes. And two years later, when Obama publicly announces his candidacy, they will be joined by a growing multitude ready to follow him.

And along the way, Bill and Seema become lovers, get married, and move in together into a house on the top of a hill, with spectacular views of a peninsular city and sparkling bay, visible when the fog permits.

15

Are our endings foretold in our beginnings?

Consider my parents' wedding. Bill and Seema had agreed they'd get married on the day Barack Obama officially kicked off his presidential campaign. In February 2007, three years after they first got together, Obama finally does so: addressing a freezing rally in Springfield, Illinois, in front of the state capitol, where a century and a half ago Abraham Lincoln called on a house divided to stand together, he issues his own call, for people to come together for the purpose of perfecting the union and building a better America.

But that happens on a Saturday, and the San Francisco City Hall doesn't perform civil ceremonies over the weekend. When Bill and Seema show up, with Fiaz and Pierre in tow, the following Monday, they are confronted by another rally: it's also the three-year anniversary of the day same-sex marriages had first been performed in San Francisco, marriages that had been voided within a few months by the California Supreme Court, citing Proposition 22. A crowd of gay and lesbian couples and supporters throng city hall to hear Mayor Newsom reiterate his commitment to win them the right to marry and reinstate their voided marriages. City hall echoes with applause and cheers, praise and gratitude.

"I didn't know this was happening today," Bill whispers to Seema.

He is disappointed that the main hall is occupied by the rally—their wedding would now be held in a small chamber instead of under the rotunda's spectacular dome—but the disappointment is overshadowed by the fear that the rally might change Seema's mind.

The rally does give Seema pause. There are many couples in the hall dressed in wedding attire, like the lesbians in the white tuxedo and the white dress. She finds herself scanning the crowd for a particular pair—of all the images of a euphoric San Francisco celebrating in the wake of Newsom's order three years ago, this is the one imprinted indelibly in her mind: The first couple to be married, Del Martin and Phyllis Lyon, founders of America's first lesbian rights group fifty years earlier. In the photo, the then eighty-three- and seventy-nine-year-olds, dressed in lavender and turquoise suits, hold each other in their frail arms, their wrinkled foreheads touching, bashful as teenagers.

But there's no sign in the hall today of Del's unruly mop of silvery hair beside Phyllis's sedate gray-brown. Were they still alive? If so, they'd been together for close to fifty-five years, married for less than six months.

They have to skirt the crowd. Bill takes Seema by the hand, searching her face for signs of doubt. Seema has, in the three years they've been together, never shown any regret about the community she'd left behind. Fiaz is the only remaining connection she maintains to her queer past.

Their sex life, too, after that disastrous start in Iowa, has more than righted itself, with some patient instruction from Seema. There's no reason to fear himself inadequate or her unfulfilled, if that morning's frenzied lovemaking is anything to go by. She'd awakened charged and aroused, with a rapaciousness that had inflamed him too. They'd fucked feverishly, Bill crying out in long tremulous sobs as he came, the shock of his orgasm coursing through him. And then he'd pleasured her to a protracted climax, tongue and fingers flicking and stroking slowly, deliberately, the way she liked.

"Bill, slow down." Seema stumbles in her high heels. "I know we decided to dress like the day we met, but repeating the ER part is going too far." She has on the scarlet dress she'd worn for the anti–Iraq War march, and Bill his blue shirt and pigeon-gray slacks.

Bill stops in contrition, and she kisses him on the cheek, whispering, "Relax, I'm not going to pull a runaway bride."

But she's glad she'd insisted on everyday clothes for their party. She'd warned Fiaz and Pierre against wearing anything fancy or bringing any wedding accessories: bouquets, balloons. She'd have felt too awkward, too guilty. Now they could be at city hall on some trivial business.

Her mother called earlier that morning, when they were dressing for the ceremony. Ammi had asked, "Will you wear a saree today?"

"No, I don't even own one anymore."

"Do you remember—how you and Tahera fought over my wedding saree?"

How she'd coveted Ammi's wedding saree, with its elaborate vines and flowers of gold zarr covering every inch of the silk, a luscious dual-toned crimson-peach, unlike the more modest dark reds that brides in their family usually wore on their weddings. She'd badgered Ammi until she'd been promised that saree for her own wedding. Tahera had to be placated, of course, so she'd offered Tahera her first three choices among the other sarees Ammi was setting aside for them, in the bottom shelf of her almirah. All those sarees that Ammi kept adding to regularly each year of their girlhood—and all the jewelry, too, the gold necklaces, earrings, and bangles, that Abba periodically brought home to enchant his two daughters with—they must have all been used for Tahera's wedding.

But Ammi said, "I still have the saree. I saved it for you, for whenever you wanted it."

The heft of Ammi's gift, like the saree's weight which belied its delicate

Banarasi weave, settled like a rock in her heart. It was a more precious gift than she'd any right to expect. Ammi had accepted news of her impending marriage quietly, as if too grateful to ask questions. Since then, their conversations have become more frequent, almost weekly, though her mother still calls from outside the home, either from Halima Aunty's or from an ISD booth. Ammi's call today had been reassuring. She'd have been disappointed, even distressed, if Ammi hadn't.

"I'm just happy you called," she'd said. "Do you want to speak to Bill?"

Ammi first demurred but then asked to be put on the speakerphone. "I wish you both a long and happy married life." Then to Bill: "Please take care of my daughter."

And Bill took her hands in his and raised them to his lips as if for Ammi to see. "I will, Seema's mother."

I don't need anyone to take care of me, she'd wanted to object. But she was silenced by the memory of all those times she'd witnessed—with anguished longing—mothers enfolding their daughter's hands into the groom's with the same tear-strained phrase.

Now waiting in the ceremony room, a pang of bitterness: if only it had been possible for her to be seated here, decked in Ammi's saree, with her groom beside her, resplendent in a sherwani—why does the gender of the groom matter?—and flanked by her parents. She's suddenly reminded of Reshmi, Prince Salim to her Anarkali, the day of the play—the closest she has come to such a configuration. Wherever Reshmi is now she is surely married and probably already burdened with several kids.

In the confines of this small bare chamber she casts the other occupants— the brides in white, carrying bouquets of demure calla lilies—in a pallor. All light in the room is drawn to her. Her scarlet dress seems to swell and pulsate, a flame of a flower, more brilliant than mehndi on any bride's hands, more fierce than any red wedding saree she could drape herself in. The registrar's gaze keeps reverting to her, even as he officiates for the couple ahead, as if no eye can resist her, no will can ignore her. She can almost imagine that Bill's tight hold on one hand and Fiaz's arm threaded about her waist are both needed to keep her seated, to stop her from whirling around the room, the scarlet swirling and flaring, even as the marriage-equality rally outside cheers, still audible over the registrar's spiel—

Do you, Seema ...?

I do. *Qabool.*

16

When Seema is fifteen, she tapes the first telecast of the movie *Mughal-E-Azam* on the only channel—Doordarshan—then available on TV. My grandfather has just bought his first VCR and is excited to put it to the test, while his eldest daughter is excited to acquire her own copy of the movie. She'll finally be able to summon at her pleasure Anarkali, or rather the actress Madhubala who portrays Anarkali with such tragic glory.

For Seema, Madhubala rules the movie, as the dancing servant girl. "Why be afraid when I merely love?" Anarkali challenges Akbar—*Pyar kiya toh darna kya?*—when he orders her to forget Salim under threat of imprisonment and death. "I'm not veiling my love from the Lord, why then veil for mere mortals?" she sings, her skirts swirling, her eyes snapping. Madhubala's lissome figure whirls in the thousand mirrors of the Sheesh Mahal, her lips curling in a mocking smile as the emperor sits frozen, only jowls shaking in anger. The scene is one of the few shot in Technicolor in the otherwise black-and-white movie.

When the movie ends, Naeemullah says, "No one can ever match Madhubala. What beauty, what grace. There will be no one like her again." Madhubala died young, succumbing to a congenital hole in her heart that brought her soaring career to a halt.

Does my mother, at fifteen, question her fascination with the movie and its heroine? Consider the complications: there's the legend of Anarkali and the legend of Madhubala; there's her father's stamp of approval on both the movie and its heroine. How easy it is, then, to confuse desire for Anarkali with desire to be Anarkali, desire for Madhubala with desire to be Madhubala, to be Madhubala portraying Anarkali.

Some instinct warns her that she risks rebuke from her mother if she indulges further her preoccupation with Anarkali-Madhubala. To persuade her mother to permit further viewings of the movie, Seema announces a plan to write a play based on it, for her school's Annual Day celebrations. And, in a shrewd move, she disarms her family by inviting them to participate in the effort.

Naeemullah pronounces it a capital idea. Father and daughter watch parts of the movie many times—with Tahera crouched by the VCR, operating it at their command—translating as best they can the poetry of the movie from Urdu to English. But the Urdu they speak at home, the Dakkani dialect, cannot compare to the purity of the courtly Urdu spoken in the movie. Urdu, Naeemullah proclaims, must be the language of love's rituals: English, even under the Romantic poets, cannot match Urdu's intricacy and intimacy. "Ask your mother," he says.

By then Nafeesa has lost her fluency in chaste Urdu. Her initial translations are feeble and hesitant, so mother and daughter pour over a dusty Urdu-to-English dictionary they find in Naeemullah's library, a relic dating from Nafeesa's college years.

The play slowly takes root, sprouts, and flowers, tended to and watched over by the entire Hussein family. *Anarkali* is pomegranate blossom.

When the play is done, and typed up by Naeemullah, with carbon copies for good measure, Seema and Tahera succeed in cajoling their parents into staging a reading at home. There's no need to discuss roles—Seema will obviously be Anarkali, Naeemullah is Akbar, Nafeesa is the queen mother Jodha Bai, trapped between loyalty to her husband and love for her son, and Tahera gets to play Salim and other minor characters.

The evening begins lightheartedly, with laughter and fits of giggling, none of them, not even Naeemullah, able to keep a straight face at first. The dialogue, dramatic in Urdu, appears overly florid in English. But as they respond to Naeemullah's coaching, something surprising happens.

"Say it like this," Naeemullah urges, lending nimble voice to the words, transforming himself from a fiery Akbar to a dulcet Jodha Bai, from an unwavering Prince Salim to a passionate Anarkali, and the words no longer seem extravagant. His wife and daughters are forced to concede the truth in his tales of excelling in amateur theater during his years of medical college. His zeal rubs off on them. Laughter is forgotten.

Seema herself is an ecstatic Anarkali.

"Not the rose, but its thorns—" she exclaims, in something approaching rapture. "Yet I do not fear the pain, for my love cannot wither."

The next step is to convince Sister Agnes, her eleventh-standard class teacher and English teacher for three years, to agree to produce the play for the school Annual Day. But after reading the typed manuscript, Sister Agnes says, "This is beautifully written, very poetic, Seema. But it's not appropriate for a class play."

Seema has thought of herself as Sister Agnes's favorite student. Two years earlier, Sister Agnes cast Seema in the lead role of Portia in a twenty-minute adaptation of *The Merchant of Venice*, a privilege that should have gone to some girl in the eleventh standard.

But Seema holds a trump card: next year she'll be in the twelfth standard and can't participate in the Annual Day play since she'll be preparing for her final public exams. She says, in her most wistful voice, "Sister, this is the last play I can take part in for Annual Day."

Her voice quavers with a quiet distress, perfected under her father's training. But to her surprise, her throat actually catches and her eyes prickle. This will be her last year with Sister Agnes; next year, she'll have the headmistress as her English teacher. Sister Agnes has been her champion these many years, and her merry eyes, wimpled face, and the long steeple-shaped mole by her upper lip have been a source of almost daily communion. The loss signals many forthcoming changes.

She sniffles and turns away from Sister Agnes, who catches her hand and says, "Come, child, don't cry. What's there to cry about?"

Seema's face is glassy-eyed and trembling. For a fleeting moment she unconsciously mirrors Anarkali-Madhubala, her eyes pooling with unshed tears, tragically brave and lovely.

Who can resist that look? Sister Agnes's eyes moisten in their turn. She promises to reconsider and later returns the manuscript with a few changes and cuts.

Soon the rehearsals start. The parts have been cast. Seema is Anarkali, of course. Akbar is to be played by Madhavi, an eleventh grader from a different section, with her shot-putter's build and strapping voice and the beginnings of a mustache. Plump, voluble Preethi is the queen mother, Jodha Bai.

As for Prince Salim: Who better to play that part than Seema's best friend, Reshmi, lanky, reserved Reshmi, taller than anyone else in class, fleet flat-chested Reshmi, faster than any other girl in school, her face angular, ascetic, noble, with knife-edge cheekbones, her hair so soft and weightless it appears molded to her skull, her voice—

It's a voice that Naeemullah has wished for his daughters! It's a voice trained in the Hindustani vocal tradition, robust yet agile, capable of both sonorous lows and ringing highs. It's a voice Seema never tires of hearing, that sends Seema's heart tripping, especially when it's inflected with the giddiness that is reserved for her alone.

Seema has given this voice only a few lines in her play. But there are benefits to this—what else does Reshmi have to do now while Anarkali spars with Akbar but hold her hand? Reshmi has little to do but gaze into Anarkali's eyes while Anarkali recites couplets of love. When soldiers are ordered to seize a vocal, unrepentant Anarkali, they first have to tear her away from Reshmi's arms. It's as if Seema, though herself prepared to play the part of the doomed Anarkali, would rather Reshmi play no other part than herself.

The next year my mother will finish her higher-secondary schooling and will leave for Bangalore to do her bachelor's in English at St. Joseph's College. She'll have chosen a college in a different city so she can stay away from home. Three years later she will leave for even farther away, to Oxford, England, for a master's. And from there to New York, abandoned by her family and leaving her first lover behind, for a fellowship at Columbia University in communication. She'll jump at the chance of staying in the United States a year later, accepting a fortuitous offer of a marketing job in a Silicon Valley just beginning to bubble up then, midnineties, excited and anxious to leave her past completely behind, seeking once again a new beginning.

17

The newlyweds have agreed that Seema should quit her current job and work for the Obama campaign. Bill will continue at the health insurance company he'd joined and will maintain their finances and benefits while volunteering on the side, at least until the fortunes of the campaign became more apparent.

Seema hopes that the contacts she made while volunteering for Dean will give her an in and lead to a job handling public relations or new media for the campaign. She writes to everyone she knows, and many promise to pass on her inquiries. She waits to hear back, spending spring and summer 2007 holding house parties and fundraisers, like she did for Dean.

Obama is the underdog in the battle for the Democratic nomination. He's deployed to crisscross the nation, speaking wherever he can, whipping up visibility and enthusiasm, his speeches at turns funny, self-deprecating, earnest, moving, inspiring, galvanizing. He's always charming and effortlessly likable. Obama fever catches on and spreads like wildfire through the progressive corners of the country.

But as summer advances, Seema has yet to hear back about a job. She complains that the campaign is closed off and unapproachable.

Bill consoles her: Obama must be flooded with applications from more experienced professionals.

Seema has other suspicions. The inner circle of staff Obama has hired is very White.

She'd been accepted by the Dean campaign, Bill scoffs, which was as White, if not more. Obama must hire the best if he's to have any chance of victory. Isn't she aware of the political landscape?

"But Obama is Black. And he's supposed to be different."

"He hasn't even started, for God's sake. Give him a chance."

This is the first argument in some time that Bill is unwilling to end, let alone concede, even when Seema throws up her hands together as if in prayer—a gesture that Bill usually uses to give in when Seema gets very heated, picked up for its absurdity from watching the occasional Indian movie.

Thankfully, there's soon news that there are to be camps to recruit and train volunteers to create field organizations in each state. They attend Camp Obama in San Francisco, led by a team of experienced organizers, including a professor from Harvard, over a weekend of communion with other like-minded activists. Bill and Seema are assigned to a leadership team for their congressional district, tasked with recruiting more volunteers and building capacity for voter registration, phone banking, canvassing, and getting out the vote in the California primary that February, less than six months away. Bill is to be their team coordinator, and Seema will be in charge of volunteer recruitment.

Raring to get started after a summer of passivity, Seema immediately hands in her resignation at her firm and embarks upon a grueling schedule of recruitment meetings wherever she can hold them, in cafés, in libraries and bookshops, in bars, in community spaces.

She has rehearsed her *story of the self,* taking naturally to the technique the Obama camp has promoted as a means to convey personal values and build connections to potential volunteers and voters, by appealing to emotion through the story of her life and why she feels called to volunteer. She declaims about being a Hussein in America, a Muslim, an object of suspicion and derision, an outsider who has to prove herself loyal all the time. A win for Obama—the skinny kid with a funny name, with a Hussein in it as well!— would mean there is a place for her, and every outsider like her, in America. Her story resonates among the immigrants and the new arrivals to San Francisco, appeals to its liberal and progressive base.

She has also begun conducting her own training sessions. Word spreads, and she's quickly in demand, invited to coach new volunteers all over the Bay Area. Between her frequent trips crisscrossing the bay and Bill's day job and evenings spent coordinating the team's activities, they sometimes see each other only in passing during the week, or at team meetings.

Meanwhile, the roller coaster that is the primary season starts. To Seema's great relief, Obama opens the year with an upset, besting Hillary Clinton in the Iowa caucus, astounding America—she'd feared he'd be snuffed out like Dean in the white winter of Iowa. But he promptly loses in New Hampshire and Nevada, only regaining momentum by trouncing Clinton in South Carolina, with only days left to the California primary.

The approaching Super Tuesday takes on the frenzied excitement of a dream. The nation is at fever pitch: more than twenty states will be voting in a few days, perhaps determining the presidential nominees of both parties. Obama and Clinton, and their surrogates, jet around the country holding huge rallies to energize their bases. *Yes we can!* has become the rallying cry of the Obama supporters: "When we've been told we're not ready or that we shouldn't try or that we can't, generations of Americans have responded with a simple creed that sums up the spirit of a people: Yes, we can," Obama had declared in a speech to motivate his supporters after losing the New Hampshire primary. "It was a creed written into the founding documents that declared the destiny of a nation: Yes, we can." This has gone viral; a black-and-white music video featuring clips of this speech has become an internet sensation, Obama's words echoed, repeated, and riffed on by celebrity singers, both Black and White.

Yes we can! Heads down, their team shifts from organizing and building capacity to getting out the vote to capitalize on the late surge of support for Obama after the South Carolina victory. Come Super Tuesday, Seema casts her vote for Obama with a sense of accomplishment—it's the first vote of her life: she'd been too young to vote while in India and had naturalized only the year before in the United States.

But the results turn out mixed. Their work pays off in San Francisco, which Obama carries comfortably, but Clinton still wins California. Nationwide, wins are offset by other losses.

Still, the Obama campaign claims victory: they've picked up more delegates than Clinton, establishing their lead, and they've managed to disrupt the media narrative of Clinton's inevitability. The media declares Obama the front-runner. The San Francisco teams celebrate, having helped limit Clinton's haul of California delegates. But at the after-party, Seema is unable to join in wholeheartedly: she'd have preferred the vindication conferred by an outright win. Despite Bill's reassurances, she cannot shake off the feeling of being let down, as on that dismal evening in Iowa four years ago.

She's beginning to fret that the campaign is not doing enough to refute the conspiracy theories intensifying on the internet: that Obama is Kenyan and not eligible to be president; he's a secret Muslim, a member of the Nation of Islam; his real father is Malcolm X; he considers himself the Black messiah; he's a socialist, dedicated to expanding the welfare state and adding to entitlements to enrich his people; he's an unqualified affirmative-action candidate. With its own nominee anointed—John McCain—the Right has begun its offensive to discredit the likely Democratic candidate. The allegations first crop up in minor right-wing sites and then are amplified in the echo chambers of conservative media. Some rumors are even given credibility by desperate Clinton supporters.

"We're not taking the threat seriously," Seema fumes. "We need to have a rapid-response media team to kill the rumors before they start spreading. Has it occurred to the campaign this is why Obama is unable to clinch the nomination?"

But Bill is dismissive, heartened by the campaign's recent gains: "No one really believes this junk."

"Oh, so you're the communications expert. People are capable of believing anything, if it's repeated often enough."

She spends a few weeks appealing to her campaign contacts to refer her for a job on the PR team. Her efforts again go nowhere, this time purportedly because she's too valuable as a trainer: they would like her to continue training volunteers in states they haven't started actively organizing in yet. Reluctantly Seema gives in and packs her bags for Pittsburgh, for the Pennsylvania primary in April.

18

It's a gray wintry March in Pennsylvania. TV channels are saturated with videos of Reverend Wright, Obama's Black pastor from Chicago, railing against America and Obama's opponents: *Not God bless America, but God damn America!* and *We have supported state terrorism against Palestinians—America's chickens are coming home to roost!* and *Hillary has never had a people defined as a non-person!* The right wing chants: Obama hates America, Obama is an Angry Black Man.

When not conducting training sessions, Seema drives to half-shuttered malls and neglected downtowns around Pittsburgh to register voters and check out for herself the effects of the uproar. Tensions rise perceptibly wherever she shows up with her Obama affiliation visible. Pedestrians stare with hostility, brusquely turning down her overtures. After trips to the restroom, she finds her table messed up, forms missing, placards torn up, with nobody having witnessed the vandalism. Posters circulating on the internet one day appear the next day on lampposts and shop fronts: Obama with his arm around Reverend Wright—*The Audacity of Hate*. Obama in an Arab headdress—*Anti-Semite*. Obama with horns and pitchfork—*Anti-Christ*.

"See what I said?" Seema rants to Bill. "They've no trouble believing Obama is a radical Black Christian and an Islamic jihadist at the same time. They can even believe he's a Muslim pretending to be a Christian so he can win. They call it 'taqiyya'—read up about it."

Obama is to address the nation the next day, in what is publicized as his first major speech on race, to try to stem the slide in the polls resulting from his relationship with Reverend Wright. The Pittsburgh office, Seema included, gathers that morning to watch the live broadcast. Speaking at a hastily arranged assembly at the National Constitution Center in Philadelphia, against a backdrop of American flags, Obama begins by reciting the opening words of the Constitution, across the street from where it was drafted and signed.

The room that starts out tense, anxious—this speech could decide the campaign's fate—is left teary-eyed, inspired. Reverend Wright is correct that the union is not perfect yet, but he is wrong that there has been no progress, that America cannot change. This campaign—the campaign of the son of a Black man from Kenya and a White woman from Kansas, building a powerful coalition of African Americans and White Americans—is proof of that. One of the organizers in the room, the youngest, openly sobs: Obama cites her story as reason for further hope in the next generation—a young White woman, who'd battled childhood poverty when her mother got sick and lost healthcare, now organizing in Black communities, seeking out allies in her fight against injustice. This is how the union grows stronger, toward perfection.

Obama is confident and authoritative, but prosaic and detached, and determined to be evenhanded: yes, Black people have been wronged in the past and continue to be wronged, but White people have their legitimate grievances too, and both sides must work together to heal the racial divide.

"Did you hear that?" Bill texts Seema even before Obama is done speaking. "This is why he deserves to be president."

Seema agrees that the speech is masterly. Obama has delivered as they'd hoped and prayed: almost immediately the media hails it as one of the most profound speeches on race since King's "I Have a Dream." What she doesn't admit to Bill is that she feels somehow disappointed, even disquieted.

For even as she accepts that it was perhaps the only strategy Obama could have adopted to blunt the Wright controversy, she can't help but wish that Obama had shown some emotion, some anger, while speaking about the wrongs suffered by his people. What if the Obama who'd given the speech today is the real Obama—passionate perhaps, but not angry, as Bill maintains, and therefore unprepared to fight back as a partisan, as would be needed, perhaps even reluctant to appear as one? What if Obama were not the fiery crusader she'd convinced herself of, but merely a cautious technocrat who prided himself on being perceived as objective, impartial, methodical? He'd promised progress as a gradual evolution for the benefit of some future generation.

In the workshops she conducts over the next days, she finds herself curiously disengaged. She's listless, too, in her interactions with her colleagues and companions. She continues to canvass and register voters but no longer outside the city. She manages to score a seat onstage with Obama for the kickoff rally on his Pennsylvania tour, to Bill's envy, but instead of excitement—this is maybe the closest she'll ever get to Obama!—all she feels is a nameless dread, as if awaiting further disillusionment.

Long lines snake outside the stately facade of the Soldiers and Sailors Memorial before the rally, despite the drizzle and gray chill of that morning. The hall is packed, center and sides, mostly students from the two neighboring universities. Mostly young, and White, and earnest but clueless, Seema thinks. She is seated with the audience onstage, on tiered risers arranged behind the lectern, in the third row. In the row in front of her sits a trio of enthusiastic older Black women, eager for Obama to appear on stage. Above her, a banner in red, white, and blue: *Change We Can Believe In.*

During the introduction, Obama stands with his arms crossed and his head bowed pensively, as if oblivious to the extravagant praise the Democratic senator from Pennsylvania uses to endorse him: the promise of the nation. What could be tracking through Obama's mind as he listens? So too would her father hold himself, to hide his gratification, at the events he'd been invited to preside over. Obama's stance of modesty vanishes as soon as he gains the lectern and launches into his speech. The transformation to an easy charm and affable authority is immediate, and familiar—she's struck again by the similarities to her father. Her senses quicken, as if alive to his slightest movement, even to the expressions on his face, though only imagined, since she's presented only his back and profile as he speaks.

But what had she hoped for in coming today? This is no more than Obama's stump speech: the invocation of Dr. King, a laundry list of the nation's problems, inspiring stories of individuals achieving their goals despite all odds, a laundry list of proposed solutions and campaign promises, ending with the appeal to hope. Obama has continued to tweak the speech—addressing issues of the day, interjecting humorous asides, sharpening well-received lines—but many passages remain unchanged. She can repeat these word for word, as if she'd memorized them for some elocution competition.

The crowd, too, must have heard some version of the speech before, though it appears not to care. It cheers frenetically at all the appropriate places, rising frequently in standing ovation. Being on stage, Seema feels pressured to rise with the others. She submits, but more and more reluctantly as the speech progresses, for even the delivery is disappointing: Obama is less fluent today, tentative at times, fumbling for words at others, defensive in the face of polls showing him trailing Clinton in Pennsylvania. He struggles to hit the highs of some of his previous speeches, his usual assurance flagging. His promises sound hollow to her ears today, for even he doesn't seem to believe them. She can imagine her father shaking his head, tut-tutting, as during one of their elocution practice sessions. If she'd come hoping for renewal, reinvigoration, she's not going to find it here.

Bill would have given anything to be here. She feels guilty for paying so little regard to Obama, mere feet away, while she is wrapped up in herself, only aware of the thunderous moments of applause, automatically joining in with the rest, standing up and sitting down in ritualized unison, like the times she'd prayed namaz in Chennai, usually during Eid, forced to by Halima Aunty—

They'd pray together, the womenfolk at home, the two girls, she and Tahera, and the two women, Halima Aunty and her mother, while their men were away at the mosque for the Eid namaz. She'd protest: Why isn't she allowed into the mosque? Why pray to a god that denies the world to her?

She could resist Ammi's bidding but not Halima Aunty's cajoling. She'd go through the prayers impatiently, mindlessly following Halima Aunty, standing up, sitting down, and then she'd wait for the men to return, restless, for everything pleasurable about Eid came afterward—Ammi's biryani, the visits of friends and relatives, the sweets, the gift of eidi that supplemented her pocket money, the chance to model her new Eid clothes. She hasn't celebrated Eid in almost two decades. The last time was before she went to England, before everything went wrong.

Obama finishes his speech to prolonged applause. He turns to shake hands with the people behind him on the risers. From Seema's vantage point, he seems less commanding now than when his face fills the TV screen. His handshakes are perfunctory—he is tired, only flitting a smile to a Black woman behind him, in response to the woman's beaming face. But that doesn't stop the thicket of hands thrust out toward him—hands thrust out as if seeking sanctification, a blessing.

Simultaneously, a recollection: At the airport in Chennai, preparing to board the flight to London that first time, they'd all come to see her off—Tahera sobbing uncontrollably, Halima Aunty consoling her, her mother discreetly wiping her eyes with her pallu, even her father cloaking distress in an exuberance of speech and laughter.

She's checked her luggage, and stands with them one last time, clutching her passport tightly like a talisman. As she turns to pass through immigration and finally onward to the long-awaited boarding gate, something unexpected comes over her.

For this is the other part of Eid she used to chafe against, when all the waiting womenfolk, including her mother, in the custom of touching their el-ders' feet on special occasions, bend down to touch her father's feet and receive his blessings, a gesture of almost veneration, which Tahera waited for eagerly every time, throwing herself at Abba's feet as soon as he returned from the mosque, and which Seema dreaded. But some obscure instinct prompts her to avail herself of that gesture now, to stoop before Abba in the airport, till her fingers and passport lightly brush his shoes. Bowed in front of him, his looming figure casting a shadow over her, she holds her breath until he gives his blessing: Jeeti raho, Beti. He raises her to standing, kissing her forehead, whispering: I know you'll make me proud.

His voice cracks, that one time, despite his efforts to control himself, and sudden relief, grief, gratitude washes through her.

Then, a recognition: She doesn't need to add to all the worshipful hands held out to Obama. Obama himself has little power to grant anything—he is here after all to seek the blessing of the White people in the crowd, a blessing that would be given only conditionally, like her father's, to be revoked any time they were displeased with him, as he himself knows well from the deference he gave them in his speech on race.

Yes, Obama could win the nomination, and perhaps even the election, but what would that change? Obama claims hope, but there is always a reality that won't budge.

Change you can believe in. What if you didn't—couldn't—believe in change? Change as something that took you someplace new, and lasting, not something that brought you back to where you've already been: three conti-nents, three countries, six cities, multiple homes, myriad loves, the ceaseless struggle, but still the same inescapable tragedy of her self: still seeking ap-proval, still seeking some way to make her father proud of her again.

19

My mother Seema as a thirteen-year-old: Sitting up in the gulmohar tree in their compound in Chennai, hiding from the world amid its fiery blossoms.

It's a Saturday, the month is July, the tree is on fire, the canopy of green bip-innate leaves overshadowed by a blaze of scarlet flames. Not for nothing is the tree also called the Flame of the Forest. Seema hides here, cradled in a nook the tree has carved out for her, her back against the trunk, legs supported on branches running fused together before they separate and disappear into the kaleidoscope of red and yellow, green and brown.

She reaches to pluck the largest unopened bud from the cluster hanging beside her head, she runs a fingernail along the pale yellow ridges of the calyx, she peels the still clinging sepals to reveal the petals—the outermost, large and white and blotched with red and yellow, and curled up inside it are the others, red and wrinkled like a baby's fingers. Within them, the coiled stamens—the filaments, curved necks so fragile it is a wonder they can support the weight of the heads, the anthers mossed with soft golden-yellow pollen. And somewhere, oh here it is, is the pistil—a hairy ovule, and a long and slender style, so completely unremarkable.

She dissects the bud and chews each detached part methodically before swallowing.

Who's she hiding from?

First, her mother. Seema knows she'll be reprimanded if Nafeesa catches her up in the tree. She's on her fifth-ever menstrual period, which arrived unexpectedly today, two months after the last one, bloodier and stronger than any previous time, so unstanchable that Seema had been scared. She'd spent the morning locked up with her mother, sobbing in her lap, drenching Nafeesa's saree with her tears.

Never had she felt so betrayed by her body before, not even that first time. Now a few hours later, secured with a pad, flouting her mother's admonitions to remain in bed, she's perched high in the gulmohar tree, chewing on crimped buds. Their pungent tartness is addictive and satisfying.

Next, she's hiding from her sister, who had stood outside their parents' room bawling as though it were her body bleeding. Tahera had pounded on the door, begging to be let in, then continued banging her head against wood until their mother opened the door. She'd refused to be sent away, lying on the floor clutching at Nafeesa's ankles, screaming as their father finally managed to lead her away: "Is she going to die? Let me go, let me go to Seema."

And last, Seema is hiding from her father.

Previously whenever Naeemullah has tended to her, it's her father she's always seen, his loving eyes, his soothing voice, not the trained professional who held office in his clinic downstairs. And always in her own room. But today, for the first time, she was summoned to his consulting room.

When she knocks, he tells her to take a seat in the tone he uses with his patients, public, practiced. She'd wanted him to hold her, to comfort her, to kiss her forehead. Instead, she has to sit down across from him, in a chair his patients use, her hands in her lap, waiting for him to look up from a book.

After a long minute, he says, eyes still on the book, "Your mother tells me you're suffering from some disorder."

It's that word *disorder* that gets to her, before anything else. Is it a disorder what's happening to her? Is she somehow abnormal? He's talking about the human body—her body—and tripping effortlessly from his lips are words, only some she's learned in biology: *ovary, uterus, uterine wall, placenta, endometrium, menarche, menorrhagia, dysmenorrhea*. He reads aloud passages from the book, explaining as he goes along, in his familiar lecturing manner that has until today been thrilling.

"Do you understand?" he asks.

No, she does not understand.

"I want it to stop," Seema cries. "Make it go away."

She wants to be told that nothing has changed, that she's still his daughter, that she's still the same person she was before, that they will continue on as they've always done, father and daughter, friends, confidants.

"It may just be temporary. It may correct itself eventually. It can always be contained," her father says. He continues reading to her from the book, elaborating on tests, procedures, treatments. Does she understand?

What she understands is that her body isn't hers anymore. She doesn't control it, it controls her. What she understands is that, overwhelmed by her disorder, her father has chosen to hide his paternal self behind his clinical self. In his voice she senses doctorly frustration masking fatherly disappointment, even distaste. She has become a problem to be fixed. What she begins to understand is that they are on different sides of a fissure that will only grow wider.

Her father closes the book and sets it aside. "Come. Your mother will be waiting for us. Lunch will be getting cold."

She doesn't want lunch. Her mother urges her to eat something but lets her go to her room.

Instead, Seema slips back downstairs and into the garden and climbs up the gulmohar tree, her pad an inconvenience to be ignored. She doesn't stop at her usual perch but continues climbing farther. She is determined to climb higher than ever before, determined to ignore the ache in her limbs, but she is forced to stop when the cramps in her abdomen become unbearable. But, although she hasn't beaten her own record, she has managed to get far enough up that she's completely hidden from view, tucked away in a fork in the trunk, cloaked by scarlet blossoms.

As she plucks petals and drops them one by one, as she plucks buds to dissect and consume, she promises herself for the first time what she'll later promise herself over and over again, in clearer and more direct terms: not to let her body decide for her what she should do, not to let her life be dictated by forces she doesn't understand or accept.

20

The evening Obama clinches the Democratic nomination, Bill picks up Indian takeout on his way home and sets to chill a bottle of champagne he's splurged on—vintage 2004, the year he and Seema started dating, the year Obama came into their lives. They're preparing to watch the broadcast of Obama's speech kicking off the general election campaign against Republican nominee John McCain.

Seema has been withdrawn ever since her return, retiring early each night, pleading jet lag and later continued exhaustion, rejecting his advances for company, intimacy. She'd become tight-lipped over the phone the last many weeks away—the tense, unexpectedly long primary season must have taken its toll—but he hopes that tonight's celebration will serve to reinvigorate her.

Barack and Michelle Obama come onstage holding hands. They wave at the crowd, its blue sea of *Change* placards. Bill waves back, lump in throat. Before Michelle leaves, she and Obama bump fists, Michelle initiating, which Bill finds strangely moving. He turns to Seema in imitation, his fist out, but Seema hasn't been paying attention to the unfolding scene, lost in some abstraction. When she eventually responds, the gesture feels forced.

He has experienced enough of Seema's periods of withdrawal to know there's little he can do but wait them out. His elation dulled, he listens to the speech distracted and irritated by Seema's inattention. Obama thanks his grandmother, and an intense yearning for Mame sweeps through Bill. If only she were by his side tonight—his lips tremble, his eyes prick with the prelude to tears, but he's stalled by Seema's apparent disinterest. He even sees her rolling her eyes at some of Obama's more obvious rhetorical flourishes.

When the speech is over, Bill picks up the champagne bottle. The cork pops with an anticlimactic whimper, the champagne fizzing onto the carpet, an acrid smell of mown grass. Seema hurries toward him with wineglasses.

They toast: "To the next president of the United States." They clink glasses, they kiss.

But it's not the evening Bill had hoped for. The one consolation: Obama and Michelle are immediately surrounded by a posse of close-cut rugged men in black suits that follow them as they mingle with the crowd—at last the secret service, prominently protective.

Seema reheats the takeout, and they sit down to dinner, the pungent spices of bhuna ghosht and achaar chicken washed down with the champagne. She's preoccupied, even as she inquires about the day's events.

They'd decided last year that if Obama won the nomination Bill would take a leave of absence, or quit if he couldn't, and they'd volunteer together in some swing state, like Florida or Ohio, for the general election. Now that the moment has arrived, Bill has to admit to some misgivings about quitting his job: he's never taken such risks before. Mame, if she were alive, would surely declare it irresponsible.

Midbite, as if Seema had been about to broach the topic herself, she says, "Bill, I've been offered a director post at my old job."

Her news, though startling, doesn't surprise him. "How come you didn't tell me about this before?"

"I'm telling you now. I start on Monday."

This confirmation of Seema's failing commitment, after the evening's apathy, is beyond vexing. "So I have to go to Florida or Ohio by myself. You're bailing on me."

"I'm exhausted, Bill," Seema says.

"But not too exhausted to take on a new job. Something's changed—Seema, what is it?"

She flares up. "Well, if you really want to know—I've lost faith in your candidate."

He sighs wearily: shoring up her confidence in the campaign has been the substance of their interactions the last couple of months.

"The state supreme court has struck down Prop 22, reaffirming marriage as a basic civil right, and what does Obama have to say?" She proceeds to imitate Obama, contorting her face into a look of sincerity and concern: "I respect the decision of the California Supreme Court and continue to believe that states should make their own decisions when it comes to the issue of marriage." Her mimicry is atrocious—her Obama sounds upper-class British—but she has got Obama's inflections and pauses right, though exaggerated to prissiness.

The court's judgment was handed down three weeks ago in mid-May, before her return, and she hadn't mentioned the matter till now. Had she been tracking the case? But, of course, with San Francisco getting ready again for gay marriages, she would have learned soon enough anyway. "Obama supports civil unions," he replies lamely.

"*You* know this—separate is not equal."

"Clinton's no better. At least Obama has made it clear he's against constitutional amendments."

"Clinton is a career politician. But Obama—couldn't he have at least acknowledged how important the ruling is?"

"If he says anything more, it will only become a distraction. Republicans will use it to increase evangelical turnout in November."

"So, equality is only a distraction? Overturning antimiscegenation laws was only a distraction?"

The dinner forgotten, the argument escalates so swiftly that Bill is blindsided. How could he suggest that gay marriages and interracial marriages are not exactly equivalent? She flings quotes at him from landmark Supreme Court decisions—*Sharp v. Perez, Loving v. Virginia*—she's evidently read up on them. She accuses Obama of hypocrisy and expediency: "He wouldn't even be here today if it had been illegal in his state for his parents to marry."

When he defends Obama's stance as pragmatic, she tears into Obama with a fury he's never seen before, in all their quarrels of four years or all her tirades against Bush and Cheney and America. Obama, too, is a lying politician. A conservative in progressive clothing. A White man in a Black body. Obama would betray everyone hoping for change. Consider the way he threw his Black pastor under the bus. Consider all the money he's accepting from the rich. Consider the inner circle of White staff and advisors he's surrounded himself with. Obama is too beholden to his White supporters to risk angering them. Obama is too infatuated with his image of uniter to fight for his people. Obama is too cowardly to force big changes. Obama is a smoke screen erected by the rich and privileged to maintain the status quo. Obama is a con man peddling empty hope to the rest.

It's a fury Bill has never experienced before. He's dumbfounded, as he watches Seema, a stranger now, her voice and features and form almost unrecognizable. He can do nothing but let her rave, the tumult within him pinning him to his chair, as he swills down the bitter champagne to fill some hole that's opened up in him.

He feels anger at her words, of course, but it's buried under everything else churning through him. There's shock at witnessing a side of Seema he's never seen before. There's bafflement at the cause for its emergence now. There's hope that Seema doesn't mean what she's saying. There's fear that she does. There's anguish that this could be the beginning of the end of everything between them.

She's spent as suddenly as she'd erupted. "So you've nothing to say?"

"We made a promise," he says. "Now this gay marriage issue has become more important to you than getting Obama elected—"

He picks at the congealed meat on his plate. He can feel the sting of her eyes on him. His heart thuds as she pushes her chair back, picks up her plate, and dumps it in the sink before leaving the dining room.

He tracks her up the stairs to their bedroom and down the stairs again to the garage; the garage door grinds open, the car throbs out. He clears the table while drinking the remaining champagne directly from the bottle. As always, her presence continues to vibrate in the air, an aroused agitated thrumming this time.

Yet he prefers that to the dull heartache of her absence in the house. He knows he should be angry with her for ruining this night. But all he feels is the relief of resignation. His guilt from earlier about quitting his job is over-run by the conviction that were he to leave for Florida or Ohio by himself, for another sustained period of separation, Seema would certainly be lost to him. He sleeps fitfully in an alcohol-induced lifelessness—their king bed is a vast desolate feathertop—only vaguely aware that Seema hasn't returned yet even as the hours stretch toward dawn.

He wakes to a pounding headache and the dream sound of rain. It's seven in the morning; Seema is in the shower. Her side of the bed is not slept in. "Did you just get in?"

"I slept on the sofa downstairs. I needed some space. I'm sorry I ruined last night for you. But we can't go on pretending like my life before you didn't exist. Like I've nothing at stake in this election."

He doesn't ask her where she was or whom she'd been with. He's too glad she's willing to discuss the previous night to hold it against her too long. He admits that Obama's stand on gay marriage is at the very least politically cal-culated. She accepts that her allegations against Obama are otherwise (mostly) baseless. She promises she will take some time before the election to volunteer elsewhere, since it would be unprofessional to un-accept her directorship now; he surmises there'll be enough for them to do for the general election in adja-cent Nevada. They both agree to forgive and forget.

But Bill cannot completely forget all that has been awakened: the anxi-eties and insecurities of their early days together; the memory of her at dinner, raging, a woman possessed.

21

A few Sundays later, end of June, Seema is at the San Francisco Pride parade with Fiaz. This year's parade is to be a celebration of the recent court victory and the marriages that have resumed since then; for the second time, Del Martin and Phyllis Lyon were the first couple to be (re-)married, and Seema hopes to see them ride in the parade today—probably her last and only chance, for Del is in her late eighties now and wheelchair bound.

Seema is here at Fiaz's pleading. Fiaz has been despondent lately, he and Pierre caught up in constant arguments. "I didn't say anything about getting married," he complains, as he and Seema wait under the rainbow flags of Market Street for the parade to start. "I only wanted us to march together in this year's parade. But—"

He quotes Pierre morosely, mimicking his scholarly tone and French accent perfectly, as if he has internalized Pierre's comments: "Parades and marriages are products of authoritarianism. I'd rather be at Mack Folsom Prison, hooded and handcuffed, partaking of homosexual delights, than marching with assimilationists and exhibitionists and look-but-don't-touch queens."

Pierre has taken off somewhere, and while Fiaz can't face the repeated questioning were he to march with his South Asian friends in Trikone—"Why didn't you bring your partner? Are you still with that French professor? Why aren't you getting married?"—he's determined to at least watch the parade.

The theme for the year is "United by Pride, Bound for Equality." Kicking off the parade are the usual Dykes on Bikes. The crowd goes delirious as dyke couples blast down Market Street on motorbikes. Today, in addition to their usual black leather or blue denim, some are attired in whites and pinks, wedding dresses straddling the gleam of their bikes, veils snapping behind them in the wind; others are suited and gowned; and yet others ride as everyday brides holding *Just Married* signs in their newlywed hands.

This is Seema's first time attending Pride in a decade. She'd grown blasé about it, limiting herself to the Dyke March, held the evening before on Pride weekend; for the last several years, with Bill, she's not even been aware when Pride came around. She feels a little like an imposter today: Does she even deserve to be here? She claps her hands to her ears against the deafening din, but the euphoria shocking the air is irresistible, the crowds larger and more exuberant than she's experienced in the past. Even Fiaz, mournful a minute ago, joins in, bouncing up and down, dragging her with him, easily overcoming her token protest.

"Any desi dykes on the bikes?" She strains to get a good view through the thronging crowd. "Any dressed like a desi bride?"

"I can't see any—" Fiaz scrambles up a lamppost base. "Anyway, it'll only be the boys dressed as brides, not the dykes. You'll see them on the Trikone float, dolled up in sarees and ghagra-cholis."

Next are the bicyclists, the AIDS Life Cycle riders, and then an outpouring of color: a surge of rainbow balloons flooding the street, as if to wash it of any lingering staidness, any straightness, and carried in by it, a swarm of multicolored anemones and jellyfish, tendrils ballooned and tethered to beautiful men and women gyrating in skimpy underwear. Bare flesh flashes, and thongs and bikinis and star-spangled breasts bob and jiggle, amid twirling streams of red, orange, yellow, green, blue, violet. The very light shimmies, shimmers.

"My eyes are getting drunk," Fiaz says.

The Pride theme float that follows is a giant wedding cake, and behind it are the various agencies and individuals instrumental in overturning Prop 22, all met with lusty thank-yous and applause. Signs of *Vote No On Prop 8* are also being toted—Proposition 8 being the Right's redoing of the overturned Proposition 22, a constitutional amendment to force a ban on same-sex marriage that it successfully added to the ballot for the upcoming November election. But the crowd doesn't let that diminish its enthusiasm. Mayor Newsom, White and straight and well coiffed, cruises by in an open-topped jeep in an open-collared white shirt, accompanied by his fiancée, and receives a homecoming hero's welcome. Seema had considered Newsom's defiance of Prop 22 a self-serving political stunt four years ago, but who is she to still argue that, in the face of this positive outcome?

"You cut social services for AIDS patients and the homeless," some voice screams at Newsom, though nobody seems to pay it any attention.

Bringing up the rear are newly married gay and lesbian couples walking hand in hand, almost sedately, the very picture of normalcy, escorting the plaintiff couples in the case against Prop 22, whom Seema has been waiting for. They ride in roofless cars decorated as wedding getaway vehicles trailing cans and streamers, waving and blowing kisses at the cheering crowd. Seema searches among them, nudging through the throng.

But no Del and Phyllis, no lavender and turquoise of their wedding suits, no wheelchair and companion. The morning's exhilaration ebbs as swiftly as it had swollen.

"Fiaz, I want to go," she says. "I'm getting a headache."

Fiaz is still hanging off the lamppost, watching intently a young man in a rainbow leotard, who'd clambered over the security fence and is running to each car, kissing each seated couple in turn and posing for selfies with them, evading the parade monitors chasing after him.

Fiaz has not heard her, and she drags him down from his perch by his jacket sleeve. "Stop drooling at the boy. He's too young for you."

"I was not drooling." Fiaz straightens his jacket with exaggerated dignity. "Not that there's anything wrong with drooling. If Pierre only limits himself to that—"

"Why do you stay with Pierre, then, if it bothers you so much?"

"He says it's only sex." Fiaz shrugs. "The way we're fighting, we may not be staying together much longer."

The light turns off in Fiaz's eyes, and Seema feels sorry for him.

"Ten years together," he says. "Even my mother is now asking when Pierre and I are getting married."

"You're lucky," Seema says. "At least she's accepting."

Seema has met Fiaz's mother during the times she has come to stay with him and Pierre: a smart, always stylish, pixie-like woman in slim tops and loose printed pants, a long narrow shawl usually wrapped around her shoulder-length bob, never missing her namaz or the thirty fasts of Ramadan.

"Next she'll want grandkids." Fiaz laughs hollowly. "Not sure, though, how much she'd approve if she found out how many dicks her favorite son-in-law sucks in his free time. You know, the only thing I asked of Pierre? Not today. Today let's march together. I want to feel pride."

Fiaz still wishes to stick around for the Trikone float, and she consents. They both watch the plodding parade with a joyless, even jaundiced eye: elected officeholders and political aspirants, various community organizations, and commercial concerns like banks and nightclubs and radio stations that have muscled in on Pride. The ethnic contingents bring up the distant tail, and more than an hour and a half later, the Trikone float comes by, a small garden of giant metallic red-pink flowers and parrot-green slotted leaves. There's only space for a few people on the float, and it's occupied by three men and two women, all dressed traditionally, the men in kurta-pajamas, the women in salwar-kameezes.

"What, no drag queens in sarees?" Fiaz is shocked. The other desis following behind are also conventionally dressed, many in jeans and T-shirts. "I thought there'd be more dhoom-dhaam today. Where's the baraat?"

Though there is music playing—*Ishq ki galiyon mein aake ghoom, dhoom machaale dhoom machaale dhoom*—appropriately from the movie *Dhoom*, the dancing, a mix of Bollywood twerking and bhangra, is energy-deprived, as Fiaz comments, from the wait to get started and the long march in the noon sun. "Nobody's even trying anymore."

He calls out to one of the dancers who signals him to join them. He looks to Seema for permission, sheepish and guilty.

"Go, you know you want to," Seema says. "I'll just go home."

Fiaz hesitates, but she pushes him toward the float, and he doesn't need a second urging. He climbs over the fence with a nimble hop, and with one backward wave—"Fuck Pierre!"—he races toward the already moving Trikone contingent, falling in with the dancers.

Seema watches until his graceful form passes from sight, twirling and skipping down the road blithely, his hips circle-shaking expertly in tight eights, his arms snaking to the music, the morning's despair seemingly dispelled. Fiaz, she assumes, would just as easily get through his current patch of misery, he and Pierre patching up their differences like they usually do. If it were only as easy for her.

She leaves the parade, but instead of returning home, she wanders toward the assembly at the Civic Center. At Powell Square there is a small contingent of antigay protestors with megaphones. They boo, they chant, they bellow, as if to drown out the cheers from the parade, brandishing their banners and posters: *God Hates Fags. Homosex Is Sin. Faggots Are Meant For Burning. Dykes Can Be Cured By Rape. America Is Doomed.* A few paraders engage with them, and the two sides shout past each other, shaking fists and pumping placards in each other's faces. One Brown protestor, in a white robe and lace cap—*Turn To Islam (before it's too late)*—is harangued by both sides; Seema feels a bitter sympathy toward him.

Some gay couples deliberately provoke the protestors by sucking face in front of them. They remind Seema of her first kiss-in with Chloe. The memory stings: the old her from a decade ago would have joined them gleefully.

The crowd at the Civic Center is bigger than any Pride she's seen. They seemed to have arrived from everywhere in the country, all sizes, all shapes, all colors, milling around, as if on a pilgrimage. There are the usual naked men and topless women, the wispy Radical Faeries and bearded Sisters of Perpetual Indulgence, the glowing and glitter-studded muscular bodies, but she's surprised by how tame the others look, as if the normal and the boring have all decided to come out finally. And unlike the earlier years, the area is overrun with couples. She's never seen so many gay and lesbian couples before at Pride.

Everywhere she looks she sees dyke couples smiling, holding *Just Married* signs. The coming threat of Prop 8 isn't stopping them.

The joke should be rewritten: What do lesbians bring to a second date? A marriage license.

There is actually a wedding in progress in one relatively empty corner of the lawn, away from the main stage: two dykes in short white dresses and long white flounces, one brunette and one blonde, a crown of daisies on each head, are being married by a pastor in a black robe and rainbow stole, surrounded by a small circle of friends. Seema wanders in their direction, stands watching for a while: the women are exchanging vows, turned laugh-crying toward each other, but she's too far away to hear what's being said over the music from the stage. She and Bill had decided to do without vows—at her insistence, of course—and were married only a short distance away.

Throughout the ceremony a South Asian woman in the circle keeps glancing at Seema. Someone from the old Trikone crowd, Seema thinks, pretending not to notice. But later, when their eyes accidentally meet again, the woman smiles and, excusing herself from her group, makes her way toward Seema.

It's too late for Seema to draw back. She braces herself, turning over in her memory faces and names. Late twenties, she guesses, as the woman approaches—she must have been a teenager if Seema had met her at a Trikone potluck when she used to frequent them.

"Hi, I'm Divya. Remember me?" A graduated bob with red-brown highlights, expertly lined eyes and lips, not too much taller than Seema, dimples. An off-the-shoulder dress in silk, sapphire. "I attended one of your training camps in the South Bay last year?"

Seema is relieved, and ashamed to find herself excusing her presence here: she'd come with a gay friend who'd since abandoned her for a bunch of guys.

"Men would do that," Divya says.

The conversation moves safely away, Divya voluble about the South Asians for Obama group she started last year. Divya's had some success fundraising in the South Bay. Actually, she's being modest—the response has been fabulous. She's been recognized by the campaign as one of Obama's top fundraisers in Silicon Valley. And Seema deserves some of the credit—Seema's camp was one of the most instructive and inspiring trainings she's been to.

Divya is chirpy, confident, upbeat. She flashes her dimples often, as if secure in presumed camaraderie. But her enthusiasm on meeting Seema doesn't seem all an act. Seema thaws—at least Divya is not twenty-two, naive, and White.

What is Seema doing for the rest of the election season? Divya is clearly disappointed when Seema admits she's not officially employed by the campaign in any capacity. Seema finds it even harder to add she has no fixed plans for the fall. She becomes defensive: "Work's very busy, I've just been promoted. I may do something in Nevada on the weekends."

Divya rallies: Would Seema consider coming down to the South Bay and doing a minisession at one of her fundraisers? Not really training volunteers, since most of the big-shot donors have no time for volunteering, but it would make them feel more involved in the campaign, and perhaps more generous. She is matter-of-fact: money doesn't buy votes but does buy staff, organizers, airtime, office space, and equipment, in more states, so they can expand the electoral map. And while small donors are important, what she does— maximizing contributions of those capable of giving more—is what will make a difference. It's the reason why Obama declined taxpayer financing, breaking his promise.

At least Divya, unlike Bill, is clear-eyed about the campaign's gyrations. Seema says she'll think about it, and Divya takes her number.

"I've got to get back. My ex just got married." Divya rolls her eyes, as if she'd prefer to have stayed out here, then the dimple again, a look and smile held an instant too long, eyelashes lowered. Her voice drops into intimacy, conspiracy, as she turns to leave: "I'll be calling you."

Seema can't help but admire the finesse. She's not surprised Divya is successful. The girl is a smooth operator, the flattery and the flirting and the networking meshed so effortlessly, only a hardened cynic would think to call her out. And the information conveyed subtly at the end about her queer ex and the signaling of her interest and availability—does Divya know about Seema's past?

It's a bitter pill to swallow, to see Divya now and be reminded of her self from a decade ago. What happened to all that pride and promise? The belief that she had all the power, all the answers, and all the fire and beauty to pull it off? She'd taken a wrong turn somewhere.

Why had she once thought this day impossible? She's missed being part of something momentous while she'd turned her attention elsewhere. And now she's too late to the party and not even invited.

She'd been considering volunteering for the No-On-Prop-8 campaign, another reason for rejoining her firm in San Francisco. But now she feels she neither belongs nor is needed there. "Come in and get engaged!" the campaign's tent screams, with a steady flow of Pride-goers bustling in and out.

Later, she doesn't tell Bill where they met—he had sulked at the mere mention of her plan to attend Pride with Fiaz—only that she'd been introduced to Divya and is considering joining in her South Bay fundraising activities.

Bill is encouraging, assuaged, she suspects, that she's found something to get involved in other than No-On-Prop-8. If he's curious about Divya, he hides it pretty well.

22

One major benefit of fundraising with Divya: Seema no longer has to deal with the Obamabots—the young, enthusiastic, mostly college-educated, mostly White Americans who've been jumping onto the bandwagon as summer progressed, all believing Obama to be their savior, a source of redemption.

The South Bay South Asian entrepreneurs, technocrats, and engineers that Seema encounters at Divya's fundraising events, on the other hand, are primarily first-generation immigrants, like her. And like her, ambivalent about the candidate. Many are confounded by Obama's upset over Clinton, having considered her predestined to be the Democratic nominee on account of her credentials. Many are skeptical that Americans would vote for a Black candidate, many question whether Obama has the necessary experience to govern, many are worried he may not be the best candidate for Silicon Valley, with taxes, immigration, regulations on the line. And many possess only green cards, so while they can make political donations, they can't vote in the election and are not excessively invested in it.

And while quite a few are willing to be convinced otherwise, even willing to buy into the Obama fantasy, many still possess the immigrant's reluctance to part with money, especially when there's no tangible return to be had, when the odds of success hover near fifty-fifty, and political donations are not tax deductible.

Despite all this, Divya has been successful. But she's set herself ambitious targets for fall, and Seema is lured in deeper. She is better than Divya at reading the facial and vocal cues of their prospects, Divya being second-generation. Also, Seema can affect rapport in Hindi and Urdu and Tamil, she can converse about current events in the Indian subcontinent and reminisce about "those days" with the long-immigrated, and her PR and publicity work with technology firms allows her to participate intelligently in the industry gossip that permeates the fundraising events.

The events—promoted as part technical, part political, and part networking—are held in the mansion of some new convert delighted to offer up his home and contacts as the price of initiation, the catering as in-kind contribution. All this keeps Seema occupied, and if she's disappointed that winning the election may come down to money, she's not surprised and is even a little relieved. It supports her hardening perception of Obama as too enmeshed in the existing power structure. Also, she doesn't need to feel guilty for not joining Bill in Nevada, driving there Friday nights, returning drained late Sunday nights after mindless door-to-door canvassing, since many of the fundraisers she organizes with Divya happen on weekends.

There's little doubt Divya is attracted to her, as she'd signaled the very day they'd met. Divya makes a game of it, flirting with her as if she believed Seema was straight and unavailable, although she must know—a casual web search would have revealed Seema's past. Seema plays along, never contradicting Divya while never lying outright either. Divya's interest in her is flattering, and equalizing, a counterbalance to playing second fiddle to someone a decade younger than her at the events. And playing a straight woman resisting seduction is amusing, even arousing at times.

The arrangement is mutually beneficial. She and Divya have a good working relationship, and their events frequently exceed their targets. Also, Seema's new intimacy with the who's who of the South Bay tech world raises her profile at her firm, adding to the success of her budding directorship.

She should have felt optimistic as summer turned to fall. Bill, too, has found his groove in Nevada, pressed into cleaning up and maintaining the state's precinct lists, a data-mining skill he'd developed working with patchy patient records at his old start-up. Obama leads McCain in the national polls, and she needn't pay much attention to the campaign itself. Even Prop 8 seems poised to fail. Support for the ban on gay marriage is polling in the low forties, according to Fiaz who's begun volunteering for No-On-Prop-8.

And yet Seema can't deny her own swelling malaise.

"I know there are differences on same-sex marriage," Obama says, accepting his nomination at the Democratic convention at the end of August. "But surely we can agree that our gay and lesbian brothers and sisters deserve to visit the person they love in the hospital and to live lives free of discrimination."

"No nominee has probably even dared to speak so openly in their acceptance speech before," Bill says. "Why are you so upset?"

Only the previous day Del Martin had died at eighty-eight. The campaign issued a statement commending Del's "lifelong commitment to promoting equality" and offering condolences to her "spouse," and Fiaz had ignited a hope in her that Obama was perhaps ready to come out in favor of gay marriage. But clearly Obama is still too much of a cautious politician for that.

She's agitated: If she's so upset, why doesn't she stop fundraising? If polls are to be believed, Obama is expected to trounce a hapless McCain anyway. Why can't she join Fiaz in volunteering for No-On-Prop-8?

She's railroaded, however, by unfolding events: McCain startles America by selecting the virtually unknown governor of Alaska as his running mate. At first it seems a desperate but futile choice, pandering to small-town America and the evangelical Right. Sarah Palin has clearly been chosen less for her credentials in governance or foreign policy and more for her anti-abortion and anti-gay-marriage stances and her rifle-toting hunting prowess.

But at the Republican Convention, Palin manages to single-handedly revive the comatose McCain campaign with an electrifying performance that leaves Seema openmouthed with disbelief. Dressed in a stylish beige jacket, pearls, and rimless glasses, her figure accentuated by her black pencil skirt and frilly peep-toe high heels—"Hot mama!" Seema murmurs—Palin plays the hockey mom and pit bull equally and exceptionally, reassuring with her folksy command and guileless delivery, while snapping and tearing at Obama with a smile and a sneer. America needs more than dramatic speeches before devoted followers, Palin swears, and more than promises to turn back the waters and heal the planet—America needs someone who can be counted on to serve and defend it, someone who can inspire with a lifetime of deeds and not just a season of speeches, and that person is not Obama.

The evangelical Republican base, which had until then rejected McCain's tepid appeals, is galvanized. Overnight, the polls that had so far been trending toward Obama immediately swing in McCain's favor, causing everyone around Seema to panic. Bill, too, is shaken, though he won't admit it, maintaining an outwardly stubborn faith in Obama's resilience, quoting campaign missives urging patience and perseverance, while his nights are restless, interrupted by bouts of sleep talking.

As she'd suspected all along, Obama's strategy of appeasing White America isn't working. She feels vindicated and shocked out of her vacillation. McCain and Palin cannot be allowed to win without a fight. Her previous doubts and misgivings now seem irrelevant.

She decides to join Bill on his trips to Nevada. In this climate of impending doom, fundraising feels too abstract and too remote from the actual work of getting voters to the polls. The advantage from all that money Obama has raised so far is illusory, easily nullified by an energized Republican base.

When Bill learns of her intention, he casts aside his impassivity gratefully, voluble now in discussing his fears, his hopes that the setback is somehow only temporary. This apprehensive Bill is new to her, needing her in a way he hasn't before.

But Divya bursts into tears when Seema informs her of her decision. At the bar where they're having drinks after work, all eyes are immediately drawn to them in sympathy: Is Seema dumping her? It doesn't help that Divya is dressed with customary stylishness—a smoky emerald-green dress, her lips pale dusk rose, eyes lined—as if out on a date. Divya takes the tissue Seema extends her, but seems unable to control herself until Seema says in a gentle voice, "Divya, my decision has nothing to do with you."

Seema waits until Divya's sobs subside. She hadn't expected such an overt display, since Divya has never given her any sign of wanting more than amusing flirtation. "This isn't about fundraising, is it?"

"I'm sorry, I don't know what came over me. It's just that—"

Seema decides to be direct. "You know I'm married. Besides, believe me, we won't suit. We're too alike."

Divya smiles wanly. She is not yet out to her parents; it's been hard dating women in the South Bay, living with her parents as she is. They're liberal in many ways for Brahmins from Pune—they didn't mind her dating boys in school and have even met a boyfriend or two, but it would be so much easier to come out if she had an eligible girlfriend to point to, in case they ask her how she's sure.

"And you are very eligible!" Divya's pouty smile and dimples are out again.

"No more flirting if we continue to work together," Seema admonishes, though she is pleased and moved by Divya's admissions. Perhaps Divya is right, but having Chloe hadn't helped her, though that was a decade and a half ago. "I can't do any more weekend events—I've promised Bill already—but I may still be able to squeeze in something on a weekday."

"Do you mind if I ask—do you identify as bisexual now?"

"I do mind," Seema snaps. "Does it matter what I identify as? Do I even have to?"

She remembers the bitter arguments that led to estrangements when she began dating Bill. Thankfully, Divya apologizes immediately, profusely, and Seema can relax. She doesn't want to have to forswear Divya too.

They work together even more closely than before, a new sense of shared endeavor and private intimacy taking root, especially as their fundraising turns more successful, the shocking possibility of Palin succeeding a seventy-two-year-old president considerably loosening the pocketbooks of their prospects. If Bill has concerns about her time spent with Divya, they seem allayed by her accounts of their fundraising triumphs.

On the weekends, Seema accompanies him on the four-hour drive to Nevada, leaving immediately after work on Friday. The days are long and tiring—she knocks on doors armed with the annotated lists that Bill has helped produce, urging supporters to vote early, and attempting to persuade the undecided—but there's benefit to not having time to think except to follow directions, to not brood in exhausting circles. She's making up for the months of doubts and distrust and disinterest, and bruised feet and exhausted trips back to San Francisco on Sunday evenings are a small penance.

She doesn't slow down, not even after Sarah Palin crashes and burns as spectacularly as she'd risen, not even when the polls once again show Obama in the lead as he emerges victorious on the debate stage, and more presidential on the national stage with his cool-headed response to the banking crisis that rocks the country in the second half of September. Bill's dread that some conspiracy could bring down Obama before election day has infected her too.

The intensity of anger and vitriol she observes on the right reaches new heights. Palin draws record crowds everywhere she goes, her supporters matching and even overtaking the loyalty and adoration that Obama inspires in his. With her trademark smiling sneer, Palin fires up her supporters, lending a benign face to the abuse and threats shouted at Obama at her rallies: Traitor! Terrorist! Bomb Obama! Kill him!

Nevada is the first state to shift from leaning McCain toward Obama, which is encouraging and gratifying. At Bill's urging, they've agreed not to discuss election outcomes or their hopes and doubts. But as November approaches, and nationwide polls predict a blowout for Obama, it's Bill who starts talking about post-November plans on their drives back from Reno.

"Would you mind moving here?" he says as they drive through Oakland, the lights of San Francisco twinkling across the bay.

He describes biking in his childhood neighborhood, down its potholed streets and past its stunted houses, with their stoops and small gardens and their multihued facades of burgundy, peacock blue, chocolate. "I'd like to buy a house here, before they all get torn down and replaced by huge-ass condos for yuppies from SF."

Seema recalls the flaming-scarlet gulmohar tree in their compound in Chennai that she loved to climb. Would it grow in Oakland?

Bill says, "I never imagined that someday I might want a house with a garden. Or that one day I'd want children who'll climb the trees in my backyard."

Bill has been dropping hints all fall about children, which she has been ignoring. This is the first time he's come out with it explicitly, and she knows she can't ignore him much longer. "Whoa, children—in the plural, Bill? We haven't talked about having one child yet!"

"We're talking now. What do you say, Mama Seema?"

"I'm not sure this world is ready for our children, Bill. I'm not even sure *I* am ready."

"Nobody thought America would be ready for a Black president. *I* never thought any of this would ever happen to me. As Obama says, we must learn to hope, and we must learn to trust."

"Let's not jinx the election, okay? Anything can happen in the next ten days. We agreed—you insisted—not to discuss these things until afterward."

"Fair enough."

Their conversation falters. A mile-long glow of red taillights greets them as they enter the Bay Bridge, and she's reminded—a trail of blood petals—of the day she'd hidden in the gulmohar tree.

She sees it in Bill's rigid grip on the steering wheel as the car swerves off the Bay Bridge onto the exit to their home: Bill is family, their home is her home, but as she well knows, even family is family only conditionally, a home may be home only temporarily. Is a child the next concession she must make?

But a child, unlike any previous compromise, is irreversible. A child is for life. The concession is a commitment for life.

A knot tightens within her, entangling her insides until even her voice sounds knotted as they drive up the dark hill toward their unlit home, indiscernible against the dark of the hillside.

23

Tuesday, November 4, 2008: Election day is a welcome lightening of the skies, after a tormenting night. Waking up in Reno alone, Bill sits glued to the TV until he sees Obama, accompanied by his wife and daughters, casting a ballot for himself in Chicago. Only then does the day begin to feel real.

The newscasters note how remarkably cool and detached Obama appears, despite the enormity of the stakes and his grandmother's death the previous day. Bill wants to scream at them: Didn't Obama shed tears while speaking about his grandmother at his rally last night? Obama had Bill sobbing like a baby. But now that it's overwhelmingly clear that Obama is poised to win, everyone seems to have heightened their scrutiny, as if already no longer willing to give Obama any benefit of the doubt.

As had Seema. The memory of their previous evening's fight clouds Bill's morning. They had originally planned to return to San Francisco Sunday night as usual. But Bill couldn't shake off the fear of some last-minute Republican shenanigans that would deliver the election to McCain. He has promised precinct captains that he'll help clean up the final get-out-the-vote lists, targeting those who hadn't voted yet—and he intends to stay, to see it through. Even if Seema must leave.

Besides, he wants to be able to observe in person the fruits of Obama's (and his) labor and savor the moment of truth as America goes to the polls. Coffee and a list of polling stations in hand, he drives around Reno as voting begins at seven, stopping first at the one closest to the campaign headquarters, in the Latino section of Reno. The line circles the block, animated chatter reaching him as he pulls up and rolls down the windows.

He'd spent the night dreading that the expected Latino turnout, key to Obama's victory in Nevada, would fail to turn up. He drives around the block relieved, exercising his meager Spanish in excited greetings and felicitations, until a policeman warns him against loitering. He flashes high fives and thumbs-ups at the campaign's election monitors. The other polling stations, too, have decent turnouts, though some seem less than busy, to his returning anxiety. But that is surely expected, given the successful push for early voting that the surge of volunteers into Nevada enabled—what Seema has been doing the past few weekends.

He wishes Seema were with him now, as he'd been there for her in Iowa. But she's decided that volunteering for No-On-Prop-8 is more important to her. She'd taken a flight back last night.

"What can you do about it in one day?" he'd asked.

"You know I wanted to stay in SF this weekend, Bill. You begged me, as if Obama would lose Nevada otherwise. You said we'd return Sunday night, that's why I agreed. But if Prop 8 passes, your Obama will surely bear some of the blame."

She'd been complaining about the missteps of the No-On-Prop-8 campaign that had made the referendum a toss-up in the last couple of weeks. The gays couldn't pull their act together, and Obama is to blame. How can Obama risk coming out in support of same-sex marriages now, when it could cost him the election?

The campaign headquarters feels strangely empty and desolate—the volunteers are in the streets getting the vote out. He'd wanted to be here, rather than stewing at home, but there's little for him to do. By midmorning there's news of record turnout all over the country. There are some rumors of voting machines not working properly in poor and Black neighborhoods, of people waiting in line for hours to cast their vote, of some voters not being given provisional ballots, but no major disruption materializes. He should be able to breathe easier. But Seema has not been returning his calls or replying to his texts.

"You never intended to return on Sunday, did you? That's why you wanted us to vote absentee," Seema had said, her bags packed, waiting for the taxi to take her to the airport. "You do what you need to do, Bill. I'll do what I need to do—"

"Why, you've become a lesbian again?"

"I—never—stopped—being—a—lesbian." Each word sharp, distinct, as if challenging him to disagree with any part of her statement.

"So what are we doing together?" The two of them in a hotel room, the campaign office a mile away, the hills ringing the town.

"I never said I'd stop being lesbian. I married you, but that doesn't change everything—"

"Have you slept with any woman since? Are you having an affair?" Both questions carry scorn, revulsion—he cannot make up his mind which one is more damning. "With Divya? Is that it?"

"No! I don't need to sleep with anyone else to remember who I am." She's gone still now, watching him warily. "Bill, you know: I love you—"

"You're a lesbian again." He yanks the door of the room open, sending it slamming against the wall. "Just leave, Seema."

Seema cringes, startled. They stare at each other for a few moments. Then she pulls out the handle of her suitcase and steps out into the corridor. He watches until she disappears into the elevator. He's still shaking, as if he'd been impacted by the door.

Thankfully, something does come up to justify his having remained here. An unexpected setback: the national hotline that the volunteers are to call, to update the database with the people confirmed to have voted, is unable to handle the deluge and goes offline. This data has to be entered manually now, and the office scrambles as calls and text messages with voter codes begin to pour in. Bill is frenetic, trying to keep up with the incoming barrage of data.

But it's joyless labor—this was to have been their day, a day together, a day of victory and celebration; he plods on, but soon he doesn't have recourse to even that as the afternoon advances and voting slows down.

It'll be four soon. He can still make it home tonight, to be there with Seema when the election is called. He looks around the office: it won't be the same here. He feels foolish. He hands over the list to a staff member, hurrying through his instructions. "Go, we've got this, go," he's told.

He pumps the accelerator as he noses it through Reno, swearing at the late-afternoon traffic like he's never done before, only the election coverage on the radio providing relief as voting closes in the eastern states. The first states are called, Kentucky for McCain and Vermont for Obama, and exit polls are trickling in.

He's just gotten through the ragged mountain slopes of the Sierras when— *Oh. My. God!*—Pennsylvania is called for Obama, not thirty minutes after the polls closed there. They'd been expecting the swing state to be hard fought, called only after a long, nail-biting night. Obama must be doing much better than even they'd expected. Bill rolls down the glass and screams out the window, the screams whisked away by the wind, so he can barely hear himself. Still he continues to scream, to the air, to the countryside, to the road, to Seema: "Seema, we won Pennsylvania!"

Her empty seat beside him is a reproach. He recalls the tone of her voice— *Bill, I love you*—so different from their frequent casual affirmations, apprehensively solemn like their earliest declarations. How could he have doubted her?

He hunts around for news on Prop 8 but can't find any radio coverage. He assumes she's probably volunteering somewhere with Fiaz and gives him a call.

She isn't. Fiaz doesn't even know she's back from Reno. He and Pierre have been knocking on doors in neighboring Alameda all day. He is despondent: turning out every "no" vote in the Bay Area has now become necessary, to counter their opponents' lead in the rural parts of the state. There's some fear that if an Obama win becomes inevitable too soon, many voters in San Francisco may not even bother to vote.

A sense of anxiety, of urgency, grips Bill. As if he needs to reach Seema now before polls close in California, to show her he is standing with her. She'd asked him: How is she to believe in all this "hopey-changey stuff"—as Palin calls it—when even Obama is still unwilling or unable—or both—to stand with everybody standing with him? He increases his speed, first seventy-five, then eighty, approaching even ninety in spots. Ordinarily he'd be worried about being stopped by cops, even when he's driving just five over the limit, which is his max.

Ohio is called for Obama when Bill's still an hour away from San Francisco. And with that, McCain effectively has no path to an electoral college majority, and the race is over even while California is still voting.

"Damn," he swears. He'd hoped to be there with Seema for this. His initial disappointment pivots to uncontainable euphoria. He finds some release leaning on the horn and switching lanes, the car shrieking as he swerves from one lane to the other and back, amid a cacophony of blared warnings. He pictures Mame's censures, Seema's alarm. He laughs and whoops, ceasing the zigzagging, but continuing to pound on the horn.

Yes we can! Yes we can! Yes we can!

Nobody else is going to get it, he thinks. But they do: first one car honks in reply, then another, and soon the entire stretch of highway slowing down through Fairfield becomes one long chorus, a rolling chant against the little town's disbelief, its dazed lights blinking—

Yes! We! Can!

So Nevada didn't matter. A twinge of regret: he should have gone to volunteer in Ohio after all. But who could have predicted such a blowout?

The evening deepens as he crosses into East Bay but seems brighter as the skies clear. I-80 swings toward the water, and he can finally see the faint lights of San Francisco beckoning across the bay. Already the landscape is rosier, dusk but also dawn. Only last week he and Seema were driving this same way, discussing what they'd do if Obama—if they—won:

A house. A tree. A child. The parameters of each are clearer: a house in Piedmont, not Oakland, if they're going to give their child the best education, as Mame would have wanted; and it must be a girl—he pictures Obama's younger daughter—with Seema's eyes and smile; and the tree must be ready to bloom a canopy of scarlet by the time their daughter is old enough to climb it.

The traffic slows to a crawl near the Bay Bridge. Is it an accident? No, it's the chaos of a street fair, a celebration anticipating the coming declaration: windows rolled down, the air rent with honks and shouts and thumping music, passengers whooping it up through open sunroofs, cars stranded empty, drivers dancing on hoods, leaping about, and exchanging high fives. The vehicles trying to get through are confounded, like lost ants, not the orderly crawl he'd been confident he'd make it through. He's on the bridge nearing his exit when voting closes in California, and seconds later the election is called for Obama.

He drives home through a city that has poured out into the streets in ecstasy: thronging, dancing, music, firecrackers, whistles. He receives texts and calls from his friends in Reno, all jubilant and boisterous. He joins in their remote celebration, though unable to silence the little voice that keeps pointing out his screwup. He calls Seema, hoping she'll at least pick up this time.

Their home stands dark. Seema's car is not in the garage. The only other sign of her return is her suitcase in the bedroom. He switches on all the lights on the lower floor, then the lights upstairs as well, some semblance of brightness to match the festivity on TV.

Fiaz doesn't know where Seema is either. He and Pierre are going to Union Square to join in the revelry and await the results of Prop 8. Does Bill want to join them?

No, he'll wait at home for Seema. He stands on the balcony chilled, watching the city, streams of gamboling headlights jolting through its streets. He can hear the distant din of triumphant horns. He remembers their first night in the house officially living together, standing huddled here, awed by the view. He calls Seema's phone periodically, checks his messages instantly—congratulations, felicitations—but none from her.

The president-elect is to make an address to the nation in a few minutes. On the screen, the tumultuous crowd gathered in Grant Park, Chicago, a block from the headquarters, anxiously awaits Obama, amid a sea of rippling red, white, and blue, a sparkle of flashes. Bill wishes he were there, or in the Reno headquarters, or even downtown with Fiaz and Pierre, where the moment would seem less unreal, less surreal, less virtual by virtue of the company of others who'd dreamed and labored for this moment.

The wait for Obama to take the stage in Grant Park seems interminable, and at the same time he wishes for Obama to be delayed till Seema comes home. He has poured out two glasses of sherry, he's microwaved the two frozen slices of cake they'd saved from their wedding party.

A hush: *Ladies and gentlemen, the next first family of the United States of America—*

Barack Obama steps out from the wings, sober and dignified, leading his younger daughter by the hand, followed by his wife and elder daughter. They are dressed in shades of red and black, the white of Obama's shirt dazzling in the blue haze of the stage. Obama's smile, when he first smiles, is almost self-conscious, without his usual confidence. His wife and daughters, too, seem shy, suddenly unsure of themselves. How tiny and defenseless they look as they walk toward the front of the stage and stand there, holding hands, waving at the enormous crowd lapping hungrily at their feet.

Bill's first instinct is to gather them in a huddle, form a protective shield around them. His second is to reach for Seema, except she isn't here. When Obama bends down and whispers something in his younger daughter's ear, and she laughs and skips, it catches Bill by surprise: the sudden collapse of his chest, as if he'll never breathe again, as if all the air in the room were insufficient to ease the strain on his lungs. The room is a blur, for there are tears in his eyes, of what seems almost like pain, and the noise from the TV is a befuddling roar in his ears.

Obama kisses both his daughters on their foreheads, then kisses his wife. His family turns and walks away, leaving him alone to face the crowd. "If there is anyone out there who still doubts that America is a place where all things are possible—" he begins. "Tonight is your answer."

"Mame, this is for you," Bill toasts, raising his glass of sherry. *Forgive me,* he texts Seema, *please come home.*

He downs the sherry but will put away the cake after the speech. For the rest of the night he will remain awake, watching the election results till the early hours of the morning, alert to every buzz or ring on his cell phone, the whine of every car winding its way up the dark and desolate road past their house.

24

At a private party in downtown San Francisco, Seema watches Obama speak, a glass of champagne in her hand.

"Because of what we did, on this date," Obama says, "change has come to America."

The on-screen audience, hungry for a line to applaud, laps it up. Seema wonders briefly what Bill is feeling—he surely must be watching somewhere— but she's still too mad to dwell on him.

She'd been standing all day on the exit ramps of Highway 101, south of the city, with a straggling band of volunteers flashing reminders to commuters to not only vote for Obama but to vote no on Prop 8 as well. *What can you do in one day?* Bill had jeered, and he was right. She'd felt too ashamed, too guilty, to appeal to Fiaz for something to do that last day; instead, returning from Reno, she'd signed up to join others like her, last-minute actors jolted out of their complacency as Prop 8's fortunes reversed.

The previous weeks, proponents of Prop 8 had sunk enormous sums of money into scare tactics: gay marriage would force the state's churches to participate in sin and its schools to teach homosexuality to children. California would be devastated by earthquakes and droughts. They'd even sent out mailers using Obama's own words—marriage is the union between a man and a woman, with God in the mix—and the Obama campaign did nothing to challenge them, beyond reiterating that it doesn't support Prop 8.

The day felt humiliating: the desperate attempts to draw the attention of preoccupied drivers, the forced cheer when one of them honked in response. Even the most optimistic of their group exclaimed as the day drew to a close, "Flinging glitter to the winds—it's just to make us feel good we're doing something."

Tired and hungry, they were shivering as the sun set, when they were asked to head back, the ramps too dangerous in the fading light. People had begun celebrating Obama's win already, but it felt to Seema, returning to an empty home, like she was participating in an ending, not a beginning. She hadn't wanted to wait for Bill, though she knew he was on his way back, furious still with his obstruction, his accusations. Nor did she want to spend the evening with Fiaz, awaiting the results of Prop 8. Divya's call was a relief, the invitation to the party an escape.

The party is in a penthouse suite, glass walls overlooking the city, the cheers and cries of celebration from the streets below only faintly audible. The 360-degree view of San Francisco is impressive, immersive—unlike the view from her home—and she feels like she's floating midair, encircled by resplendent towers, the landscape and sky a mute, remote background. The interior is dazzling as well: white marble floors, blazing chandeliers, scattered furniture imposing like sculpture, a glossy grand piano, majestic and white. The TV, despite its huge screen, cannot compete with this glitz, and Obama appears washed out, outshone, even his voice sounding thin and tame.

Divya is giddy. She's on her third glass of champagne, prattling away as she weaves through the crowd, dimpling as she greets the Silicon Valley movers and shakers. There are few Asians here, few technocrats, few women—the assembled are mostly venture capitalists and angel investors, the majority White, and almost all men. And Divya moves among them—in her midnight-blue mesh gown, with its silver-threaded spider web and its plunging V-neck—like a princess. No, a courtesan.

Seema had been in no mood to dress up in anything more fancy than a teal flared dress, and initially she'd felt self-conscious arriving at the party, although Divya assured her she looked gorgeous. Still, under the champagne's influence, she finds herself slipping again into old habits of performing charm—easy laughter, rapt attention, the occasional admiring glance—as if competing with

Divya for the approval of these men. If nothing else, the performance serves to take her mind off what awaits her in her own life.

She'd turned her cell phone off, vowing not to check her messages or the internet until she's in a calmer frame of mind. But there's a buzz building in the room that she can't avoid hearing. Originating from the cluster of men by the piano, well-groomed and obviously gay, the bitter murmurs ripple through:

Prop 8 appears likely to pass, though the votes in urban areas like San Francisco have yet to be fully counted, and the result may not be known till the morning. The expanded turnout for Obama is surely to blame, for exit polls show that a majority of Black voters in California supported the ban on same-sex marriage.

What swirls through her?

It is cloying, vindicated disappointment: she'd expected this, had reason to expect this—to be disavowed and abandoned, like Prop 22 had done eight years earlier, like her father had done in the decade before that.

It is vindictive, expanding anger: Against Obama's feckless expediency, Bill's half-hearted support. The Black community's betrayal, if that truly was the clincher—surely Blacks must know what it means to be discriminated against. The No-On-Prop-8's myopic White leadership, fearful of airing ads with loving gay or lesbian couples in order to allay the fears of straight White people, while ignoring input from minority organizations and shunning out-reach in minority communities. The whining gay White men here, conveniently forgetting the much larger numbers of Whites who must too have voted in favor of Prop 8 for it to pass.

And herself, for she's been such a sellout, with nothing to show for it—

What swirls about her? The dazzling constellations of lights, the glass windows, the glowing marble floor. Or is it she who's swirling, champagne-flushed, in this brilliant hall of glass and mirrors, with its thousand reflections, refractions, distortions, sipping Bollinger from crystal flutes, waited on by earnest tuxedoed attendants roving with platters of hors d'oeuvres? A veritable Sheesh Mahal—a flash of recollection—and she's performing for their entertainment but without Anarkali's audacity to challenge and subvert.

A quartet of men surround her and Divya, leaning in under guise of appreciation, corralling the two women in. Divya doesn't seem to mind, intoxicated by the night and her successes.

Seema grips her by the shoulders. "Divya, chal," she says, rough and urgent. "Bas, kahin aur chalen."

"Chal?" Divya struggles to refocus attention on her. Her accent even on that simple word is Americanized. "Where to?"

The men around are nonplussed, eyes darting from one woman to the other and back.

Seema ignores them. "Hum in goray aadmiyon ke khilone nahin." She's quoting—or misquoting—some long-forgotten movie dialogue, echoing its outraged intonation accurately. The men boxing them in draw back instinctively, to her satisfaction.

Divya seems unsure how to respond. It's even unclear if she's comprehended what Seema means—they've never conversed in Hindi or Urdu before. She chuckles tentatively, seeking clarification from Seema, indulgence from the others.

Seema is unrelenting. "Aati ho kya, ya main jaoon?" Divya must leave with her, a victory snatched from these men. Her gaze holds Divya's, boring into Divya as if to impel her to acquiescence.

Something in her gaze—some entreaty, some promise, some threat—makes Divya drop her eyes and nod yes.

Seema takes her by the hand, flits a quick kiss on her cheek—a first—a reward. "Excuse us, gentlemen," she says, a triumphant smile further subduing the circling men, "but we have to go."

She leads Divya out of the circle, who follows her meekly, her previous light-headedness replaced by a nervous tripping across the room. Seema steadies her, conscious of all the eyes in the room on them. She holds on to Divya's hand while they wait for their coats: trophy, security.

"Seema, what's going on?" Divya asks, when the elevator doors close, leaving them alone together. Her voice rasps, breaks.

In reply, Seema takes Divya in her arms, tilts her face toward hers in preparation for a kiss. Divya pulls back, pointing to the security camera at the upper right corner, but there's no mistaking her trembling hand, her shallow breathing, her quivering body.

Seema thrills: between the security camera's silvered lens and the elevator's gilded mirror, here too are more reflected visions, like the trick cinematography so beloved of Indian movies. She pulls Divya toward herself, presses her lips to Divya's ear in a whisper—Pyar kiya toh darna kya?—then plants them on Divya's lips. Whether Divya recognizes the allusion to Anarkali or not, she sighs, allowing her lips to open, Seema's tongue to find hers.

She should have dared to kiss Divya upstairs, in the penthouse, in full view of all its entitled men, this same way, if only to suck the air out of that ponderous room.

In the lobby Divya asks, "What now?" She suggests—diffidently still—that she spend the night at Seema's place, since she's too drunk to drive back home to the South Bay.

Seema recalls she'd told Divya earlier that Bill had chosen to remain in Reno, to explain why she accepted the invitation to the party. A momentary hesitation, confusion, thinking of Bill waiting at home for her, then she says, "No, let's get a room nearby."

25

It takes Seema another year to decide to separate from Bill. During that time Bill's desire for a child hardens to a demand. Seema asks for some time apart to ponder the matter, away from the charged context of their home, and Bill agrees.

But is it merely chance, or fate, that when they get together on the eve of a more final dissolution they come to conceive me?

Consider: Before returning one last time to her home with Bill, Seema has chosen to have her IUD removed, despite its considerable alleviation of her menstrual suffering, despite the protection it provided from the consequences of unplanned nights like the one in Iowa that resulted in her miscarriage. And that final coupling in the fog—

Had some part of my not-to-be mother come willing after all to concede to a lifelong commitment? Had she come searching for some new beginning in that ending?

Just like I must search for a way past her ending, lying silenced on an operating table, toward my own beginning.

Three

2010

I

I'm born of insecurity and need, of my mother Seema's desire to fashion a family and home for and by herself.

Even so, it's not until a few weeks after learning about my incipience that my mother comes to accept my inclusion in her life. During that time, the promise of me battles with the threat I pose: the disruption I presage, the additional responsibility for someone else's happiness that I entail. She withholds from my father information of my conception when they meet to sign the summary dissolution, afraid Bill may convince her to keep the child, to raise the child together, or even to get back together, before she has time to decide for herself. But afterward, the task of delivering me, of raising me single-handed, is too formidable, too frightening to consider. *You'll never be ready for a child,* Bill had said, and she believes him.

What changes her mind?

Is it to a happenstance, her sister's visit to San Francisco, that I owe this life?

Consider: Receiving Tahera's call out of the blue after her separation from Bill, Seema nearly discloses her pregnancy, conjuring up a future that definitely includes me, so she can better arouse Tahera's sympathy and pity. Later, she feels guilty: she'd come close to trotting me out as an actor in her play for her sister's compassion. Now she can't compound the guilt by deciding to abort me. Her guilt makes me real. I'm born of guilt.

When Seema agrees to have dinner with Tahera's family on that visit, it is to prove to herself that her sister doesn't have anything she needs or desires. But despite her impulse toward disdain for the virtuous domesticity presented to her, she can't help feeling envious of her sister's life, echoing as it does the vibrance of her exiled past. "Wait till you're a mother yourself," Tahera says, as if that prize is out of Seema's reach. I'm born of envy and rivalry.

Another way to look at the visit: Seema hasn't decided yet to keep me. She spends the day with Tahera's children. She sees my potential in them, and her mind becomes fixed to something more definite—perhaps these eyes, perhaps this voice, perhaps this way of holding the world both in an embrace and at a distance. I become real to her. By the end of the day, in some deep and unconscious stirrings of her mind, she has formed a resolution to give me a chance. I'm born of hope.

2

My to-be mother knows the risks associated with bearing me at her age. But she'd not been overly concerned until learning of Nafeesa's condition. In the last two weeks, witnessing her mother's decline heightens her awareness of how quickly the pillars of our lives—hers and mine—could collapse, how suddenly the ground could shift beneath us. We are, after all, in a land of earthquakes. She's single, and she needs to assign a substitute parent for me.

But in asking Tahera to be my guardian, isn't she motivated by another reason too? In addition to securing someone to take her place were something to happen, isn't she also trying to find someone to take her mother's place? The prospect of being set adrift again, unmoored, when Nafeesa's gone, agitates her. Who else can she turn to but Tahera?

And so she comes up with this way of testing her sister, of checking how solid the walls separating them might be. Some ancient compulsions persist, she hopes, despite the barriers built up by history and time. That a dammed-up stream of love may yet find its way through and flow again, ending years of drought.

On that rain-cocooned afternoon when Tahera, breaking down, accepts provisional charge of me, Seema believes both prayers to be answered. Afterward, Tahera sits by Seema's feet, watching the rain make patterns on the windowpanes, while Seema finishes braiding her hair. A peaceful silence has descended between them.

For what more can be said, with both sisters unwilling to imperil the fragile, dearly bought peace?

Presently, Tahera gets up for the asr namaz. Seema moves her chair so Tahera can use the corner for her prayers, but she continues observing: There's a fierce grace to Tahera's motions, a strength in their sureness, each gesture, each posture unfolding without hesitation, as though inevitable. As though ordained.

3

Sweet Grandmother! Sweet mother of my to-be mother and could-be mother! You do not know yet of the reconciliation between your daughters—however unspoken and tentative—when you hobble into the living room as day turns into evening. You are unrested from your nap. All afternoon you'd been worried that the pain, returned since the morning like a spring refilling a well, would overflow the confines of your body, once again no longer yours to conceal. It has receded to more manageable levels now.

But look—Tahera and Seema in twin plaits!

Your two daughters pose, showing off their hair. You immediately recognize each daughter's handiwork: Seema's shoulder-length hair much harder to braid, but precisely done, and you can picture Tahera's fingers moving with the same sureness and concentration of years ago; Tahera's hair longer, done looser, with escaping strands, especially toward the tip, showing definite signs of her sister losing patience. You can almost hear Seema complaining, as in the past, "But Tahera, your hair takes too much time, it's so long, ask Ammi to do your hair today."

The memory makes you momentarily forget your pain, and the hasty step you take toward your daughters causes you to wince. But what is a little pain today amid all this happiness! You'd gladly accept more of it if this evening's flush were to last forever. How young your daughters look in their twin plaits, and how playful they are together, holding the tips of their braids crossed at their upper lips to form a twirled mustache and beard, as though they've assumed their childhood selves.

They insist on doing your hair too, and though you're reluctant—your hair is so wispy now—you submit to their wheedling, and join in their glee, as they shape what remains into some semblance of plaits.

How does the evening go? There's sweet chai and sitting by the window and watching the rain as it lets up. Then clouds begin to disperse, and fleeting golden rays of the setting sun pour through the window.

"Will there be a rainbow?" Tahera asks.

The eastern sky cannot be seen from the apartment, and Seema suggests Tahera check from the rooftop.

There's no rainbow, Tahera finds. "But, Seema, your rooftop's very pretty, with great views. And there's a full moon tonight. Why don't we have dinner up there, like we used to in Chennai?"

Tahera brushes aside every one of your objections: The cooking is simple, and won't take her very long. She will bring the food up to the rooftop herself. There are tables and chairs already there. They can use shawls if the evening turns cold.

Her only concern is that the three flights of stairs may be too much for you, Grandmother, but you let yourself be carried away by her enthusiasm, and you claim you can handle them.

A whirlwind of activity follows. Tahera flies around the apartment, straightening objects and furniture, returning everything to its proper place, as though any excursion for pleasure must wait on tidiness. And then the maghrib namaz. This is the quickest you've seen Tahera pray, like in the black-and-white film clips from your youth—Gandhi and the freedom fighters at the salt march all scurrying like insects! Up she goes, down she goes, now she bends, now she rises, first she turns her head to one side, then to the other, and there—she's done.

"That was very quick," you say.

"That's normal—I don't have much time on weekdays."

You and Seema are infected with Tahera's energy and want to help. But she waves you away: "Go make sure Seema's packed and ready for the hospital. I can cook faster by myself."

The kitchen comes to life. Cabinets and containers open and close, pots and pans clang, the knife goes chop-chop, mustard seeds splutter, ladles scrape the sides of pans in a frenzy, water whooshes in the sink, papads sizzle. A parade of aromas tickles your nose—curry leaf, asafetida, turmeric, onion, frying oil, rice steam, cilantro.

Meanwhile, you and Seema have little to do because Seema has already packed her bag for the hospital. So you look into her closet and take out my belongings, newly purchased or gifted, and you show her how to correctly fold my little outfits, not in quarters, bunched up, but with sides folded in, as they were laid out in the store. Seema doesn't complain but returns the stacks to the closet and brings you more things to fold, including some of hers.

"Everything's ready," Tahera calls out before you know it. "I just need to finish my isha namaz."

The dining table is laid out with plates, silverware, napkins, covered dishes, moons of papad, glasses, water—just like you used to do, for your daughters to carry up to the rooftop. You're impressed by Tahera's speed, but saddened too: some things you've taught her, and some things life has.

She's taken a shower, and is dressed again in her hijab and jilbab. Her twin plaits have disappeared, and with that her previous frenetic, animated self. Her isha namaz is back to its unhurried deliberation. She packs plastic bags with the picnic material as methodically.

Seema leads the way up, you follow, Tahera behind you with the bags. The stairs require grim determination—the pain intensifies with each flight, especially the last, and you proceed slowly, sustained by the sliver of the luminescent sky visible through the door.

San Francisco, lit by a thousand lamps, including a giant one in the sky, lies twinkling before your eyes: the sky a deep peacock blue, the moon saffron, the bay glistening with silver reflections, the city crisscrossed with garlands of light like strings of jasmine. Everything gleams—rooftops, railings, leaves, walls, roads—polished by the rain. And though this is *not* Chennai, it *is* a city under the moon, and cities under the moon everywhere have the same ethereal loveliness.

Tahera unpacks the bags while Seema points out the various landmarks: the Christmas-tree-shaped Transamerica building, the double necklace of the Bay Bridge, the blazing Market Street, and across the bay, as though on another continent, the faint shimmering lights of Oakland and Berkeley.

Having served the food, Tahera calls you to dinner. You recognize the mother she has become: she could be you from years earlier. You and Seema return to the table. You take your seats, and then wait, without touching your food.

"Bismillah," she says. "Let's eat."

With that, Tahera transforms again, as though having taken care of everything, she can now shed the pretense of adulthood. She's a daughter again, asking you anxiously how the food tastes—is everything cooked through and adequately spiced and salted?

Everything needs to be perfect tonight. You assure her: everything is as it should be.

Seema goes into raptures: "I forgot how great these simple dishes can be. The grated carrot and ginger in the curd rice. The peanuts in the lemon rice. The potatoes—spicy and blackened just the right amount. And the moonlight makes everything more delicious."

How your daughters' faces glow, their eyes shining! How they scrunch at their papads like they used to as girls, the papads initially round as their faces, and then slowly waning like the moon! How they laugh, how they call on each other to supply missing details to reminiscences!

A light breeze blows this way and that, playing with their voices, now bearing them away, now drawing them nearer, so you can't quite hear everything your daughters say. They're too quick for you, anyway, leapfrogging from one topic to another like they used to. You're content to sit back and let their voices wash over you like the breeze and the moonlight. Everything is a balm on the pain throbbing through your body until it feels distant, like it belongs to someone else.

"Ammi's become very quiet," Seema remarks.

You'd taken advantage of a cloud curtaining the moon to close your eyes. When you open them again, everything seems dazzlingly bright—across the table, your daughters' faces flare at you, and you can't distinguish between them. Who's sitting where? Who's pregnant, who's wearing a hijab? Your eyes take a moment to readjust.

"Are you in pain, Ammi?" Tahera asks. "Do you want to lie down?"

"No, I was just enjoying listening to you both. I was trying to remember the lines Tahera used to recite during our rooftop dinners at home. About the moon—do you still remember?"

"I was reading it just this morning, in the book Seema got me," Tahera says. "What is there in thee, Moon! That thou shouldst move my heart so potently?"

When yet a child I oft have dried my tears when thou hast smiled.

Thou seem'dst my sister. Hand in hand we went from eve to morn across the firmament . . .

You haven't heard Tahera recite in two decades. Her voice rings out, silvery and sparkling. Listening to Tahera reminds you of her father. How like him she sounds now. But you don't want to be reminded of his absence tonight.

When Tahera finishes, she says, in her normal voice, but still addressing the sky, "Seema asked me to be Ishraaq's legal guardian." She glances at Seema briefly.

"In case something happens—" Seema fiddles with her plate. "And Tahera agreed."

Both sisters look at you, waiting for you to say something. You recognize that your daughters are offering you this as a consolation. You're moved, but also vexed: Why must the gesture of reconciliation include an allusion to calamity?

"Nothing will happen," you manage to say gruffly, not knowing which emotion to give expression to. Your eyes fill up; you shiver. To cover your reaction you pull the shawl tightly around yourself, surreptitiously swiping it across your eyes.

"Are you feeling cold, Ammi?" Seema asks.

"Just a little breeze." Seema suggests you drape your shawl around your head to cover your ears, and Tahera leans over to help you.

You don't want to leave this place: the air rinsed clean by the rain, the city flickering solicitously, the luminous sky soft like a shawl, the benevolent moon presiding. And Tahera and Seema—in the telescoping moonlight, it's as if you're seeing all visions of them superimposed, not only as they are, but also as they were, and as they will be—daughters, sisters, mothers, grandmothers. Their hair black like the new-moon night, their hair silvered by the full moon; their faces unlined and smooth, their faces creased by shadows. You realize that the Tahera and Seema you want to continue seeing are not the Tahera and Seema of the past anymore but the ones before you now. You want more than the glimpses you've been afforded so far.

You want more. You want more! But what to do? The only way is through Time, and Time has already forsaken you.

How the moon smiles, Grandmother, so serenely, as though it were making you a promise or offering you a reprieve.

4

What is this tightness in my chest as I consider my three foremothers together on the rooftop? I have no words for it—I can't even say that I must be out of breath, for I haven't taken a single breath yet. I'm struggling with feelings I cannot describe; they seem to change and elude me even as I seek to comprehend them.

O dearth of human words! Roughness of mortal speech!

Even that lament isn't mine, but courtesy of my could-be mother, from her favorite *Endymion*. I hear the words in her voice, passionate and declamatory, the way she'd recited to the moon other lines from the same poem.

Woe! Woe! Is grief contained in the very deeps of pleasure, my sole life?

The way my grandfather Naeemullah had taught her, the words saturating the mind and lungs till every nook and recess echoes with them, shocking the body into resonance before they break free of its confines.

I clutch at the words, trying to hold them inside me the same way, to suffuse my body with them so they can become my own. For I have lived but only vicariously until now, and I have nothing else to turn to.

5

Maybe there's something to be grateful to my grandfather for, after all.

"Why poetry?" Naeemullah had argued one afternoon in the presence of his two daughters, and set their lives on the track that has led to this moment. "We may as well ask: Why life?"

I see him facing his reluctant audience of white blouses and blue pinafores, hemmed in by the line of white habits and gray wimples. He's looking into the distance. To whom is he speaking? For surely most of what he says goes over the heads of anyone paying attention, including his daughters, the elder listening to him disinterestedly, concerned more with what his speech implies about her performance and whether she has executed well enough to win, the younger seeking clues to help gain her father's favor. Sister Josephine is perhaps the only one following him, and she too wears a perplexed smile at times, paused in the act of running the beads of her rosary through her fingers.

Maybe he was really speaking to me all that time ago.

If life is a picture, then poetry is the faint flickering light that illuminates it, he says. If life is a lamp, then the stirring overlapping shadows it casts all around us are poems. We cannot apprehend the one without the other.

And the poet is life's prophet.

Look around you: we are gathered here now in this bounded space, enclosed by these walls, but we are in reality in a city, in a country, on a continent, on a planet, in a solar system, in a galaxy, in a universe that is so vast we can scarcely imagine its limits. We can never comprehend the full extent of the world and the life that surrounds us, even with the most powerful telescopes and microscopes that science can invent.

Adding to the enormity of this task is an additional complication: even with the things that we can perceive readily, we have become so accustomed to them that we can no longer see them clearly. The best we can hope for is that someone lifts from our eyes—at least for a moment—the fog of familiarity that obscures from us the wonder of our being, to create anew for us the universe we have become indifferent to.

No, science is not the answer. The scientist looks at the rainbow and thinks: raindrops, electromagnetic radiation, refraction, reflection, dispersion. We need something different, something that will re-create for us the thrill we felt when we first witnessed a rainbow. And failing that, something that will point out to us what we are missing or have misplaced, and how, if possible, to recover it.

This is where poetry, and poets—prophets!—come in.

"My heart leaps up when I behold a rainbow in the sky," Wordsworth writes. "So was it when my life began, so is it now I'm a man."

How important is it that he continues to experience the rainbow this way? He can't imagine a life without it. *So be it when I shall grow old, or let me die!*

And what is it that allows Wordsworth to always feel such thrill on seeing a rainbow? *The child is father of the man; and I could wish my days to be bound each to each by natural piety.*

It is the purity of childhood that makes it possible. The thrill that children—you children—experience on first witnessing a rainbow is pure joy and wonder, simple, instinctual. In much the same way a bird sings to greet the sun each morning. We have to hold on to this purity of nature if we are to continue experiencing such joy, such wonder, in our lives.

So Wordsworth says, and I agree with him. But the poem enacts a larger, more complex truth as well. Wordsworth's heart may leap up, for sure—but is the joy he feels now the same joy he felt the first time he saw the rainbow? Isn't his current experience of the rainbow already different from his experience as a child, including as it does the memory of other times in his past when he has witnessed one, the hope that he will continue to experience a similar thrill in the future, the fear that he may not?

Wordsworth the man can only wish he is able to maintain that same simplicity and purity he possessed as a child. The very act of writing this poem proves to him—and us—that his wish cannot come true.

Wordsworth is a prophet. Like all prophets, he describes what should be, while at the same time admitting to what is, what cannot be, and what is beyond his understanding. Like all prophets, he has been blessed not with the whole truth but with that part of the truth he can grasp and convey. Like all prophets he is beset with self-doubt.

But even speaking half-truths, he points us toward the whole. The light he casts flickers, illuminating some part of the picture of life for one moment, only to cast it into shadows and doubt the next. But that flickering gives us a glimpse of the truths that mark our lives.

This is the best any human being can do in the face of the complexity of the universe, and most of us will do much worse.

6

So this is what it is, that feeling, almost akin to helplessness: my being so happy in my foremothers' happinesses that my heart aches, and a drowsy numbness pains my sense. As though of hemlock I had drunk, or drained some opiate one minute past, and toward unconsciousness had sunk . . .

Keats again to the rescue, his ode to the diminutive nightingale that transfixed him one night—as if my could-be mother's influence is growing in me, my future already decided.

Or am I merely dizzy, running out of the oxygen that has so far maintained my link to my mother? Am I to be forced to take a breath soon, to breathe in this world before I'm ready to enter it, before I've had my fill of this moment, my mothers together in momentary happiness?

As if Time is ready to forsake me too. I must press on, if I am to learn the full truth of my journey.

7

Tuesday morning, Seema wakes to an abdominal pain. But since her organs are squeezed to the back to accommodate me, the pulsing cramps feel more like her back is seizing up. She assumes her earlier backache has intensified.

Nafeesa blames herself: "I shouldn't have let you climb all those stairs last night."

Seema must stay in bed this morning—Nafeesa will not hear of anything else. Seema drinks her chai, brewed strong and milky and sweet, sitting in bed with the pillows piled up behind her. Breakfast, too, is served to her: toast and an omelet, despite protests that she's not hungry.

Later Nafeesa and Tahera discuss the menu for dinner the next day, for Fiaz and Leigh. Seema lies back against the pillows, languid in the soft hum of their voices. They are planning an elaborate meal: mutton biryani, chicken curry, brinjals fried in oil, onion raita, a vegetable salad, perhaps kheer or halva for dessert—all contingent of course on finding halal meat and the other ingredients.

"What if I go into labor by then?" Seema objects but is brushed off. Her mother and sister have taken over her kitchen, and her house, and her life, as she'd feared. But they seem so taken with their plans—debating which recipes to use, recalling past feasts—that she admits to knowing a good Middle Eastern butcher in the Tenderloin, where Bill used to buy goat, and a Pakistani store near it that usually stocks the small round baby eggplants.

The next point of discussion is how to do the grocery shopping. Nafeesa and Tahera both agree that Seema should rest, even as she complains, "I can't stay in bed all day."

A decision is made: Tahera will do the shopping, taking a cab. But Seema, guessing how uneasy the sketchy Tenderloin would make her, suggests Fiaz accompany her.

"He won't mind," she assures Nafeesa, who balks at inviting someone to dinner only to set them to work. Fiaz is promptly requisitioned: he'll come pick Tahera up in the afternoon.

Although Seema rebels against it all morning, lethargy slowly seeps into her body. As if now that the finish line is visible, her body has decided to slack off.

"Sleep as much as you can," Nafeesa advises. "Once the baby's born, he won't let you rest."

So Seema half closes her eyes and lets the house fall away to a gauzy haze. From the kitchen float Nafeesa's and Tahera's voices, engaged in making a shopping list, her mother specifying quantities. Sometimes they argue over the amounts, to Seema's amusement. She can picture her mother gesticulating gracefully like a dancer, palm cupped, thumb traversing the length of the fingers to indicate various amounts, as she does in Chennai, giving instructions to their maid.

By the bed, Leigh's lilies droop more than yesterday, the cream a shade duller. Seema idly wonders what Leigh is doing at that moment. It will be a while before they're able to snatch some time alone again, after the delivery. But she doesn't want to think about it now. The future will have to take care of itself.

8

Tahera's period has arrived earlier than expected. She discovers the spotting while preparing for her morning shower. In the past, her cycle has always been very regular, always preceded by a slight discharge and a soreness of breasts, but here it is a few days early, unannounced.

Perhaps this explains the lassitude she'd woken up to. In the cold pale gray of the morning, the elation of the previous night's moonlit escapade had seemed remote and improbable. And her call to Irvine tested her patience: Ismail agitated, unable to find the clothes Amina was adamant about wearing to school; Amina extra clingy and whiny; and even Arshad peevish, dissatisfied with the lunch Ismail had packed, his father having forgotten to thaw the food she'd left in the freezer. Life seemed to be unraveling without her, and she'd ended the call feeling guilty of deserting her family, and dejected.

The malaise intensifies without the solace of namaz or the Quran; she cannot bring herself to pray, or even read the Quran, during her period, even though she knows that the injunction to refrain from doing so during menstruation is disputed by some scholars.

Forgoing namaz for any reason leaves her feeling lost and rootless. But it's perhaps because she's aware of her attachment to the act of praying that she's willing to give it up on the days of her period—giving up namaz resembles fasting during Ramadan, and the pangs of loss she feels are almost like the pangs of hunger. Her streak of austerity welcomes these deprivations. But at least in Irvine, she can draw strength from the frenzied structure of her days, both at the clinic and at home, a sufficient distraction from the unsettling void that the absence of namaz opens up in her.

The planning for the feast gives her something to focus on. She enters into it with a determined enthusiasm. This is the most animated she's seen her mother so far, and Tahera finds comfort in that, submitting tolerantly to Nafeesa's varied and often conflicting suggestions. A marked change from Ammi's state during yesterday's trip for Seema's checkup, Alhamdullilah, a small miracle. Almost as if her mother has somehow been restored in spirit, revived perhaps by the rooftop celebration. She is happy to indulge her mother so that the effect endures, accepting with only slight misgiving all the extra work to cater to her sister's friends.

Her equanimity restored, despite going without the zuhr namaz, she checks in with her clinic, to discuss with Khadija the patients left in her partner's care. She dips into the book of Keats's poems as she waits for Ismail's call after he's brought the children home from school, hoping to rectify her disaffection from the morning.

It's a subdued Amina who lets slip the news to her, in a roundabout way: They were not allowed out during play period that morning. The playground was closed for the day. She's sad because her favorite swing is burned. Then, clearly prompted by Ismail, she tells her mother not to worry, she's not going to cry, she's going to be brave.

"But how did the swing burn?" Tahera presses Ismail.

"I told Amina not to tell you, afraid you'll be worried." There had been a small fire in the children's play area the night before.

"Do they know how it started?"

"Nothing for sure yet." He's deliberately vague. Only when she persists does he admit that the police may be investigating it as a case of suspected arson, and a possible hate crime—it is an Islamic school, after all.

9

Seema is roused from her listless post-lunch nap by a call from the campaign office.

The campaign has just obtained reliable intel that supporters of Kamala Harris's Republican opponent are planning a blitz of ads the week leading into the election: a huge buy, upward of $10 million, flowing in from outside the state. They want to revive Prop 8 as a campaign issue in a bid to energize the demographic that voted to ban same-sex marriage. The same groups that worked to pass Prop 8—including the Mormon Church—were apparently getting involved in the attorney general's race.

Can Seema come in for an emergency meeting?

Seema's backache hasn't improved. Ammi will make a fuss about her going, but she can't say no. Only one concern gives her pause: "Is Divya there?"

Divya will be at the meeting, but she can't hide from her forever. Seema consents and gets ready.

Thankfully, her mother is too caught up in dinner preparations to do more than cluck her tongue and suggest, "Why don't you tell them you're not feeling well?"

"This is important, Ammi," Seema says, hunting around the apartment for her laptop accessories. "There's a lot at stake."

She hopes that either her mother or sister will inquire into what exactly is at stake—this would be a good opportunity to introduce the topic of same-sex marriage without exposing herself directly—but neither is paying attention to her.

Seema had not taken part in any of the protests and candlelight vigils held in San Francisco after the same-sex marriage ban was added to the California constitution. She'd been too preoccupied with her own grief, and guilt. Obama had won, but he'd thrown the gay community under the bus to secure his victory. Issuance of marriage licenses to same-sex couples was stopped that very day.

Seema also had to deal with the repercussions of her feckless night with Divya.

She's not proud of her cowardly evasions during the year that followed, keeping both Bill and Divya dangling, until she'd felt able to take control of her life again. She'd not confessed to Divya that election night was a mistake of judgment but instead had simply insisted that nothing further could happen between them while she was still married to Bill.

One consolation: Obama is certainly as craven as she is. Two years after his election, he still hasn't come out in support of same-sex marriage. He still supports only civil unions for gay and lesbian couples, even after a federal court ruled Prop 8 unconstitutional, two months ago. He's worried now about his reelection prospects, perhaps waiting for the political winds to turn more favorable—only four states have legalized same-sex marriage, and opinion polls have yet to show a majority of the nation in support, despite rapidly changing attitudes of the younger generations. Meanwhile, he has left himself open to his views "evolving."

As she climbs down the stairs, the exacerbated pain makes her wince and groan, a clenching that I respond to by kicking. But she's been given a chance to make up for her previous nonparticipation in the marriage war, and surely that is worth some minor suffering.

10

Grandmother, you'd like an early start on the preparations for the feast tomorrow, but without the groceries there's not much you can do. You go through Seema's cabinets and cull what you can. You earmark which of her pots and pans, spoons and ladles, to use for which dish—you need an extra-large pot for the biryani, for example, one that can be sealed to hold the steam in. Thankfully Seema has an old pressure cooker that will do. You rinse Seema's dining china and glasses, even though Tahera has said she'll take care of them, warning you not to overexert yourself.

But Tahera has been unavailable for much of the afternoon, on the phone with Irvine. At first with her clinic, and you don't want to disturb her. You are proud of what she has managed to create—you know the struggle it has been, the initial scarce years at her clinic with barely any patients, and how she slowly built up her practice by making house calls to the Muslim women in her community. You listen to the authority and assurance in her voice with pleasure.

But later with her family, you know something is wrong—she lowers her voice whenever you enter the living room, but there's no mistaking the tension and urgency. Whatever is being discussed between husband and wife is surely causing the strain on her face.

Are they quarreling? You blame your son-in-law: Why did he have to spoil what was turning out to be a sweeter time than you'd imagined? You're worried, too, about the time—doesn't Tahera need to finish her asr namaz before Fiaz arrives?

When Fiaz buzzes, Tahera is still on the phone, almost scrunched over it in her seat by the window, keyed up like a spring-wound toy. You hover around her in a fret of indecision.

"What?" She looks up, exasperated.

"Fiaz is here, he's waiting downstairs."

She gazes blankly as if she doesn't remember her commitment. But then she takes a deep breath and signals you to hold a minute.

You back away to give her some space. She concludes the call in a whispered consultation and snaps her phone shut. She dresses as you watch, hurriedly pulling on her jilbab and fixing her hijab. You hand her the list, relieved.

"Everything okay?" you ask, though you don't want to bring up anything that might cause her to change her mind.

Just some matter with the children's school, she says, giving you a forced smile before heading down.

With both your daughters gone, you can finally admit it to yourself: the afternoon's activities have exhausted you. You try napping, but you're too wired—perhaps the excitement of planning, perhaps that extra cup of chai. You sit down and wait for your daughters in the quiet of the living room.

You feel bad that you've paid so little attention lately to Tahera's life. Surely whatever's the matter with the children's school can't be too concerning? Perhaps Tahera's right—you've been so caught up in Seema's pregnancy that you have ignored Tahera and her family. You've barely spoken to your grandchildren and Ismail since you arrived. But what can you do? You have only so much energy, and time, left.

You've been pondering Bill's request at odd times of the day since his visit. But with Tahera around, you've been unable to catch Seema alone. Or perhaps you've been using Tahera's presence as an excuse to put the conversation off.

Last night on the rooftop, when your daughters told you of their guardianship plans, you could have seized the opening. But their offering had meant so much to you, so much to them, how could you have spoiled the moment and told them then what you've come to think:

No matter how good Seema is going to be as a mother, you cannot approve of keeping a willing father away from his child. Perhaps Seema is letting her feelings toward her own father blind her to her child's needs. If the baby is Black—and seeing Bill the other day has reminded you that I'm not just Seema's child but his as well—then he needs his father to help him navigate what you know of America's tortured path to the present. Yes, America has finally elected a Black president, but if Seema is to be believed, half of America cannot tolerate being governed by him. And Seema speaks of protests in Oakland, even at this moment, against the shooting of that poor Black boy by White police officers in a train station. Also, if Tahera and Ismail were to become the child's guardians—heaven forbid anything happen to Seema—no matter how hard they try, they will still not be able to offer him the same kind of love and guidance his father can.

But, perhaps, you can still do something about it.

You call Seema and ask when she'll be back. In about half an hour, she says. You give Bill a call next, extracting his number from where you'd squirreled it away. Without allowing time to second-guess yourself, you ask Bill if he can come over to Seema's apartment within the next half hour, as quickly as he can—you'll explain when he gets here.

Yes, he says, a little surprised, and promises to leave immediately.

You want him here before Seema arrives, so she can't deny him entry. And afterward—

Seema will no doubt be very angry. But she'll have to forgive you, won't she? And you'd have at least made an effort—and not kept putting it off for later. For who knows what tomorrow holds?

II

Picture Bill in the chair by the window, Nafeesa in the futon opposite, both looking to the door as the key turns in the lock. The hardwood floor is ablaze in golden bands, light slashing in through the slats in the drawn blinds, but the room itself is shrouded in the gloom of twilight, with the occasionally dazzling mote of dust. It's nearly dusk, and Nafeesa has not yet turned on the lights.

As the door opens, Bill makes to rise, but Nafeesa gestures—wait—and he remains seated. Seema lumbers in, hands bracing her back, as if to counterbalance the massive globe containing his son. He hasn't seen her up close recently, and the size of her comes as a shock.

She heads straight to the futon, sighing and grimacing, exclaiming, "Ammi, I'm so tired. And my back feels like a thousand knives."

It's a voice he hasn't heard her use before, a child's voice pleading for things to be made better, and watching her labor across the room he feels a spurt of regret and shame at his absence from her side. He swallows and keeps still, as if that would allow him to disappear into the shadows.

"I told you not to go," Nafeesa scolds.

Seema hasn't noticed him yet. She sinks down to the futon and Nafeesa wipes Seema's face with the edge of her saree—like the way Mame would clean his face with a wet rag when he'd come in from playing outside, though Nafeesa is far more gentle.

"That feels so nice, sweet Ammi." Seema leans back with closed eyes, and Nafeesa gets up to massage her face and brow, then her shoulders, bending over her.

Bill has seen Nafeesa and Seema together just once, at the dinner at the aunt's house in Chennai. Nafeesa hadn't been overly demonstrative then: apart from the long initial embrace, she'd seemed guarded, almost reluctant to show affection. The aunt had to coerce Nafeesa to allow Bill and Seema to touch her feet—a ritual explained to him as asking for Nafeesa's blessing—and even when she'd agreed, she'd sounded flustered as she uttered the words—*Jeete raho*: live long and prosper—that accompanied the ritual.

And this evening, waiting for Seema, Nafeesa had sat up straight the entire half hour, rigid and unbending, reminding him so much of Mame that he's surprised now at this other side to Nafeesa, her maternal ministering.

It's hard to reimagine Seema as being close to her family, as even having a family, so little had she spoken about any of them in all their years together. It had only been the two of them. Seeing her now with Nafeesa, allowing herself to be tended to, a sudden pang: for what they could have been, for what they never were.

He's anxious now to make his presence known, afraid that if he were to wait any longer, he'd become privy to some further intimacy that would blunt his ability to face Seema. He clears his throat.

Seema looks around the room and sits up with a jerk. In the half light, her eyes flare, larger every moment as if taking over her face, and he's transfixed by them. He stands up and takes a few uncertain steps toward her, stopping in a vague panic when the room darkens further, the shadow of some intruder cast on it. Except he's the intruder, blocking the light through the window.

"Seema, I asked him here." Nafeesa cuts in, imploring. "Don't be upset."

In response, Seema pushes herself up and trudges past him to the apartment door. Does she mean to leave or to insist he does? Nafeesa scurries after her.

Bill finds his voice: "Seema, wait, please listen to me just this once. I promise I won't bother you again."

As if she hasn't heard him—"Why were you sitting in the dark, Ammi?"—Seema flicks on the switch by the door.

The room flashes, the walls spring forward, then steady themselves. Bill blinks. Seema's apartment feels less menacing now, but he is in the spotlight. Seema stands by the door, one hand on the doorknob, ready.

"Seema, come sit down." Nafeesa takes her by the elbow.

Seema shakes her off. "I can listen from here. What does he have to say, Ammi?"

She's looking at Nafeesa, not him. He looks to Nafeesa too, who opens her palms in a sudden gesture of resignation: it's up to him now.

He paces once around the room. Everything he'd tried to rehearse still feels inchoate, incoherent. What can he say that he hasn't said to her in so many emails and messages before?

He realizes he must appeal to her mother, get her to continue playing a part. She'd gotten Seema to at least accept his presence.

"Mrs. Hussein, I want you to know how sorry I am for behaving so badly toward your daughter. Seema deserves better. She's the best thing that ever happened to me, and I let her down. You can't imagine how many nights I've laid awake wishing I could roll back the past year. There's nothing I wouldn't do to go back to where we were. And there's nothing I want more than to be a good father to my child.

"Mrs. Hussein, I know the part elders play in your culture. They do in mine too. You are honored and respected for how much you sacrifice for your children, for how you love and guide them throughout their lives. You're the only elder Seema and I have left now. I promise in your presence that if Seema were to forgive me, I will never give her any reason to regret it. I promise—"

And most naturally, as if he's done this all his life, he bends down to touch Nafeesa's feet. He doesn't know how he came to do it, but it feels right. "Please forgive me."

Nafeesa pats his shoulders unsteadily, urging him up.

He can't meet her eyes now, or Seema's, for he's afraid he'll tear up. He steps back and picks up his jacket from his chair.

"Seema!" Nafeesa's voice is a sharp command. "You must listen to what he has to say. I don't know what happened between you two. Things always happen between husbands and wives. I know you pride yourself in making your own choices, but this one time I want you to consider carefully what Bill says. For your son's sake, if not for your own."

Bill glances at Seema's face. At first he thinks she wears the same intransigent expression he knows so well, but now there's something else there too—a crumbling: doubt, and weariness. The authority in Nafeesa's voice had startled him too.

"I'm exhausted, Ammi." Seema shuffles away from the door. "Can we do this some other time?"

Nafeesa hesitates, throwing him a questioning look as she helps Seema back to the futon. He's sure Nafeesa understands there won't be a better time. "I can come back later, Mrs. Hussein."

"Please sit," she says, slipping a cushion behind Seema. "Tahera may be back soon. Seema, would you like something to eat? That will make you feel better. Bill, you'll have something too."

She hurries out before he can demur.

He pulls his chair to the middle of the room, closer to Seema. There's an air of the reprimanded child about her, a shrinking, a sulking—she is the one now who refuses to meet his gaze.

They haven't been alone in a room together for more than half a year.

He squeezes his hands together and begins in an undertone: "Your mother tells me you're volunteering for the Harris campaign. How's it going?"

It's the right opening: she lets out a sigh, as if she's been holding her breath, and turns to face him. They'd always started this way, he recollects, discussing political matters before venturing into the personal, even the evening they'd decided to separate. At least that has survived between them.

She matches his quiet tone. "The race is tight, it'll be down to the wire. What do you lawyers think of her candidacy?"

"Her 'Smart on Crime' slogan is good." He smiles at Seema. "She could be the next Obama."

"Let's not talk about Obama. He's managed to keep one promise. He's united the country as he said he would—only it's against himself."

"You're still disappointed."

"I had high hopes. And you'd think I'd have learned a lesson from that, but no." A quick smile and a shrug. "But Kamala is half-Indian, and a woman."

"You've only given up on men then?" He hadn't meant to raise this, but his recent nights have been tormented by sightings of Seema with the girl in the hat. There's no mistaking the nature of their relationship.

Seema stiffens, scanning his face. He can't hide from her that he knows. She casts an anxious glance toward the kitchen, as if worried her mother may overhear. But doesn't Nafeesa know?

"Why are we wasting time like this?" she hisses. "What did you want to say to me?"

He fears he's lost her with his misstep. He stammers: "You never replied to my emails and messages."

"I've been busy." She points to her belly. "I've been having a child, as you can see."

"Seema, I understand why you're angry. What I did was wrong." He'd like to pull his chair closer, but even leaning forward makes her retreat. "There's no excuse for what I put you through. Punish me if you want. But don't punish my child."

"What do you mean punish your child? My son is no longer your child, remember?"

"I just meant—he needs a father. It's not going to be easy."

"Are you implying I won't be able to take care of him? That I won't be a fit parent?"

"Seema, don't twist everything I say." He wishes he could start over again. "I know you'll be a great mother. But not even two mothers can protect him as I will. Even if you don't want me back, let me—"

"Is that what's bothering you—two women bringing up a child together?" She struggles to her feet, crying out: "Ammi, what were you thinking? How could you do this to me?"

She's assumed that childlike voice again, now childishly shrill.

"Seema, what I meant was—"

He's thankful when Nafeesa hurries into the room. She's carrying two bowls of cut fruit in her hands.

Seema turns to her mother. "Do you want to know what happened between us? Do you know what he wanted me to do? He wanted me to have an abortion. He wanted me to kill my baby."

"Seema, you know that was a misunderstanding." He rises, taking a step toward Seema, wondering how to calm her down. She waves a hand as if to ward him off.

He appeals to Nafeesa. "Mrs. Hussein, please—"

But in Nafeesa's face he sees fear now. There's no missing it: those widened eyes, the frozen lips. Her hands begin trembling, he's afraid she's going to drop the glass bowls.

It takes him many seconds to realize how he must appear, towering over them both.

"Mrs. Hussein, I—" he says, stepping back, stumbling against the chair, his hands up to show he's backing away. "I've never hurt Seema. I could never hurt her. Tell her, Seema."

But even as he speaks, Nafeesa moves to interpose herself between him and her daughter.

And Seema says nothing.

He looks at Nafeesa and Seema, one protecting, the other almost cowering behind—as if he were a monster. He is not a terrible person, not a man to be afraid of—

A strange bitter taste fills his mouth, like the cod liver oil Mame forced him to take every morning.

He can perhaps understand Nafeesa's reaction, but how could Seema do this to him? She remains still, not saying anything.

"You know, Seema—" He wags a finger, keeping his voice as level as he can manage. "I can have the consent form revoked. Any court would void it if it's not in the child's best interests."

He grabs his jacket, resists the urge to kick the chair aside, and strides out of the apartment.

12

The Tenderloin reminds Tahera of Chennai: Fiaz's car lurches through its jammed streets amid the sound of grating brakes and revving engines, cabs honk, pedestrians surge forward ignoring traffic lights, potholes pockmark the road, dust rises from everything and is everywhere. Pavements are littered with paper, plastic, discarded clothes. The buildings look grimy, their walls rain-stained, their paint peeling.

Fiaz finds the store Seema had indicated, but there's little parking. "Shall I drop you off here? I can keep circling the block and pick you up."

But Tahera can't keep discomfort off her face: A group of men in hoodies pulled over their matted hair, clutching garbage bags of possessions to their chest, loiter in front of the store. And the store itself is intimidating—the legend *halal meat* barely visible on its run-down facade, its dingy storefront criss-crossed with brown tape to hold the glass in place. Why had she agreed to this ill-considered errand?

Fiaz, after a quick glance at her, announces that he'll park in a garage a few blocks over and accompany her.

On the walk from the garage, Tahera feels an urge to edge closer to Fiaz as they approach the men outside the store. She's thankful for the hijab and jilbab but at the same time rues the attention her attire provokes. She's used to stares and undisguised curiosity by now, but today the news from home has made her particularly self-conscious.

The pictures of the desecration of the mosque hadn't affected her as much. On her phone's small screen, the busy and hard-to-decipher graffiti seemed almost toothless, the work of some angry attention-seeking malcontent. Though she knew it was their mosque, it might as well have belonged to some other town lately in the news. And it was easily painted over. But this arson at the school—even if unconfirmed—how could she not take it as anything but a direct threat to her children? And who were these people who could set fire to a children's playground, and what if they were capable of more?

As she crosses the staring men, she braces herself for some kind of attack, either verbal or physical. The store's seedy interior, with its chipped white-tiled floor, faded blue walls, and fluorescent lighting, is a relief.

And there behind the counter—her heart leaps up: a Muslim! Gray-haired and bearded, clearly Middle Eastern, in a fraying prayer cap. Behind him a sticker with an ayat from the Quran, and beside the cash register a photo of the

Ka'ba. She'd forgone namaz, had been unable to even touch the Quran today, and must have been craving these visible signs of practiced faith, totally absent from Seema's apartment.

"Assalamu Alaikum!" She flashes a wide grateful smile. She wishes she knew more Arabic.

His acknowledgment is reserved. "Salaam. What can I do for you, sister?"

It's an odd transaction—she is effervescent, he formal: Sure, he has goat meat. What would she like? Big pieces, not too much fat. Is the meat fresh, tender? Yes, it comes from Sacramento every week. How much does she want? Three pounds, not too many bones. Her mother's going to cook goat biryani. She's not had her mother's biryani in so many years!

He reaches into the refrigerated glass case stacked with meat, picks up a pink-red, fat-marbled slab. Does she want it cut up? He feeds the slab through an industrial-strength electric meat saw and gathers the cubes in a plastic bag. He shows her the reading on the scale, slaps tape around the bag, and hands it over. The meat looks very good, shukran! Does he have chicken thighs too? Bone-in is fine, it adds rich flavor to curries!

The chicken is packaged as well, and he calculates the total.

Fiaz reaches for his wallet.

"No, you're our guest." She taps Fiaz's hand away. "Seema warned me you'd try to pay."

She's more relaxed on the way back to the garage. Allah keep you safe, the storekeeper said as she left, and though the phrase is customary, she needed to hear it. Somehow it's easier to ignore the men outside—she barely even notices them.

Conversing with Fiaz is easier too. She describes the biryani at family weddings in Chennai. But her mother's biryani, she asserts loyally, would rival any she'd eaten at any wedding.

"I'm glad we found the meat, then," Fiaz says. "I can't wait to taste it."

Tahera hesitates: Should she tell him the real reason for her state of anxiety? Fiaz is a Muslim, but he's a friend of Seema's, and like Seema, he has probably lapsed in his faith. But, he'd mentioned a mother who prayed at the mosque he took Tahera to on Saturday, and brought up in the United States, he may understand better than Seema and her mother.

"I'm tense about what's happening in Irvine—" She gives him a brief account of the events: the fundraising for the community center, the desecration of the mosque, the suspected arson at the schoolyard.

The vigor of Fiaz's anger is both surprising and satisfying. A mosque anywhere has a right to exist, and Muslims everywhere have a right to their faith.

Tahera asks: Does he pray namaz regularly?

No, but he accompanies his mother to the mosque during her visits.

She shouldn't have expected more from a friend of Seema's, so she drops the matter, asking instead about his mother. It turns out she is a retired nurse, living by herself in Sacramento after his father's death. She visits him frequently but refuses to move. At some point, when she needs more care, he'll have to persuade her more forcefully to move in with him.

"It's nice to have your mother close by," Tahera says. A flash of guilt: for a panic-stricken spell that afternoon she'd argued with Ismail about catching a flight to Irvine that very night. Ismail reminded her why she was in San Francisco in the first place, dismissing her return as unnecessary, her fears as overblown. "I wish I could care for my mother better."

"I'm sorry to hear about her illness. Seema told me," Fiaz says. "This is a tough time—I hope Allah gives you all strength."

Their next stop is the Pakistani grocery store. The store is quite small—two aisles, dimly lit, with a musty, unaired smell, stacked high with spices and grains—compared to the ones she's used to in Irvine. But the store does have the baby eggplants and the green chilies in its refrigerated section, as well as the aged basmati rice and all the nuts and spices on her list. She needs Fiaz's help to reach some of the upper shelves.

At the checkout, Fiaz browses through the compact discs on the counter. "Cheap—five bucks each. And they have Urdu ghazals. Do you remember which singers your mother likes?"

Some names seem familiar. Tahera points to Begum Akhtar and Noor Jehan, faded women on faded disc jackets, from the 1940s and '50s. She remembers tapes playing softly some afternoons when she and Seema returned from school to find Ammi in bed, eyes closed, listening to songs they'd make fun of as nasal and old-fashioned—Ammi would shut the music off to prepare the girls' tiffin. And Ghulam Ali, from Tahera's youth, whom she also liked.

Fiaz says he'll buy all three, and Tahera is touched. She hadn't gotten her mother anything from Irvine. Why hadn't the thought occurred to her?

One last stop is required, for mint, cilantro, yogurt, lemon, onions, tomatoes, milk, cream, oil. Fiaz says he'll take her to the Safeway on their way back. It's dark already, everything taking longer than she'd expected because of the traffic and parking. There's no maghrib namaz—because of her period—but she'd like to talk to her children before they go to bed.

Compared to the previous stores, the Safeway is large and brightly lit, aglow against the hills of San Francisco. They're back in the America she knows. The bulb-ringed marquee perched atop a tall column, like a torch, overpowers the lusterless orange moon in the city-lit sky, though the moon is almost as full as it was the night before, only a tiny sliver missing. Glimmering shopping carts and shiny cars litter the busy parking lot.

Inside, Tahera is back among the labeled aisles and preoccupied customers pushing overloaded carts, familiar to her from every other chain store she's visited. This is America going about its business.

Her earlier uneasiness floods back. She is small in this huge hall, hemmed in by strangers—mostly White, no Muslims—crowding the aisles. She is a black blot, in her jilbab and hijab, against the cheerful color of the rows of merchandise. Alert once again to glances cast her way, she suspects shoppers of avoiding her, or plowing ahead, ignoring her, as though to claim the space for themselves.

She's ashamed of her earlier reaction to the men outside the halal market— it's not those harmless men but "decent" people like the ones here she needs to beware. It's decent Americans like these behind the warnings and threats, the profanities and blasphemies: Go back to your savage lands, with your bombs and your burqas, your sharia and your polygamy. You're not wanted in America. She'd only read about it on the news and on blogs before, but now it's here at her doorstep.

Arshad's question echoes in her mind: *Why do they hate us so much?*

At times, she finds herself instinctively scuttling out of the way when a White shopper approaches. And then, in retaliation, she lingers over her selection, to hamper an overeager shopper, taking her time to make her choice, determined not to be cowed. What were they thinking? If only they said it out aloud, so she could challenge them.

An image of the burning playground persists. She imagines Amina caught in the flames, on her favorite swing, shouting to her mother to save her. The thought of being unable to reach her daughter in time sets her heart racing, her feet tripping in panic. The anonymous voices around her blend into an ominous soundtrack to the flickering flames. She wishes Ismail were here; she needs his comforting presence.

Fiaz's playful patter helps take her mind off of Irvine. He has lively opinions about everything, including which brand of vegetable oil to use. She searches for the one he suggests, but when she turns around to place it in the cart he's pushing behind her, he isn't there anymore.

For one long moment she freezes: she's been abandoned here. Then, still clutching the bottle in her hand, she rushes to the end of the aisle, scanning the store for him.

A relief: he's standing by an adjacent checkout counter. She's about to call out, when she observes that he's conversing with two men: one White, one Black, both in very tight V-neck T-shirts and indecently short shorts, their limbs and chests muscular, smooth and hairless. The three men are laughing and talking, completely at ease with each other. The clerk rings the men up and they collect their bags and take leave of Fiaz, who kisses them both on the lips.

Tahera knows the men are a homosexual couple, one of the many San Francisco is notorious for. And the fleeting look—guilt? shame?—on Fiaz's face as he turns around and catches sight of her is enough to confirm another suspicion: Fiaz is gay too.

It's obvious now—how could she have been so blind? How Seema and Fiaz must have laughed at her naiveté, scorned her "narrow-mindedness." A deep flush reddens Tahera's cheeks.

"Were you looking for me?" Fiaz has regained his composure. He takes the oil from her and heads back to the cart. "Do you know why the frying pan liked the oil? Because it was so refined!"

But now that she's wise to him, she is no longer susceptible to his banter. She maintains a studied silence for the rest of the trip.

13

Tuesday night is soccer night at the mosque. Imam Zia had wanted to cancel the session, but the boys wouldn't have it, and he has roped in Ismail to better control them—many have only learned of the recent incidents at tonight's isha namaz. Ismail has brought Arshad and Amina along, giving in to Arshad's wheedling.

This is Arshad's first time here, since only those in high school and older are allowed to participate. Imam Zia says Arshad can take part in the training at least, like his friend Jemaal, who usually accompanies his much older brother to isha namaz on soccer nights. Amina is content with her coloring book, but Arshad is glad to be among the men, on the alert for anything more he can learn about the fire in the schoolyard.

Little had been shared at school, and Arshad and Jemaal have already discussed their meager store of information to exhaustion. Only the swing and the slide had been affected, their charred frames standing out starkly in the cordoned-off play area. The police had made a brief visit that morning.

Before starting, Imam Zia warns: No more discussions and speculations, no venting their anger in aggression on the field. He has heard outbursts, cuss words, proposals of retaliation. Any such displays, either in word or action, and he'll end the practice immediately.

Even so, furious whispers buzz around Arshad as they warm up, first jogging laps, then stretching. His ears are on fire: he hears *gasoline, fire bombs.*

Their anger seeps through the dribbling and passing exercises, bubbling open as they practice shooting goals. Jemaal's brother Emir comes closest to defying Imam Zia. "Burn in hell," he muffles his scream as he sails the ball into the net. The twins, Rizwan and Sohail, are quiet, as usual, but even they appear on edge, with a grim determination that Arshad can copy without arousing his father's ire.

His father had insisted it was nothing, a small fire, probably started accidentally, maybe by a discarded cigarette. An accident! Imam Zia, too, would do nothing, other than once again admonish his jamaat to have patience while the police investigated, like after the defiling of the mosque and the besmirching of the Prophet. As if the police cared enough to catch the cowards who had set fire to his little sister's swing just because they couldn't accept the supremacy of Islam over their supplanted religions.

The scrimmage is to be seven a side, with Arshad and Jemaal sitting it out. Imam Zia whispers to Arshad's father: Better that they have the troublemaker Emir on Imam Zia's team to keep him under control. Ismail can take the twins, who usually respond well to him.

Amina has put aside her coloring to come cheer for their father. Arshad is torn between loyalty and blossoming admiration: Emir is small but quick and ferocious, and he's everywhere on the field in the wink of an eye, fearless in tackling larger opponents, unconcerned with hurting himself. He slides to kick the ball away, misses, goes slithering down the synthetic turf, but bounds up again instantly to limp back into play, rolling up the ripped hems of his tracksuit.

Imam Zia admonishes Emir twice. When it happens a third time, Imam Zia sends him to the back of the field, to the relative passivity of goalkeeping.

Imam Zia then takes charge of the game. A sorcerer with the ball, he now feints, now swerves, now chops and cuts, steps over and turns, the ball magically tethered to his feet throughout. Stumped at first, unable to even get close to the ball, the other team regroups, energized to wrest it from him amid roars of appreciation and competition. Jemaal runs up and down the side of the field as if drawn along by the ball, hoarse with breathless commentary.

Arshad watches with mixed feelings his displaced hero's artistry on the field, while Emir languishes by the goalposts. But when Emir is finally allowed to return to his former position, now chastised and deferential, he joins his teammates urging to be passed the ball when Imam Zia is surrounded and immobilized by determined opponents. Obeying Imam Zia's instructions, he and the team then press the ball forward toward the goal in well-placed passes.

They should have dominated the game, scoring goal after goal, were it not for Sohail and Rizwan—Arshad has switched his support back to his father's team, after the surrender of his latest hero—two pairs of eyes on the ball, two trunks and four pairs of limbs reacting like some coordinated whole, an equally magical defense that even Imam Zia can break through only rarely. But Imam Zia manages to get the ball past them, scooping it over to Emir, who springs into a header. The ball soars past his father's inadequate arms into the net, while Emir runs screaming back to Imam Zia for a high five.

"Jemaal, we must do something, you and me," Arshad cries out in sudden anguish. "Nobody else will do anything."

14

"Tahera knows about me," Fiaz announces in a stage whisper. Having helped carry the groceries in, he has stopped by Seema's room, knocking conspiratorially on her door. "She saw me with Ben and Percy at the Safeway. Not very difficult with those two."

My mother is in bed, working with her laptop on her belly, the extra warmth spread like a cozy comforter over me. She gestures to Fiaz to pull the door shut behind him. She's half-relieved, half-aggrieved: one less deception, one more complication to deal with. Should she have, as Leigh has held, been completely open with her mother and Tahera from the start? But it hadn't seemed possible before their arrival: Would her mother have come, would her father have let her mother come if he too found out? "How did Tahera react?"

"She has barely spoken to me since." Fiaz smiles ruefully. "We were getting along very well before that."

Seema sighs, puts the laptop away. She's not ready yet to give up the lurking hope that Tahera has moderated since sending her that letter twelve years ago, just as America itself had, to at least tight-lipped tolerance. "I was going to tell you, I've asked Tahera to be my son's guardian."

He raises both eyebrows. "Tahera, really, why?"

"Who else? You've already said you can't, and I'm assuming you haven't changed your mind." The shamed look on his face is confirmation. "And it's too early with Leigh. There's no one else."

"Why not Bill? He's the father, after all."

"You know why not Bill," she snaps. "Everyone keeps pushing Bill on me. Has he gotten to you too?"

"Ouch. What's going on, Seema?"

"I'm sorry, I'm dealing with a lot." She pats the space beside her. "Come sit by me for a minute? Bill was here. My mother had some crazy idea of bringing us together. They just ambushed me."

"That sounds horrible." Fiaz sits down, massages her shoulders. "How did it go?"

Two memories arise: when she'd first set eyes on Bill that evening, and when she'd hid behind her mother. She's ashamed of her reactions to both moments: the instinctive desire to welcome his reassuring presence into her life again; the despicable cruelty with which she'd repulsed him, afraid he'd betray her to her mother.

"He left threatening to void the consent form," she says. "He could fight for custody."

"Don't worry about it now. We can deal with it if it happens."

"One silver lining: my mother stood up for me in the end. I was so relieved, I couldn't even be angry with her for setting it up. But I need to have something signed about guardianship before I go into delivery, just in case. Isn't it sad that after all these years living here my only two options are an ex who wanted me to get rid of my baby and a sister who still probably doesn't approve of my *lifestyle?*"

"You do know, Seema, that if I didn't have Pierre—?"

"Do I know?" Her smile is inquiring, a little bitter. "But you do have Pierre. At least Tahera agreed. I can always change it later, depending on what happens with Leigh."

Fiaz stretches himself on the bed alongside her and drapes his arm over me, as he's done before. "I'm ready to sign up for diaper duty whenever Ishraaq needs me."

"Guess what? My mother thinks you and I are together. After Bill left, she asked if there was anything between us. I suppose after her plan with Bill misfired, she decided to settle me on you. I said we're just friends, but I don't think she believed me. And she won't, if she sees us like this."

"Uh-oh, dinner's going to be awkward tomorrow."

"I'll think of some way to disabuse her by then," Seema says. "And don't worry, silly—I won't tell her all your secrets."

Fiaz laughs uneasily. "I got these CDs for her. Hopefully that'll be enough to keep me in her good books."

15

Grandmother, you're inspecting the mutton when Fiaz offers you the CDs. Preoccupied with the meat—the butcher should have made the pieces larger, so they won't fall apart in the biryani—you thank him cursorily. Only after he leaves, and you and your daughters are done with your simple dinner of rice and rasam, do you examine them.

"Arre, where did he find these?" You flip through them, excited. You've been searching for these discs for many years, the cassettes you owned not playing anymore. You try to remove the cover of the Noor Jehan CD, but your hands shake too much. The collection has the very best of Noor Jehan's songs and ghazals.

Tahera takes it from you and turns on Seema's music system, lying dusty on the lower shelf of the bookcase in the living room. Seema has returned to her bedroom, claiming she's working on something for the campaign, though you suspect she's avoiding you for having forced Bill upon her.

The lilt and melody of the opening song transports you immediately to your childhood home in Coimbatore, to the hiss and crackle of the LPs playing on your father's—my great-grandfather's—gramophone, and to the jasmine-scented, song-silenced evenings in your parents' bedroom, your father in the rocking chair by the window, your mother cross-legged on the floor, stringing buds plucked from the garden. And you, on your father's lap, rocking with him, or sprawled on the bed doing your homework with your sister when you were older.

You are aware of the years that have intervened since that past. You clasp the empty plastic case to your chest to steady yourself. What a precious gift from someone you've scarcely known for a week. Only a friend, Seema insisted. "So thoughtful of Fiaz, and I didn't even thank him properly," you say. "Come, sit and listen with me, Tahera."

Tahera says she'll clean up in the kitchen and then join you. Unfortunately, your daughters were never admirers of these old classics. You rest your head against the futon, close your eyes, and let Noor Jehan's voice steal its way back into your dying body. It's an unexpected pleasure, something you hadn't imagined finding here on this trip or, for that matter, ever again.

Now here's Noor Jehan singing, "Mujhse pehli si muhabbat mere mehboob na maang." You've been both waiting for and dreading this song, for all the memories it holds for you. You had recited that Faiz Ahmed Faiz poem, one of your favorites, at a jubilee celebration at your college. How different your life would have been if your husband hadn't come to that event with his friends. He said he'd fallen so in love with you that evening, he'd moved heaven and earth to find out who you were and forced his parents to approach yours for an alliance. And you were so charmed, you allowed yourself to be swept off your feet and forget everything, including the warning in the last lines you had recited: *There are other satisfactions than the satisfactions of love.*

You'd wanted to teach Urdu and write your own nazms and ghazals, perhaps even sing them. You locked away all your dreams, along with your bridal finery, in a chest you've rarely opened since.

You murmur along with the closing refrain through trembling lips.

You're aware Tahera has entered the room. You're glad for the interruption, otherwise the song might have set off your tears. You sense Tahera watching you: some part of the story of this song is cherished family lore. You're grateful for the moment she gives you to compose yourself before she sits beside you.

She squeezes your hand. "You never told us you wanted to sing too, Ammi."

"I never trained. I never even asked. Your Nana wouldn't have let me. It wasn't something we did." The truth is, it had never seemed important to you what anyone wanted. You could want so many things, you believed then, but the world would only give you what it's willing to give, what has been set aside as your portion. You didn't believe you could bargain with the world. "You never told me Amina sings so well. Perhaps my granddaughter—"

"If Allah wishes." She sounds despondent, not the blossoming you've come to expect whenever she talks about her daughter.

"What is it, Tahera? You've been acting differently all day. You even skipped your namaz."

"It's just my period."

You wait, knowing there is more: you can see in her eyes that the commiseration in your face is welcome today. Usually she withdraws at any sign of pity or compassion.

She opens up hesitantly. There's all this anger in America against Muslims like her. And it's not just name-calling and abuse. Their mosque in Irvine has been vandalized, the children's playground has been burned.

You're shocked and saddened. You know so little of Tahera's life here. You don't know what to say. You've never understood why both your daughters, given a choice, always seemed to choose the path that required more hardships. You'd get upset, thinking they were being thoughtless and obstinate, not considering you at all. If they cared for you, they wouldn't act that way.

Perhaps the Faiz poem is written in their voice, addressed to you: *Don't ask of me that earlier simpler love. The world holds other sufferings than mere love.*

You'd given up what you wanted without even trying. You'd convinced yourself that all you ever wanted was that your daughters lead happy lives. But you never asked them what would bring them happiness. The least, and the most, you can do now is listen. You don't yet know the full sum of their struggles and sorrows.

Tahera's eyes are downcast. You lift her chin up, as you would when she was a child to force a smile, and she complies, and you let your own eyes rest on her face, as if to take in all her pain and add it to yours.

16

Seema is in bed in San Francisco, waiting for her mother to come to her. Seema is in bed in Chennai, waiting for her father to come to her.

In San Francisco, Seema listens to the faint buzz of conversation between Tahera and Nafeesa in the living room. During the lulls, she can make out—barely, because the volume is turned down low—the songs her mother has been playing all evening.

In Chennai, Seema listens for the determined rhythm of her father's steps up the stairs. He hadn't come to the airport to receive her—he usually does when she arrives before dawn, but due to a snowstorm in London she'd been delayed till the evening. He wasn't home for dinner either, and she's waiting for her father to look in on her, as he does on the nights of her homecoming.

In both places—San Francisco and Chennai—Seema is sick with anticipation and apprehension. Except that in San Francisco, she is additionally burdened by the ghost of that long-ago night in Chennai, revived and clamoring.

The Seema in Chennai has made up her mind. The questions her father has asked her over the phone about "her friend Chloe" have convinced her he suspects, informed by one of his friends at Oxford, most likely Uncle Rajasekharan, who has seen her with Chloe on a few occasions. Her father has also started to talk about her marriage. How much does he know? And what does he have in mind? She will be firm about refusing marriage. She has rehearsed what she will say.

She is eager to get the confession—the confrontation?—over with as soon as possible. If only Chloe were here to blunt her anxiety. Any noise suggesting her father's approach makes her sit up and clutch her damp bedsheet, twitching as though her organs are pulsing alongside her heart. Her palms are bathed in sweat despite the grumbling fan and the chill December night.

But still she's optimistic: Abba loves her, he's proud of her. Her mother has said nothing so far, and she takes this as a good sign. If anything, she expects her mother would be more upset, being more traditional, less doting. Abba had supported her decision to study in England over Ammi's strenuous objections, persisting until Ammi had come around.

The Seema in San Francisco is no longer afflicted by the daring optimism of youth. She finds it absurd that the Seema in Chennai expected her father would support her, commending her on the courage to agitate for what she wanted, as he'd done many times before. How naive that younger Seema must have been for failing to recognize the difference between a transgression that challenged her father and her past harmless exploits.

She's been holding everyone—her mother, her sister, even her lover—at bay for the last few months, bracing herself for a repeat of that earlier abandonment. But the last few days have softened her defenses: having experienced once again the comfort of their love, the prospect of losing them for the second time wrenches at her.

She owes it to Fiaz to correct her mother's misconception about their relationship, and to Leigh for standing by her patiently. But mostly she owes it to herself, so she never reacts again with the kind of fear that the threat of Bill's disclosure had aroused that evening. She will speak to Ammi tonight, as she should have done earlier. She owes it to Ammi, too, to give her a chance to come through. Perhaps her mother's desire to see her partnered will yield a different outcome this time, this second coming out.

In Chennai: footsteps first, then a soft knock, then her father's voice, muffled.

She gets up and opens the door.

He's come directly to her, not having changed his clothes. He holds her by her nightgowned shoulders, kisses her on her forehead. "I'm sorry I couldn't be at the airport. Was the delay too taxing? Did you eat?"

She's relieved to still hear tenderness and concern in his voice. She reaches for the switch to turn the light on.

"No, you should go to sleep," Naeemullah says. "You must be tired. We'll talk tomorrow."

"I'm jet-lagged—I won't be able to sleep anytime soon."

They compromise: she gets into bed, Naeemullah pulls a chair to her bedside.

The room is lit only by a night lamp. He is a dark shape sitting beside her, stroking her hair. They converse in whispers, even though Tahera has her own room now, next door. They talk about Oxford, which he has fond memories of. She talks about college, and the courses she's taking. She has one semester left.

And then what?

She hesitates: she's thinking of a doctorate.

"Wonderful! Both my daughters will be doctors." Tahera has surprised everybody by opting for medicine after her schooling. "But don't you think," he continues, pressing her hand, "it's time to get married? Your mother already had you at your age."

In the shadows, she can't quite make out the expression on his face. Is that what gives her the courage?

"Abba—" She hopes he's smiling. "There's something I've been meaning to tell you—"

In San Francisco: her mother gets ready for bed, as unobtrusively as possible—the lamp remains off, she barely opens the closet door to retrieve her nightclothes, her footsteps are as soft as the moonlight streaming through the window. And then she arranges herself rigid and narrow, toward the edge of the bed, as if to minimize her presence.

"If you scoot any closer to the edge, you'll fall off," Seema says, her eyes still closed.

Nafeesa sits up, surprised: "I thought you were sleeping."

"I was waiting for you."

"Why did you wait up for me? As if I need help to come to bed. You need your rest." Tsk-tsking, Nafeesa lies back again. "It's late. Let's go to sleep."

But instead of abiding by her own proclamation, Nafeesa continues, "I was listening to the songs Fiaz brought me." And, after a pause, "I never thought I'd hear them again before I—"

The hush in the bedroom is then punctuated by quick sharp intakes of breath, Nafeesa's desperate attempts to stifle her sobs. As with Tahera the previous day, Seema doesn't know how to react. This is the first time her mother has alluded to her impending death, displaying open grief at the prospect. She reaches a tentative hand toward her mother, but Nafeesa brushes it away.

In the darkness, an immense abyss opens up between mother and daughter, in the space between their bodies in bed. It is Seema who lies rigid now, not breathing, as if even that could pierce the distance separating them. Her world turns soundless, complying with her mother's wish that the moment simply pass by unacknowledged. Nafeesa's sobs are someplace else, in a different room, a different continent. Only unmoving shadows remain, the dark curve of the calla lilies arcing over Seema in the ghostly moonlight streaking through the window.

Gradually, as Nafeesa regains control over herself, sound returns. She hears her mother say: "Seema, I want to say something—"

In Chennai, Seema's rehearsed speech starts off well. The darkness is liberating: she won't be distracted by her father's reactions. She is the performer, her father the audience. She has prepared an impassioned argument, incorporating much that he has taught her, much that he should recognize as his own values. He will be proud of her—she will make him proud of her, not for nothing is she his daughter.

When does she realize her performance is coming up short? When Naeemullah listens but his grip on her hand tightens, his face looming large and featureless? His impassivity makes her falter. Her prepared words sound trite and unconvincing. She panics, losing the thread of her oration, digressing into explanations and justifications she hadn't intended. Still he's silent. She clings to the belief that she can salvage this. She only needs to find the right words, the right way to declaim them, and her father will respond with his usual applause and approbation.

She repeats sentences, phrases, rehashing herself in increasingly desperate constructions and combinations until she finally stops with a strangled gulp of air, her father's grip painful around her wrist.

"You're hurting me, Abba," she sobs, trying to reclaim her wrist from the vise of his hand.

In San Francisco, Seema turns toward her mother, ashamed at having allowed her to cry alone. She takes her mother's hand, lifts the bony knuckles to her lips for a kiss—dry lips to dying skin—as her mother had done earlier that evening, consoling her.

Mother and daughter curl toward each other in the dark of the room, their bodies adjusting to the space occupied by me, their faces almost touching.

"What is it, Ammi?" Seema asks, the words whispered to Nafeesa's clammy forehead.

"Forgive me, Seema," Nafeesa says, her fingers tracing—awkwardly given the constraint of closeness—Seema's face, the bridge of her nose, the springy curl of her eyelashes, as though she needs to make sure that Seema is here.

Forgive her for what?

For everything, for all that she should have done but didn't, for all that she did but shouldn't have.

For not having understood, for still not understanding fully—

Nafeesa is both coherent and disjointed, forthcoming and hesitant, precipitate and pensive, the bridge of her words sometimes stretching across silences, sometimes hanging midair unfinished.

Seema responds with caresses and kisses, with noises of encouragement, not wanting to say anything for fear of upending the moment and bringing it to an end. A trembling half joy, a shimmering sweet sorrow fills her. She has never felt this close to her mother before, never before seen her as an equal in regret and pain and heartache. That long-ago night with her father in Chennai is forgotten. Any lingering resentment toward her mother dissipates.

Tomorrow, she promises herself, with Fiaz and Leigh there, she will tell Ammi everything. Her apprehensions for the future fade away, as a glimmering optimism takes hold, even as she recognizes how little time together she and Ammi really have.

17

I take it all in, hungrily, greedily: Nafeesa's remorse, Tahera's fears, Bill's disillusionment. Arshad's anguish, Seema's optimism. America's turmoil. As if I need to inhale this world into the very cells of my body, every element of it simultaneously, before I can bring myself to take a single breath of its air.

I taste most sharply my could-be brother's anger and despair. For isn't Arshad someone in whom my to-be mother had seen a possible model for me, convincing her of my viability? A child who seemed so sure of himself and his place in the world that she could picture him rising to meet the world hand to hand, eye to eye, the kind of child she could picture herself raising.

The kind of person she'd believed herself to be before that fateful evening in Chennai, when her performance had failed her. And ever since, she's been convinced she's merely going through the motions, performing a pale simulacrum of herself.

If I could give her that moment of radiance. How differently the world would have unfurled for her. I reimagine that evening, seeing it as she imagined it would play out. I become the audience she desired, willing to be captivated by the power of her performance, waiting to be converted by the persuasiveness of her words:

Abba, you taught us to look beyond subsistence, beyond what is needed to keep mind and body together. You taught us to probe the universe for hidden truth and beauty, to seek sustenance only in the true and the truly beautiful. You taught us to question everything else—rituals, tradition, faith, ties. You taught us to embrace everything that life challenges us with: we are to always strive beyond what we are capable of, beyond what we cling to for comfort.

You taught us to love: to love those discoveries that bring unexpected joy, to love those moments that press us to the brink of new discoveries, to love those beings who make each moment burn and crackle with the promise of illumination. You said that it's precisely there, in these moments, that true poetry resides.

I love someone like that—beautiful, wise, brave, strong. In their presence the universe reveals its hidden beauty, in their presence the universe shines with a new light—

Isn't someone like that worthy of love? Isn't love like that worthy of our deepest gratitude?

18

The city sinks into the night.

Blessed Sleep, quiet defender of the still midnight: Close, with your careful fingers, our gloom-beleaguered eyes. Protect us with your watchful attentions, lest the fugitive day slip in and even at our pillows inflict many wounds. Save us from ravaging consciousness that roams ready, with sabers drawn.

Seal us in. Root out treachery. Expel from us our treasonous minds.

19

Imam Zia speaks: How magnificent the universe is, my brothers and sisters. So vast that no human being can take full measure of its vastness, so beautiful that no human eye can perceive its every beauty, so mysterious that no human mind can comprehend all its mysteries.

Yet every part of the universe—from a massive galaxy to a minute neutrino—follows every law that has been prescribed for it by the creator, Allah, the Exalted in Might, the All-Knowing. Every part of the universe submits to the will of Allah, which is the essence of Islam, and thus every part of the universe is Muslim.

The stars are Muslim, the sun is Muslim, the moon is Muslim. Does not the Quran say, "The sun runs his course for a period determined for him: that is Our decree. And the moon—We have measured for it mansions to traverse till it returns to its withered state, like a stalk of date. It is not permitted for the sun to catch up to the moon: each swims along in its own orbit according to Our law"?

And here on earth, every mountain is Muslim, every ocean is Muslim, every river is Muslim: they all follow the natural laws that have been laid down for them. Every animal is Muslim, every tree is Muslim, every bird is Muslim: from birth to death every organ, every tissue, every cell in their bodies follows the laws that have been designed uniquely for them. Can the nightingale sing any other song than has been ordained for it? Every note that it sings has been written for it. It can no more change its song than it can shed its wings.

But what of man? On the one hand, every man is born Muslim, because every part of his body, from the nails on his toes to the hair on his head, is regulated by Allah's laws. His heart is Muslim, his brain is Muslim, his tongue is Muslim: his body is bound to follow every law that Allah has decreed.

On the other hand, Allah has bestowed on man a mind: a mind that can think and judge and choose. And with this mind, man has been endowed with a free will: he has the freedom to embrace or deny any faith, the freedom to live by any code of conduct, the freedom to react in any way to the conditions of his life. With this mind, he can choose whether or not to be a Muslim.

How can man's mind and body be brought in harmony with each other?

Only if his mind consciously submits to Him whom his body already submits to intuitively. Man completes his Islam by surrendering back to Allah the freedom he has been given, by consciously deciding to obey the slightest of Allah's injunctions.

Now his feelings are in harmony with his heart, his thoughts are in harmony with his brain, his words are in harmony with his tongue. Now his actions are in harmony with his body, and he is in harmony with the universe: he obeys with both his mind and body Him whom the whole universe obeys.

He has finally become a Muslim, in this brief life. And for that he will be rewarded for eternity in the afterlife, with everything his heart desires, with all the joys of Paradise.

20

John Keats speaks: Forgive me that I cannot speak to you definitively on these mighty things.

Is there another life? Shall I awake and find all this a dream? No voice will tell: no God—no demon—deigns to reply, from heaven, or from hell.

You perhaps at one time thought there was such a thing as worldly happiness to be arrived at. I scarcely remember counting upon any. I looked not for it if it not be in the present hour—nothing startled me beyond the moment. If a sparrow came before my window I took part in its existence and picked about the gravel.

Man is a poor forked creature subject to the same mischances as the beasts of the forest, destined to hardships and disquietude. If he improves by degrees his bodily accommodations and comforts, at each stage there are waiting for him a fresh set of annoyances. The whole troubles of life are frittered away in a series of years, and what must it end in but Death?

The most interesting question is: How far, by the persevering endeavors of a seldom appearing prophet or philosopher, may mankind be made happy? Can I imagine mankind's happiness carried to the extreme?

In truth, I do not believe in this sort of perfectibility. The nature of the world will not admit of it.

This is human life: the war, the deeds, the disappointment, the anxiety; the weariness, the fever, and the fret. All human, bearing in themselves this good: they are still the air, the subtle food, to make us feel existence, and to show us how quiet Death is.

Do you not see how necessary this world is to spirit-creation, to school an intelligence and make it a soul?

Intelligence there may be in the millions: atoms of perception—they know and they see and they are pure, in short they are God—but they are not souls till they acquire identity, till each one is personally itself, to possess a bliss peculiar to each one's individual existence.

How are souls to be made then? How but by the medium of a world like this, effected by three grand materials—the mind, the human heart, and the world—acting the one upon the other for years?

The world is a place where the heart must feel and suffer in a thousand diverse ways, for the heart is the mind's experience, the teat from which the mind or intelligence sucks its identity: as various as the lives of men are so various then become their souls, and thus does God make individual beings from the spark of his own essence.

I'm certain of nothing but the holiness of the heart's affections—they are all, in their sublime, creative of essential beauty.

21

The city sleeps.

Magic sleep, comforting bird: you brood over the troubled sea of the mind until it's hushed and soothed. Night of silvery enchantment, full of tumbling waves and moonlight: we welcome your merciful renovations.

But: Dazzling sun, enduring lamp of the skies, that lures us back into the labyrinthine world—why must we show gratitude for your daily resurrection, our imprisoned liberty? What doesn't unfurl beneath your burning light for many a day but withers and dies?

My mother's last day on earth is here, and the sun will too soon rise over the hills of the East Bay to preside over it.

22

In some parts of the world, the sun has already breached in preparation for the new day. How effortlessly the sky appears to give birth to the sun, how willingly it allows itself to be transformed in return, from a speckled nighttime indigo through a burning daybreak orange to a jubilant sunlit blue, and how confidently the sun traces its arc through the sky, blazing its fiery path around the earth—the result no doubt of all that repetition and practice, the eons of strict observance of every natural law there is.

But my mother's pregnancy has taken a turn that few other pregnancies do. The abdominal pain she's been suffering from since yesterday is only the beginning. The medical term is *placenta abruptio*. The placenta that has kept me nourished and thriving, and is only to be expelled from my mother's body in an act of afterbirth, has begun to separate from the uterine wall, even before I am delivered to the world outside. As if it's in a rush to sever our connection.

I'm the first to sense this, a vague discomfort, as though there's something in the fluid enveloping me that makes me screw my face up so, eyes squeezed shut, brow furrowed. My thumb—my left thumb, for I must be left-handed—has acquired a taste that I can't find satisfying, no matter how much I continue to suck on it.

23

Wednesday morning: Arshad struggles through fajr namaz, unable to concentrate. Even after being up most of the night, he still can't settle on which symptoms to fake to persuade his father that he must stay home.

Arshad has no experience faking illness. If his mother were home, he'd never have agreed to Jemaal's plan—he has too much respect for her professional acumen. Fortunately, Arshad needs to convince only his father, who is usually preoccupied these mornings getting Amina ready for school.

Arshad can't decide between a stomachache and a fever—but what is he to do if Abba insists on checking his temperature? Also, he can't overdo the symptoms: Abba may then decide to have him examined by Khadija Aunty or may choose to remain home to take care of him. This first hurdle must be surmounted if the day is to succeed according to plan.

"You're daydreaming, or what?" Ismail taps Arshad lightly on the back of the head.

Arshad is still on his knees wondering which dua to pray for help with the day's enterprise. Startled, he hurries through the rest of the tasleem, staggering to his feet afterward.

"You don't look well," Ismail says. "Go sleep some more, you can read the Quran in the evening."

Fajr has brought some respite after all. Arshad returns to bed, heartened, after a glance in the mirror: he does look peaked and fatigued from the sleepless night. He may be able to get away with a low-grade stomachache, with generalized weakness thrown in for good measure. As though in answer to his dua, by the time he needs to get out of bed again, his body appears to have fallen in with his designs, sick with anxiety. He shuffles through his morning preparations, his sighs and groans are only slightly exaggerated, and when he doubles up clutching his stomach, the pain feels real.

Amina, his only audience, is easily convinced. "Abba, Bhaiya's sick," she runs downstairs crying, lending him credence.

His mother's call, coming then, also ends up working in his favor: she's not worried since he doesn't have a temperature, she announces, and he'll be fine if he stays home and rests.

Abba leaves him with solicitous instructions; Amina's eyes brim with sympathy and concern. He's reenergized when they depart, the feverishness his body had assumed fading even as his father's car turns into the street. The ease with which the first hurdle was overcome seems auspicious.

While waiting for Jemaal, he makes a list of possible targets, looking them up on his father's computer. When Jemaal arrives, Arshad feels once again the rush of blood through his body, making him light-headed with excitement and apprehension.

"Have you seen this?" Jemaal pulls up a video on a website. It features a boy about their age, speaking directly to the camera: "In recent weeks people may have been telling you what to think of us Muslims. They say that you should fear me. But I'm no different from other American teenagers—"

"What is this? We have to beg them to leave us alone?" It's similar to a video his father has shown Arshad, *My Faith, My Voice.* "While they can do whatever they want to us? Are you chickening out?"

"Nah! I was just showing you what Sajjad and Bilal want to do. They're all bull, no balls."

"Let's not waste time then. You were late." Arshad shows Jemaal the list he's made.

They argue about the criteria: the churches should be within bikeable distance, of course. But not too close to each other—this is Jemaal's condition—to create a sense that their crusade is far-reaching.

Arshad proposes, as a symbolic gesture, the Episcopalian church opposite their mosque, though he worries that it might direct suspicion toward their congregation.

"Let them suspect," Jemaal says, "they won't be able to prove anything."

They settle on it as their first stop. Jemaal picks the next one—a megachurch near the freeway that dwarfs the Islamic center being built. This is some distance away, so they decide to pick two more churches along the way, completing a circuit.

They look at photographs. A tall glass facade clinches one choice. For the final target, Jemaal says they need to include a Baptist church—he's heard that Baptists hate Muslims the most. After poking around the internet, they settle on one that looks enticing with its row of blue stained-glass windows. It has the added bonus of being the oldest Baptist church in the city.

There's one last decision to be made: What should they call themselves?

Jemaal suggests "The Avengers"—he's a fan of Marvel comics. It's Arshad's idea to look to the Quran, and happily they soon alight on one they can both agree on: Ar-Ra'd. The Thunder. The name seems appropriate: it's the title of the surah that speaks of unbelievers demanding of Allah signs of His omnipotence.

"The Thundering Avengers has a nice ring!" Jemaal says, but Arshad prefers the simple Arabic name.

Jemaal goes downstairs to pick rocks, while Arshad designs their "calling card." They'll make copies on sheets of paper that they'll fasten around the rocks. Arshad has given up on including the surah—it seems blasphemous to allow parts of the Quran to be crushed, or trampled underfoot—so the sheets will simply contain the takbir, Allahu Akbar, and their group's name.

Jemaal returns with his backpack loaded, he has chosen the rocks wisely: they fit easily in the palm, they're neither too heavy nor too light, and they appear hard enough, unlikely to crumble. They wrap a sheet around each rock, two rubber bands per rock, and split the rocks between their two backpacks. They lock the house and leave on their bikes.

They arrive at their first target, stopping by their mosque, square and squat in the tarmacked parking lot, its green dome dazzling in the midmorning sun. Diagonally across from it, at the far end of the block, is the church, hunched in the shadow of oak trees on its small rectangle of a lawn, only its steeple rising above the foliage.

The two boys dismount from their bikes. No glass is visible from where they stand.

"Let's go around," Jemaal says.

They cross the road, get on their bikes again, and cycle slowly up the block and around the church. There are small windows on the side, but the prospect is disappointing and anticlimactic.

Ah! There, in the back—a large wheel window with amber glass set high up on the wall, probably directly overlooking the altar. But, they won't be able to take a good shot at it from the road—they will have to aim from the lawn, directly beneath the window.

"I'll keep watch," Jemaal says.

Arshad crouches behind the trunk of an oak tree, ready to sprint, a rock in each hand, looking back occasionally at Jemaal standing by the street corner to get a better view of the roads, which have a constant trickle of cars speeding by. Arshad's bike is leaning against the tree, but he still has his backpack on—he's worried removing it may delay the getaway.

Twice Jemaal says, "Now!" But both times Arshad's feet refuse to cooperate.

"You have to do it as soon as I give the signal," Jemaal says.

He offers to take Arshad's place, but no—Arshad steels himself—he will see this through.

"Now!"

He's running, the rocks heavy in his clenched hands, the straps of his backpack pulling down on his shoulders. He's out of the shadows of the oak trees, cutting diagonally across the lawn.

The green of the lawn is a blur, the white of the walls flash past in his peripheral vision, the amber disk of the window hangs suspended like a full orange moon. He's aware of little else—not his pounding heart, nor his pounding steps, nor his dark little shadow scurrying just half a step ahead of him. His right arm is already swinging, but he knows his physics: he'll impart a velocity in an unwanted direction if he doesn't come to a complete halt before he takes a shot.

He digs his heels in, pivots toward the window, winds his torso, and releases. The rock leaves his hand and sings through the air. He doesn't wait to see if it has found its mark, he's immediately preparing the other projectile: wind and release again.

Alas! He's not ambidextrous. Even as the second rock leaves his left hand, he knows it's going to fall short—the thrust is simply insufficient. But he's already running back now, with hardly a sideways glance. He knows by the crack and clatter of falling glass that at least his first missile has been successful. He fumbles with his bike and leaps onto it.

Whir go the wheels, whir goes the gray of the road beneath him—relief, then exhilaration, surging through him. Swoosh goes the exhilarating air. He's vaguely aware of Jemaal's bike nosing his, the splotches of sunlight dancing over him, the blazing disk of the sun as he emerges momentarily between trees.

He races his bicycle down the block away from the scene of his triumph, zigzagging now as a delirious jubilant laughter bubbles through him. He wants to whoop, to let go of the handlebar and pummel the sky. He turns back to Jemaal who's also huffing with laughter, even as he's calling out to Arshad to stop.

Arshad has only one regret: that he didn't think to call out the takbir— Allahu Akbar!— as the rocks soared from his hands. The next time, he promises himself, the next time!

24

In San Francisco, Tahera wakes looking forward to a day spent with her mother. She now claims the dinner for Fiaz and Leigh as a gift Allah has bestowed on her, one of her last opportunities to cook a feast with Ammi.

She's grateful for it. She won't let her knowledge about Fiaz distract her; his conduct is a matter between him and his Maker. Who is she to judge, besides, whose is the graver lapse? She's ashamed now of the jealousy that had consumed her when she'd thought that he and Seema were a couple, destined for an open-armed welcome from their parents. Fiaz has been a support to Seema—she must have met him during her wayward days, which she must have renounced before her marriage to Bill—and Fiaz has brought joy to Ammi. What more can Tahera ask from a relative stranger? Judgment is up to Allah.

Last night's conversation with Ammi had been different from all the others since her arrival. Perhaps the music allowed Ammi to return to some earlier, less burdened time. Ammi didn't try to bring the conversation around to Seema, like in the recent past, but instead persisted gently in learning what was bothering Tahera. She could finally let her guard down, about the events back home and her concerns for her children's safety.

Ammi listened, without the derision Abba and Seema might show for what Abba has often labeled the results of her "Allah business." Her mother gave a look of understanding that Tahera had recognized and reciprocated: Look at what we've been forced to accept, what changes the world has wrought in us.

Tahera holds on to that look, for the hope it brings her: to give and seek solace from each other, as many times as is still possible. The efforts of the day, and the trip, will be worth that reward.

The day has already brought a few annoyances, but she's determined not to let them bother her. Her period has been heavier than usual, and she's had to change pads a couple of times already. Also, on her call with Irvine, Arshad seems sick, but hopefully not enough to be worried about.

She'd like to start on the cooking, but her mother first insists she check on Seema.

Seema has been experiencing a few contractions. The two sisters sit side by side on the bed, knees up, backs against the headboard. Tahera is glad for this moment of respite, before embarking on the long session that dinner will entail, for her heavier bleeding portends increasing nausea and headache throughout the day.

Seema grimaces every time one convulses her, biting her lips to contain her cry, clamping her hands tightly around Tahera's. This is the second one in the last half hour, and in between, the sisters have maintained a drowsy companionable silence to the sounds of Seema pecking away at her laptop. Tahera finds the pressure on her forearm, where Seema's nails dig in, strangely soothing—it makes her forget her own discomfort.

"And this is just the beginning?" Seema asks, after a particularly intense contraction.

"These are just Braxton Hicks. True labor contractions will grow progressively closer and become more intense, lasting up to a minute."

"I can't imagine how painful those will be."

Seema sounds scared. Tahera is reassured: here's the Seema she'd grown up with, the Seema who'd turn to her in moments of pain.

"You'll be okay." Tahera realizes, with some shame, that she'd looked forward to her sister's vulnerability, the only moments she'd felt needed, and appreciated. "You can always take epidurals if the pain becomes too much. And we'll be there as well."

A momentary bitterness: Who had been there for her, during her pregnancies? Her mother had wanted to come for her first pregnancy, but she'd refused her, aware of her parents' disapproval of the life in Islam that she and Ismail were creating for themselves. And she'd been glad for it: going through the process with only Ismail and Islam for support had brought her closer to both. She had fallen in love with Ismail then, the way he and his faith steadied her, finding a peace in the rituals of their life together. And doing namaz together till the last moment had allowed her to get through the delivery without needing an epidural herself.

But those times seem almost idyllic now, compared to what is currently happening at home. There are too many issues to reconsider. Perhaps the expansion of the Islamic center is misguided, and perhaps Ismail should rethink his involvement with it. And how to protect Amina and Arshad if the situation escalates? Maybe it wasn't the wisest decision to send them to an Islamic school. Maybe they should dress less differently, less conspicuously in the future—

But pondering these issues serves no purpose other than to aggravate her headache, sapping the energy she wishes to reserve for the day.

"I have to go help Ammi with the dinner," she says, pushing herself off the bed.

"Tahera, wait." Seema restrains her. "I need you to witness this."

Seema reaches over, awkward in her bulk, to pull a folder from the bedside table. She takes a printed sheet from the folder and fumbles in the drawer for a pen.

"It's my will—it names you as Ishraaq's guardian."

Tahera holds out her hand, and Seema hesitates but gives her the sheet. Tahera scans it without really taking it in, except for the line where her name appears: printed like the rest of the sheet. "You already made this?"

"I like to be prepared. You're still willing?"

"Am I allowed to sign this? My name appears in the will."

"I'd like something signed before I go into labor. I'll ask Fiaz later."

But Tahera hasn't spoken to Ismail yet. She hadn't expected to be confronted by anything official so soon. Also, she'd meant to clarify with Seema the matter of her child's upbringing in Islam. Tahera cannot agree to anything else, of course. But given the events in Irvine, she's not prepared to have that discussion now, when she herself is conflicted about the wisdom, though not the rightness, of some of the choices she's made for her children.

Meanwhile, not waiting for her answer, Seema has uncapped the pen and sprawled her signature across the bottom of the page. Then, while extending them to Tahera, Seema calls out to their mother, "Ammi, can you come in here for a minute?"

Perhaps Ammi would object to the making of a will today, deeming it inauspicious, affording Tahera a delay. But Nafeesa merely dries her hands on her saree and, taking the pen and paper from Seema, signs and dates the form as a witness.

Tahera cannot refuse now: she cannot appear to be backing away from her promise in the presence of her mother. It has brought her mother some happiness in her last days, and she can't take it away. She also cannot bear to introduce discord into today. She signs and dates beneath Nafeesa's signature, trying to recapture the moment that had led her to accept Seema's request: her face in Seema's lap, her arms around Seema, with both Seema and the baby comforting her, each in their own ways. It had truly felt like Allah's answer to her istikhara, that the guardianship and the renewed intimacy with her sister were right and good, for both Tahera and her faith.

And with this signature I formally gain a could-be mother.

25

Grandmother, you're glad to get the day's preparations started. There's a mound of red onions and tomatoes to be sliced, bunches of mint and coriander to be picked, almonds to be blanched and slivered, garlic and ginger to be peeled and ground to paste, meat to be cleaned and trimmed. And of course Tahera is doing most of it. She keeps an eye on you to make sure that you don't take on anything too taxing, and you keep an eye on her to make sure everything's done right—she tends to slice the onions too thickly, for example, which won't meld into the biryani as they should, but she blames it on how unusually pungent they are, making her eyes water so. Seema has closeted herself in her bedroom to avoid the fumes.

It's tedious work, and both of you labor quietly through the morning, you making light of your aches and pains and she of her period-related discomforts, so you can embark on the actual cooking in the afternoon. She has mentioned a few times already that she's lucky to be able to learn from a master, and you hope you haven't lost your touch.

You begin with trepidation.

But how redolent Seema's apartment soon becomes, Grandmother! First the toasted aroma of oil being heated, then the roasted sweetness of frying cardamom, cinnamon, cloves. Then onions fried till they're translucent, then the meaty ginger and garlic, then green chilies and fragrant coriander and mint. How the odors harmonize, how they swell and fill the apartment.

Seema says, coming out of her bedroom, "We'll never be able to get rid of this smell now."

But she's not complaining—her eyes are closed, a beatific smile plays on her lips. She decides to work at the kitchen table too, finishing her edits on the matter for the campaign. There's the spitting and sizzling from the pots, the occasional splutter of some whole spice exploding, and overlaid on these, the sounds of mothers and daughters working: chopping, stirring, typing, murmuring questions and directions.

By unhurried stages the distinct aroma of biryani assembles itself, at first fugitive and evanescent, but then lingering longer and longer, as though being coaxed out like a shy child.

Seema is overwhelmed. "This is too much. I'll be so sated by the smell that I'll hardly be able to eat any of it."

You know what she means, how filling just the aroma can be—you and

Tahera will be content with just a taste of the biryani when you're done. Gratified by her response, you shoo her back to her bedroom. You taste for salt the simmering sauce of the yakhni that Tahera spoons out to you, you check its meat for tenderness and give your approval.

You are relieved, though you still cannot be perfectly at ease until the very end—when the seal to keep the steam in is broken, and the basmati rice, added to the yakhni while still a little short of fully cooked, budded at the core, has absorbed the spices and liquids and blossomed to a perfect tenderness, releasing to the biryani its own distinctive fragrance. And this you will not know for an hour or more.

Even Tahera relaxes. She's been an efficient assistant all day, quick in executing your directions. But she's also been dogged in her efforts, as though she cannot afford to smile until the success of the biryani is assured. She smiles now. She insists you rest, while she takes care of the remaining dishes. But you want your hand in every dish today. As a compromise, you suggest some music to lighten the afternoon, and she agrees, even to ghazals.

So while Tahera gets the ingredients ready for the chicken, the crackling of Begum Akhtar's inimitable voice, the breathy harmonium and the bright sitar, the comforting percussion of the tabla, infuse themselves into the kitchen as well. It's your favorite ghazal: "Woh jo hum mein tum mein qaraar tha." *The understanding that we had between us, you might remember or not: that promise of steadfastness.*

It's a song for lovers, but it seems appropriate to you this afternoon, so reminiscent of those long-ago festival days in Chennai with the house buzzing this same way. The magic of Begum Akhtar's voice possesses you to exclaim that you wish your granddaughter would one day be able to sing this very song.

Once again Tahera hedges, like last night, and you have to draw it out of her: Masha'Allah, Amina has been bestowed a supreme talent, the way she picks up songs after listening to them a few times, reproducing long melodies with a nimbleness of voice, even if she has to substitute words she doesn't know with made-up lyrics. Yet the question of how—even whether—such talent should be nurtured is not easy to answer. It could be in violation of the Prophet's teachings if it serves merely to distract and arouse—so the Hadiths say. Ismail himself considers it to be something best enjoyed as a gift, a source of private and personal happiness.

You listen, old sorrows and frustrations resurfacing. You remember the first time you saw Tahera in a hijab, when she and Ismail had come to receive you and her father at the Dallas airport, your first visit after she'd followed Ismail to the United States. You were meeting Arshad for the first time—your first grandchild, two months old then—and though Tahera was holding the baby up, it was her face you couldn't drag your eyes off, a face small and scrunched in the hijab's clutch.

Tahera has maintained that it was her decision to don the hijab. The decision to later robe her body in loose-fitting jilbabs was hers too, she'd claimed, for the freedom of movement it gave her, as well as freeing her from wasting time worrying about her personal appearance, time she could little spare after Amina was born. She has defended Ismail: Ismail held that he could advise her on the teachings of the Quran and the Hadiths, the various fatwas by learned Islamic scholars, but she must make the judgment call and decide for herself what is required by Allah, as must every Muslim, for Islam was revealed as a forward-thinking religion, meant for all ages.

How different her life would have been if she hadn't insisted on marrying Ismail. Even from America, as her father wanted, there were other proposals. But she picked Ismail. "What's wrong with being a practicing Muslim?" she'd argued. At least she wouldn't be led astray on sinful paths, like Seema. She'd forced you and her father to give in.

"Why do this to yourself, Tahera?" you say. Meaning: Why burden herself with additional considerations, like whether the singing that gives one so much joy is a violation, or even namaz during one's period if it gives comfort, as if life isn't difficult enough already?

"Sometimes I wonder too," she says, a little shamefacedly. "I worry I'm failing my children, especially with what's happening in Irvine."

In the warmth of an afternoon spent in the kitchen, when everything—the smells, the sounds, the company—reminds you of an earlier time, a time when you were presiding, when your daughters would poke their excited faces into the kitchen to inhale the aroma and then pinch their noses shut "to trap heaven inside their heads," ready to acquiesce to anything you wanted from mere anticipation of the treat in store, in that heady fog of nostalgia and relived memory, you are compelled to speak:

Living in America is like living in an in-law's house, you say. When one marries into another family, one needs to learn their rituals. One needs to adjust and accommodate, one needs to continue charming and beguiling well-wishers, one needs to win over naysayers and adversaries by surrendering a little, by learning how to become indispensable to their well-being. One cannot survive by segregating oneself, by giving others reason to treat one as an outsider. One survives by learning how to fit in.

By the rigidity of her faith and practices, isn't Tahera opening her family to charges of fundamentalism, especially at a time when America has good reason to be suspicious of fundamentalists? Isn't Tahera making it harder for her children to succeed in America by not teaching them the skills they will need to flourish in its culture? If not for herself, she should at least think of her children. This is the lesson to take from the events in Irvine.

While you speak, Tahera continues cooking—she chops, she stirs, she holds out the ladle to you to taste, she inquires about next steps. She doesn't flare up, and you grow bolder and bolder in your pronouncements, heartened: maybe you are finally getting through to her.

Too late you notice that her eyes have hardened. You've said more than you intended, led astray by some miscalculation about her receptiveness and a trick of time that made you forget where you are. An unease settles in the kitchen, like from the first day.

"Say something, Tahera."

She remarks, in an offhand manner, "Did you know Fiaz is a homosexual? Is that the sort of American culture you want your grandchildren to be exposed to?"

She doesn't wait for your reply but turns back to the stove as if she'd simply made an insignificant observation, unrelated to anything.

You don't have an answer to Tahera's question. It's not that you're dumbfounded by the idea. Various details click immediately into place: Fiaz's almost effeminate good looks and sense of style, his implied bachelorhood and reticence about his home life, his easy relations with Seema, his love of fine things.

Dully, you begin pondering the implications of Tahera's revelation. Is Tahera mocking your intentions for Fiaz and Seema? Is that why she brings him up now, to demonstrate how little you know about life in America?

You feel small: how presumptuous, how foolish your advice to her, thinking her incapable of considering her own situation carefully. You will have to ask her forgiveness, as you'd asked Seema's last night. You had promised yourself that you'd listen, not try to fix what you don't understand.

"Shall we check on the biryani?" she asks.

A welcome distraction: you brighten with gratitude at this conciliatory gesture on her part. She lifts the lid and pries away the sheets of paper towels covering the mouth of the pressure cooker to absorb the steam.

Ah, there it is! That final elusive note of the aroma! One sniff, one glance at the rice—the grains fuzzy yet distinct—and you know the biryani will be perfect, you don't even need to taste it.

Tahera gives the pot a final mix, and then samples the biryani straight from the ladle. "One can't ask more of even Jannat than biryani like this. Seema's friends are lucky." There's an edge to her voice, but at least she's smiling.

"It's not only for Seema's friends," you say. "It's for you too."

The last couplet of the ghazal resonates—*Whom you once counted a friend, whom you once considered loyal, I'm still that same smitten one, whether you remember or not*—and you wish you could take Tahera in your arms again to remind her of those times. But she's returned to the chicken, skinning it with a matter-of-fact ferocity, and you fear you've squandered some opportunity that'd been granted you this afternoon.

26

Amina is waiting after school for Ismail to pick her up. In Arshad's absence, she stands by herself, by the main entrance just inside the lobby, which is emptying slowly of its inhabitants. Her friends have all left with their parents.

She wonders what her brother is doing at home. Is he feeling better? She'd remembered to say a dua for him at lunchtime, her hands joined in prayer, right after saying her Bismillah.

But her father is late. She's not concerned yet, comforting herself instead with an alternate vision: perhaps her mother will pick her up today!

Ammi will arrive and wrap her jilbab around her and drop a kiss on her head. And then they'll drive home, and Bhaiya will be there, and her Asma doll, and Ammi will give her a cupcake to eat—with frosting and sprinkles!— and chocolate milk to drink.

This catalog of pleasures keeps Amina occupied. She swings her lunch bag, she skips from one end of the doorway to the other, stopping in the middle to peer at the parking lot.

Her backpack begins to feel heavy. She takes it off and presses her face against the glass doors to peer around the corner, farther up the driveway. She's supposed to stay inside—Abba warned her specifically while dropping her off that morning—but Bhaiya, when he's with her, usually disregards this injunction and leads her to the playground at the end of the parking lot, claiming they can keep a better watch for their parents from the platform above the slide.

Except, of course, the playground has been spoiled—her face falls at the memory of the burned swing and slide. Nobody was allowed to go near the playground during recess or lunchtime today either.

But where is Abba? As minutes pass, the fear that she's been forgotten mounts. The teacher on watch is engrossed in her cell phone—Amina pushes open the door quietly and trudges to the end of the front porch, toward the parking lot, dragging her backpack behind her. Here she waits some more, dangerously close to tears, chewing at the corners of her hijab even though she knows she's not supposed to. But it feels as though everyone has forgotten her—including the teacher on watch—and with a stifled sob, she slips under the yellow tape into the enclosure of the playground.

It's a desolate and strange new country. In the center of the playground the charred structures tower over her like skeletons of dinosaurs. Huge blobs of deformed plastic are scattered beneath them, blackened animals in various attitudes of agony. The colors she admired—bright reds, greens, blues, yellows—are sooted. The soft white sand she liked to scuff is streaked through with gray ashes and debris. The odor of burning—Amina scrunches her nose—still lingers over everything.

And her favorite slide is no more. Only a tongue remains at the very top, twisted and fierce. Underneath it is a shapeless lump of plastic, which the tongue reaches toward as though it wants to lap it back up. Her stomach knots, like whenever she imagines something happening to Asma doll.

She whimpers: Who would do something like this to her slide?

"Bad men," Farah Miss had said in class that morning.

Farah Miss is Amina's favorite teacher. Farah Miss is young, tall, wise, kind, and always pretty in her light-colored hijabs and jilbabs—cream, lavender, rose. Allah will punish the bad men, Farah Miss explained. There are two angels writing down everything a person does, one sitting on the right shoulder, Raqeeb, who writes down all good deeds, and one sitting on the left shoulder, Atheed, who writes down all bad deeds. And one day when everyone is standing in front of Allah, Allah will consult with Raqeeb and Atheed and decide whether to reward or punish. On that day the bad men who had burned the playground will be thrown into the fires of Jahannam.

Farah Miss made the children recite their kalimas, Allah being the only one powerful enough to protect them from the evil work of the Shaitan and his helpers. Farah Miss then made them blow into their palms and down their chests to create an armor around themselves, so the evil Shaitan couldn't harm them. And Farah Miss went around the room, blowing on the forehead of each child, before starting the day's lessons.

The prayers work their magic again: standing with her eyes closed in the playground, Amina recites the kalimas—the first few fully, the last couple mumbled where she's forgotten some words—opening her eyes only after she's done blowing down her chest. Now all that remains is to walk around and blow over every object here, both fallen and standing.

She blows over the melted slide, the seesaws, the merry-go-round; she blows through the chain links of the melted swing. She blows into the air toward the sky, she blows onto the sand as she slowly spins around, so that her breath can reach every part of the playground.

A glitter in the sand catches her attention: it's one of two plastic figurines that were attached to a rotating drum mounted on a climbing structure. This figurine is the princess, with yellow hair and rosy cheeks and dressed in a sparkling white gown with a gold tiara on her head. Amina has asked Ammi many times for something similar to the tiara for Asma doll, but Ammi has always refused—tiaras are not for Muslim dolls. Amina picks the figurine up, brushing the sand off it.

The princess is unharmed except for a small fused section of the tiara. The prince is missing—Amina searches futilely in the sand—he must have melted in the fire with the drum. She cradles the princess close to her chest, singing to the princess the song her mother sings to console Amina when she's hurting.

At first Amina sings softly, whispering the song into the ears of the figurine. But she's alone here, with nothing around her but the ruins of a place she has spent happy hours in. She begins singing a little louder, as though she wants what's left of the playground to hear her. And then louder still: to the sand, to the air, to the skies.

Her voice is clear and ringing even to her own ears, and she revels in the sensation the song produces in her throat, in her chest, in the upper reaches of her nasal cavities as she strains for the high notes. She'd started the song plaintively, but as it works its way into her body, it transforms into something subtly joyous, the notes a little brighter, the tempo a little quicker, the cadences lilted toward the sky.

In the new universe she's singing into existence, the princess figurine has been restored to its original condition and united with the prince, the playground has been re-created, her mother has returned, her brother is well again, and she is safe at home, surrounded by everything familiar and dear to her.

When her father calls, she spins around startled, dropping the princess. Her father beckons from the car parked close. She fumbles to pick up the figurine, then sights her backpack, shrugs it on, and races toward the car, almost forgetting to duck under the yellow tape. Beside her father sits Arshad. No mother, but her disappointment lasts only a few seconds. Her brother must be feeling better; she's pleased he has accompanied their father to collect her.

But why does Bhaiya not get out of the car and help her into her booster seat as he usually does? Is he still sick? It's Abba who helps her, strangely stern and silent. Bhaiya doesn't even turn around to look at her.

"Look, Bhaiya, what I found—" She holds out the princess, remembering only belatedly that her father may not approve, but thankfully he's busy pulling out of the parking lot. Her brother, too, ignores her offering, giving no indication that he's even heard her.

"Are you still not well, Bhaiya?" Her fears for him, from the morning, return.

"No, he's not well." It's her father who replies. "He will go straight to his room when we get home."

On his face is a forbidding expression she's never seen before. There's none of the concern he'd run up the stairs with, when she'd called him to her brother's side that morning.

Something has changed, she senses. It's not a foreboding she can give words to, it's more an impression that some fire has passed through the world she knows, and everything—the playground, Abba, Bhaiya, perhaps even herself—has been melted and transformed into something dark and strange. She hides away the princess doll under her books in her backpack.

27

Leigh arrives at four o'clock, hours earlier than expected.

Tahera buzzes her up, looking in on Seema to announce her untimely arrival. Tahera appears frazzled, her face shiny with sweat from the heat and steam in the kitchen, her hair plastered to her head. She then retreats to the kitchen, picking up her hijab on the way.

Seema is herself surprised. What could Leigh want? Seema pictures a scene where Leigh races up the stairs and sweeps her into her arms to kiss her, while her mother and sister watch openmouthed. The prospect is both unnerving and exhilarating.

In the early days of their relationship, Leigh often acted in impulsive, unpredictable ways: turning up at Seema's office with takeout from their favorite

Burmese restaurant, slipping into Seema's apartment to light candles for when they later returned, kidnapping Seema for a day trip to a spa. But lately there have been few such incidents, which Seema is thankful for—Leigh's spontaneity can be exhausting, and the stunt with the candles was dangerous— though Seema also misses the excitement.

Today Leigh arrives empty-handed. "Don't mind me," she tells Nafeesa who has hurriedly washed her hands and come out of the kitchen to greet her. "I knew you'd be busy, I thought I'd take Seema off your hands, perhaps go for a walk?"

Nafeesa hesitates, looking back to Tahera in the kitchen for guidance.

"Ammi, I'm not in labor, don't worry," Seema says. "I'm not going to have a baby in the next hour—even the contractions from the morning have stopped. I could use some fresh air, and Leigh will be with me if I need help."

"What about your backache?"

"I took something for it. It seems to be working."

Nafeesa gives in. Will they drink tea before they leave? It will be ready by the time Seema has changed.

Leigh follows Seema into the bedroom, ignoring the warning shake of her head, and launches into a rapid patter about upcoming articles and interviews, Raj Goyle, the Indian American running for Congress in Kansas, and Jeremy Lin, the first Chinese American NBA player, clearly intended for Nafeesa's and Tahera's ears. As she helps Seema into something more suited to a walk outside, she stoops to cover Seema's shoulders and belly with swift giggling kisses, which Seema decides, keeping an eye on the open bedroom door, is wiser to yield to than protest.

Back in the living room, cups of chai in their hands, they sit conversing as though they hadn't just given in to teenage giddiness a few short moments ago, until Leigh puts her cup down and says, with an air of innocence, "Ready?"

They wait till they round the corner to hold hands. And then at the next corner Leigh leads Seema into a cul-de-sac, where they kiss, feverish and long, standing in the entrance of a recessed garage.

Afterward, Leigh sighs: "I needed that."

"I know, I missed you too." Seema chooses her words carefully.

At least San Francisco has conspired to give them a perfect October day for walking, for making up. The late afternoon sun is perched high above the hills to the west, skimming the hovering clouds, flooding the Mission with a light that clings to everything with a honeyed sheen—skin, hair, clothes, houses, streets. Above, the sky has yet to lose its limpid blue, and around, the air is humming with a warmed-over buzz, the city everywhere stretching languorously.

Seema tells Leigh about the ad against Prop 8 she'd written for the Harris campaign. They've rarely discussed the topic of marriage, both wary of broaching the subject, but this seems a safe step in that direction. Besides, Seema is proud of her work.

"That's awesome," Leigh says, with a kiss. "I must treat you to ice cream."

There's a line outside their favorite shop. They join it, still holding hands.

"When's the baby due?" the woman behind the counter asks, as she hands them samples.

"Any time now," Leigh answers for Seema.

The woman says, "Good luck, enjoy your baby! Is this your first?"

The woman's glance includes both of them. Leigh looks to Seema as if for confirmation, a hint of expectation in her eyes.

"Yes," Seema says, "my first." She adds a smile to involve Leigh in complicity, hoping that would suffice, but Leigh's shoulders drop. But what else could she have said? They're not there yet, however much Leigh (or even she) might wish otherwise.

At the bottom of the path, they pause so Seema can rest a little before the climb up. They watch the couples in the tennis courts swinging their rackets and missing their serves with easy laughter. Beyond the tennis court, men battle on an uneven soccer field with animated shouts and grunts. And beyond them, on the slopes of the hill, are the afternoon sunbathers.

Where do they come from—Seema wonders, as she's done before—the sunbathers and the tennis and soccer players, the people lining up for ice cream, partaking of the afternoon's store of pleasures with such familiarity? They made happiness seem easy, as though they could sense the universe's pulse and knew exactly where and when it was ready to offer up its coffers. A customary bitterness: she's not one of them. Happiness has never come easy to her.

A memory: A Sunday morning in bed, Leigh spooning Seema. They'd fucked already, but Leigh's hands start moving once again, in spirals, across the swell of her belly, down to the cleft of her thighs. Leigh stops herself. "I wonder what the baby makes of all this."

"The baby's happy if the mother's happy."

"Is the mother happy?" Leigh's lips on Seema's nape.

"Very happy." Drowsy and content.

They'd eventually gotten out of bed, and then this same walk to Dolores Park. The day had seemed cozy, like the bedroom they'd left: made to hold just the two of them. But later that same evening came the call from her mother about the diagnosis.

"Leigh," she says now, "last night I almost told my mother about us."

"But you didn't." Not an accusation, merely a statement, but resigned.

"It wasn't the right time." Seema is defensive. Leigh hasn't had to worry about her parents' acceptance. "My mother was crying, and I couldn't comfort her. I felt so bad. I'll tell her tonight after dinner."

They climb up the hill in silence to their spot at the top of the park, Seema holding on to Leigh's hand for support.

But how unlike that other day, when holding hands wasn't enough and they stopped periodically to touch each other: face, hair, the small of the back. At the Dolores Cafe, while waiting for their coffee, Leigh held her, hands resting on her belly, and they swayed to the sounds of the café and the street, oblivious to the crowd. They raised cups in a toast to perfect Sundays. They ambled up the hill, washed a vivid green by the September sun. Their bench was free, lit by a dazzling beam of sunlight. They took bites of each other's cupcakes; they fed each other spoons of yogurt.

And sitting there, they'd talked about everything and nothing: Leigh's dreams of going to grad school for journalism, the upcoming elections, Seema's work for the Harris campaign, the baby.

"Have you decided on a name yet?"

"I don't know how to pick. Nothing seems to call out to me."

"Maybe I can help." Leigh's hand on her belly, stroking it.

Raising Leigh's hand to her lips. "Yes, I'd like that."

"What are you thinking about?" Leigh asks now. They're sitting side by side on their bench, the city spread at their feet.

What Seema would like to say: I want to know what you see in me. Why do you want to be with me?

She senses the futility of the question, for no one could answer it fully, truthfully. At best an answer would contain truths, half-truths, and fictions one wanted to believe. Leigh has answered before: because Seema is beautiful, Seema is resilient, Seema doesn't let the world push her around.

But her resilience has come at the expense of keeping everyone at bay. She recalls her family, her friends, her lovers, her homes, the many she's left behind or escaped from, so easily, so cavalierly, over the years. Only to foolishly grasp at the next whoever or whatever offers passing succor. Like Divya, and perhaps even Bill. At least she has resolved the matter with Divya: yesterday, after the meeting at the campaign office, she'd told Divya she shouldn't have led her on, that she has no current intention of leaving Leigh.

If Leigh asked her the same question, Seema might reply: because Leigh is at ease with the world, Leigh makes life look easy, Leigh makes her happy.

She only knows how to fight the universe, as if there were no other way to access its secret store of happiness. Leigh is one of these afternoon revelers, who know what they want and are willing to accept it when offered.

If Seema were forced to be more truthful, she'd have to add: because Leigh also reminds her of her first and truest love, because she also fears having to bring up a child alone.

Perhaps it's better to accept without scrutinizing the reasons too deeply, to not try to separate them into truths and fictions but value them as a whole. Much like religions do—she's thinking now of Tahera—like faith does: For isn't love just like religion, this faith in someone other than oneself to help steer through the flow and ebb of life, to give meaning to life?

"I'm thinking about you," Seema says.

"What about me?" Leigh says.

"I'm thinking I can't go through the delivery without you by my side."

This at least is the truth. She is not promising anything beyond it—she cannot. She will speak to her mother—and if needed, her sister—about this. "I'm so happy," Leigh says, but quietly, resting her head on Seema's shoulder.

It must count for something that she, in some way, contributes to Leigh's happiness. She takes Leigh's palm and presses it to her belly. "Feel how strongly he kicks. He's ready to meet us."

It's a signal of my growing distress, but they don't know that. The sun is setting behind them, the city is flaring in front of them. She holds Leigh's palm there, as they sit in their favorite spot—steeped in light that's growing thick and darkly honeyed now, under a sky that sings in reds and oranges, then in pinks and purples. My two could-have-been mothers watch as the city first bursts into flames, then dies to ash-blue embers.

28

Tahera is on the terrace, the dinner ready, the kitchen cleaned up, seeking a moment to herself before Seema's friends arrive. But she must call and check on her children, and she's stressed, too, by how to tell Ismail about Seema's will. The usually restoring namaz is not a possibility today, and her body is leaden with exhaustion, having plowed through the day's exertions while battling her period.

Over the phone, Ismail announces that Amina has been crying all evening, and he can no longer soothe her. "She's not listening to anything I say. She wants you."

Tahera hears Amina in the background: thin whimpering cries, different from the gusty sobs when she misses her mother. Drained of the energy to determine the cause of her daughter's distress, she suggests that perhaps Arshad can calm her down. He's so good with Amina.

"I've asked Arshad to stay in bed," Ismail says.

"Does he have a fever? Why didn't you call me earlier?" she asks, moved to guilty concern for having forgotten about Arshad's illness until now.

"I can take care of Arshad," Ismail says. "Just calm your daughter, please."

She recognizes in the way he'd inflected his words—*your daughter!*—
that he, too, is close to a breaking point. She braces herself to face Amina's
querulousness.

How is mother's sweetheart doing? Why is she crying?

A jumble of sounds answers her: sobs, swallowed words, panic-stricken
wails. Tahera can't get a word in edgewise. Amina isn't listening: she has created a wall of sound around herself to keep her mother out. This is no time
for words or reason, the ways Ismail must have attempted to quiet her. She
knows what her daughter needs at this moment, and the knowledge helps her
overcome her weariness.

Tahera begins by hushing her daughter, patiently repeating the shushing
sound over and over again, a little louder each time, like a rising tide. Next she
croons a lullaby, from her own childhood days, the song she sings whenever
Amina wakes up frightened by nightmares.

Slowly Amina responds, her wails giving way to sobs, then to sniffles, then
to silence.

So Tahera asks, "What is it, Munni? Why are you so upset?"

"Bhaiya said I'll burn in Jahannam for playing with the princess doll,"
Amina says. Bhaiya snatched the doll with the tiara and threw it away. Bhaiya
threatened to never play with her again.

Amina's voice breaks, and Tahera is once more forced to pacify her. "Your
Bhaiya would never do anything to hurt you, Munni. Did you bother him?
You know he's not feeling well today."

To distract Amina, Tahera explains what happens when someone becomes
ill: how germs invade a body, how the body grows feverish and the mind grows
tired and irritable as white corpuscles in the blood fight the invading germs.
Eventually her Bhaiya will return to his normal loving self.

"Please come home, Ammi, make Bhaiya better. Abba is upset with
Bhaiya. He won't even speak to him."

Here Ismail interrupts, taking the phone away from Amina. In response
to Tahera's queries, he denies Amina's report: Nothing's going on with Arshad,
the boy has perhaps been acting up a little, from not feeling well. When Tahera insists on speaking to her son—she must learn how he's really doing, and

besides, it's so unlike him to frighten Amina—Ismail becomes evasive. She has enough to worry about with her mother and sister. Isn't Seema's delivery approaching? He's taking care of this. What can Tahera do from there anyway? He'll tell her when she returns.

Panic-stricken, like her daughter had been a little while ago, Tahera sputters: What is wrong with Arshad? How can she wait till she returns, worried as she is about her son? She has every right to know now.

Ismail finally tells her: Arshad was only pretending to be sick. Jemaal's uncle Selim was driving to his construction site when he happened to see Jemaal and Arshad on their bikes during school hours. They wouldn't stop when he called out to them, and he had to follow in his car to catch up to them. They gave every kind of excuse for being outside, and when he inspected their backpacks to see what they were hiding, he found rocks in them. They were planning to stone many churches in town. Unfortunately, by then they'd already inflicted damage on the church next to the mosque.

At first Tahera is too relieved to comprehend the extent of Arshad's transgression: a broken window is surely a small forgivable offense. "Should we offer to pay for the window?"

"Do you want to call attention to your son?" Ismail chides. "The fools left a trail. They wrapped paper around the rocks, signing themselves Ar-Ra'd or some such nonsense. The police are investigating. One window, and the boys will be labeled jihadis for life, with the FBI after them."

She hadn't considered this. She blanches: What will happen if Arshad gets caught?

"We can only pray that nobody saw them," Ismail says. He talks vaguely of keeping Arshad out of sight for some time. If Tahera were there to take care of Amina, he could take Arshad out of town. Perhaps he can coordinate with Jemaal's father.

But what about Arshad? What do they tell him? Surely they can't ignore what he did. What if it leads him down some terrible path?

"First, let's get the situation under control, then we'll worry about that," Ismail says.

"Let me talk to Arshad," Tahera begs.

No, Ismail says, not now. "I've already spoken to him, but everything I say only seems to make him more willful, more defiant. We'll have to be careful how we treat this. I'll talk to Imam Zia. Arshad won't listen to anything you say anyway."

Ismail hangs up before she can protest. His matter-of-fact assertion that she can do nothing to help her son stuns her with its authority, its truth. She's tempted to let his father and Imam Zia handle him their way.

But there's this: the anguish in Arshad's voice when he'd asked her, barely three days ago, "Why do they hate us so much, Ammi?" And she'd forsaken him, convincing herself his father was the right person to counsel him.

And also this: Amina's voice on the phone, trembling at the mention of the brother she loved, her desperate plea: Come home, Ammi, make Bhaiya better. As if Amina sensed—but how? by what sisterly connection?—some fever waiting to carry her brother away, some tragedy poised to change their lives.

But what can she do?

What has she ever offered Arshad, anyway? A son to whom she has never felt the way she should feel toward a son and who, perhaps in retaliation, treats her with the same remote and ambivalent affection. A son who slipped away from her even as he slipped out of her, and now may be slipping away even further.

She'd been pregnant with Arshad during her residency in family medicine and felt resentful at the disruption to the career she needed in order to rebuild some semblance of the life she'd left behind in India. Following the delivery she'd left Arshad in Ismail's care, to return almost immediately to her rotations. Had Arshad sensed her resentment? After her daughter was born, she'd smothered him with the same affection and endearments she lavished on Amina, but perhaps by then it was too late. She had to be content with his forbearance, his quiet eyes always watching her as though he could see through her.

She has failed not only her son but also her daughter, who loves him, whose happiness depends on him. Just like Tahera's happiness once depended on her sister.

She recalls her mother's words from the afternoon: Why do this to yourself, Tahera? You must learn to fit in. If not for yourself, at least think of your children.

Meaning: there is no one to blame but herself.

She feels it in her body, a sharp and searing pain: a grief deeper than she has ever known. For she's not just grieving the past but also some cherished future for her family, which seems on the brink of collapse. It includes the losses of the past—a sister, a father—and the losses yet to come—a mother, a son, perhaps even a daughter. The grief comes upon her so suddenly that she has to grip the terrace wall to hold herself up, as though the bones in her legs have melted.

But no! The floor under her has vaporized. She's hovering over the city of San Francisco, whose trees and houses and streets and hills are shimmering under her, awash in a fiery light she hadn't noticed until now, as though the city were burning and its flaming tongues were leaping toward her, threatening to swallow her up. The scorching flames of the guilt and remorse of mothers, daughters, sisters, unable to love or incapable of protecting those they hold dear.

This is Jahannam, she thinks, this is how it feels to burn in hell. Jahannam is the fire of grief, Jahannam is the fire of guilt and remorse. And above her the sky blares its reds and oranges. The sky is a warning screamed at her.

How long does she stand there looking at—but not seeing—the city as it slowly turns to cinders? Here's what she sees when the fire has finally burned itself out:

Up the street, two figures, hand in hand. The way one of them waddles instantly identifies her, even from this distance. At the apartment entrance, precisely below her, they turn toward each other and kiss. It's a long lingering kiss, meant to satiate some deep hunger. Then they part and, amid laughter, disappear into the building.

29

Evening's here, so come home please. I know no peace, there are no words for my heart's longing.

Noor Jehan sings, and you, Grandmother, are struck yet again by the pathos she wrings from the words. You've listened to the song a few times since yesterday, but twilight is the perfect time for it—as the sky darkens against the windowpanes and the universe shrinks to the room you're in, while promising to expand to the moon and stars.

"The resurfacing moon and stars revive your memory, pledges of your love," Fiaz translates from the song with a sigh. "But that's beautiful. Thank you."

Eyes half-closed, you both listen to the song. It seems to you, Grandmother, that Fiaz too is no stranger to this long wait at dusk.

"Why do *you* thank me?" you say. "It's *I* who am in your debt."

"For introducing me to Noor Jehan," Fiaz says. "I may never have listened to her otherwise."

You've been waiting to express your gratitude since he arrived half an hour ago. But the words have been difficult to pin down: so weighty, yet they flit like wary dragonflies. He arrived with flowers—brilliantly colored gerbera daisies. He followed you into the kitchen praising the aroma of the biryani, peering into the dishes for dinner, lavishing you with fulsome compliments in high Urdu, which made you laugh. He then busied himself arranging the flowers in a vase and later prowled around the living room on the lookout for Seema, until the song cast its spell, and you both fell quiet in its enchantment.

"You are such a good friend to Seema," you say. "You take such good care of her."

"She's like the sister I never had," he says.

"Then you're like the son I've never had." You hesitate, then continue, "You'll make someone a very good life partner one day."

You stumble on the phrase *life partner*—how cumbersome it is. But that's the only phrase you know and the only way you're comfortable talking about what you think of as his condition. You can't look at him as you speak, so you gaze out the window. You wonder if he'll acknowledge your clumsy attempt at declaring your acceptance.

"That's the nicest compliment anyone has given me," he says. "I have a partner. He knows how lucky he is to have me."

There, it's said. Now an uncomfortable silence settles as you both readjust to this new intimacy.

You cough. Fiaz clears his throat and wonders aloud: Why isn't Seema back yet? And where is your other daughter?

You say Tahera is still on the rooftop. And Seema and Leigh should be back soon.

You peer out the window, as if expecting to see them from up here. And having taken one plunge, you're primed for the next: "Are Seema and Leigh partners?" you ask.

The alarmed look on Fiaz's face is sufficient confirmation. You feel guilty for putting him on the spot, but how much longer could you have held back, after your suspicions were aroused by the way Seema and Leigh sat primly sipping their chai, like the many times you've witnessed Seema and Tahera put on a show of innocence after having concocted some mischief? The air around them had crackled with some shared secret.

"Seema didn't tell you," Fiaz replies, half question, half statement.

You're grateful again to Fiaz for not evading you. "I guessed."

He comes and stands beside you. "What are you thinking, feeling?"

"I'm glad," you say. But it's only a half-truth. You're sad, too. It explains what happened between Seema and Bill, but you don't understand it any more than you did years ago. "If it makes her happy. And it'll be better for the baby."

How challenging your promise from last night is turning out to be: to try to understand Seema. "Please don't say anything. I'll talk to her later, when we're alone."

You wipe your eyes and turn away from Fiaz: "Are you hungry? Maybe I should start heating the food."

Luckily, Seema and Leigh trip in, with apologies for being late: the sunset was so breathtaking they couldn't drag themselves away. Both of them glow, as though they've bottled up the last rays of the sun and brought it in with them.

"You said you were going for a short walk," you chide Seema.

You chide Leigh, too, for breaking her promise to bring Seema back early. She listens meekly, and you feel like a fretful mother-in-law.

After helping Seema to the futon, Leigh takes the chair opposite. They continue their pretense of being only friends, carefully monitoring their behavior for any slips.

You want to tell them: I know, so you don't have to hide any longer.

You want to say: Leigh, you should sit next to Seema.

You want to see them together, so you can reassure yourself of the value of what they have together—love, if that's what it is. But Grandmother, you don't, because—

"Where's Tahera?" Seema asks, looking around.

30

It's a while before Tahera returns to the apartment.

Nafeesa says, "What were you doing on the rooftop for so long? I even sent Fiaz to call you. You look chilled, dressed so lightly."

Tahera gives no answer. Yes, she's almost numb, but the warmth of the apartment is more jarring than welcome. She'd been pacing in the cold pale reality of the rooftop with only the moon for company, like the many times as a girl in Chennai, but there was only so long she could avoid the gathering in her sister's home.

Fiaz rises to greet her, Leigh waves. Tahera returns a perfunctory smile, a mere tightening of her lips, and fends off her mother hovering about her: "I have to pray my isha namaz."

Ignoring everyone in the room, she rummages through her suitcase for a fresh set of clothes, a fresh pad, then heads for her shower. A wadu will not be sufficient today, she will need to do a full ghusl. Her period isn't over yet, though the major flow has perhaps ended, but there is still some bleeding. But she can no longer go without her namaz. She needs its strength to face a world that feels even more hostile than it did just yesterday, with everything that has happened since the news of the arson. The room, with Ammi and Seema and her friends, feels almost like a battlefield she must steer through warily.

Tahera leaves an awkward silence behind her. Fiaz raises an eyebrow at Seema, but Seema is herself baffled. "I don't know," she mouths. Tahera has made no mention of Fiaz all day and had seemed happily engaged in the kitchen with Ammi when she'd left with Leigh. She looks to her mother for a clue.

Nafeesa murmurs, "Some things back home are upsetting her." She wishes now that she'd not provoked Tahera that afternoon. Or that she'd asked forbearance from Tahera for tonight, but she'd been afraid she might only make things worse.

Fiaz asks, "Was there more trouble at the Islamic center?"

"What trouble?" Seema asks, and Fiaz explains, an eye out for Tahera's return.

Nafeesa is surprised that Fiaz knows and Seema doesn't. "Seema, you should pay more attention to your sister's life."

Seema runs through her various conversations with Tahera in the past few days—how is she to know if Tahera doesn't talk about it? She has heard about the protests at Ground Zero in New York, of course, but hasn't followed the news. It wouldn't have occurred to her to connect it to Tahera and her family, anyway. She feels abashed at her ignorance. "Has it really gotten that bad?"

"I did a report on the protests at Yorba Linda and Temecula—people waving flags and chanting 'God bless America' in front of mosques," Leigh answers. She recalls how taken aback she'd been by her first sight of Tahera in her hijab and jilbab, and is conscience-stricken learning about Tahera's ordeals. "I'm not surprised worse is happening in Texas."

They're conversing in low voices. When Tahera comes out of the bathroom, the discussion halts. She's had a shower and changed her clothes—a dark brown jilbab, a light gray hijab with large indigo flowers, which strikes Nafeesa as pretty and unlike anything she's seen Tahera wear. Perhaps it's intended for the guests? Nafeesa notes that Tahera hasn't dried her hair properly—drops of water drip down her face—but before Nafeesa can say anything, Tahera walks straight through the room toward her belongings, as if there's no one else in the room. She picks up and unfolds the janamaz with a flick and spreads it out in her usual spot.

"Tahera, you should pray in Seema's room," Nafeesa says, a little sharply. "We have guests."

The walk across the room has required all of Tahera's resolve. Like with the men in front of the meat shop in the Tenderloin and the shoppers in Safeway, she is the target of stares and whispers, judgment and contempt. She's sure

Seema and her friends, even Ammi, have been discussing her affairs, pretending concern, but in reality, judging her for her beliefs and practices, as Ammi had done that afternoon. Thankfully they don't know about Arshad, but if they did—the shame burns brighter. They would judge her as negligent, condemn her son as hateful and out of control.

She trembles. She'd unfolded the janamaz out of agitation and habit, but the reprimand in her mother's voice stings. What is so discomfiting about namaz that it needs to be out of sight, as if Seema's guests can't abide it? Perhaps because it reminds them of what they owe Allah. She feels compelled to continue where Seema and her gay friend and her lesbian lover can watch.

She starts her salat with the takbir, but in her haste has forgotten to mentally voice her niyyat—*Allah, I intend to pray four rakaat as fard for isha namaz, facing Ka'ba*—and must start over.

If she'd been concerned earlier that her namaz may not be accepted for praying while her period isn't over, she has more reason now, riddled as her namaz is with makruh acts caused by her lack of concentration. For though she's facing the corner walls, she's unable to dismiss the presence of the others. She struggles on, feeling none of the peace of mind she'd sought in the namaz.

Fiaz does notice Tahera's small mistakes: arms not clasped when they should be, an extra sajda instead of sitting up in jalsa. Tahera is clearly becoming frustrated, fumbling even more as she tries to recover.

"Let's go to the kitchen," he whispers to Seema, "and let your sister pray in peace."

He leads the way, and they stand awkwardly around the dining table, until Nafeesa says they may as well set the table while they wait.

They set the place mats, the plates, and the cutlery. Seema is to sit down, since she's experiencing some pain, as if contractions were resuming. The three work quietly so Tahera isn't disturbed. And then the food is transferred to serving dishes, except for the biryani, which must wait until Tahera joins them so it doesn't get cold.

Their muted actions are still too loud to Tahera's ears. Even as she strives to focus on her namaz, she recalls the evening she arrived—was it less than a week ago?—when Seema and her mother were setting out dinner. She'd been right to be anxious then, for hadn't Seema already wreaked havoc on her life once? She had come, anyway, to support her dying mother and offer what aid she can her sister, because that's what her mother wanted. And this is what it has led to: while her own life in Irvine threatens to fall apart, she's here participating in Seema's licentious life.

There is no getting away from it: Seema and her community talk of tolerance, and the Quran warns about judging in Allah's stead, but Allah could in no way have intended that she be accepting of what He has denied His creation. If she had known that Seema had returned to her former ways, she still may have come to San Francisco, for Ammi's sake, but she would have known to hold her distance from Seema.

Maybe this day is a warning, that the permissive comforts from her past life, which she'd been slipping back into so easily, are really distractions to her faith she needs to guard against, whatever Ammi may say.

If she needs proof of how easy it is to forget the teachings of the Quran and the Prophet, then an account of her visit provides a list of temptations: the non-halal chicken the very first night, the book of poetry, the steadily impairing association with Seema's friends, Seema's request of guardianship, the music, and tonight's dinner. She's been led to this point, step by step. If the Shaitan needed a helper, he couldn't have done better than use her sister. And she'd fallen for it: she'd been on the verge of letting Seema back into her life, even believing it to be the answer to her istikhara.

Why is she still here? She has better things to do: she has her own family to tend to, a daughter who needs her, and a son whom she's failing. She is unable to even find the immersion she craves in namaz—each sound from the kitchen yanks her back into a depraved world.

Finally, the sounds stop. She's done with her rakaat for isha but decides to pray a few more for the optional prayers. And also duas for forgiveness and mercy, if Allah is indeed unhappy with her lapses, and for Arshad's safety and well-being. Perhaps his act was intended by Allah to remind her of her true life in Irvine, to return to it immediately. This must be what her vision of Jahannam on the rooftop means. She'd mistaken that, too, imagining in that moment of grief that the loss of sister and of son were alike. Until her eyes had been opened to Seema's continued transgressions.

She raises the volume of her recitation, so the buzz of the surahs can fill the living room and infiltrate the rest of the apartment, cleansing it.

In the kitchen, Seema succumbs to irritability. Surely Tahera is keeping everybody waiting to call attention to how namaz is more important to her than the dinner she'd spent all day cooking for Seema's friends. Like the martyr Tahera used to like playing as a girl.

"I'm hungry," Seema frets. "At this rate, I'll be in labor by the time she finishes."

Nafeesa looks: Tahera is still moving through her prayers. It would be unseemly to start dinner without her—especially since the dinner owes its existence to her—but Nafeesa is nettled by Tahera's disregard for their guests. She decides: "Why don't you and your friends start? I'll wait for Tahera. She won't mind."

Fiaz demurs, but she ignores him. The aroma of biryani fills the room as she transfers the fragrant rice and mutton to a serving dish.

Fiaz breathes in the aroma, his chest and frame expanding as though to suck in all the air in the room, a smile on his face. "How can I say no to this?"

Nafeesa is gratified. "Eat, eat," she urges. "I hope it's to your liking."

She searches for bigger chunks of meat to serve him and Seema. And Leigh as well—at first hesitantly, unsure if Leigh likes Indian food, and then with growing assurance as Leigh praises the dishes.

Satisfied, she settles down to watch them eat. The way they pass the food around, the way their eyes exchange smiles—like a family, she thinks. Something intimate is being shared, without words, through the very harmony that permeates their eating together.

Tahera faces the quiet dark of the living room corner. Behind her is laughter, the sounds and smells of a celebration, from which she is excluded. She can picture the scene, as if she were observing by the kitchen door: Seema and her lover and her friend all focused on their plates until the first throes of hunger and desire are sated, while Ammi, having prepared the feast, would barely be eating, her eyes more on their faces than on her own plate, feeding off their pleasure. A new family coming together.

Whatever be the rewards in the afterlife, Tahera has no doubts now that she is to be punished here on earth, shunned by family and country alike, for never straying from the straight path, while Seema, who has only ever pursued her own desires, is to be feted, rewarded with this new family. And soon the pleasures of a son, while Tahera is to be left with the pain of failing hers, which too could be traced back to the day Seema walked out of their home. The evening fires from the rooftop may have diminished, but now they spark and flame again, only this time with anger.

31

Grandmother, you hear Tahera finally moving around in the living room and you call out, "Tahera, come to eat. We're waiting for you."

There's no response, and you decide to check on your daughter.

"Tara," you start, and then stop at the sight of the red suitcase lying open on the living room floor, her clothes and belongings stacked in piles around it. "What are you doing?"

"I'm packing," Tahera says.

"Why do you have to do that now?"

"I'm leaving. I'm going back to Irvine tonight."

You stand still, not knowing what to make of her statement. Tahera is down on her knees, stowing her clothes in the suitcase. "Why? What's happened?"

"My son is ill," Tahera says.

You bend over Tahera's suitcase, not sure whether you mean to help her pack or unpack. What could an eleven-year-old be suffering from that suddenly required his mother's presence? Tahera must be overreacting. "How can you leave now? Seema will be in labor soon. Is Arshad really that sick?"

"What does it matter? He's my son. I have to go. I want to go." She dumps the last of her belongings into the suitcase and slams its top shut. "I'm not needed here anyway. You all can manage very well without me. Go, enjoy the feast I cooked for Seema and her friends."

You place a hand on your daughter's shoulder to help her rise, worried now. You lower your voice: you don't want anyone in the kitchen to hear you. "I didn't want to keep our guests waiting. I'm sorry I asked them to start without you. I still haven't eaten. Come, don't behave like a child. You'll spoil the evening—you put so much effort into it."

Tahera, squatting on the floor, stares up at you—she seems to have shrunk to the willful child you once knew her to be, though never as wayward as Seema. She shrugs your hand away, and struggles to rise, lifting the suitcase at the same time.

"Yes, I'm the one spoiling the evening. It doesn't matter that Seema already has. She gets to do whatever she wants, and you'll still fly to her side, even feed her your biryani."

"Tahera, please!" you say, gesturing her to calm down. Surely Seema and her friends must be listening—the sounds of eating have ceased. You glance back at the kitchen door—at least no one's watching. You lower your voice even further: "What's all this about?"

"Ask her what kind of relationship she has with her friend." She resists your attempts to lead her to Seema's room. "I thought she'd given up all those haram activities."

You're perturbed: How did she learn about Leigh? But more importantly, what do you tell her? Grandmother, how do you speak when you haven't made peace yet with Seema's choices yourself, even though just a few minutes ago you'd been grateful for the friendship and love surrounding her?

"Tahera, this is not the time to discuss this," you say in Urdu, so Leigh won't understand—you wish you hadn't been speaking in English before. "They will hear. Please."

"So you knew, already," Tahera replies, still in English. "You knew and didn't tell me. What you must think of me, that I wouldn't help if I knew, even if my dying mother asked."

You shrink at her anger—where does it stem from? You want to deny knowledge, you want to say: I learned of it only today, I learned of it from Fiaz. You know she's seeking reassurance that she's a good daughter, and you want to assure her you know of her love and thoughtfulness and kindness toward you. But you're so focused on preventing further disruption to the evening, that instead you say, "Tahera, they are our guests. What will they think?"

"Let them think what they want. I've done nothing to be ashamed of." She turns toward the kitchen. "I'm not the one violating Allah's decrees. And for what? Just because Seema wants to draw attention to herself, she wants to think herself different—unique—so she can look down her nose on the rest of us, as though we're mindless sheep for following the Quran and the Prophet."

She makes a quick round of the room, as if searching for something. You follow a step behind her, trying to gather your courage to hold her by the arms and calm her down, if you still have the strength to.

You know your words from the afternoon rankled: she includes you when she talks about being looked down upon. You want to tell her: it wasn't just frustration that drove you but sorrow too. You know as well as, if not more than, anyone else the effect of the constraints on one's lives, real or assumed, imposed from the outside or by the self. For hadn't you let yourself be ruled by your husband's dictums all these years and paid the price for adhering to them, and for breaking them? The price in both cases was crippling.

But you can't say this, because you know your comparison won't be welcome. You can't tell her, when she's this angry, that you understand Allah can demand a heavy price from His creation. That you understand she believes she has no choice in the matter. Just like Seema does.

Tahera sees the Quran and rehal on the bookshelf, grabs them, and darts to open her suitcase to put them away.

"Tara—" You touch her arm, grieving for both your daughters. Why should they each struggle separately, when they have each other and could use each other's support? "Don't judge your sister so harshly. She doesn't deserve it."

"Always thinking only about Seema." She spins around to strike your hand away. "I'm not doing any judging. But Allah will. She will burn in Jahannam if she doesn't correct her ways."

The upright suitcase, latches released, falls open. In Tahera's haste to prevent its contents from tumbling out, she lets the Quran and rehal slip from her hands. The hardback suitcase halves crash to the floor anyway, followed by the thump of the Quran, and the clatter of the rehal.

You'd stepped back to avoid them landing on your feet, and you stumble. You're afraid you too will fall, but someone catches you. It's Fiaz, and behind him Seema and Leigh, pale as ghosts.

"Look what you made me do—" Tahera blazes, at you, at everyone behind you.

32

"Enough, Tahera, enough," Fiaz says. "We respect your choice—to live according to your strict interpretations of the Quran. It's not the only way to be a Muslim. You don't have to insult us."

Seema has never heard Fiaz this forceful before, or this stern. He stands between her and Tahera. She's ashamed of hiding behind him, like she hid behind her mother with Bill yesterday. She hadn't expected she would feel this sick to her stomach even after it was clear how Tahera would react.

A stranger stands before her, a stranger in her stark attire and implacable face, with the Quran in one hand, silhouetted against the light from the floor lamp. She's unrecognizable as the sister of her youth, or even the sister from just days ago—not the girl in twin plaits who'd looked up to her, nor the woman who'd cried in her lap after braiding her hair. And not even the sister from just that morning, the one who'd reassured her that she'd be there with her for the delivery.

"Seema can speak for herself," this stranger says to Fiaz. "What *you* do is no concern of mine."

"What your sister does is no concern of yours either," Fiaz says.

Their mother cringes at Fiaz's tone. "Son, please—" Nafeesa restrains him with a hand on his arm. "Tahera, let it go."

"Son!" the stranger sneers. "Your son and daughter are birds of the same feather. You must be proud of who they are."

Even this Tahera, the one with the dark flint inside her, seems to have some power over Seema: Leigh squeezes Seema's hand, but Seema instinctively withdraws it.

What does my mother continue to want from this sister?

Now that she is on the verge of being deprived of it, my mother can admit it to herself: she wants what that day spent with Tahera's children promised.

"Will you come visit us?" Amina asked, and even as my mother sought a lie to let down the child, she grasped at the prospect of a permanent mooring, which has eluded her since her exile, where she could access again and again the unadulterated happiness of that day, reminiscent of her childhood where she didn't have to fight the world for it. Even her happiness with Leigh doesn't compare, accompanied as it is with the fear that it isn't meant to last.

Did she conjure up, for herself and for me, the hope of visits between siblings and cousins, like in Chennai, so that it wouldn't be just the two of us—mother and son—dependent only on each other for any sense of stability and continuity? And had she even contemplated paying the price she'd once rejected, the shameful silence that would enable it, if both parties agreed? With my grandmother's prognosis, it had felt urgent. And only this morning, with Tahera signing the will, it had felt possible.

Tahera touches the Quran to each eye, then collects the rehal from the floor and makes protective space for them in the suitcase lying open at her feet. The rest of the strewn contents she stuffs haphazardly back in and closes the suitcase. She tightens the hijab around her head, picks up her handbag from beside the futon.

"Tahera, don't go," their mother pleads, in Urdu. "Seema, say something."

"If she wants to go, let her go," Seema rasps, in English. "I'm not going to stop her. You came to see Ammi. Well, now you have—"

"Are you saying I'm a bad daughter? As if you are perfect."

"Seema, Tahera, stop—" Nafeesa wrings her hands, but both sisters ignore her.

"I know I'm not perfect," Seema says. "But even I can see what Ammi needs now."

"Yes, this is what Ammi needs now!" Tahera waves a contemptuous hand at Leigh. "So you and your lover are going to take care of Ammi? Seema, you've never taken care of anyone but yourself."

"You don't think we can?" Seema takes Leigh's hand back in hers, aware that she and Leigh have never discussed this before. But Leigh doesn't pull away.

"You people are selfish. You only think about yourselves. Did you even stop to think what effect this will have on Ammi's health? Of course you didn't—the same way you didn't think about us when you ran away to pursue your selfish sinful desires."

"Now you're simply being hateful, Tahera," Fiaz says.

Tahera turns on him. "At least I am trying to live honestly and quietly, and by my understanding of the Quran. I will be able to answer to our Maker, but will you and Seema?" She pauses as though expecting Seema to respond.

"Yes, you live very quietly!" Seema bites back with spite. "With your fat-was and your jihads and your suicide bombs. No wonder everyone is afraid of you, even in Irvine."

Tahera pales, pulls her jilbab tighter. "If that's what you believe, then why did you ask me to be your child's guardian? Why didn't you ask your lover? Or your best friend? Nobody who shared your *liberal values* was willing?"

Leigh's hand in Seema's goes slack. "You asked your sister to be Ishraaq's guardian?"

"Oh, you didn't know?" Tahera's laugh is bitterly strident. "She had us witness her will just this morning. I wonder why she asked me and not you or her ex-husband. I don't know how long your kind of relationships last. Maybe she doesn't expect to stay with you very long. Knowing Seema, she may have already found somebody else. But who can say what Seema is really planning? It's hard to guess—" Tahera's face scrunches up. "Maybe she thought if she asked me, I would be happy to stay and do the cooking and cleaning and be the unpaid midwife as well. Be careful, she may only want you as a babysitter."

No one attempts to stop her: there's no stopping her, she flings her arms after each accusation as if to block any response from getting through to her, the flared sleeves of her jilbab her shields. "I'm sure that's why she married Bill, too—so Abba would take her back. You're a user, Seema. You use and throw people away, you don't care who you hurt—"

Every shaft finds its target. But Seema has something new to worry about: Leigh has pulled away and grown still.

"Is she right, Seema?" Leigh says. Her lips seem to hardly move, but Seema feels the burn in her words. "Is that all you want from me? A babysitter for Ishraaq?"

It's an assault from both sides: a thwarted sister, an anguished lover. Who is Seema to respond to first? And how to deny the half-truths on both sides?

You're a user, Seema.

How to speak when the truth is not simple, when everything she says will need qualifications, and those qualifications will need further qualifications, and so on. How to explain in a moment what has taken a lifetime to accrue?

And here's something else, working from inside my mother's body, undermining her further: a rift is opening up between the placenta and her uterine walls. A trickle of blood—an embryonic spring—is welling into the uterus and pooling around my amniotic sac. She registers it as a discomfort in her abdomen—she shouldn't have gorged on the biryani, or is this perhaps the beginning of labor? An invading languor, an apathy almost, renders her unequal to the task of facing her sister and her lover. I register the reduced supply of oxygen and glucose as an irregular heartbeat, a climbing chill, a fickle tipsy consciousness.

Can my mother sense my distress? Her mind is elsewhere, grappling with what to say to the two women confronting her. She finds nothing that can heal the rifts, has little energy for it now. The two women continue waiting.

Leigh gives up first. "I should leave."

Nafeesa, harassed, depressed, says, "Look what you've done now, Tahera."

She gestures to Seema to do something to stop Leigh, but what is Seema to do?

There's not much time anyway: Leigh moves quickly, stooping to collect her jacket and bag. Without even pausing to put on her jacket, she gives a thin smile to Nafeesa, whose hand is extended out toward her, and letting herself out of the apartment, clatters down the stairs. The door to the building opens and shuts.

The silence is broken by Tahera: "I didn't ask her to leave. I asked nobody to leave. I said *I* was leaving."

"Then leave," Seema says. "Everybody leave. I don't need anyone's help, I don't need anyone. I didn't ask you all to come here. Just go. Please go."

She turns toward her bedroom, without a glance at her mother or sister. Fiaz makes a movement toward her, but she stalls him. "You too, Fiaz. I'm tired. I'll call if I have *use* for you."

She shuts the bedroom door and locks it. She doesn't turn on the light. She climbs into her bed and pulls her comforter over herself. She ignores the knocks on the door, the rattle of the doorknob, Fiaz's strained voice, and places a pillow, her mother's pillow, on her face to block all light from her eyes, even though the room is already dark. The smell of the coconut oil her mother uses assails her nostrils, and she turns the pillow over to the faint scrubbed fragrance of detergent.

This dark is a blessing. This solitude is a blessing. She takes a few deep breaths, and her lungs fill with relief, as if she'd been holding her breath not just the last few minutes, not just this evening, or even this week, but all her life.

The pillowcase is cool against her eyelids, like leaves with the drip of summer rain after long dreary days of oppressive heat.

Her mind glides toward calming thoughts: flowers budding in gulmohar trees, mangos ripening in fragrant stillness, monsoon suns smiling through shiny eaves, sweet Reshmi's cheeks, a smiling infant's breath.

And all the while, blood continues to pool and swirl around me, in shifting fleeting patterns that neither of us can see.

33

Poor Tahera. Her sister has locked herself in her room. Her dying mother regards her with eyes that threaten tears at any moment. And though Fiaz stands by Seema's bedroom door, he appears to be present everywhere she looks, judging and condemning her. What is she to do?

A part of her wants to apologize, to throw herself around her mother's neck, to knock on Seema's door and beg for forgiveness. But these actions would constitute an admission of guilt, which she cannot bring herself to do. For to do so would be to accept the enormity of her offense, not only against her sister but against her mother as well, and her own understanding of the teachings of the Prophet. So she tells herself: Allah as her witness, she has done nothing wrong. She stands irresolutely by her suitcase, clutching her handbag to herself.

"I'm going to catch a taxi to the airport," she says, testing her power to leave.

Does she want Nafeesa or Fiaz to make another effort to persuade her to stay? And if they did, would she give in? But the option is not presented: Nafeesa is still bereft of speech, and Fiaz is ready to take Tahera at her word.

"I'll drive you," he says.

He makes his offer without any rancor that she can detect. Is he simply determined to get her out of Seema's apartment? Does he mean to take her to task on the way? Or is he laying claims to being the nobler Muslim? Her indignation gives her the strength to leave: "There's no need. I can manage by myself."

She looks toward her mother for a last sign of protest, then picks up her suitcase and heads to the door. The suitcase is heavy; she cannot make a quick exit like Leigh did: she struggles to hold the door open while hauling her suitcase through. Fiaz appears behind her, and this time she accepts his help. He descends first with her suitcase, and she follows with her bag.

She is halfway down the stairs when she hears her mother cry, "Tahera, wait."

Nafeesa's footsteps sound behind her, but she continues down the stairs and out the building entrance—Fiaz holds the door open for her—into the cold San Francisco night.

"Thank you." She takes her suitcase back from Fiaz. It's a stroller; she pulls the handle out, then waits for her mother to join her.

Nafeesa shivers as soon as she steps out onto the street—she has on only her thin sweater.

"Go back, Ammi, it's cold," Tahera says, but her mother appears too dazed to respond.

The three stand by the entrance to Seema's building, like actors who have forgotten their lines. Tahera nods to Fiaz—she wants him to leave, she knows her mother will say nothing in his presence. "I'll be able to find a taxi myself, Allah Hafiz."

"Good night." He accepts his dismissal politely.

He extends his hand to Nafeesa, who returns a squeeze. "Aunty, tell Seema to call me."

He turns and runs lightly down the street, leaving Tahera alone with her mother.

And still her mother says nothing. Even a reprimand would be welcome. Tahera is bitter: her mother has chosen Seema. The prodigal daughter has returned, and the long-dutiful one is to be turned out for misbehavior, without even a chance to explain herself. Seema has stolen her mother as well. She tells herself she cannot forgive her sister, even if it means she cannot ask for forgiveness herself.

There should be taxis around the corner, two blocks away, and she begins dragging her suitcase in that direction. But first she must, she will, say goodbye—this could be the last time she sees her mother alive. She will not let herself be cheated of this moment too.

She turns around, sees Nafeesa following her. Tahera waits till her mother catches up.

They walk to the sound of suitcase wheels rumbling over the uneven pavement and the slap of Nafeesa's slippers against her feet. The street is dark except for dull light bleeding out of a few lit doorways and bright white halos under the occasional streetlamps. When will her mother say something? Under one of the halos, Tahera allows herself a quick glance. Nafeesa's blank gaze is on the pavement, as though mesmerized by the patterns there. She's accompanying Tahera mindlessly, stopping when she stops, stepping off the pavement to cross the street when Tahera does. Her mother has escaped to some other world, become lost there.

Now they're near the bustle of the main street. Time is running out, and Tahera has only to reach that brightly lit corner for her world to be altered, perhaps irrevocably. *Say something, Ammi*, she wants to cry out. She prays for something to change the course she's on—perhaps she won't find a taxi, perhaps she's too late for the last flight to Dallas, perhaps she's left her purse behind and cannot buy a ticket or board the airplane—even as she realizes that it's in her power to turn back. Yet how powerless she feels.

At the street corner, she rummages through her handbag: she does have her credit cards and license. Is there anything she's left behind? The only thing that comes to mind is the book of poetry Seema had given her. She'd seen it lying forlorn beside the Quran but had not packed it. Forlorn! The very word is like a bell to toll her back to herself.

And here is an empty yellow taxi drawing up at the traffic light. Is it a vision or a waking dream? Automatically she raises her hand to flag it down.

"To the airport." Her voice is surprisingly firm, yet appears to be spoken by someone else, not her. Is she awake or asleep?

She cannot bear to look at her mother. The driver—Middle Eastern, maybe even a Muslim, she thinks inconsequentially—springs open the trunk and swings her suitcase into its depths. Deprived of its weight she feels untethered, as if she could float up into the fog-hazed skies to join the fading moon, leaving the streets, the lights, the city's inhabitants—her mother and sister—behind.

The driver thumbs open the passenger door for her and climbs back into the car. She turns, finally, toward her mother in a hungry embrace, almost throwing herself at Nafeesa, as if to not give her a chance to resist. She buries her face in her mother's hair. She would like to press Ammi into her body, to inhale Ammi into her lungs, to kiss Ammi's cheeks and eyes and forehead and hands, to memorize the feel of every inch of her skin.

What she still cannot bring herself to do is meet her mother's eyes.

"I must go," she mumbles into Nafeesa's hair, fighting a sudden and terrible urge to justify her decision. She cannot maintain the embrace any longer without breaking down. She releases Nafeesa, then scampers into the taxi, pulling the door behind her with extra force, afraid her mother might follow her inside. The crash resounds in the cab, and the driver asks, "Were you trying to break the door?"

She doesn't reply. She has her face pressed to the window, her eyes fixed on the figure at the street corner: small, crumpled, and diminishing, while the moon continues to stalk her.

34

Say: You who tread a different path! I do not revere what you revere. Nor do you revere what I revere. I shall never revere what you have revered. Nor will you want to revere what I revere—

To you your path, and to me mine—

35

Grandmother, where are you? What's keeping you? Please return soon. There's hope yet: there's life in us still, and blood still trickles through your daughter's veins.

Her hand, still warm and capable of grasping, would, if it were cold and in the grave, so haunt your days and chill your remaining nights that you would wish your own heart dry of blood, just so in her veins red life might stream again and your conscience be calmed.

See, here it is—she holds out her hand, she cries out to you.

36

My mother's last conscious moments with me: She struggles up in the dark of her bedroom, unable to comprehend what has woken her. The liquid warmth of her blood is a shock, but so familiar from her childhood that she presumes herself in Chennai, waking up to a familiar if infrequent deluge.

"Abba," she calls out, "Ammi—"

The blood has soaked through her clothes to the sheets, and she pulls her knees in to escape the wet patch, even though in the dark she can't make out its extent. But her own body prevents her, a protrusion growing out of her, solid, globe-like, unexpected. It's then she panics, awash in realization, one thought screaming through her mind: Ishraaq!

For one long paralyzed minute she wills Bill to be here, to help her out of this puddle of blood and carry her away, as he'd done once before. But, of course, Bill is no longer by her side, and neither is Leigh, and Tahera has left, and she's sent Fiaz away and locked her mother out. Her father is oceans away. She's all alone, like she'd always feared.

She fumbles for the switch of the bedside lamp. Her hand strikes a vase and sends it crashing down—first the splash of water, then the shattering, loud in the confines of the room. She forgoes the hunt for light and lurches out of bed, her only thought now to get out of the room toward help—for her baby, her baby!—for whom she would bear the pain of stepping on glass, though she tries to avoid where she expects the shards to be.

But it is the water that undoes her, slimy from the stems of calla lilies soaking in it for two days. The first hobbled step on the slippery hardwood floor, and her foot slides. She teeters for a moment, for the second time in a week, poised as if time itself has paused, and then her world pitches backward. Her hands flail, seeking a reprieve, something to intervene, but this time there is no sister to pull her to safety. Her head strikes the bedside table.

Her last gesture before she loses consciousness: one hand strokes feebly the dome of my world, offering and seeking comfort.

Oh, that each moment could be an age. Then we could live long in little space, and Time itself would be annihilated.

37

Grandmother, you're sitting on the front steps of Seema's building. When you return from seeing your younger daughter off, you find the door locked—it locked automatically behind you. There's no response when you buzz Seema's apartment, and you decide to sit down for a while, because it occurs to you that you don't want to return immediately to Seema's home. You will rue this lapse soon, Grandmother, you will beat yourself up over it.

The truth is, Grandmother, just as you couldn't find it in you to be angry with your husband all those years ago, you can't fault Tahera for her departure now. You don't disagree with everything Tahera has said. Though you want to be, you're not yet entirely comfortable with all the choices Seema has made. And you're not unaware of Seema's shortcomings—unlike your husband, you've mostly had a clear-eyed understanding of your elder daughter's sometimes manipulative and self-serving nature. Some of Tahera's accusations have insinuated new misgivings in your mind, which you don't know what to make of yet.

In your defense, Grandmother, you've had only a few hours to digest the reality of what your elder daughter is asking of you for the second time.

"I'd rather have no daughter," her father had proclaimed the first time, during one of their many rancorous fights on Seema's last visit from England, "than one who makes me hang my head in shame."

"I cannot lead a life of falsehood," your daughter had declaimed in reply, "just to save your face."

What life she wanted to lead, you didn't ask then—because you couldn't imagine that life as being anything other than impossible, unhappy, fruitless. Even the words to describe it—*homosexual, lesbian*—have sibilant, sinister overtones. You refused to use the words and dismissed the matter as another of Seema's attempts to shock you. You reproached her for her willfulness, you begged her father for forgiveness on her behalf.

Even on the morning you found Seema gone—her room bare, her clothes and suitcase missing, pale rectangles on the wall where her favorite photos used to be—you didn't take her seriously, thinking it a ploy to bring her father around. You thought she'd gone to your sister's house, where she'd been spending a lot of time during that trip. Only when you learned she was not with Halima did you start panicking.

You've seen today—finally, at the dinner with Seema's partner and friend—the contours of the life Seema could lead. But you've not been given time to grapple with the knowledge; you've once again been asked to pick sides, this time between the two daughters you'd hoped to bring together as your last act of motherly consideration. The rift you'd come to heal has ripped open wider than it had been before.

You want some time alone with your sorrow—your multiple failures as a mother—before you face your elder daughter again.

Presently you rouse yourself. You press the buzzer and speak into what looks like the intercom. Still no response. You're more irritated than alarmed—Seema has locked herself in her room and perhaps can't hear the buzzer. You know none of the neighbors; you gather your courage and buzz the floors below and above. A man responds to your second attempt. He grunts at your flurried explanation of being locked out and buzzes you in.

At least the apartment is open. The smell of biryani overwhelms you as soon as you enter. You look into the kitchen: dishes and plates as they were left, remains of an unfinished dinner. You cannot bear to see these signs of a ruined evening. You had such hopes.

You clear the table, scrape the food off the plates into the garbage. As for the dishes and the biryani—will anyone have the desire any longer to eat them? Still, you can't throw them away. You make space for them in the fridge.

Only then do you knock on Seema's bedroom door. First timidly, then peremptorily. You rattle the doorknob, you push against the door. It won't budge, and there's no reaction from inside.

Now you're frantic: you call out her name, hysterically almost, a heavy hand squeezing your heart.

What are you to do? You are alone, thousands of miles from anything you're familiar with, with no idea how the world works here, no knowledge of its rules and protocols. Whom to call?

Tahera may be at the airport already, and it would take her a while to get back, and—yes, Fiaz, but alas, you don't have Fiaz's number. You do have Bill's number though.

Your hand trembles as you fumble for it. You pray that he will pick up, that he will listen to you, despite what happened yesterday. Was it only yesterday? The first ring, then the second, then the third cut short as Bill answers, and before you hear his voice—

"Son, son," you sob in Urdu, because for what you have to say, and even for what you can't find the words to say, it's the only language that moves your tongue at this moment. But, of course, he doesn't understand you. You panic that he may hang up, you force your tongue slowly around words that feel foreign to it now, you force yourself to give voice to your fears clearly and specifically.

Yes, Bill says, yes, he will be over, they should call 911, call an ambulance, he'll call them, what's the address again, is there anyone else in the building to help, he'll be over, don't worry, it will be all right, it will be all right, it will be all right.

You want to believe him.

How do the next minutes go? You must have run upstairs to the neighbor who let you in and somehow convinced him to help. Did he try to break the bedroom door down before the ambulance arrived? He must have tried, he must have given up. Did the ambulance come screaming down the street pulsing blue and white? You must have been watching out for it on the fire escape, you must have run down to meet the two paramedics stepping out of it. You must have shown them the way up. The three of them—the paramedics and the neighbor—must have forced the bedroom door open. Someone must have turned the bedroom lights on.

Seema is on the floor beside the bed, lying on her side. Her head is raised, propped up at an unnatural angle in the niche between the bed and the dresser, her eyes closed. One hand is thrust up, as if trying to hold on to the side of the bed. A dark red smear on the sheets trails off at the edge of the bed where her fingers curl. Under the curve of her belly, which looks enormous, as if she were pregnant with a lifetime's worth of babies, a thick wide pool glistens red-black against the hardwood floors. Merging into the pool of blood is a colorless pool of water, with scattered flowers—the calla lilies—lying in it, among shards of glass.

You stagger back to the splintered door, unable to stand any closer, unable to take your eyes off her, unable to watch. The two paramedics bustle around her, setting her on a stretcher. They call out to each other instructions and observations that you can't comprehend. They ask questions that you don't realize are directed at you, because they're looking at your daughter. The neighbor repeats them to you, nudging you out of your trance.

You must have tried to answer their questions. They tell you that your daughter's pulse is present, though weak, since she's lost much blood. They think they can still hear my heart beating. They won't know for sure until they get to the ER. You clutch at the small glimmer of hope their words give you.

They must have carried the stretcher down. You must have remembered to grab Seema's maternity bag before you followed them. You don't remember locking the apartment but do remember noticing for the first time the color of the carpet that covers the stairs—crimson—and the dark mahogany-red stain of the handrails.

Bill must have arrived by then. You feel relieved: you're no longer alone. At least there's one other person to share the unbearable weight of this moment with you. You embrace him, grateful he's here. Bill must have asked what he can do to help.

Call Tahera, you tell him. You must have been able to recall Tahera's number. You wish you had Fiaz's number, and Leigh's, too. You wonder what your husband is doing right then.

One of the paramedics says you can ride with them. Someone must have helped you into the ambulance and handed you Seema's bag. Bill says he will follow in his car, he must have found out where they were taking you.

The ambulance screams through San Francisco's streets to the hospital. Yet how long the ride seems to last. The inside of the ambulance is lined with equipment of every kind but apparently none that can help your daughter. Was it only two nights ago, that dinner on the rooftop beneath that full promising moon, when you'd declared with so much certainty, "Nothing will happen"?

You imagine her calling out to you as her blood began to spill out of her body. You recall that day from long ago—the day your newly menstruating daughter bled uncontrollably—when you attempted to soothe her fears as she lay crying, her head in your lap. Both these daughters, the past and present Seema, lie on the stretcher beside you now, as do all your imagined versions of me, and you would give anything—your blood, and your life, too, for what use is what remains of your life anymore?—anything to keep us with the living.

Coda

I

At his home in Chennai, a husband, father, grandfather is busy with his daily correspondence. There are decisions to be made: Which proposals to support? Which speaking engagements to accept? Which invitations—to meetings, dinners, and receptions—to decline?

He has a routine he adheres to religiously since his wife's departure. After waking up, he goes for his morning walk in the park around the corner, stopping first at the neighboring restaurant for his morning cup of tea. On his way back he picks up his breakfast from the restaurant, his usual order kept ready for him: two idlis and two vadas, the sambar and chutney packed in small plastic bags. He shaves and showers, dresses, then eats his breakfast reading the newspaper. When the maid arrives, she'll clear the table, wash and put away the plates and dishes he's used, then sweep and clean the house, while he works in his study.

Now he consults his calendar and makes plans: he has a full day, ending with the keynote speech he's to give at the Indian Medical Association's annual convention. When the maid is done housekeeping, he leaves the house and won't return until bedtime. He looks over the speech, about the responsibilities of doctors in the twenty-first century, and makes a few final edits.

He ponders for a moment whether he should call his wife. But why should he? They should be the ones calling him.

2

In Irvine, a father watches his daughter fall asleep. She lies in his bed, the side where her mother usually sleeps, whom she's cried for all evening. She is silent now, but her face, even in repose, is tense. He strokes her hair, waiting for her body to slacken, and studies in the half gloom the worried creases of her fore-head, the tight thin lines of her lips.

Eventually, when she has slipped into a sufficiently deep slumber, he lifts her into his arms to carry her to her own bed. But he pauses by the door of the children's room, suddenly reluctant to enter. He turns and carries her back to his room, her body a comforting weight against his chest.

Later, he's ashamed: Is he afraid of his own son? He lies awake in bed pondering, then persuades himself to return to check on the boy. His son is sleeping peacefully, his chest rising and falling with the grace of a bird riding a gentle breeze, his face serene, lit by Allah's own words and the ceiling's glowing universe.

3

At the San Francisco International Airport, a daughter, sister, mother waits by the departure gate for her flight to Dallas: she has bought a ticket on the last flight leaving that night.

When her phone rings—displaying a San Francisco number—she's quick to answer, on the hope of hearing her mother's voice again. But it's a voice she hasn't heard before, a man claiming to be her sister's ex-husband. He tells her that her mother asked that she be informed about her sister: bleeding, emergency, ambu-lance. He gives her the name of a hospital and is in a hurry to hang up.

But she *needs* to be at home, by her children's beds, looking down at their sleeping forms. Hasn't she been punished enough for her decision to abandon her son and daughter? She has her boarding pass in hand, her luggage has been checked. Surely her sister will be all right—

She remains rooted to her spot.

4

In the halls of a hospital in San Francisco, a wants-to-be father paces the marbled floor, one end to the other, spinning visions of the future: the joys of accidental fatherhood, perhaps even an unexpected restoration of his ruptured family. Any doubts he's harbored have been replaced by the simple longing to hold the baby, and the mother, in his arms, even if he has to—as he will, as he wants to—accept the inclusion of a fourth into the family.

He'd never really believed life capable of granting him this. But now he feels a strange stirring of hope, of pride almost, of attaining some kind of happiness. Like the day two years ago when a man in his image was elected president of his country.

Surely it is a sign that he's been called to be present here today. He has declared himself the father of the baby to be born; he neglects to correct the nurses when they refer to the mother as his wife.

He's not unaware of the dire peril to mother and baby. A nurse has tried to reassure him: they're doing everything they can. He has willed himself to believe the doctors capable of miracles.

5

In one unlit corner of the waiting room, a mother, wife, again-to-be grandmother stands with her back against the wall. She feels safer in the relative shadows, away from the light, as if by doing so she can escape the malevolent attentions of the universe. Every time someone—a doctor, a nurse, an orderly—enters, she shrinks a little as if to render herself invisible, preferring ignorance to bad news about her daughter and the baby.

But as the minutes pass uninterrupted, a slow anger builds: Will no one— no doctor, no soothsayer, no god?—reveal to her the outcome of this waiting and free her from this particular hell? She's been patient long enough. The time allotted to her is even now running out.

Until then she'd accepted her impending death with resigned equanimity, much as she'd accepted everything that happened as simply how the world worked. But now she wants more than just the knowledge of the well-being of her daughter and her baby:

She wants to hold and coddle her grandchild, to be there when he takes his first steps, when he utters his first words. She wants to teach him Urdu, to sing him Urdu lullabies and ghazals. She wants to see her daughter settle down with her partner; she wants to cook for them the most delicious meals they've ever eaten.

She wants the world—for herself, for her two daughters, for all her grandchildren—more fiercely now that she's confronted with a world slipping away from her.

A figure approaches, haloed under the light, unearthly, otherworldly. He's a doctor, a healer—like her husband, her daughters' father, but not him—and as he draws nearer:

Oh, what comfort does he bring?

6

Inside an operating room, a not-to-be mother is laid out on a table under the cool annular brilliance of surgical lighting, her domed belly exposed.

She's unaware, of course, of where she is. Her heart continues to pump what feeble blood it can. Her lungs continue to inhale and exhale a straitened air. She's hooked up to machines that monitor her body for signs of life, to tubes that dribble into her the blood and fluids her body has lost and the anesthesia that will deaden her to any pain her mind can still acknowledge.

Around her assemble doctors and nurses, their hair covered, faces masked, bodies gowned, hands gloved. Scalpels and scissors, forceps and suction tips— these are the tools at hand for these robed figures: inadequate, but the best they have. A scalpel slits through the skin and fat covering her belly and slips into her womb.

Blood seeps out of her like a spring. Gloved hands probe the interior of her split womb, seeking to lift out her blood-smeared baby. The umbilical cord connecting her to the child is snipped. Her body struggles to hold on to the wispy flame of life still flickering through it. Others bear the child away.

7

Here I am, breached into this world, all twenty inches of me, all seven pounds, with all my features and appendages in their place. The downy mammalian hair that once covered my entire body is gone. I'm fully and independently human now, even if I haven't yet taken my first breath.

To think that only nine months ago, I was a mere leech, the size of a grain of rice, clinging to my mother's walls. And then a lump of flesh, pea-sized, formless and shapeless, just a week later. I was an inch, head and heart in place, limbs budding, when my mother decided to keep me. My urogenital folds had fused and extended out to form the spongy shaft of my penis, clarifying my boyhood, by the time my father rejected me. I was beginning to make my presence known, pushing out against my mother's abdomen, when she first met her current lover.

Two days earlier, when my mother's sister accepted guardianship of me, I was ready—my intestines already functioning, fashioning and storing what will be my first stool, black and tar-like, while my lungs, the most developed of my organs, lay compressed but ready to assume from my mother's lungs the task of providing oxygen. I was as prepared as I'd ever be to leave behind the three shells that had protected me from the world's harsh brilliance: the placenta that nourished me, the uterus that harbored me, the body that housed me.

When I emerged from my mother's womb and the umbilical cord was severed, a reflex triggered by a hunger for air should have made me gasp, and I should have taken my first breath. My lungs, until now a crimped-up mass of solid tissue, would have then expanded with their first taste of air, and my blood would have begun to flow through them, to be renewed there. The respiratory muscles that line my rib cage and diaphragm would have become engaged, forcing me to take my second breath, and then my third.

But I don't respond this way, and someone slips a suction tube into my mouth to clear my windpipe and induce me to start breathing. Someone else wipes me clean of the blood and mucus smearing my face and body. They thump me on the back—part encouragement, part prod—to shock my body into responding. My collapsed lungs resist, and someone places a mask over my nostrils to force air into me. My stubborn lungs strain with the pressure, but even as I convulse and splutter, they expand only slightly.

As if, by some grace, I've been given the power to choose whether I wish to enter this world or, by holding my breath, forsake it.

8

On a ship sailing from England to Italy, a poet despairs—a storm rages outside, and a storm rages within. He's confined to his cabin in this wooden coffin taking him away from everything he loves. It's not fame he lusts after anymore, nor the moon's otherworldly beauty.

His friends and supporters have chipped in generously to finance this convalescence in Rome, in the hope that the merciful Roman winter would grant him a reprieve, allowing him to return to his world—to his fiancée and friends, to his poetry. But he knows there's to be no return from this journey. The symptoms are recognizable—blood, phlegm, a wasting away, a hollowing of chest and body. Hasn't he nursed and lost his mother and brother to the disease's ravaging clutches?

He has asked the friend accompanying him to buy him some laudanum for seasickness—a drink of that could put an end to his suffering. Who would have thought the human heart capable of containing so much misery?

The sea outside, the very air, heaves and strains.

9

In the basement of a church in Oakland, a to-be father who will never know his son serves a much delayed breakfast to hungry children. There are three tables, each with twenty kids, and they've been waiting for food the last thirty minutes. They've been led in their daily pledge already—I pledge to develop my mind and body to the greatest extent possible; I will learn all that I can in order to give my best to my people in their struggle for liberation; I will discipline myself to direct my energies thoughtfully and constructively rather than wasting them in idle hatred—and one of his Panther comrades has given them an impromptu lecture on resistance and history, but they have less than half an hour to get to school, and they are restless and ravenous.

He arrived at the church early that morning only to find the storeroom ransacked—the flour strewn around, the fridge emptied, the eggs smashed, the milk spilled—and one window busted open. There had been little time for anger or investigation, but he's sure he knows the perpetrators: the pigs in uniform.

He'd immediately set about trying to forage supplies for some kind of breakfast to feed sixty hungry kids, leaving his comrades behind to clean up the mess—he refused to even consider turning the kids away. He stopped at the pad to scrounge for whatever cash he could find and managed to procure grits and sausages and a few cans of orange juice concentrate.

He's in the kitchen dishing up the next batch of plates, listening with pleasure to the laughter and joking in the next room that returned once breakfast was announced, when there's an abrupt silence. And then the bellow: Who's in charge here?

Sounds of a scuffle, chairs and trays being shoved aside, shouts and screams, the whimpering of kids, the protests of his comrades. He rushes to take a look, finding trays on the floor, an orange-yellow mess of grits and juice. The children cower in their seats, their faces frozen in fear. His two comrades are lined up against the wall. Covering them, with guns out, are three White cops, weaving and blustering, while a fourth stands guard at the entrance to the basement.

Instinctively, he darts back into the kitchen and picks up the pistol he keeps hidden behind the fridge, in anticipation of such occasions.

10

At the airport, some passengers notice a woman hurrying away from the departure gate. This wouldn't have bothered them except that she's wearing a hijab and is covered from head to toe in a dark-brown gown. She looks frantic, almost disturbed. They debate whether this is cause for concern and decide they'd rather be safe than sorry.

They inform an airline employee, who passes on their concerns to a security agent, who after some consultation institutes the following precautions: the terminal must be thoroughly searched for any unattended baggage; all carry-ons must be examined manually on every flight leaving the terminal; all flights with possible Muslim passengers must be flagged and delayed till the agents are able to identify the fleeing woman.

Many passengers—some frustrated, some scared, some angry—call friends, family, lovers to advise them of the delay, and to hear their voices for what could perhaps be the last time.

II

In the Castro, a lover returns to his apartment earlier than expected and finds it empty. Not wishing to spend the rest of his evening alone, he sets out in the hope of locating his boyfriend at one of their usual haunts. But repeated text messages go unanswered, and after checking bars for some time, he gives up and returns home, changes into pajamas, and climbs into bed. He gives a friend a call to check on her, to offer and seek sympathy, but gets no answer from her as well. He'll eventually fall into a fitful asleep. Later, he'll be vaguely aware of another body joining him under the sheets. He'll turn automatically to his side, so that the length of his partner's body is pressed against his, comforting, the way he likes it.

In Oakland, in her small tomb-like studio a lover lies awake in her bed, dry-eyed, alone. When the phone rings, she springs to answer, but it's not her girlfriend, and right now she doesn't want to speak with anyone else. Her mind replays the evening, reenacting the moments so it doesn't end the way it did: banished from the only world she wants to inhabit, the enveloping warmth of partner and child. She'll drift through the night, waiting for the phone to ring.

12

In Washington, D.C., a president who'd once proclaimed the virtues of hope has woken up in the middle of his sleep, despondent. His party is poised to be trounced in the upcoming midterm elections, and with the House passing into opposing hands, he may not be able to achieve anything more before his current term ends. He may even be denied a second term.

I am firm in my belief that the interests we share as human beings—justice and progress, tolerance and the dignity of all human beings—are far more powerful than the forces that drive us apart.

He's feeling a little sorry for himself: his opponents are proving more adversarial than expected, united in the goal of denying him any success, viciously rooting for his failure. He'd tried working across the aisle, as he'd promised he would, wooing them with concessions and compromises, which they'd rejected, rousing their base against him.

He's a little bitter too: his own supporters seem to be turning against him as well. They already seem to have forgotten that he inherited an economy on the brink of collapse, a military mired in two wars, a nation under terrorist threat. Instead of having his back, they take pride in whining about how disappointed they are, condemning any compromises, and protesting pragmatic steps as too little, as if perfect failure were somehow more admirable than imperfect success.

All of us share this world for but a brief moment in time. The question is whether we spend that time focused on what pushes us apart, or whether we commit ourselves to an effort to find common ground.

Yes, he'd campaigned in poetry and is governing in prose, but surely adapting to the way the world actually works is the only rational thing to do: he has no power, after all, to compel the world to comply with his wishes.

We have the power to make the world we seek, but only if we have the courage to make a new beginning.

He must continue to hope.

13

At the airport, the woman weaves wildly through the passengers heading in the opposite direction, indifferent to the startled eyes trailing her. There are no taxis waiting outside the terminal—she's on the departures level. The few cabs dropping passengers off don't stop for her, despite her frantic waving. She must seem hysterical, she imagines, a tiny woman running toward them with her hijab fluttering, her jilbab billowing in the cold Bay Area breeze.

In desperation, she darts in front of a cab speeding away. It swerves to avoid her but does come to a stop. She clambers in, breathlessly announcing her destination, hoping the driver knows where the hospital is. The driver begins to protest in his gruff Russian accent, but something in her demeanor must be convincing of some emergency, for he nods and turns the meter on.

She's riding the same route she'd taken scarcely a week ago, except this time she's alone. But not entirely, for the ghosts of her mother and sister accompany her—a mother abandoned, a sister spurned. Sitting on the edge of the seat, she keeps her eyes fixed on the road ahead to avoid the sight of the empty seats beside her.

When the cab climbs up the final hill into San Francisco, she can see very little, the hilltop blanketed by a fierce swirling fog. When the taxi crests and swoops down the hill, she is dizzy, as though she is falling off a cliff whose base is hidden somewhere deep in the clouds of fog rising to meet her.

The city has been obliterated, erased with some vicious white marker, and in its place is a smoking void. Only occasionally the billowing fog parts enough, to reveal at times feeble pinpricks of house lights, at times glowing rivers of headlights like molten lava overrunning a hillside.

Somewhere in that are her sister and mother. It strikes her now that she's riding into its fiery ruins for some definite trial and sentencing. For doesn't the Quran warn of grievous penalty when the sky issues forth a smoky mist to envelop the people?

Perhaps her punishment is to be that her sister and mother are forever lost to her, erased from her life. She recalls that evening decades earlier when she'd walked into her sister's room, only to find it bare, stripped of every sign—her sister disappeared with meticulous care. And—Allah forbid!—if something were to happen to her sister or the baby now, her mother would never forgive her. As she would never be able to forgive herself.

She'd allowed herself to behave hatefully. What had gotten into her, she who has always prided herself in her righteous ways? Her son's face rises before her eyes—she imagines it at the moment the rock flew out of his hands, the set of his jaws, the line of his brows—but no, she cannot blame her son for her actions this evening. She sees it clearly now—whatever hurt, whatever anger, whatever hate drove him to such an act, it surely also belongs to her.

For a brief urgent moment she contemplates asking the driver to turn back to the airport: she needs to be in Irvine right away, something hanging there in the balance. Otherwise she may be too late, returning to her son only to find every loving trace of him erased. Hadn't her husband spoken of whisking her son away? But then there's the threatened erasure, too, of her sister and mother. Why is Allah forcing these dilemmas on her?

The cab is hemmed in by the traffic brought to a crawl by the fog, too far from the airport to make it back in time for her flight. Surely Allah knows best: He is, after all, the Most Beneficent, the Most Merciful. She can only hope she's being led to some sort of redeeming test, her son's and her sister's fates somehow linked and connected.

Allah, she prays, Allah, spare my son and my sister, let nothing happen to them.

The driver turns a startled face toward her: she has spoken the prayer out loud. Please hurry, she tells the driver, please hurry—

The car revs and lurches forward into the fog, the pale nebulous light opening and closing around them. And the car swings and zips down blurred streets lit by milky lamps, past drowsy traffic lights, past phantom buildings, through the ghostly remains of a shrouded city.

All the while she repeats the prayer under her breath, sitting on the edge of the seat and rocking herself back and forth, the way her daughter sometimes does. It's a child's prayer, repetitive and insistent—she's slid back into a practice of praying from her childhood days, unmediated by a surah from the Quran or a dua, unmoored from regular offerings five times a day, from a time when prayers were part entreaties, part demands, part inveiglements, part threats, part negotiations, scripted by the needs of the hour and whispered over and over again to the universe.

She includes in her prayer everything she is in danger of losing: Allah, give me back my sister. Allah, give me back my son. Allah, spare my mother pain. Allah, protect my daughter from harm. Allah, secure my husband's love for me. Allah, save my sister's son. This is all I ask from you. You have to hear me this one time. I'll never ask for anything else ever again.

The cab glides to a stop in front of a shimmering building that extends into the hazy heavens like a portal.

14

In Irvine, in a still-possible future, a brother says to his sister: Come, I'll show you something.

He looks excited, and his sister drops what she's doing and follows him. He leads her down to the garden, away from the house, and picks up the hose lying there.

She's wary but goes to his side: Bhaiya, don't get me wet, I just got ready for asr namaz.

It's an afternoon in late fall, a limpid sky stretching across their heads. The sun shines above their rooftop, above the treetops, behind them.

This is the best time for this, he says. I'll show you something beautiful.

He points the hose in the direction of their shadows extending on the lawn in front of them. He turns the hose on: a fine sheet of water sprays out in a wide V shape from the nozzle and falls to the lawn in a graceful curve.

Look, he says, and sweeps the nozzle up and down, as though he were washing the air in front of them. In the delicate scrim he creates from the water glinting in the sunlight, there appears—broken at first, and then more fully—a rainbow, large enough that it hovers like an arch made for the two of them, and near enough that they could easily leap through it.

Bhaiya, it's lovely, she exclaims, clapping. It's like magic.

Not magic, he explains: When the sun is behind us and low enough, some of the rays striking the water are reflected back from the inside surface of each droplet. But since different wavelengths of light are refracted a little differently, the light is separated, as through a prism. Depending on where we're standing, only some of these rays reach our eyes, from droplets that lie in a narrow arc, the reds from the outside of the arc, and the violets from the inside.

We're each seeing a slightly different rainbow, he says. A rainbow, like beauty, is in the beholder's eye.

15

At some point, when the hydrogen in its core is exhausted, the sun's nuclear reactions will cease. The sun will have expanded to more than a hundred times its current size by then, engulfing the earth and its moon. Perhaps that is the description of the dawn of Qiyamah, the day of resurrection.

But this is billions of years in the future, and the inventories of my own futures interest me more.

In the normal course of events, this is what should happen after my lungs expand for their first taste of air: My vocal cords will quicken for their first cry. My lips will seek a nipple for my first suckle of mother's milk. In a few hours, my bowels will move. In a few days, my stomach will increase from the size of a marble to the size of my fist.

I'll learn to recognize voices, faces, smells, in a couple of months. My eyesight will become capable of distinguishing primary colors, then the full rainbow spectrum, over a period of five months. I'll sit up, then crawl, then take my first step, then walk, then run, over a period of two years. I'll gurgle, then babble, then speak, first in words, then in sentences that will grow more confident, more complex, over a period of six years.

My first set of teeth will erupt, then fall away one by one, to be replaced by a permanent set, by the time I'm twelve. Sometime around then my testes will increase in size, my scrotum will descend, the shaft of my penis will grow longer, thicker, and pubic hair will begin to sprout. My testicles will produce the first of the millions of sperm they'll churn out over my lifetime. I'll experience my first ejaculations. My vocal cords will shorten, and my voice will drop an octave lower, to my adult voice. I'll be sixteen when these changes are complete. I'll have grown from my current height of twenty inches to my adult height by the time I'm twenty-one.

Meanwhile, the hundred billion neurons in my brain—formed during my first six months inside my mother's womb—will form hundreds of trillions of connections with each other, rapidly at first, as my newborn brain responds to every attention and stimulation, then slower and slower, as newer experiences serve mainly to reinforce some connections, weeding out others.

I'm a blank slate at birth, with an infinity of futures available to me. With each neural connection that is made, that my brain fails to make, that is pruned, the futures are whittled down, until if I were alive long enough, there's only one life I could possibly live.

Call it fate, call it destiny. Call it qismat, call it the will of Allah. Call it following the laws of nature, call it acting in accordance with our natures. Say it's been decided by evolution; say it's in our genes, in the secretions from our glands, in the pathways in our brains. Say we're the products of our environments, our upbringings, our histories.

Aren't our lives circumscribed, in any case, by powers over which we have little control?

16

Seema, I held our son in my arms. They had swaddled him in a blanket, to keep him warm, so only his face was visible—your face: heart shaped, an obstinate set to his lips, his eyes tightly shut. But his hair was all mine. I wanted to hold him without the blanket but didn't know how to remove it. I was afraid I would drop him if I tried to unwrap him with one hand.

I asked a nurse to help. She looked at me oddly at first, as if she didn't understand, but then she took him to the table and undid carefully the bundle of him. When she handed him back to me, holding him in one hand, with his body resting against her forearm and his neck supported by her palm—oh how tiny he was, how beautiful, blue-black all over, with just a hint of pink on his lips—I couldn't figure out how to take him from her, how to hold him, with his arms and legs dangling and in the way.

How easy she made it look. Like this, she said, hold your arms like this. She made me raise and hold one arm bent, with my other hand below it, palm facing upward. To support the body, she said.

17

Grandmother, waiting outside you're unaware of what's transpiring in this operating room, even though the force of your mind is bent here.

Here's how your elder daughter, Seema, dies: After plucking me out of my mother's womb and handing me over to a nurse without even a glance, the doctor turns his attention back to my mother's body on the table, attempting to stanch the flow of blood that is quickly draining her of life. But how to force the blood to remain in a body that seems intent on expelling it? He's only human: he continues to try even after your daughter's heart ceases pumping.

As for me: What real chance did I have? My body has always known what awaits it: acids have been building up in my bloodstream, and my brain has for some time been slowly strangled of oxygen. Detached from my body, my mind has all along been hovering—fluttering, skittering, skipping—suspended like a trill clinging to the air, straining to keep afloat, to keep away the final dying cadence.

But what a glorious song, Grandmother! Death sings in ways Birth cannot. It takes a lifetime to perfect that purity of tone, the vibrato of lament.

It has taken me all of three minutes.

Don't pity me, Grandmother: I may not have experienced anything real but the inside of my mother's womb, but I still have the song Death sings through me.

In that respect, I'm perhaps no less fortunate than others with more life: for aren't so many of their songs merely wishful or fanciful, lined with desire and regret and envy, about what might have been but never was—or merely bitter and dissatisfied, lined with anger and remorse and guilt, of what was but never should have been?

I share this song with you, Grandmother, so it might bring you some comfort. I have mere moments to live. You will soon learn of our fates—my mother's and mine—without needing to hear the words spoken by the doctor, for the expression on my not-to-be father's face will convey everything you need to know.

Grandmother, somewhere in this building your other daughter, Tahera, my other not-to-be mother, is searching for us. She is lost: the maze of corridors that separate us—identical and blandly monotonous—have confused her. She asks for directions but is too impatient, too agitated, to heed them. Now, in the desperate hope that she'll somehow be led to us, she's hurrying through corridors picked at random, clutching to herself her jilbab, which trails her raggedly—the sleeve and skirt were caught in the car door as she made haste to exit the cab, the fabric ripping when she yanked to extricate them.

Grandmother, you will be resting your head against a wall, your gray hair against the white tile, your gray face in the shadows, when she stumbles on you. Bill will be seated by you, holding the shell of me in his arms, the two of you inches and miles apart. Tahera will catch one sight of you and freeze, transfixed.

Will the three of you grieve together, Grandmother, help each other grieve? So much depends on the answer.

There's what's left of your life, and Urdu ghazals and Faiz's poetry and Noor Jehan's voice. There's Bill's and Tahera's lives, the lives of their loves, both current and future. There's the lives of my now not-to-be siblings, both born and as yet unborn.

When you sense Bill shudder, will you let your hand stroke his hair like you've stroked your daughters' hair so many times before? When Tahera unfixes herself, will you let yourself rise to take her cloaked and ragged form in your arms, as you've done so many times in her childhood? Don't you see, Grandmother? It's that past Tahera, too, who runs toward you with her arms open.

Will you forgive, Grandmother, and let yourself be forgiven? Console and be consoled?

Yes, there could be a hereafter. Perhaps we'll all be resurrected, all our loves and our loved ones, our bones put together, then covered in flesh and skin. Maybe breath will then move our bodies, and maybe breath will then move us. And perhaps we'll have forever for what may be granted us: kind words, a touch, maybe even a kiss, a caress. Perhaps we'll be held, or be able to hold.

But in this cold clinical room there's only the three of you.

18

The light dazzles my eyes, yet I catch a glint of the blade approaching.

Father, was I born for this end?

19

Come with me, quickly. There isn't much time left, and I want to show you something beautiful: here by the entrance to the hospital, where the fog swirls fiercely, hiding the city and its comforting lights from us, hiding the universe from us.

Wait here, on this ridge overlooking the concealed city, till a car comes by, as one surely will very soon, its headlights aimed directly at us as it swings into the parking lot. No, we won't be blinded by the lights, we'll face the other direction, toward the open hillside.

Here comes a car now—don't be scared, don't turn around—and here is the fog rising off the hillside in front of us, and here are the headlights illuminating the fog for us.

Look! Strangers approaching us through the glowing fog, from the direction of the hidden city, treading through the air, floating over the hillside! And can you see? Shimmering around them: a perfect halo! And what's that circumscribed within the halo? They're trailing folded wings behind them!

How the figures loom larger and larger as they approach us, and then how suddenly—when it appears as though they are reaching out to greet us—they take wing and disappear!

No, they're not angels descended from some heaven, nor visions from some dream world. These radiant fugitives are created by us: they're merely our shadows cast on the fog, their wings bestowed by these rails that are protecting us from falling off this ledge.

And the glorious halo is a fogbow—like a rainbow, only with the colors tightly braided—produced by the light from the headlights reflecting off the inner surfaces of the millions of tiny droplets of water suspended in the air in front of us, obscuring the hillside, the city, the sky. So tiny that the droplets of water interact with the very particles of light.

But we are minuscule ourselves compared to the universe, and we are innumerous as well, and there is indeed light cast upon us, so perhaps we too can—

Acknowledgments

When I began this novel, I knew that the poetry of John Keats and the words of the Quran would be integral to the development of Ishraaq's voice. Aside from the explicitly attributed quotes, I've allowed myself the license of incorporating lines and phrases inspired by and adapted from these sources, as signs of Ishraaq's journey.

Imam Zia's sermon (Part Three, Section 19) is inspired by Abul A'la Maududi's *Towards Understanding Islam*. The ideas presented there are Maududi's, from the opening pages of his masterful treatise on the nature and meaning of Islam, which I read in a translation from the Urdu by Khurram Murad.

The John Keats speech (Part Three, Section 20) is comprised almost entirely of Keats's own words, a mash-up of various poems and letters. The main ideas are from a letter to his brother and sister-in-law, dated April 21, 1819. Section 18 (Part Three) makes heavy use of his sonnet "To Sleep," while Section 21 (Part Three) adapts lines from "Endymion," and Section 35 (Part Three) repurposes "This Living Hand." Elsewhere, I've drawn on lines from "A Song About Myself," "Endymion," "Ode to a Nightingale," "Ode on a Grecian Urn," "To Autumn," "After Dark Vapors," "Why Did I Laugh Tonight?," "To J. H. Reynolds," "La Belle Dame Sans Merci," etc.

For the quotes from the Quran included in the novel, I've consulted the

Yusuf Ali translation, along with that wonderful online resource Quran.com, which makes available several other translations, as well as the meanings of individual Arabic words. Section 34 (Part Three) is adapted from the surah Al-Kafiroon.

I've also used dialogues and lyrics from the movie *Mughal-E-Azam*; President Obama's public speeches, including excerpts from the Cairo speech (Coda, Section 12); lines from William Wordsworth's "Solitary Reaper" and "My Heart Leaps Up"; Faiz Ahmed Faiz's "Muhjse Pehli Si Muhabbat"; and Momin Khan Momin's "Wo Jo Hum Mein Tum Mein Qaraar Tha."

I owe a debt of gratitude to my agent, Anjali Singh, and my editor, Dan Smetanka. I couldn't have asked for better guides and champions. Many thanks, too, to all the teams at Counterpoint Press for their amazing work in bringing this book to life. I started the novel more than ten years ago, at the Helen Zell Writers' Program, University of Michigan; the faculty and my cohort there are still among the first I turn to for counsel and support. I'm also grateful to the residencies—MacDowell, VCCA, Yaddo, Djerassi—and the organizations—Kundiman, Lambda Literary—that have provided much-needed encouragement and community along the way.

Many friends have read various drafts and given valuable feedback. Many more have sustained me with their companionship. My family has always cheered me on; my partner has never failed to cheer me up. To you all, my abounding love. This book wouldn't have been possible without you.

NAWAAZ AHMED was born in Tamil Nadu, India. Before turning to writing, he was a computer scientist, researching search algorithms for Yahoo. He holds an MFA from University of Michigan–Ann Arbor and is the winner of several Hopwood Awards. He is the recipient of residencies at MacDowell, Yaddo, Djerassi, and VCCA. He's also a Kundiman and Lambda Literary Fellow. He currently lives in Brooklyn. Find out more at nawaazahmed.com.